Red
Sky at
Morning

BOOKS BY
MARGARET KENNEDY

Red Sky at Morning
The Constant Nymph
The Ladies of Lyndon

RED
SKY
AT
MORNING

BY
MARGARET KENNEDY

PUBLISHED BY
DOUBLEDAY, PAGE & CO.
GARDEN. CITY, N. Y.
MCMXXVII

To
Virginia Kennedy

"Il n'y a qu'une manière de refuser demain:
C'est de mourir."

PROLOGUE

PROLOGUE

THE PUPPET-SHOW

CATHERINE FROBISHER was one of those women who are more conspicuously successful as widows than as wives. Intensely loyal, she was inclined to be intolerant of faults in a beloved object. Her imagination was stronger than her memory; she was lenient to the dead, she was generous to the past, but she dealt with the living in a temper of irritable, affectionate inclemency. She was an idealist and a romantic to the end of her days.

Her career turned upon this capacity for sentimental retrospect. Her husband was not undistinguished in his lifetime, but he did very little, positively, to deserve the enormous reputation that Catherine achieved for him after he was dead. By sheer persistence she impressed his name upon the world, and within five years she had won for his memory a place that had never been accorded to him by contemporaries.

The chief merit of Charles Frobisher had been his faculty for making friends with abler men than himself. He kept excellent company. He knew everybody and went everywhere. His correspondence was enormous. He was, besides, a poet and a critic, but most of his work was so good and so dull that nobody read it more than once. It would have gone for very little if he had not had a "circle," and if he had not managed somehow a little to survive a very interesting generation. He was the inevitable second-rate luminary that becomes for posterity a type of its age: a sort of common denominator of late Victorianism. So that when people thought of the 'seventies they thought of Frobisher rather than of his more distinctive companions. He presided over the age, a burly, bearded, jovial figure, laughing heartily at his own puns and implacable in his hatred of anything French.

It was with a half-conscious sense of this that his widow began her task of editing *The Life and Letters*. She took great pains to keep up a correspondence with all his old friends, and to maintain those links with the past that are so important if a tradition is to be preserved. She continued to live, with her two children, at Water Hythe, the Elizabethan farmhouse in Oxfordshire where Frobisher had entertained his most distinguished guests. And gradually she succeeded in turning this house into a shrine; it was thrown open on Saturday afternoons, so that the public might have an opportunity of seeing the yew parlour where Meredith used to smoke his pipe, the library where Jowett had argued with Herbert Spencer, and the fireplaces that Ruskin had said were all wrong. She altered nothing, the walls of the drawing room were still decorated with little water-colour landscapes by the first Mrs. Frobisher, the beautiful, unhappy Adelaide. For Charles, in accordance with the tradition of the period, was married twice, and his first wife ran away from him, after twenty years of unconcealed misery. He was nearly sixty before he found happiness with Catherine, who was the daughter of his old friend and neighbour, Bartley

Trevor of Monk's Hall, and his first child was born when he was sixty-three.

The marriage had been a great surprise to the neighbourhood, and it was generally agreed that Catherine had done very well for herself. Nobody had supposed that she would ever get a husband, for she was plain, rather clumsy, and apparently content to live at home and keep house for her father. The beauty and wit of her younger sister Pamela had been an additional disadvantage to her. But in the end it was Catherine who prospered and Pamela who came to grief. For Pamela also married a poet—a better poet than Frobisher. Superficially, it was a brilliant match. Norman Crowne was young, handsome, rich, and well born. He was possessed of a dazzling if fitful genius, and in his brief heyday, he attracted a good deal of attention. Frobisher did not like him.

"I feel bound to warn you," said Catherine to Pamela, before the marriage. "Charles does not like him. He distrusts him. He says he is afraid that Norman has no ballast."

Norman, when informed that Charles thought he had no ballast, made a historic remark, which is still remembered to his credit.

"Poor Charles," he said, "is *all* ballast."

But Charles was inevitably right, though he did not live to see the bad end that he had so often prophesied for his brother-in-law. The crash came some three years after his death, at the close of the century. Norman Crowne's career came to an end in a downfall as sudden, as spectacular as his rise to fame. Like a meteor, he exploded one day and disappeared into darkness. He was arrested and tried for murder.

His misfortune lay in being too successful. It might have been better for him had he encountered worse luck at the outset. A little adversity and hard work might have preserved his sense of proportion. Living in a world of phantasy, he lost his bearings and became unable to distinguish between the possible and the impossible, the permissible and the forbidden. He believed quite literally that he might do as he pleased, and it pleased him to do some things that he regretted later.

It had been his intention, on his marriage, to blot out from his mind certain incidents of the past, to free himself from certain associations that had become distasteful to him. But he found himself in a trap. Reality asserted itself too late. The past would not leave him in peace. Continually he was haunted by shadows of an evil world, by dark memories, by threats of exposure. He was at no time a very sensible man, and he lacked sound friends to whom he could turn for advice or help in his difficulties. Gradually he allowed himself to become the victim of a secret and rapacious persecution, which overcast the whole of his short, unhappy married life. Even before the death of his much-loved wife, he had begun to ponder upon desperate remedies, and he fell thereafter into a condition of mind that looked very like insanity.

He shut himself up and would see no friends save one, a very doubtful companion, the evil genius of his life. And this was not probably from choice but because he had no other alternative. It was proved later that he had come to be entirely in the power of this man, that he had every reason for wishing him out of the way, and that he had, more than once, expressed some obscure intention of violent measures. The friend died, in suspicious circumstances, and Crowne was charged with the crime. Many people believed in his innocence, but nobody could disregard the history of squalid vice revealed during the trial. Crowne was, in any event, a ruined man, and an acquittal could bring no escape from the disgrace which had fallen upon him. His children must bear through life a tarnished name, though they were, at the time, too mercifully young to be aware of their fate.

"But they'll have to be told sometime," said Catherine. "And what can I say to them? How can I ever tell them that their father was hanged?"

She said this to Philip Luttrell, the young rector and squire of Water Hythe and Ratchet, who had called to condole with her. And as this was on the first day of the trial, he felt bound to express a hope that Crowne might not be hanged after all.

"But, my dear Philip! Everybody knows that he did it."

"I've met a good many people who would dispute that. When I was in Oxford last week, I came across some men who knew Crowne very well indeed when he was at the House. They all agreed that he probably didn't do it."

She took no notice of this. She had at times a concentration upon her own point of view only possible to the very determined or to the deaf.

"It's a most marvellous instance," she said, "of my dear husband's foresight. He was a wonderful judge of character. He always said something like this would happen. He never liked that man. He never trusted him. I remember his saying once to me: 'There's a false glitter about his work that I don't like.' I thought that was so good. A false glitter! It just sums up one's feeling about those early sonnets. My husband had a deep suspicion of that sort of cleverness. He thought that it was meretricious. I remember he called it the iridescence of corruption. And the chemist identified him as the man who bought all that arsenic."

Philip reminded her of the most puzzling feature in the case. The victim, according to medical evidence, had not died of arsenic poisoning.

"I know all that," she exclaimed impatiently. "But you must admit that it looks very bad. What did he want arsenic for? He was planning the murder when he got it. Of course he was."

"Probably. And it certainly looks as if he had argued himself into believing that it would be right to rid the world of such a wretch. That's what these friends of his were saying the other day. Their view was that he lived entirely in a world of his own, and if he found himself in a difficulty, he flew into an unreasoning, childish rage. He was fantastically indignant. He could not understand the idea of yielding to necessity. It was just like him to go off openly and buy a lot of poison. It was a gesture."

"You mean he was posing? But then, if he meant to do it, that's surely just as bad as if he had done it."

"He won't be convicted unless it can be proved that he did actually do it. You see the law——"

"Oh, my dear Philip, you needn't explain the law to me. I've heard all that you are going to say, years before you were born."

Philip held his peace, as he always did when she referred to the years before he was born. The difference in their ages gave her the right to take this tone, and though he was her rector he was a little frightened of her. They had been neighbours all their lives, and he could never forget the days when she had been a grown-up young lady and he a little boy, the playmate and contemporary of her young brother, Bobbie. This brother had gone into the army, and his absence in India at the time of the Crowne trial was deplored by Catherine as a heavy misfortune.

"If only Bobbie were here!" she sighed. "I know he would have done something. He would have stopped this horrible business. He was so fond of poor Pamela; he never approved of her marrying that man. He would have arranged all this. He would have advised Norman, and seen the lawyers, and that sort of thing. And he would have been such a help to me. I do miss him."

"You must make use of me," said Philip gently. "You must let me help you in every possible way."

She assented, not because she had very much reliance upon his judgment, but because she had the Victorian widow's traditional respect for the clergy. In the absence of Bobbie, she turned instinctively to her rector, and Philip, in the following distracted days, did all that a kind heart could suggest for her comfort and relief. She would not leave Water Hythe on account of her children, and she would not read the newspapers because it was all so sordid, so that he had to impart to her the details of the trial from day to day. He sent many telegrams. He arranged for the future of the Crowne children, who were to be placed thenceforth entirely in the charge of their aunt, whatever the verdict might be, and he went himself to bring them from London to Water Hythe. Catherine was grateful, but she considered that he had done no more than he ought.

"I must say you've been very good to me," she said on the last day, as they sat in the firelight together, waiting for the end. "I shall never forget how helpful you've been, all through this terrible time."

"Why, Catherine! What else could I do? I'm so glad you've let me be of any use to you."

"There was nobody else," she told him with a certain bleak candour that was hers. "But, oh dear! I wish it were all over. Why doesn't that telegram come?"

It had been a shattering day. The children, oppressed by a trouble that they could not understand, had surpassed themselves in naughtiness. It had rained so incessantly that nobody could go out. Nervous, exasperating storms had swept the waiting house. The winter dusk was closing in and no message had yet come from London.

Philip and Catherine were sitting in the hall, a great

barn of a room, always smelling of wood smoke, with a log
fire at either end. The stone floor and heavy rafters showed
it to be the oldest part of the house, the living room of a
fortified grange built by half-savage yokels. Nineteenth-
century pictures, two Leightons, a Millais, and a portrait of
Frobisher by Watts, looked odd and smug upon its walls. A
massive door led out through a deep porch into the garden,
and a row of small irregular windows gave upon the same
view, a square lawn flanked on the left by a dovecot, and on
the right by a little church. In the distance were the flat,
wet river fields and a row of pollarded willows. But now
grass, river, church, and dovecot were all lost in a blur of
misty twilight. The storm wind blew in the wide old chimneys, and rain came hissing down upon the logs.

At the farther end of the hall, by the other fire, a deafening
noise was going on. Charlotte and Trevor Frobisher were
quarrelling over a game of Beggar-My-Neighbour, while
William and Emily, the twin children of Norman Crowne,
were rushing aimlessly about. They were too young for any
systematic game, but they had an idea that they were trains,
and a good deal of whistling went on. Every now and then
a siren hoot would signify that they had become boats, or a
terrific growl would turn them into lions and tigers.

"It's just possible," shouted Philip over the din, "that it
mightn't be over to-day after all. When I telephoned from
Oxford, they said that the judge had only begun summing
up."

"Oh, I do hope it won't drag on another day," said Catherine in alarm. "This suspense is quite intolerable. Now,
Charlotte! Don't whine! You must let Trevor have his turn
at dealing. And please stay on your side of the room. Don't
keep coming over here. Go away now. I suppose that at the
worst he could appeal? Couldn't he appeal on the ground of
insanity? Personally, you know, I think he should have

pleaded guilty at once and then tried to get off on the ground
that he was insane. Because the Crownes are all queer, you
know. There was an old aunt who . . ."

Her voice sank and Philip lost it in an outburst of hooting
from William and Emily. He signified that he could hear
nothing, and she told him to come into the drawing room,
where it would be quieter. Protests and tears at once broke
out from the twins.

"Oh, Aunt Catherine . . . you . . . you . . . you . . . you
mustn't . . . you . . . you mustn't . . . you . . . you . . ."

"William! Don't get so excited! Finish your sentence.
It's just a silly trick, talking like that."

William collected himself with an effort and said:

"You mustn't go off that rug. It's a boat. You'll be
drowned."

"I'm sorry. I'm afraid I can't play now. I'll play at boats
with you when I come back, perhaps."

"All right," he said, pacified.

And they heard him say confidentially to his sister:

"I know what I kin do. I'll make the whole house be a
boat. They've just gone to another sort of . . . sort of . . .
sort of part of it. I told them to. I'm the captain."

Philip followed Catherine up a little flight of stone steps
into the panelled Tudor drawing room. He said, as he went,
that William was very like his father.

"Like his father! Like Norman Crowne!" Catherine looked
shocked. "How can you say such a thing? They're not a bit
alike. Not a bit. William is a dear little boy."

"So was Crowne, once, I daresay. And still is, from one
point of view. That's the whole trouble. Crowne never quite
grew up. He went on thinking he could make houses be boats
long after he ought to have known better."

"He was mad," said Catherine with conviction. "I'm
quite sure of it. This thing that came this morning, while

you were at Ratchet, proved it to me. I meant to tell you before. I don't know what to do about it. It came addressed to the twins, but really . . ."

She pointed to a large box in the corner of the room. Philip took off the lid and peeped inside and saw little dolls. He asked if it was a toy.

"I suppose you'd call it that."

"For William and Emily?"

"Their father sent it!" she told him in a horrified whisper.

"Haven't you given it to them?"

"No. It's most unsuitable. In any case, they're too young to appreciate it. It's a little theatre. A beautifully made little toy, but most unsuitable."

It was certainly a beautifully made little toy. Philip was amazed at the perfection of its detail as he and Catherine took it out of its box and set it up. There were several changes of scene, a curtain, footlights, and a whole set of cardboard puppets to be worked on wires.

"I believe he made it himself," whispered Catherine. "He was very clever at this sort of thing."

He had made it himself. It had occupied his time during that last half-crazed week before his arrest, when he should have made a bolt for freedom and got out of the country. That he made no such bolt was taken by some people as a proof of innocence and by others as significant of guilt. For six days, he never left his house at all. He scarcely ate and never slept. When the police came they found him in an attic, working on his toy theatre in a great confusion of glue, paint, cardboard, and empty champagne bottles. And now it appeared that he had left orders for the dispatch of this toy to his son and daughter. Philip immediately wanted to play with it, but Catherine looked at it with disfavour. She repeated:

"It's not a child's toy at all. Those are horried little dolls."

He inspected them and agreed with her. The cardboard figures were wonderfully lifelike, but they were not agreeable.

"This piece," he said after he had examined them all, "is to be acted entirely by villains, I should think."

"The play is here. He's written it himself, in blank verse."

Catherine fished a notebook out of the box and held it out to Philip, cautiously, as though it might blow up or bite them. He, aware that this latest work of Norman Crowne might very possibly be the last, could not help a small thrill as he began to read. Written in a clear hand and almost without correction, it was not difficult to decipher. Full directions were given as to changes of scene and the manipulation of the puppets. Philip read on for a few minutes, caught up in the old charm of Crowne's delectable style. Then he flung the book back into the box again, exclaiming:

"The man was as mad as a hatter."

"That's what I say! All the Crownes are mad. He ought to have pleaded insanity. There were things that poor Pamela told me—it's a mercy, really, that she died when she did. At least she was spared this. For she was fond of him, you know, in spite of everything. But she went so far as to say to me one day that she thought all Crownes . . . What is it, Trevor? I thought I told you not to come in here."

Trevor had poked his head inquisitively round the door, and now, disregarding his mother's reproof, he came up to the table and looked with interest at the puppet show.

"What's that?" he asked.

"Never mind. Go away now."

"It's a theatre!" he decided. "A little theatre. Is it for me?"

"Trevor! Obey me this instant or . . ."

"A theatre! A theatre! I've got a theatre!"

He began to shout and jump up and down. Charlotte, who

had followed him into the room, began to shout in chorus. And the twins, hearing the din, came stumping up the steps with hoarse demands to see the little theatre, too.

"What ought one to do?" sighed Catherine helplessly.

She was not quite herself. The troubles of the day had been too much for her. At any other time, she would have made short work of her naughty son.

"A theatre! A theatre!"

"Kin I see? Please, Aunt Catherine, kin I see?"

"Don't touch it, Car. It's my theatre."

"'Tisn't. It's all of ours."

"It's mine."

"Who said so?"

"Please kin I see Trevor's lovely little theatre?"

"I said bags."

"Mother! It's not his, is it?"

"It belongs to neither of you. Leave it alone and go away, all of you. I'm very vexed."

"But who does it belong to?"

"To the twins."

"The twins!"

Trevor and Charlotte began to grumble.

"The twins are too little. They'd break it. They wouldn't know how to play with it. Who gave it to them?"

"It will be put away till they are older. Run along!"

"But can't we play with it till then? We wouldn't hurt it. We could play with it and they could watch us."

"No."

All four children burst into loud howls. It was the climax of a disastrous day. Philip, who had swept together all the little puppets and put them with the book on a high shelf, suggested to Catherine that there was, perhaps, very little harm in the theatre itself. It might ensure quiet for the rest of the evening if the children were allowed to play with the scenery and footlights. Catherine agreed. She was glad to compromise, for she was very tired. The toy was taken into the hall and put on a low table, and the Frobishers obligingly played with it while the Crownes looked on. For the twins were really too little to care for it much. They gaped agreeably for a few minutes while Trevor raised and lowered the curtain, and then they went back to being trains.

"But it was naughty of Trevor," murmured Catherine. "He is getting very disobedient, and I give in to him too much. If it hadn't been the end of a tiring day, I should have punished him. Really, he needs a man over him. I wish Bobbie would come home and settle down. It's his duty."

She did not exactly mean that her brother should cut short a promising career in order to come home and beat his nephew. When she talked of Bobbie's duty, she was thinking of Monk's Hall, her father's house, lying deserted among its trees half a mile up the river. It had been empty since Bobbie went to India, and she wanted him to come back and live there.

"I wish he would marry," she said. "But not out there, of course. Anglo-Indian women are impossible. Nearly always ill bred. I couldn't bear to see one in my mother's place. What's that? Is it somebody at the garden door?"

The telegraph boy from Ratchet had lost his way in the darkness and had missed the front door, which was among farm buildings at the back of the house. He wandered round in the gray sheets of rain, amid the groaning of hidden trees, till he found the garden porch. Seizing the huge old knocker with both hands, he struck a ringing blow which drowned the howling of the wind. Philip and Catherine wrestled with bolts and locks. A wild drift of rain blew into the hall, and some wet, dead leaves came floating in from the darkness. Catherine took the telegram to the light while Philip fought with the wind and got the door shut again. The children, startled by this sudden incursion of excitement into a safe world, glanced up from their play. Catherine was saying:

"Thank God! Oh, thank God!"

"Acquitted?"

Philip took the telegram and read the reassuring word.

"For the children's sake . . . oh, thank God!"

They became aware that Trevor and Charlotte were listening with open mouths. Trevor, who was a sharp little boy, asked if it was about his Uncle Norman. He had heard the servants gossiping.

"Yes, dear," said Catherine after a moment's thought. "It is. This is very good news. We must be glad for the twins' sake. Your uncle was accused of a terrible crime, but he has been proved to be innocent."

"What was he accused of?" demanded Trevor and Charlotte at once.

"I can't tell you the whole story now. You'll know when you are older. It might have been very terrible, but we have all been spared a great trouble."

"How was he proved to be innocent?"

"He had a very clever lawyer," said Catherine, when she had reflected.

"But was he really innocent? Did the judge say so?"

"The jury, Charlotte. You remember, I read to you in *Britain's Story* that it is always the jury who . . ."

"Yes, I know. But will the twins go home now?"

"No, dear. They will go on living with us."

"But why? If Uncle Norman isn't put in prison . . ."

"Hush, Trevor! He will be going abroad for some time."

She said this with great determination, and she spoke for the whole of England. For everybody said, over the paper next morning, that Crowne was lucky to get off and must now live abroad. He had made his own country too hot for him.

"But, Mother, can't the twins go abroad, too?"

"Why must he go? Did he really not do it?"

Trevor looked suspicious. But his mother told him not to ask so many questions. She again exhorted them to rejoice for William and Emily's sake.

"They aren't even listening!' he said scornfully.

Nor were they. This crisis in their destinies had not disturbed them. They had gone back to their private enchanting little games, immune in the delicate radiance of infancy. Only for a moment, when the great door swung open and strange winds blew in, had they looked up and wondered. A dead leaf still clung to Emily's silvery curls. But when the door was shut, they forgot the night and the leaves and the messenger who had come. William, with fair hair all tossed back and a glowing face, was going through tunnels, wriggling himself under all the sofas with piercing shrieks. And Emily, able at last to get near her own toy, was playing with the puppet show. She had found a picture of a little castle on a steep crag with pine woods all round it— a little white castle with red turrets. She knew it. She had seen it before, very long ago, when she was a baby. Her father had shown it to her from the window of a train, in some almost forgotten mountain country. To find it now made her remember the mountains; it was like a secret message which nobody else could understand. Very softly she touched it with one finger and found herself back in that land. The little castle entranced her. Its smallness made it seem more real because it was within her compass. Philip heard her calling names over to herself as her finger travelled from one object to another.

"There's a tree. . . . " she said. "An' there's another tree . . . an' there's another tree. . . ." And then, a little uncertainly, in the words of that country: "*Baum?*"

It was indeed a mercy that she should be so young.

PART ONE

CHAPTER I

THE TWO HOUSES

I

NORMAN CROWNE and his misfortunes were soon forgotten. He fled, immediately after his acquittal, from a world that had turned against him. And the rest of his life, that broken and shattered thing which had been flung back to him, was spent in a shamed obscurity. Nobody quite knew where he had gone, and when, two years later, he died in South America, his friends had got into the habit already of referring to him in the past tense.

But though the man himself was forgotten, his case was remembered. The Crowne scandal still attracted a good deal of attention: it lived on and acquired, with continual canvassing, an extraordinary romantic patina. A new generation, less susceptible of shock than its forbears, discussed the points at issue with new zest. The poems were more read than ever. Their reputation abroad was tremendous, for it is generally believed in Europe that no English poet can be worth reading unless he has been ostracized by his countrymen. The reverberations of the affair were to be encountered in many parts of the world.

They were least felt perhaps at Water Hythe, for Norman Crowne was never mentioned there. The Frobishers did not discuss him, nor did they read the volumes of personal memoirs and reminiscences, published from time to time, in which the Crowne case always got a chapter to itself. The children, growing up under Catherine's care, were scarcely aware of anything amiss. They learnt in time the story of the trial, and they took it for granted, as children will. But Trevor and Charlotte were far more conscious of a mystery than were the little Crownes.

"I believe . . ." said Trevor at last, some six years after the trial, "I'm almost sure, Car, that Uncle Norman really did do that murder. Why did he go away at once? Why mayn't we talk about him? If he didn't do it, I daresay he did something worse."

Charlotte pointed out that there was nothing worse than murder.

"Well, but what is all this mystery? Why is he one of those Wait-till-you're-older-dear things?"

"I read something in the paper once," said Charlotte, "that said he was one of the greatest tragedies of the age."

"There you are, then!"

They both felt that such a father was wasted on the twins, who never made capital out of a personal advantage. Trevor said sourly:

"I wish my father had been a murderer."

"Trevor!"

"Well, I do. Then perhaps we shouldn't have quite so much ancestor worship going on in this house. I believe our father was a fearful old bore, as a matter of fact."

Charlotte was inclined to believe it, too, but she thought fit to look a little shocked.

"We ought to be sorry for the twins," she said primly.

"Why? They're so stupid. They don't appreciate it. And, for another thing, I'm getting tired of this idea that we're all so fond of each other. It's all humbug. Mother will keep telling everybody that we love each other, just like brothers and sisters. Even if we did, it wouldn't be anything very much. Most brothers and sisters hate each other. It's humbug to talk as if they didn't."

"But we are fond of William and Emily, in a sort of way."

"Yes. In a sort of way. We don't hit them or jump on them or pull out their hair."

"And we always find it dull when they're away. We've said over and over again, these holidays, how dull it's been."

The twins had spent the greater part of the summer on a visit to a Crowne great-aunt who felt forced sometimes to take a little notice of them, and Trevor had to admit that things had been very slow.

"But that's simply because four are more fun than two, for games and things. They aren't particularly amusing in themselves. The best thing about them is that they have good tempers and do what we tell them."

"They have good ideas, sometimes. They invented some of our best games."

"Yes, they can invent things. They can make plans. But they never get anything done. They aren't sensible. We use all their ideas."

"Still, I'm glad they're coming back to-day."

"So am I. But I'll tell you what, Car. I won't go this time and meet them at the station. I'm sick of this idea that I'm so impatient to see young William that I have to rush to the station when he comes. I see too much of him as it is. If he's put into my dorm at Bassett's next term, I shall see a lot too much of him."

"I shouldn't have thought he'd be much trouble."

"He says his prayers too quickly," complained Trevor. "It's disgraceful. He's no sooner down on his knees than he's up again. I've told him he's jolly well got to stay down till I tell him he can get up. Everybody in my dorm has to stay down for two minutes and seventeen seconds."

"That's only because you want to work your stop-watch."

"Well, what's a stop-watch for?"

"If Mother says you're to go to the station, you'll go."

"It's soft enough to even like one's cousins . . ."

"Trevor! You're disgusting!"

"I will split my infinitives if I want to. I shall say to Mother that it's soft enough to even like one's cousins, but that meeting them at stations is a work of—of supererogation!"

"And Mother will tell you not to show off."

"'Tisn't showing off to read the Thirty-nine Articles. I always do in sermon-time: it's much more interesting than listening to old Philip."

"It's showing off to say things out of them."

"To tactfully show off," he stated, "is the way to get on. You and I both show off, Car, but you do it badly and are ashamed of it, while I do it well and take a pride in it. At Bassett's they call me clever Trevor. William and Emily never show off, and they'll never get on. Nobody pays the slightest attention to them."

He was in a perverse mood, and he even began to split his infinitives at lunch. But his mother seemed to find this simply amusing, so he gave it up. Evidently she thought that he really knew no better—a disconcerting idea. She had a direct method of dealing with his moods that could only have been devised by a person with a large sense of humour or with none. Unintentionally, she would take the wind out of his sails and leave him feeling silly. There was no spirit in him when she asked, in the tone of one proffering a treat:

"And which of you is coming with me into Ratchet?"

He merely mumbled that it was his sister's turn. But the base Charlotte would not let him off.

"Trevor doesn't want to go," she said.

"I think family scenes at railway stations are very trying," he explained warily.

"How silly you are," was Catherine's comment. "But you can't come in any case, for I remember that I've arranged with Mr. Stryde to take you for Latin this afternoon."

That was the end of Trevor, and a very poor end, too. He hated these coachings with Mr. Stryde, an old retired pedagogue at Ratchet. He agreed with his mother that he ought to get a scholarship at his father's old school, but he expected to be able to do this without any extra tuition. The September sunshine was inviting, and he did not want to stay indoors.

He looked very glum as, from the dining-room window, he watched his mother and sister setting off in the dogcart. Charlotte, just before they got out of sight, looked back and put out her tongue at him. But she was ashamed, almost immediately afterward, of having descended to so childish a piece of vulgarity. She drew herself very upright and tried to seem as mature as possible as they bowled along the dusty high road to Ratchet.

Between them, the mother and daughter contrived, in their shabby dogcart, to look infinitely more important than the chance travellers who were whirled past them in expensive cars. They might have owned the country. And in Catherine there was actually a certain fundamental resemblance to the land where her fathers had lived for so many centuries. A good many objects in the landscape had a look of her. She was like the hens, as they scurried into safety by the hedges, and she was like the large, untidy haystacks, leaning confidentially together in the rick-yards.

The years had turned her into a large, gray woman, ungainly in movement, short-sighted, and perpetually entangled in the chain of her eyeglasses. Her clothes were always black and shapeless, and she had never in her life walked on high heels. On great occasions she wore round hats with little black ostrich feathers moored firmly to the crown, or, in the evening, an extra quantity of valuable lace, sewn bunchily on to her velvet because she would never cut it. Her hands were rough with gardening and a little gnarled by rheumatism, but she always wore several beautiful rings. These, and a kind of subtle, innate dignity prevented the pilgrims to Water Hythe from ever mistaking her for the housekeeper.

Charlotte was like her. She, too, would be large and plain, and her mouth, moreover, was made hideous by that badge of her race, age, and class, a wire contrivance to keep her teeth straight. This glittering horror was a great torment to the poor girl, and she often stopped herself from smiling for fear that people might notice it.

Catherine, raking the countryside with a possessive eye, said that they were very late with the harvest. She scattered abrupt, condescending greetings among acquaintances upon the road, and when they happened to pass Philip Luttrell, she called out to him a command that he should come to tea with her at Water Hythe.

"Wait there for me! Don't go till I come back!" she cried as they left him behind.

He shouted something inaudible, but she merely waved her whip at him and drove on, remarking to Charlotte:

"I must ask him about Trevor's coaching. I don't think poor old Mr. Stryde gets him on nearly fast enough. Perhaps Philip would take him himself, for a bit."

"Trevor wouldn't like that," said Charlotte.

She knew that this was treachery, but she did so love to

be treated as the eldest and to discuss the other children with her mother.

"Won't like it? Won't like it? Why not?"

"He doesn't like Mr. Luttrell. He calls him Parson Bumpkin."

"Trevor talks a great deal of nonsense. I know he thinks he's being clever, but he merely gets silly and above himself."

"But, Mother, do you think that people ought to be clergymen unless they're really religious?"

"Of course not. But Philip Luttrell is a perfectly good churchman."

"He preaches very dull sermons."

"He has no gift for it. Many good men have not. I never knew before that Trevor attached any great importance to sermons."

"He says that people shouldn't go into the Church unless they have a . . . a vocation."

"That's nonsense," cried Catherine with energy. "The Church is a profession, like any other. Philip's father had the living in his gift, and he very naturally provided for his younger son in that way. You must remember that it was before the elder brother died. And even when Philip eventually came into the property, he couldn't have afforded to give up the living. There were all his brother's debts to pay. I think he did very wisely."

"I know. I told Trevor all that. But he says he's a socialist. He says that people oughtn't to be able to give livings to their sons. He says the landed gentry ought to be abolished. Isn't it dreadful, don't you think?"

"He'll get over it, my dear. He only talks in that way for effect. He's picked it up from some newspaper."

"No. He says he's come to that conclusion because of having the awful example of Uncle Bobbie before his eyes."

"What do you mean, Charlotte?"

There was an ice in Catherine's tone that told Charlotte she had gone too far. She wriggled in her seat, and said at last, half defiantly:

"I suppose he means the way Uncle Bobbie just sticks at Monk's Hall . . . and . . . and never does anything. I mean . . . if he'd stayed in the army . . ."

She ran aground and could say no more. An insatiable curiosity had emboldened her to start upon this topic, but her courage failed her when it came to the point. For her Uncle Bobbie, like her Uncle Norman, was never mentioned at Water Hythe. And this was the more embarrassing because he lived at Monk's Hall, less than a mile away. He had left the army five years before, but he never came to their house nor did they go to his. All inquiries from the children were snubbed.

But they had seen, in church, the cause of the trouble— a yellow-haired lady called Mrs. Grainger, who lived at Monk's Hall, too, and went everywhere with their uncle. They were aware that this lady was an evildoer long before they had guessed at her sin. But the day eventually came when Trevor, who had been learning his catechism, communicated his conclusions to his sister in private. He was certain, he said, that Mrs. Grainger must have broken the Seventh Commandment; but the twins had better not be told, since they were so young. Everything bore out his theory, especially his mother's flurried severity, when questioned, which was a sure sign that sex was in the air. She put on the same manner over the meaning of strange words in Shakespeare, or when one of the dogs had to be shut up. For all these things lived in the same pigeonhole in Catherine's mind.

It did not occur to Trevor until later that his uncle was of necessity implicated. For some time the children believed that Mrs. Grainger was the only offender: but at last they were forced to suppose that Uncle Bobbie had committed adultery, too. The idea was however almost fantastic, and Charlotte longed to get direct confirmation of it. But she feared that she had been too bold. She stole a frightened, sidelong look at her mother.

Catherine appeared to be thoughtful rather than angry. As it happened, she had been wondering lately whether Charlotte was not old enough to be "told." She now saw an opportunity, and after a short pause she began, very solemnly:

"You are right, Charlotte. Your uncle's life has been a very sad one. And you must have guessed why, haven't you?"

Charlotte took the precaution of looking as doltish as possible. She mumbled:

"I know we don't go to Monk's Hall."

"No." Catherine looked stern and sad. "I've not been there for years, and it is my old home."

She sighed. Charlotte was afraid that she might not, after all, come to the point, and helped her a little.

"Is it," she suggested, with a blush, "is it because of that Mrs. Grainger?"

"Yes, dear. I don't feel I can go to Monk's Hall when that woman is there. And I think, Charlotte, that it is time, that you are old enough, to know a little how we all feel about it. Your—your uncle got entangled with this woman in India. It's ruined his career. She was the wife of his colonel, and he had to leave the service. It's spoilt his life and cut him off from the position that he ought to have here. For, of course, nobody will call on her. And I understand that he goes nowhere unless she is received, too. It's a very bad example to the village. For he can't marry her, I believe. Her husband . . . won't divorce her."

Catherine dropped her voice at these words, as though the hedges might hear and be scandalized. And Charlotte, in spite of a certain angry embarrassment, felt excited and important. These confidences were a mark of maturity, like the new stays to which she had lately been promoted, which had one bone in them and fastened with clips, while Emily still wore the old buttoned sort.

"Is that why he keeps pigs?" she asked.

"Not necessarily," said Catherine rather crossly. "But he must have some hobby, I suppose, poor man. Nobody goes there."

"Some people do," said the tactless child. "Milly's sister was in service there, and she said they give quite big dinner-parties sometimes."

"Men go there, I believe."

Catherine's voice was like the east wind. It sounded awful. Charlotte shuddered at the frightful immorality of it. Then she recollected another piece of gossip.

"Mr. Luttrell goes there."

"He has to," said Catherine quickly. "He is their rector."

But he went much too often, as everybody knew. His old friendship with Bobbie could not justify him in going nearly so often. In fact, he had at one time got himself unduly talked about with this Mrs. Grainger. Catherine had even heard that he called the person by her Christian name, but she hoped that this was not true. For in most things she was satisfied with Philip.

"You must understand," she said, without further comment on the situation, "you must realize what a grief all this has been to me. Bobbie is my only brother, and we are cut off from each other."

"But wouldn't he make it up if——?"

"If I would call on Mrs. Grainger? I daresay he would. But I can't do that. I don't regard her as his wife, and I never shall. One has one's principles."

She had said this for five years. But principles are awkward things. Perhaps if she had known at the outset that this situation was likely to last so long, she might have taken up a different stand. Naturally, she had thought, everyone had thought, that the Grainger would soon tire of Bobbie and his pigs. She would need gayer company. For Bobbie had always been reckoned a dull dog, even by his family, and since the untimely indiscretion that wrecked his career, he had grown duller. Only the Grainger had not, apparently, grown tired of him, and it really began to look as though she might be established at Monk's Hall forever.

"Of course, I trust you, Charlotte, to say nothing of this to the others. I have only talked to you because you are the eldest."

"Yes, Mother."

Charlotte looked forward to teasing Trevor. Of course, she would not tell him, but she would let him know that she had been told. They drove on, through Ratchet, stopping at one or two shops to give orders. Respectful tradesmen stood bareheaded in the sun and listened to Catherine. And then the dogcart turned into the white-railed station yard. Upon the small platform, they found themselves face to face with Bobbie Trevor, who was also waiting for the train.

This sort of thing was always happening. There never seemed to be a time when Ratchet platform was safe. If Water Hythe did but call for a parcel, Monk's Hall was sure to be calling for one, too. It was the penalty that they all paid for Catherine's principles, and nobody ever knew what was the right thing to say or do. Fortunately, Mrs. Grainger was not in sight at the moment, so that a word or two might be exchanged between the brother and sister for the sake of appearances, though, as a matter of fact, the two porters and the stationmaster all knew how things stood between the two houses. Catherine repented her confidential mood during the drive when she saw the round eyes that Charlotte

was making at her peccant uncle. Sharply, she bade the child
go out into the yard again and hold the horse.

"Well, Bobbie?" she greeted him. "Where are you off to?"

Bobbie left off staring at his boots and smiled sadly. He
was a handsome creature, with a soldier's head upon a farm-
er's shoulders, a narrow skull and very long arms.

"I'm not off anywhere," he said. "I'm here to meet Lise.
She had to go to London on business."

"Oh. How are the pigs?"

She resented the tactless way in which he proffered information about Lise Grainger. He should not have mentioned
the woman at all. A silence fell between them. Bobbie said
that the train was signalled. Along the shining ribbon of
line, under the bridge, they could see a black dot and a puff
of smoke. Presently it enlarged itself into a train. Just before
it was upon them, he let loose a most petrifying piece of
information.

"Grainger's dead."

He said it so casually that she did not immediately comprehend him. The train had slowed into the station before
she took in the possible significance of it. Grainger was
dead, and his wife was therefore free. It was too late to make
any further inquiries. Farmers and country people were
crowding out on to the platform, and he had hurried forward
in search of Lise. The twins were nowhere to be seen. Very
probably the little scatterbrains had forgotten to change at
Oxford.

If Grainger's wife was free, she might marry Bobbie. It
was more than likely. And Catherine could not immediately
decide whether this was a misfortune or not. She caught sight
of the woman getting out of a first-class carriage and looking
most dreadfully conspicuous. Climbing out behind her were
the missing twins.

Lise Grainger could never be overlooked, and on this small platform she blazed like the sun. She had an unfortunate voice, cheerful and booming like a gong, so deep as to be almost a bass. She was booming away now to the porters, who were both of them struggling with her luggage. For she still had something very Indian about her and always managed to look as though she were travelling with a suite. The stationmaster himself was swept into her service. Golf clubs came out of her carriage, though it seemed odd that she should have taken them to London on business, and a hat-box, and a green kid dressing-case (what a thing! thought Catherine) and last of all two modest little suitcases belonging to William and Emily.

"Hallo, Bobbie!" boomed the cheerful voice. "How nice of you to come! Look! I've salvaged these two infants. They'd lost their tickets."

She pushed the twins toward their uncle. Catherine, looking very black, bore down upon the group and claimed them.

"Why, children!" she cried. "What happened to you? Why did you travel first class?"

William and Emily were growing up rather tall. They were thin, fair children, of a serious demeanour, very polite to everyone and as like as two peas. If Emily's ringlets had been shorn and her petticoats put upon William it would have been impossible to tell them apart. They stood in a courteous uncertainty between Monk's Hall and Water Hythe, waiting for orders, and William explained that Mrs. Grainger had paid for their tickets from Oxford.

"Very good of you," said Catherine coldly to Lise. "How much do I owe you?"

"That's my affair," Bobbie was moved to assert.

"Oh, but really . . ."

"My nephew and niece . . ."

She saw that it was undignified to argue, and she murmured that they must settle up later. Then she scolded the twins for having no money of their own.

"We had some," said William, "but we lost it with the tickets. It was all in Emily's handbag."

"Such a lovely handbag," mourned Emily.

It was the very first handbag that she had ever owned. Only yesterday was it given to her, and now it was lost. The skies were black.

"Poor little thing!" boomed Lise, who had heard all about the handbag on the way from Oxford. "Isn't it a shame? But we must get her another."

"We lost it at Oxford, you see," explained William. "And if Mrs. Grainger hadn't bought us new tickets we should have had to walk here, begging our bread on the way. I expect it would have taken days and days."

Emily would have liked that. They would have sung for their suppers in the villages as they passed through. Probably they would have collected quite a lot of money. And at nights they could sleep in the haystacks. By the time they got to Water Hythe they would have been all in rags, so that Aunt Catherine would not have recognized them. Charlotte would cry: "Oh, look, Mother! Two beggar children at the gate. . . ."

"Come, come, Emily! Don't dawdle! Get up, child! Get into the cart quickly!"

Charlotte, perched upon the back seat of the dogcart, was smiling a toothy welcome. Emily scrambled up, wishing that her skirts were longer or her legs shorter. She could not help showing her drawers when she climbed over things and into things. William clambered up beside his aunt, and they all set off for home. The Monk's Hall trap pursued them for a little way, but they were soon caught up and left behind. Lise waved to the children as she passed, and Catherine gave her a stiff little nod. They jogged along in the dust of the high road, and Catherine said to William:

· "You shouldn't, as a rule, accept help from strangers."

"But Mrs. Grainger isn't a stranger," he pointed out. "I know her quite well."

He pondered for a moment, and then, with a little giggle at his own waggishness, began to chant:

> "Oh, when you are in danger
> Beware of Mrs. Grainger!
> Remember she's a stranger!"

"Don't be silly, William."

"But, Aunt Catherine, if the man who fell among thieves hadn't known the Good Samaritan, ought he . . ."

"You and Emily did not fall among thieves."

"There was a person in the train who looked like a robber."

"How did he look like a robber?"

"Well, he had a beard. I daresay he stole Emmie's bag."

Emily, on the back seat, sniffed. It had been a suède bag with a mirror and a memo tablet on which she had carefully written the date of William's birthday (also her own) and a powder box in which she had meant to keep silkworms. She would have enjoyed showing it to Charlotte, who was asking in a disapproving voice why her hair was done that way.

"Aunt Belle likes it."

"Well, Mother won't. Curls are very middle class. I expect you'll have to plait it as soon as you get in."

"Yes," said Emily dolefully.

She was miserable. Her handbag was lost, and she was an orphan, dragged about like a little doll, plaited by one aunt and curled by the other. She would have no redress if they took to beating her, and starving her, and shutting her up. They could murder her, if they liked. Childhood, endless and dreary, stretched away before her. It was an immensely long road that she must walk before she could be grown up and free, before she could run away to London and live in a darling little house with William. She hated being a child. She hated Water Hythe. The telegraph posts and the dusty hedges swam together in a mist of tears.

Behind her back she felt a little poke. William, without turning, had thrust a hand backward through the bars of the seat between them. She did the same, and very secretly they crooked their little fingers together. This they always did when they came to places, carried, as they often were, unwillingly, by a horde of kindly relations. It was a sign that the Crownes also were a family, a solid unit in the midst of a world that, for some obscure reason, was always just a little too benevolent toward them.

2

Philip Luttrell had been waiting at Water Hythe for more than an hour in obedience to Catherine s command that he should stay until she came. He chafed a little at being forced to spend a busy afternoon in such a manner, but a long habit of obliging good temper kept him at his post.

This melancholy mildness of disposition had been the blessing and the bane of his life. He took the line of least resistance over everything, not so much from laziness as from a sort of inborn fatalism. He had no ambitions. His father had told him to be a clergyman and he had obeyed, though he would have preferred the Bar. Like many unambitious men, he had a very lovable disposition, and a number of warm friendships was the most positive element in his life. The ladies of the neighbourhood had often tried to find a wife for him, but he showed unusual determination in resisting these attempts, and lived in great comfort at Old Ratchet Manor, a pleasant little early Georgian box of a house, within a stone's throw of the larger of the two churches in his cure.

The only excitement in his career had been occasioned by his loyalty to his friend, Bobbie Trevor. Some of his parishioners had objected to it. A letter had been written to the bishop, complaining of his many visits to Monk's Hall. It was said that he disgraced his cloth by consorting with people who lived in sin. He had been beside himself with indignation. For a couple of weeks, he had gone about in a black rage, almost prepared to give Communion to Bobbie and Lise, should they ask for it, which was not likely. But nothing had come of the affair. The bishop's chaplain mislaid the letter, and so many months elapsed before the question was taken up that the attacking party lost heart. Philip went on visiting Monk's Hall and, in time, his parish got used to it. Excuses were found for him by everyone save Catherine, who was always a little affronted, though she disapproved of the appeal to the bishop. Her grievance was personal; she had stifled her natural affections and broken with Bobbie, and she thought that all loyal friends ought to have followed her example. She was never able to like Philip quite so well again, but she refrained from any open remonstrance, allowing an unbroken silence to signify her disapproval. This was seemly and effective, and Philip had not the courage to defy it. He never spoke to her of Bobbie or of Monk's Hall; inwardly he excused himself on the ground that this policy released him from the necessity of taking sides.

"Though I'm a craven!" he thought, as he sat cooling his heels in the hall at Water Hythe, "I ought to go about fighting people more."

He wondered what would happen if he told her straight out that he was going over to Monk's Hall that evening to see if Lise had come back from London. The afternoon was too hot for such combative measures. It was drowsy and dazzling. The house dogs lay snoring on the sun-baked stones of the garden porch; the pigeons, strutting about on the grass in front of the house, were too languid even to coo. Sometimes a punt creaked lazily upstream, but the river was so low as to be invisible, and it seemed as though the summer hats and parasols and white flannels were gliding by some magic over the dry, green earth.

Philip amused himself as best he could by glancing through a little book which he found put out conspicuously on one of the tables. It was called: *My Green Garden and Other Poems*, by Charlotte Curtis Frobisher, and it was printed privately. In his impatience he was inclined to be a little critical of Charlotte's verse, nor was he mollified by the unambitious childishness of her style and theme. She wrote in simple ballad stanzas about clouds and larks and all the pretty things that fall naturally within the perceptions of a sensitive child in a cultured home. He considered that far too many of her poems began with the words "I saw" and "I sat." His young friend Emily, whose work he was occasionally allowed to see, was also subject to this failing. She sat and saw rather monotonously. But then she sat in strange places and saw strange sights. He had a copy of some lines of hers that began:

> I sat in the churchyard all walled in white
> Where tombstones stand at the dead of night.
> And I saw how the hosts of earthy ghosts
> Crawl out of their graves by the cold starlight.

There were seventeen verses of this poem all full of winding-sheets and coffin-worms. Emily had assured him that she meant to write a great many more when she had time. He wished that she and not Charlotte would publish a book. And instantly he remembered that she had better not. It would never do; for people would never forget whose daughter she was. She could never write well enough for that.

He had witnessed, some months before, a sinister demonstration of Emily's bondage to a name. Coming one day to call at Water Hythe, he had happened upon a dancing class. All the little girls of the neighbourhood were being taught the court curtsey by a weekly visiting instructress from Oxford. And he had sat down to watch, among the mothers and governesses, because Emily's joyous little hop of greeting had been so attractive. He thought that her dancing was perfect. He adored her strenuous gravity, the twinkling of her long black legs, and the thumping of the pigtail on her back. When she sawed the air with her thin arms and bounded across the room in a series of artless pirouettes, he could not help whispering to his neighbour:

"Isn't she enchanting?"

The lady, who was a stranger, agreed rather doubtfully. In a lower whisper, but with considerable relish, she said:

"That is Norman Crowne's little girl, isn't it? I thought so. Poor little thing!"

Whereon he perceived that Emily, despite her charm, her infantine gaiety, might never be able to escape from being a poor little thing. A sufficient amount of pity will undermine any moral constitution, and she would always find that people were anxious to be sorry for her. Ladies like this would meet her at every turn. Really, it was a wonder that she had not begun already to feel the effects of this miasmic compassion. Some children, so situated, would have become quite odious: Charlotte, for instance, would have been terrible. But then, Charlotte was a minx; he called her a minx several times, as he turned the pages of her book, and then he reproached himself for intolerance. It was not the poor girl's fault that she was so plain or that her mother kept him waiting.

His tedium was scarcely relieved by the companionship
of Trevor, who came in very sulky, after a profitless session
with Mr. Stryde. The two shook hands without enthusiasm,
and the boy, with the air of searching carefully for a topic
that might interest his visitor, inquired solemnly:

"How is your horse?"

"My horse," said Philip, "is well."

"How nice!"

Then, seeing the book in Philip's hand, he asked in
tones of genuine and lively interest:

"What do you think of Car's poetry?"

"Not bad for her age."

"She asked to have it printed for her birthday, you know.
She would have it, though Mother said it was silly. And so
do I. It's a pity to rush into print. I sha'n't."

"No, Trevor. Don't!"

"Not until I've left school."

"But you mustn't deprive us too long, you know."

Trevor said nothing, for he did not like Philip's tone of
voice. Secretly, he was very much annoyed by this march
that Charlotte had stolen on him. He ranged round the
room, fidgeting and eyeing Philip balefully in the hope that
some opening for insolence might be given to him. At last he
said:

"I've quite made up my mind, you know, to sell all these
pictures when I own this house. Don't you think I'd better?"

Philip looked at the Leightons and the Millais and the
portrait of Frobisher by Watts and suggested that they were,
after all, very interesting.

"Horribly interesting," agreed Trevor. "This house will
never be fit to live in while it's so interesting. It's no better
than a museum."

"I see your point. But how would you decorate the place
if it were yours?"

Trevor had no idea. His young faculties had got no further than incoherent, rebellious criticism. But he climbed on to a chair and took down one of Adelaide's water-colour sketches in order to show Philip how much better the wall looked without it. At a scuffle in the passage, he returned the picture to its place very nimbly. His mother's voice was heard outside, giving orders.

"I think I'd better go and see if the twins have come," he murmured wanly, as he disappeared through the garden door.

Catherine, just outside, was being peremptory about two teas, one in the drawing room and one in the schoolroom. Usually, they all had tea together, and Philip knew at once that he must have been kept there to discuss something private and important.

"Where's Mr. Luttrell?" he heard her ask, as though she could entertain no doubt of his having waited.

In a moment she was greeting him:

"Ah, Philip. You haven't waited long," she stated. "Tea is just coming. I'm so glad I caught you, for I want your advice."

He promised to see about better coaching for Trevor, and he gave his opinion as to the best way of mending the garden roller. But he had an odd feeling, while they talked, that her mind was elsewhere. She gave him the impression of not having come as yet to the point. All through tea he was waiting for a clue, aware that something was on her mind, that she was most anxious to discuss it, but that she could not begin. At last she demanded, with a little laugh, his opinion of Charlotte's poems, adding:

"She'll regret it later on, poor child! But one has to allow them to make their own mistakes. One has to compromise with them—with life. . . ."

He agreed, in some surprise, for he thought the sentiment unlike her. She began cautiously to develop the theme.

"One has one's standards . . . one's principles. One tries to maintain them. But it's all very difficult. Things are so complicated. Circumstances . . . as one goes through life. . . . Time does make a difference, doesn't it?"

Philip felt that all this could hardly refer to Charlotte's book. Positively, they must be getting to the root of the matter. After another difficult pause, she revealed it all in a most disturbing question:

"Er . . . have you been up to Monk's Hall lately?"

He mastered his amazement and replied that he was going up there in a few minutes. Inwardly, he prepared for battle.

"You've heard their news?" she asked.

"News? No!"

"Colonel Grainger is dead. Bobbie told me this afternoon. I saw him at the station."

Then Lise . . . then Lise . . . He could find nothing to say. For years he had wondered what it would be like to hear that Lise was free. He hardly knew what he felt. It was so sudden.

"Of course," Catherine was saying, "this may mean great changes in poor Bobbie's life."

"He'll marry her," said Philip, pulling himself together.

"Will he? Are you sure of that?"

"Quite sure," he declared, discovering with a small guilty shock that it was a definite relief to be quite sure.

"Poor Bobbie!" sighed Catherine.

"I think he's a lucky man," stated Philip firmly. "I have a great esteem and . . . and affection for Mrs. Grainger."

Catherine had no doubt of it. But that most deplorable side of the business did not, for the moment, concern her. She had other ends in view.

"If he marries . . ." she began.

Philip was disappointed in himself. He had always implicitly believed in the hopeless constancy of his passion for

Lise Grainger. Loyalty to Bobbie had insured its hopelessness, for he looked upon her as Bobbie's wife; but he could not entirely account for this sense of personal relief that descended upon him as soon as he had assured himself that the marriage was bound to take place.

If this news had come five years ago, it would have upset him very much. He thought of a thousand foolish things he had once said and done for her sake, of all the excuses he had invented to be near her and to see her, of all the nights he had lain awake, just thinking of her. He must have changed since then; but perhaps she had also changed. She was not very young when first she came to Monk's Hall: she was older than either Bobbie or Philip. But she had been, somehow, more exciting than she was now, more golden and joyous, a more vital contrast to the slow-moving English landscape round her. She had been so gay under bleak skies, so generously disposed toward a world that had not treated her very kindly. It was no wonder that they loved her. And she was, surely, all these things still. It was he who had changed. His love had lost its intensity, but it had waned so slowly that he was only now aware of it.

Catherine was still talking about standards and principles and compromises.

"Of course, I've never been there. Nor have I received her here, while the whole thing was so irregular. But if he marries her . . . one will be in a difficult position. It was largely for the children's sake that I felt I ought to be firm. One can't be too careful, with growing girls. But now . . . I don't know. Naturally, they begin to notice, and it might be easier, especially if he marries her. . . . Charlotte was asking about it all only this afternoon."

"Charlotte must surely have suspected something," he suggested. "They see her in church every Sunday, and they must have wondered who she was."

"It's such bad taste on her part to come to church at all," complained Catherine. "I mean, to Water Hythe church. Especially with the Monk's Hall pew just behind ours. In the old days, it used to be so nice, the two families practically sitting together. But now it's very disagreeable. Why can't she go over to Lyndon, where she's not known?"

Water Hythe church was very small; indeed, it was more like a private chapel than a church, for it could only be reached through the Manor House garden. Philip read Matins and Evensong there, on alternate Sundays, to a tiny congregation of cottagers who could not get as far as Ratchet. He knew that Lise went there simply to annoy Catherine. He had himself expostulated with her for bawling *Lord have mercy upon us* quite so loudly down the back of Catherine's neck when the Seventh Commandment was read.

"But don't you see"—Catherine had got to her point now—"don't you think it might really be much better, under the circumstances, if some sort of understanding . . . if there is really going to be a marriage it would make such a difference that . . . I was wondering if you could tell me how they stand."

He saw it now. She wished him to understand that compromise was not impossible, but it was a bitter task, since she took a pride in the inflexibility of her principles. If a marriage took place, she would force herself into a little civility toward Lise, for the sake of appearances. But she wanted to be sure of her ground before she committed herself.

"I'm sure he will marry her," said Philip, "and I think I see your point. But I'm not certain, you know, that she will be as anxious for a reconciliation as you are."

"I'm not in the least anxious," put in Catherine quickly. "It's only that I'm thinking of the children and Bobbie. And I don't want to do anything in a hurry. I'm not at all sure, even if he does marry her, that I could bring myself to receive her here. It's the thin end of the wedge, you know. If once one lets those sort of people into the house, it is supposed that one has no standards. Personally, I've not the slightest desire to know her any better. Not the slightest. I don't suppose we would have anything in common."

"Yes, and I expect she feels that, too. I daresay she may feel that nothing is to be gained by a reconciliation."

Catherine could not believe this. She became voluble and indignant:

"You don't mean to say that, having wrecked poor Bobbie's life (and you must admit, Philip, that she has wrecked his life, though I know that you have found something to like in her which I don't see, and I daresay she has a great many good points), even now, when he's marrying her (which I can't see that he's absolutely bound to do; I suppose he must, but I do think he is behaving very well by her), she's going to go on, for the sake of a petty grudge, cutting him off from all his friends? Will the woman never consider his interests?"

"She has never cut him off from his friends, Catherine. That has been their doing, entirely. If she now meets the advances they may make, I'm certain that it will be because she does consider his interests. She's the most good-natured, generous creature alive."

Catherine ignored this. She considered that Lise ought to be only too grateful for the recognition of honest women. But she did not say so, as she wished to placate Philip and to make him her go-between in the first advances.

"I daresay you'll find," she said drily, "that Mrs. Grainger is more amenable than you expect. But I should be very glad if you could find out for me if and when the marriage is to take place."

He would make no promises, and after a little more fencing he took his leave. For his own part, he was far from approving of such a reconciliation. It was likely to be more uncomfortable than the old feud. The two ladies would never really forgive each other, and he would always be the buffer between them. It was a prospect that filled him with profound depression and uneasiness.

He walked slowly across the footbridge at the bottom of the garden, and through the fields. He was not in a hurry to get to Monk's Hall, and he wanted time to think things over. His first excitement, his mysterious relief, had been succeeded by an equally mysterious melancholy. It stole over him and through him like a cold and clinging fog. He could not find out where it came from, since he had just assured himself that nothing was going to be changed and that Catherine's news had no real significance at all. He had always thought of Lise as Bobbie's wife, and now she would be Bobbie's wife. He would continue to be the devoted friend of both of them. And yet a sense of finality had closed in on him, as though something very important had come to an end.

For Lise had been the love of his youth, the great emotional adventure of his life. There had been a time when he had hardly known how he was to get on without her; but, as years passed, he had got used to his trouble, and at last, by infinitely small, slow degrees, he had got over it. Now it was finished. Nothing was left of all that he had so passionately felt save a vague warmth of kindliness. The love of his youth had been barren; it had borne no fruit either of the body or of the spirit, and he did not suppose that he would ever feel anything so much again. This regret that now invaded him was for the young man who had once possessed so great a power to suffer and who existed no longer. It was the first time that he had ever scanned the face of the past with any sense of envy or remorse.

"This," he thought, "is growing old."

He climbed over a stile that led out of the sunny fi[
into the woods enclosing Monk's Hall. These, even on
bright afternoon, were dark and mysterious. They were ve. ,
silent. Not a bird rustled in the shady thickets, and his feet
pressed noiselessly on a soft mast of last year's beechnuts
and dead leaves. Twice he swung round, almost imagining
that he heard footsteps padding behind him. But in the
long green rides he could perceive no followers.

He could remember that wood in a spring, five years ago,
when it was drenched in a sea of bluebells, and tufts of prim-
roses, like little yellow cushions, grew along the path. During those weeks he had often gone over this same ground
with a heart on fire because he should so soon be seeing Lise.
He had been violently unhappy; he could not candidly say
that he wanted to go through such agitations again.

"I ought to be thankful," he told himself. "I've been
through it. And the chances are that I've now got a peaceful
old age in front of me."

For he was still young enough to entertain extravagant
hopes.

The path wound through the wood and brought him at
last within sight of the house. It was a gloomy building, but
not without dignity. Its gray stones belonged to an ancient
monastery that had been burnt down some two centuries
earlier. The farm buildings huddled behind it were much
older than the house and had a decidedly ecclesiastical look.
Trees hemmed it in on every side, but the ground in front had
been cleared a little where an imposing flight of steps led
down from a terrace on to a circular lawn. But there was no
real view from any of the windows, and the whole place had
a northern aspect. Bobbie himself, wandering round the lawn
with his dogs at his heels, and gouging up occasional dande-
lions with an old clasp knife, had just such a melancholy,
overgrown look as his house. He cheered up, however, when

he saw Philip, and responded affably to an inquiry about the pigs.

"I've just built some new sties," he said. "Come and see."

They picked their way over the middens in the kitchen yard, while he told Philip that he had planned these sties himself and practically built them single-handed, with a little help from old Beazeley, the village carpenter.

"There you are," he finished triumphantly. "You see!"

Philip looked and exclaimed:

"Why! They're in two stories!"

"That was my idea. They sleep up above."

Philip choked back his laughter at the idea of the pigs going upstairs to bed, and gravely praised the masonry.

"I've got these yards to drain properly, you see. And that's a thing I've never done before."

Bobbie leant on the low wall of the sty and surveyed his handiwork with modest pride. Then he said:

"Grainger's dead. Did you know?"

"I had heard . . . yes."

"Goin' to get married," mumbled Bobbie.

"That's good," said Philip, trying to be hearty and feeling foolish. "Where's Lise? In the house?"

"Think so. Want to see her? Had tea?"

"Thanks, yes. But I'd like to see her."

"Well, I think she's in the drawing room. You go in. You'll excuse me. I've got to see about boiling this mash. Go in the back way, won't you? It saves time."

Philip knew the back way very well. When he had come over as a boy to play with Bobbie, he had been far more familiar with these long stone kitchen passages than with the polite grandeurs of the rooms in front. Even now, he could scarcely pass the green baize door leading from the offices to the hall without a slight sensation of awe, and a feeling that he must be careful to "behave." But the hall in

those days had been a good deal more impressive than it was
now, for the whole place was in a bad state of repair and
looked dilapidated. The staircase was very fine, springing
up in a double flight on each side, with a wonderful turn
of strength and grace, but several banisters were broken, and
the walls showed bright squares where pictures had been
taken down and sold. Bobbie had no faculty for making or
keeping money; he grew poorer every year. And his house
palpably lacked a mistress. The curtains and hangings were
dingy. Nothing was ever clean. For Lise had made no
mark upon the place: she had lived there, but the uncertainty
of her status and a discouraging lack of means had prevented her from attempting any renovation or improvement.
Philip hoped that she might in future make more effort.

He found her in the drawing room, half asleep on a Récamier sofa, a bright bold intruder among the faded ele-
gancies of the old *régime*.

"Why, Pip!" She reared up her shapely bulk and took
both his hands. "Have you heard the news? I'm going to
make an honest man of Bobbie."

"What luck for Bobbie," said Philip, still trying to be
hearty. "Tell me, what do you want for a wedding present?"

"What don't we want! A few suites of furniture would suit
us nicely. There's scarcely a chair left that's safe to sit on.
And we can't refurnish on the hire-purchase system, because
we'd never be able to meet the monthly payments. We're
ruined, you know. On the verge of the poorhouse."

"You've been that, my dear Lise, ever since I can remember."

"Oh, but we really are now. Bobbie mortgaged the last
acre the day before yesterday."

"The pigs 'll pull you round."

"Not they. We put more into those pigs than we'll ever
get out of them. They're Bobbie's only vice. In every other

way, he's very nearly perfect. I wonder what would have become of me, Pip, if he'd turned me off instead of marrying me."

Philip murmured something about its being a pity to talk nonsense. He supposed that, if Bobbie had turned her off, he would have married her himself, for old time's sake. It was not easy to imagine what would otherwise have become of her. She was not so beautiful as she had been when she first came to Monk's Hall. England had tarnished her, poverty had battered her. She had the sort of showy magnificence that requires an opulent setting, and that quickly becomes a little tawdry in shabby surroundings. A stranger, meeting her now for the first time, might have marvelled at Bobbie's taste. By some standards, he was certainly treating her well.

"Poor Bobbie!" began Philip.

But she flushed and interrupted him.

"Please don't call him that. I can't bear it."

She looked, in a moment, ten years younger. And Philip remembered that she adored poor Bobbie. It was very odd.

"I hate it when you call him poor Bobbie," she cried. "I have a feeling that everybody does, as a matter of course. And it's my fault. He might have made something of his life if it hadn't been for me. But then I couldn't know that it was all going to be like this: that it would be such years before we could marry. And what have I done to him that's so dreadful? You'll say I've cut him off from his family. What if I have? I shouldn't think that sister of his is much loss. She seems to be a very rude, disagreeable sort of woman. And her children don't look a devastatingly attractive couple, do they? The only ones I'd like to know better are the little Crownes, poor little dears."

But here Philip protested.

"There's nothing in the least poor about them. As a matter

of fact, they're very rich. The surviving heirs of a large and wealthy family, you know. Every few months some old Crowne, some cousin or great-aunt, dies and leaves them another million."

"Oh, but you know what I mean. Everyone will always remember who their father was and expect them to turn out queer. And they are a bit odd, to my mind. I travelled with them from Oxford to-day, and I thought them very old-fashioned little things. I lent them money for their fares, and small thanks I got from their aunt."

"I think," ventured Philip, "that you might find the atmosphere a good deal more genial in that quarter, nowa-days."

"Oh, really?" Her face hardened. "Has she said so, pray?"

"I think, for Bobbie's sake, she'd like to climb down."

"If he married me, you mean?"

"In any case, I think she's weakening."

Lise said nothing and he added, with some hesitation:

"Of course, it rests with you. You are the one who's been badly treated. If you don't care to forgive . . ."

"Oh, but I do. I shall." She looked up, kindly and frankly. "Of course I shall. Why shouldn't I? Bobbie would be pleased. And after all, what does it matter?"

"That is, of course, the generous view."

She lay back again on her sofa, looking defeated and old.

"Five years ago," she said musingly, "I wouldn't have talked like this. But time's a funny thing. It reconciles you to most things. Time's gettin' on, you know, Pip. We're all of us gettin' old."

"Don't let's talk about it."

"I was no chicken when I came here, and I've gone off a lot since then. I'm turning very fast into what the old gentle-men call a dam'-fine-woman-still. And I've learnt to know what time means. It's most extraordinary, Pip, what a dif-

ference that makes. When one is young, one simply doesn't
know that such a thing exists. But in the end, it's the only
thing we know anything about. We don't know ourselves;
we only know what time has done to us. We think at first
that the world stands still and that we move and make
something of life. But we get to learn that it's life that moves
and makes something of us."

Her voice trailed away mournfully. Perhaps she was thinking of the Curragh, where she had rattled through her gay
and thoughtless girlhood, and her marriage and the voyage
out and the fun of being the prettiest woman in Simla. The
clocks had ticked no slower in those days, but she had never
listened to them.

Philip said nothing at all. He was wandering round the
room and peering at a large, dusty old china cabinet. As
long as he could remember, he had been fascinated by the
collection behind its glass doors. Everything was there, as
it always had been, the same curious jumble of Dresden
figures, shell boxes, miniatures, knickknacks of ivory and
tortoise shell, carved chessmen, and two painted fans.
Poked away behind it was an ancient ruin of a harp that had
stood there for sixty years. He twanged faintly at the one
unbroken string, just brushing off a faint note, a ghost of
a sound. It floated through the long, dim room like a knell
for lost youth. Lise started from her reverie and began to talk
again, more to herself than to him.

"You might say we have no choice at all. But we have.
We can let it make us wise. By not fighting against it. By
taking things lightly and letting them go lightly. Only fools
try to fight against time, and they always get beaten. And
nobody is really sorry for them. If Bobbie's sister is nice to
me, I shall be nice to her. Because that's the place in life that
I've got to now."

It seemed strange to Philip that this woman should be

submitting to the years so much more simply than Catherine. For though Catherine had told him that time made a difference, she had spoken in the grudging tone of one who makes a bitter discovery. He did not believe that she would ever let it make her wise. She might be forced to compromise, but always under protest.

Anyhow, they were all getting old together, he as much as they. He had survived his love. And he would be older. He would survive much more than this. He saw as he thought the rest of his life, and how year after year he would potter about the flowery lanes, growing a little slower in sense, a little deafer, a little wiser, the spirit dwindling.

On the way home, he tried to temper his melancholy by rejoicing in the beauties of the evening. But he was less successful than usual. The woods seemed strangely autumnal, and he thought he could detect a faint whiff of bonfires on the breeze. His mind turned inevitably to the falling leaves and the short twilights of winter.

3

The two houses of Monk's Hall and Water Hythe were hidden from each other by a piece of rising ground called Ash Hill. It was not really a hill at all, but a low mound; the flatness of the surrounding country gave it a look of height and turned it into a landmark. From the river bank it rose sharply on the Monk's Hall side, and at the top there was a very tolerable view of the water meadows, the woods, and the chimney stacks of the houses. The stream, crawling round its base, meandered away through the uneventful fields into a landscape that never changed. Always the same long, low train of clouds seemed to hang on the horizon, and the same smoke rose, year after year, from the Water Hythe chimneys, blown away over the trees by the prevailing westerly gales, or sometimes, in the stillness after rain, rising into the air in a straight, thin column.

The sides of the hill were shaggy with rough grass and crooked thorn trees, but on the flat summit there was a clear space where seven very old ash trees stood together in a group. And in the middle of this grove Bobbie's great-grandfather had built a small, ridiculous temple, a round dome supported on six white pillars, like a marine band-stand. The erection was an eyesore for miles round; it was entirely out of keeping with its setting, afforded little shade in summer, no shelter in winter, and was raked by every wind that blew over the hill. As a pleasure house, it was use-less, ugly, and dilapidated. Nevertheless, the four children regarded it as the choicest spot in the whole countryside; it was, in their eyes, most romantically beautiful. They had a picnic there every other day, and boiled their kettle under the dome on a flat stone that they hopefully suspected of having been a heathen altar.

Inside this temple, and opposite the door, there was a sort of niche that had been intended for a statue. Anyone standing in this niche could see out through the ash trees for a long way, across the river to the south, where a blue haze of woods sheltered Ratchet Village. But nobody ever did stand there except Emily, when she had a mind to play at being Venus, a game she much favoured in spite of the ridicule of her cousins. She would climb up there and stand for whole minutes at a time, listening to the hymns of a de-vout congregation. And she would look out of her niche to see, not Ratchet, not the homely fields whence she would so soon take wing, but the blue waves of the Ægean. She would sniff the sea wind exultingly. There was a picture of Venus in her Hero Book, a white marble lady in a little temple on the rocks, dreaming alone in the bright salt airs. One lovesick youth was bold enough to invade that wave-washed solitude, and he lay for long hours on the cold pavement, his forehead pressed to the feet of the goddess. And after a night and a day, he was given three golden apples.

She meant to go one day to Greece with William; but in the meanwhile this little temple did very well, if only her worshippers had been more obliging. Trevor was horrid when he had to be the youth; he always said something rude, like *Thanks for those few nuts*, when he took the apples. And even William would not pray for nearly long enough. He always wanted it to be morning so that he could go and run races with Charlotte, who was Atalanta. In fact, it was better to play this game alone, which Emily did, peopling the temple with really devout youths who made no bones about kneeling as long as they ought. She watched the punts as they came creaking round the bend of the river and turned them into sea craft, flashing triremes, bringing back heroes from battles and long sieges in strange lands. Swarthy sailors, bending to their oars, would send a hail to the Sea-Born One, and Catherine's guests, taking a little turn on the river after tea, were really on their way to Troy. Emily had no use for grown-up people, unless they could be woven into the fabric of her dreams. She looked at them with unseeing eyes. The spectacle of her Aunt Catherine and the mysterious Mrs. Grainger being punted by her Uncle Bobbie did not in the least amaze her; she did not exclaim as Trevor or Charlotte would have exclaimed. She saw nothing unusual in the group. They did very well for wayworn mariners, scudding home before a storm, and she, being in a ruthless mood, determined to drown them.

"Then winds," she cried, "blow up! Let them perish! Let the fishes gnaw their bones."

To her immense satisfaction, a few large drops of rain began immediately to spatter among the trees. The sky turned to an inky blue, darker than the water, and a fierce, blustery gale blew all the willow leaves with their silver sides upper-most. The ash trees creaked together. Quite obviously, the wayworn mariners were going to get very wet.

They had been foolish to come out on such an afternoon, but anything was better than conversation in the Water Hythe drawing room, on this first occasion of family com-promise. They had braved the weather, and now they were paying for it. Bobbie flourished his pole, and both his ladies worked away with their paddles, but the wind was too strong for them and they were blown farther and farther away from the Water Hythe landing-stage. A great rack of rain came drifting over the country. In their efforts to get home, the three were more united than they would ever be again. There was but one thought between them.

Emily, beholding their struggles, was enchanted. She fully believed that she had made this rain, and it showed that she really could control the weather, if she tried hard enough. Perhaps, if she could do this, she might manage to fly, and to sing two notes at once, both of which feats had hitherto baffled her.

Charlotte, Trevor, and William, who had been sprawling and scuffling on the grass outside, now came into the temple for shelter. They asked at once why Emily was making those funny noises, and recommended that she should not stand with her stomach stuck out.

"I'm trying," she said, from the niche above them, "to sing two notes at once. I shall do it in a minute."

"You can't," Trevor told her. "I've tried. Nobody can."

"Ah, but I can do things that other people can't," she said confidently. "I can fly. I can make it rain. I made this rain, really."

"Did you?" asked Charlotte drily. "Then make it fine again."

Emily tried. She stiffened herself in a transport of effort, but the rain continued to fall. Her cousins mocked at her. They demanded to see her fly. With a frantic inward prayer to her guardian angel, she flung herself forward and outward and fell with a crash on to the pavement just below the niche. Trevor and Charlotte, frightened, jumped up and ran across to her.

"You little idiot! What on earth did you do that for?"

"Are you hurt?"

"No." She sat up. "Of course I'm not hurt. I was flying."

"You'll break your neck one of these days."

"We never meant that you were really to fly. You don't seem to know when a game's a game. How can you be so stupid?"

"I was flying," she repeated sulkily.

And William supported her. He insisted that she had gone much farther than a mere jump could have taken her, and that her fall had been very slow, like a sort of glide. He even surmised that with practice she would be able to go long distances quite soon.

"After all," he pointed out, "you fell off your bike very often when you were learning, Trevor. But you'd have been quite annoyed if people had said that you weren't bicycling."

"That's perfectly different."

"I don't see any difference."

"My good fool! It's possible to bicycle, but it isn't possible to fly."

"You only say that because you've seen people bicycling and you haven't seen them flying."

"Well, and that's quite a good reason for saying it."

"You've never seen people being eaten by sharks. But you believe that they are. Why do you?"

"Because books I can trust tell me that they are."

"How do you know the books don't tell lies?"

"I use my common sense."

"Well, and so do we use ours. Once there were people who thought the sun went round the earth. They were people like you. And there were other people who thought the earth went round the sun. They were people like us. They were right."

"They had some reason for thinking differently from everybody else. They had telescopes and things."

"So have we got reasons. We've got secret reasons for knowing we shall fly, but we can't explain them just yet. When you see us flying from here to Ratchet, you'll feel pretty small."

"When we see it, I'll lick your boots, young William. But till then I shall go on saying you're both complete fools."

Trevor was getting quite angry, not at William's obstinacy, but at his confidence. For the twins were not merely arguing for fun, as anybody might have argued. They half believed in their case, and a logical defeat could not shake them.

"I get tired of hearing all that William and Emmie are going to do," he said at last to Charlotte. "I think it's time they really did something. They're going to fly, but at present they don't even walk very well. They always fall over things, because they don't look where they are going. They never have sixpence in their money-boxes, but when they grow up they are going to be very rich."

"So we are," said Emily, cautiously patting her bruises. "Everybody says so."

"It's true," agreed Charlotte. "I asked Mother once. She was very cross and said we weren't to talk about it. But I could see that it was true."

Catherine had indeed done her best to suppress the topic. She thought that the prospect of great wealth might be bad for the twins, who were always getting ideas into their heads. They received the same pocket-money as their cousins, and their clothes were made to last quite as long. But this did not prevent them from making many fantastic plans as to the spending of their money when they grew up, and the substratum of reality, the actual fact of genuine money somewhere in the bank, put these particular romances beyond the reach of Trevor's sarcasm. He could prove that they were silly, but he could seldom deny that they were possible.

"I say," he persisted sourly, "that you never will be rich. You'll lose your money. Just think how William always loses his offertory. It's an absolute nightmare. Punctually every Sunday, as soon as the collection-hymn begins, I know it's going to happen. I go hot and cold, waiting all through the service for the moment when the plate will come to our pew and young William will begin to turn himself inside out."

"Awful!" agreed Charlotte. "The choir and the schoolchildren all turn round and stare, and Philip Luttrell is left singing the hymn all by himself because his back's turned and he can't see what's going on. Last Sunday, when he stood up there singing: *Time like an ever-rolling stream bears all its sons away*, I thought to myself, well, it always bears William's money away."

"I don't like that hymn," observed Emily dreamily. "That about Time! I think it's horrid of it to. And we sha'n't lose our money, you know, because it's all in the bank."

"You'll speculate," Trevor told her.

This was puzzling. She knew that speculation was a form of thoughtfulness, to which she and William were much addicted, but she had never heard before that it cost so much money.

"And you'll buy stupid things," prophesied Charlotte. "Pianolas that won't work."

"I shall buy Monk's Hall," said William with a flash.

"I won't sell it to you," retorted Trevor immediately.

"It won't be yours."

"Yes, it will. When Uncle Bobbie dies. I'm his eldest nephew."

"I shall buy it before he dies."

"No, you won't."

"Yes, I will."

"What would you do with it, anyhow?"

"I should live there with my friends," said William glibly, "and we should drink out of skulls at midnight."

This was really rather hard on Trevor, for it had been his habit to entertain the others with long stories of all that he would do with Monk's Hall when it was his. He had originated the touch about skulls at midnight, and William had adopted it simply in order to be exasperating.

"What sort of friends do you think you'll have?"

"Poets," said William, obstinately faithful to tradition.

"Poets! What sort of poets?"

"All sorts. I'm going to be a poet myself."

"You'd better hurry up and write some poetry, then."

"I've written some."

"That's a lie. It wasn't finished. You've never finished a single thing in the whole of your life. Nor has Emmie. You can only boast, and I'm tired of it. After tea we'll go through the lists of our writings. We ought to, anyhow, before the end of every holiday. And if you can prove you've written more than us, perhaps we'll believe you can fly. Now get tea for us."

A fire was built by the Crownes under the supervision of the Frobishers, for in all practical matters the twins were entirely under the domination of their cousins. The kettle was boiled. And after tea Trevor called a meeting of the Young Authors' Guild, a secret society they had founded two years before. Emily, who was the secretary, was instructed to read out the complete list of works produced by the Guild. This list was kept under a loose stone in a corner of the temple and was, in consequence, a little earthy and marked with snails. It was very long, for the four children had waded in ink ever since they could first hold a pen. They meant to be worthy of their fathers.

Charlotte, a little self-consciously, suggested that a separate list should in future be kept for works published by the Guild. But the others snubbed her; they regarded *My Green Garden* as a piece of showing off.

"But when our lives come to be written . . . " She protested.

She had begun to prepare for her own biography ever since the publication of her father's Life in two volumes. But Emily said mulishly:

"All this won't count a bit. It'll go into childhood and early years, and that's always the shortest chapter in the book."

"Though goodness knows it seems long enough at the time," sighed Trevor. "Never mind, Car. We'll keep an album for press-cuttings."

Charlotte had one press-cutting, and she doted on it, though twenty-two of its thirty words referred to her father and not to herself. At night she took it to bed with her. She grew very red, under Trevor's sarcasm, but she said nothing. Emily began to read:

"*Alonzo and the Moorish Infanta*, an unfinished Drama by Emily Crowne."

"Unfinished!" yelled the Frobishers.

This was true. Her desk was full of magnificent beginnings, but neither she nor William had much perseverance. With a sigh she rubbed out *Alonzo* and continued:

"*Bloody Dick*, by Trevor Hartley Frobisher.

"*An Elleggy*, by William Crowne.

"*The Haunted Buttery Hatch*, a Tale of Mystery and Imagination, by Trevor Hartley Frobisher.

"*Ode to Liberty*, by William Crowne.

"*Isabella, A Novel*, by Charlotte Curtis Frobisher.

"*Mediatation on a Grave*, by Emily Crowne.

"*My Green Garden and Other Verses*, by Charlotte Curtis Frobisher.

"*The Perjuror*, by Trevor Hartley Frobisher.

"*Ode on Napoleon*, by William Crowne.

"*Advice to Parents*, by Trevor Hartley Frobisher.

"*The Truth About the Princes in the Tower*, by Charlotte Curtis Frobisher.

"*The Pollipantos, an Imaginary History of an Island*, by William and Emily Crowne."

"Not finished!"

"Oh," she implored, "such a lot of it is written. Really, it's very long."

"You must finish it."

She looked rebellious. She loved *The Pollipantos*, an idea that had come to her after reading Gulliver. But it was true that this imaginary history was not yet finished, nor was any sort of end in sight for it. The theme was inexhaustible. The Frobishers had never been allowed to write any of it, although they were sure that they could do it a great deal better than the twins, and had started, contemptuously, a rival *History of the Fricassees*.

"You must finish it," said Trevor severely. "That's the law in this Guild. I'm sorry, Emily. Go on reading."

But William was in a mood for dispute.

"Who says it isn't finished?" he began mildly.

"I do," Trevor told him. "Go on, Emmie."

"Why?"

"Because it hasn't got an end."

"I know. It can't. It's history. How can it end?"

Trevor avoided this and observed that he was the best judge, being the eldest.

"I'm the best judge," contended William, "because I wrote it. I say it is finished."

"Say it till you burst. It won't go on to our list."

"Yes, it will."

The placable William was getting quite flushed, as the ancient feud between the Frobishers and the Crownes, which had been simmering all the afternoon, rose suddenly to boiling point. The old hostility was in their bones, and Trevor, when he lorded it over his cousins, when he took advantage of their instability and their want of practical resource, was taking unconscious revenge for all the mockery that their father had heaped upon his.

"Why should you decide for us?" shouted William.

"Because I'm the eldest."

"That's nothing. I daresay Pontius Pilate was older than Jesus Christ."

"William! How dare you?" This from Charlotte. "That's downright irreverence."

"Your father was older than my father. But he didn't write such good poetry."

"Oh, yes, he did. He wrote better. Your father, young William, couldn't write poetry at all. If he hadn't done a murder, nobody would ever have heard of him."

Charlotte, with a gasp of horror, leapt to her feet. She felt quite sick. And Trevor himself was uneasy. He had been half in joke, but he knew at once that he had gone too far. With an attempt at a laugh, he turned away and pretended to be looking to see if the rain had stopped. But a scream from the girls warned him of William's attack. The two boys rolled together down the temple steps, William hitting out angrily, and Trevor, good-naturedly enough, trying to push him off. But every time the smaller boy was pushed away he came for his cousin again, with set teeth and blazing eyes, until at last he had to be knocked down.

"There!" cried Trevor. "Now do shut up. I'm sorry if I insulted your father. It was only in fun and I didn't mean it.

You shouldn't lose your temper like that. If you don't take
care, you'll be murdering somebody yourself, one of these
days."

But William was past reason, and his next move horrified
them all. Snatching a smouldering stick from the bonfire, he
waved it around his head, dancing and yelling:

"I'll burn you! I'll burn you!"

Trevor took to his heels, and they dodged in and out among
the bushes. The rain soaked through their jackets and eventually cooled William's torch. Then Trevor came out of cover,
sat upon his stomach, and lectured him upon the ungentle-
manliness of trying to burn people.

"I'd apologized for saying what I did about your father.
Of course I didn't mean it."

"Yes, you did."

"I didn't, I tell you. Nobody really supposes . . ."

"I do," said William, getting up from the wet grass and
shaking himself like a little dog. "I've always believed it
myself."

"You have?"

"Yes. And I expect he was right. I hope he did do it. Your
father wouldn't have dared. He'd have been afraid of being
hung."

Emily, hopping on one leg up and down the shallow temple
steps, clinched this argument by shouting:

"So there!"

The Frobishers gasped. For once their cousins had completely silenced them.

CHAPTER II

THE BUBBLE

I

IT WAS no surprise to anyone who knew Catherine that her son and daughter should disappoint her as they grew up. Her pride in their outstanding cleverness could not blind her to their failings, and she made no bones about admitting that they were not going to take after their father. They lacked his solid qualities. Before they were out of their 'teens she had decided against a literary career for either of them. It would merely entail a waste of time, for their work would never be other than second-rate. Trevor had better go to the Bar, where he might succeed, if only he would apply himself. And for Charlotte a husband must be found as soon as possible.

The preliminary skirmishes, consequent upon this decree, had scarcely got under way before war broke out. But this was, to Catherine, a mere postponement of the issue. If Trevor was spared to her, she would insist upon his going to the Bar as soon as the war was over, and Charlotte, temporarily employed as a V.A.D., should be taken eventually for a Season in London. Nothing was to be changed, if Catherine could help it, and when peace was declared they all began again, just where they had left off four years earlier. For Trevor was among the survivors, contrary to all her miserable forebodings, and in answer, as she believed, to the anguished prayers which she had put up, day and night, on his behalf. He was twice wounded, had fought on most fronts, and been mentioned in dispatches. She was unspeakably proud of his gallantry, but she still believed that he was mistaken in considering himself a poet.

"I feel," she explained to Philip, "that the war ought to make no difference. Except that it's put all these young men back in their careers, so that they will have to work all the harder to make up for the years they've missed. I want Trevor to lose no time in getting settled, now that he's out of the army. It would be so bad for him to waste any more time."

This was on the very afternoon of Trevor's final homecoming, after his demobilization, and Philip could not help feeling some sympathy with the boy. Catherine was probably quite right, but she was in too much of a hurry. She should give her son time to look round; it was tactless to hurl his future at his head on the very instant of his arrival.

"I think I understand how he feels, Catherine. You know, I find this return to everyday life very unsettling myself. We've got so used to giving emergency values to everything. We've almost lost any sense of permanence."

"You'll take Orders again, of course," she told him.

"I suppose I shall. There doesn't seem anything else to do."

He had given up Orders because he wanted to join the army. And now, having spent three years in the Near East, he found himself back at Ratchet, trying, a little half-heartedly, to pick up the threads of his old life. His want of spirit annoyed

Catherine; it was tiresome of him to say that he felt unsettled, just when she wanted his support in settling Trevor.

"It's quite simple," she proclaimed. "We've all got to consider where our next duty lies. During the war, we developed quite a high sense of duty, and we mustn't lose it now."

"I agree, Catherine. But it may take us a little time to discover what those duties are."

"But it's obvious. We must all get back to normal ways as soon as possible. We must try to put the war behind us."

"The world we live in is changed. It won't be the same again. The normal conditions that we must try to establish can never be pre-war conditions."

"We must all try," she repeated obstinately.

"But don't you feel yourself as though everything had come to a sort of standstill?"

She did indeed. Ever since the signing of the armistice she had felt as though she scarcely knew what to do with herself. During the war, it had all been so plain and clear. She had to be brave, to fortify herself against all possible disasters, to uphold the courage of others by a conscientious optimism, to economize in food and fuel, and to refrain from an unChristian hatred of the Germans. But the relief, now that it was all over, was almost oppressive. Ever since her secret burden of anxiety and fear had been removed, she had felt quite light and giddy. She, who had gone about her war activities with so much silent determination, now pottered round the house and garden in an oddly aimless way. She forgot things. She fussed. Sometimes she told the same story twice. The future before her was immense and empty.

Time and trouble had left but little outward mark on her. She was still the same gray, upright, rather formidable woman. But it was significant that in the village they had begun lately to refer to her as "old Mrs. Frobisher."

"Yes, I think we are all of us a little *désœuvrés*," she agreed, with a shake of the head. "But we must fight it."

She got up and went across to peer out of the window, saying, "I thought I heard something; but it's much too early yet, of course. His train isn't even in. Will you have some more tea, Philip?"

"No, thank you, Catherine. I really think I must be getting home, as a matter of fact."

"Oh, you mustn't go yet. You must stay to dinner. Trevor will want to see you."

"Will he?" Philip looked dubious.

"Our oldest friend! Of course he will. Stay to dinner and you'll have a moon to ride home by. Oh, and will you excuse me, Philip! I think, if you've quite finished, I'll send the tea-pot out. And then, when Trevor comes, he can have it fresh. No, don't ring! I'll take it out myself. The maids will be at tea."

She trotted off. Really, she could not be still a moment. All day she had been like this, never able to be quiet. When she had taken the tea-pot into the kitchen, she just ran up to Trevor's room to see if his sheets were well aired.

"Of course I sha'n't say anything very much about it for the first day or two," she was explaining as she came back. "It would spoil his welcome. To-night I want us all just to be happy together. And of course I want him to have a holiday, poor boy, after all his hard time. I shall be delighted to have him here for a month or two, and perhaps we could ask some of his friends down. But I do want him to make definite plans for the future, at once."

"A few weeks may make all the difference to the way he feels about it," suggested Philip hopefully.

"I know. I know. I don't want to force him. In fact, I never have coerced them. It's useless to try."

"Worse than useless, I'm sure."

"Charlotte, now!" Her voice grew harsh and bitter. "I never argue with Charlotte. I just let her do as she pleases. To-night she wouldn't stay at home, though she knew I wished it. She's gone over to tea at Monk's Hall, and she won't be here when Trevor comes. It's all just done to assert her independence: it's the modern attitude, the belittling of family ties. I said nothing. I just let her go. One can't coerce them."

She said a good deal more, in the same strain, and Philip could not quite understand what she meant. For he was very sure that she intended to get her own way. But after a little while a light broke in upon him. She would not argue with her children, or reproach or exhort them, but the strongest of all silent arguments was at her disposal and she meant to use it. They were without independent means, for their father had left all his property, unconditionally, to his wife. Not that she was ungenerous; she would have given her last penny to Trevor if only he would be sensible. But she considered that she owed it to Charles Frobisher not to allow his children to live in idleness upon his honourable earnings. Their allowances were dependent upon her approbation, and she did not consider this coercion.

She was outlining to Philip her own conception of her duties as a mother when the old house dog, sleeping by the fire, broke into excited barking. There was a bustle in the hall. In an instant, she was out and on the front-door steps. A car purred in the darkness, while figures dodged round the headlights. Trevor's voice was heard saying:

"Hullo, Mother! Do I pay for this now, or does it all go down on a bill?"

He came into the hall, out of the windy dark, and kissed her, and never saw, in the flickering lamplight, that tears were running down her worn cheeks.

"Well, Mother!" he said again. "It's very good to be home."

"Oh, Trevor," she said. And then she turned from him abruptly and called out of the front door:

"Have you got a nozzle?"

"No, Mum!" replied a voice from the night.

There was a good deal of lamentation. It appeared that Trevor's car should have picked up in Ratchet a new nozzle for the garden hose. Conflicting instructions were given. A piercing wind coursed round the hall and doors slammed. Golf clubs and luggage were carried in from the car outside, and Catherine, pausing for a moment in her harangue about the nozzle, called out to the maids to leave the things, because Mr. Trevor would carry his own luggage upstairs. The young man, standing uncertain in all the draught and confusion, felt that his homecoming had been flat and bleak. He was repelled by his mother's ungraciousness, and told himself that she cared more for the nozzle than anything else.

He left her still scolding at the front door, and wandered into the drawing room, where he found Philip installed like some disagreeable, inevitable piece of furniture. The irritating, eternal past rose up around him in all its familiarity and staleness. Everything was as it always had been. On the journey he had felt a real exhilaration at the thought of getting home, and he had determined to be very charming to everyone. But he had forgotten how stupefying home could be. And really, he could not see why he should have to carry his own luggage upstairs.

"Well, Trevor!"

"Well, Philip!"

They shook hands.

"Well, Cæsar! Hullo, old boy. I say! He *is* getting old."

Catherine's offer of fresh tea was refused, for he had had some on the train. He tried to be genial and to adorn the short replies that a tired man likes to give about his journey. He exerted himself to inquire after everybody. But a numb-

ing depression had invaded him, and he set it down, per-
versely, to the presence of Philip. It was so typical of Philip to
be there at the very beginning, such an unnecessary re-
minder of callow, childish rebellion.

"I suppose," he thought, "that he's been brought here to
discuss my future. Damn him! Blast his neck! I wonder
Uncle Bobbie hasn't been dragged in, too!"

And he asked how they all did at Monk's Hall. Catherine
shook her head.

"They've decided to sell the house, or let it," she said.
"All the land is mortgaged, and now that rubber is paying so
badly, they can't possibly afford to go on there."

"Where will they go?"

"They thought abroad somewhere. It's easier to live
cheaply."

"Rough on Lise."

"It's a great deal harder on your uncle," said Catherine
quickly. "He was born there."

"All the more reason for wanting to get away. Nobody
should live in the house they were born in. Who are they
going to sell it to?"

"That's the difficulty. Nobody wants large houses nowadays. It's not easy to get any price for a house that size."

"Especially when it's"—he was going to say "such a
mouldy old hole," but from respect for his mother's feelings
he modified it and said—"got a northern aspect."

"The back windows face south," said Catherine, who
thought that her old home was faultlessly beautiful.

Trevor suggested that it might do for an institution of some
sort; an asylum or a nursing-home. He said this partly out
of mischief and partly because it really struck him as a good
idea. But she took the remark simply as a tasteless joke,
and the conversation languished into silence. Fortunately, it
was almost time to dress for dinner, and she went off upstairs,

pausing on her way to see if Trevor's fire was burning nicely. Generally, she did not allow bedroom fires, but this was an exceptional occasion, because Trevor had come through the war and would have to unpack. And it was a very cold spring night. Her own room struck as chill as a vault, as, shivering, she took off her black stuff bodice. She hurried into her red flannel dressing gown.

Trevor, down in the hall, would not go to dress. He wandered about vaguely, examining the books that lay on the tables and grunting at their dullness. Occasionally, he muttered a remark, half to himself and half to Philip. But he got no answer. Philip's short mood of sympathy was over, and he disliked the young man as much as ever. The moment when Catherine ran to the door had been beautiful and moving, but it had not lasted. The beauty had shivered and collapsed before Trevor's boorishness and Catherine's harsh disappointment. Philip took up the *Times* and buried himself behind it.

"Emily sent you a message," said Trevor at last.

This was a provocative opening. The newspaper came down at once.

"She wants to know who wrote the Catechism," Trevor hastily improvised. "I said you'd probably know."

"Why does she want to know that?"

"Couldn't say. Probably she's in love with a bishop."

Trevor hoped that this would be black news for his companion. But Philip merely inquired how the twins were.

"The same as ever. They never vary much, do they?"

"No. I must say, I was surprised, when I last saw them, to find them so little changed. One would have thought the war . . ."

"Yes, wouldn't one? But the war never affected William and Emily very deeply. They didn't take it seriously, you see. They take nothing seriously except perhaps a few things that the rest of the world calls nonsense. Look at William! Barring the fact that he could never remember which his right hand was, he made a very good soldier. He's so entirely biddable. He likes doing what he's told because it saves him trouble. But he didn't take it seriously. You know, when they were teaching us to bayonet sacks, all the men used to curse horribly and jab away at the sacks as if they were Germans. We were encouraged to go at it like that. But old William must needs call his sack a 'lousy lickspittle,' which made all the men laugh just when they were getting nicely worked up. His sergeant nearly killed him."

Philip recognized the essential levity of the Crownes in this anecdote. Long before the war, he had observed, with a slight twinge of anxiety, that the twins were somehow incapable of growing up. They got taller but no older. They travelled no farther from the East. It was as if they lived in a world that was free from the continual pressure of time. They put on the outward shows of maturity; they were confirmed; William's voice broke and he bought a razor; Emily was promoted in her turn to boned stays. But these things were, to them, little more than a sort of dressing up. At an age when most young people are stormy and rebellious, they kept the beautiful serenity of childhood. They dealt with their seniors in a spirit of acquiescence that was sometimes mistaken for common sense. They did what they were told, and they never criticized, for their grasp on the actual world around them was so slight that they could have no quarrel with it. The war came to them simply as another circumstance to which they must submit, another whim of the people set over them. William went to the front, and Emily made shells, but they still waited, as they had always waited, for the time when they should be grown up and free and able to live together in London. And now they had broken away and had bought a house in Kensington. Their aunt had done her best to stop it, but she could do very little, for they were of age and had free command of their very handsome fortune. Extraordinary rumours had already drifted to Water Hythe of their enormous personal and social success, so that to Trevor and Charlotte they appeared to be the most fortunate creatures in the world. To Trevor specially, on this night of home-coming, the very different lot of William seemed a little unfair. He could have done such amusing things himself, if only he had possessed an independent income. For he feared that his mother was going to be obstinate. Everything about her welcome, with its emphasis on old times, had been depressing to him.

The sight of his room, when at last he went up to dress, was enough to sink him still further into a slough of bitterness. Not even the bright firelight could make the place agreeable to him. His mother, with misplaced zeal, had collected and carefully set out all the treasures of his boyhood, so that he might feel entirely at home. His eye was continually falling on some object that was intended to encourage him to be a boy again. Most of these relics caused him acute shame, for nothing is more disconcerting than the memory of past enthusiasms. He had grown old enough not to have enthusiasms or to go about collecting things any more. He despised himself for having bought those Medici prints; they were donnish. And his edition of Kipling appalled him.

"God! How awful home is!" he thought.

The birds' eggs and stamps and butterflies were less compromising. Their date was further off. At fifteen he had been ashamed of them, but now they were amusing and rather pathetic. They were such small collections and so childish. He liked to think of himself as a little boy, but he could not bear to think what a callow youth he must have been. For there was nothing callow about him now. He had grown up into a good-looking, dapper, alert little man, with the reputation of a wit. That was how he thought of himself.

Charlotte, who ran in to greet him just before dinner, found him in a terrible state of depression.

"Hullo, Car!" He kissed her. "Nice sister you are. Why weren't you here when I arrived?"

"Because family reunions are so dreadful."

"You've said it! But I daresay it might have gone off better if you'd been there."

"Didn't it go off well?"

"No."

"What happened?"

"I was a brute to Mother."

He grew pale with contrition.

"She won't remember it," said Charlotte.

"I know. But I shall. I shall be very sorry when she's dead."

"Oh, dear! I'm always thinking that myself."

"You? My dear, you're a pattern daughter."

"No, indeed I'm not. But we get on better than we did. I try to remember that she's really devoted to us, and I avoid struggles as much as I can. I just let her talk. I say nothing. You know, the secret of getting on with them is to remember that old dogs can't learn new tricks. They can't change or adapt themselves and we mustn't expect them to meet us halfway or understand our point of view. We must do it all."

"I wish," said Trevor, "that one could be born without parents. It's a hopeless relationship. I'd thought things were better between Mother and me; but now I'm afraid they'll never really improve much."

There had been a better understanding during the war, because the issues were so much simpler. The small irritations and disputes of their daily life had been superseded, and were forgotten in his long absence from home. He had been able to admire and appreciate her calm, courageous fortitude. But now it was clear that this state of things had no permanence.

"What happened?" asked Charlotte.

"Oh, I don't know. We just sat about, and couldn't think of anything to say, and got on each other's nerves. It would have been better if Philip hadn't been there."

"Oh, was he?"

"Yes, my dear! *And* to dinner! The first night! Quite like old times, isn't it? And what's more, Car, I'm quite right; he is in love with Emily. I always said so. The only civil look I got from him was when I talked about her."

"That's no proof."

"With Philip it is. He's such a cold-blooded fish. The faintest interest, in him, is equal to a violent passion in anybody else. I don't mean that he wants to marry her, or anything carnal like that. But she's his Blessed Damozel. And I don't blame him, if he admires Botticelli. I daresay I'd be in love with her myself if she weren't my cousin. Just look at the time he took to prepare her for confirmation! It's my belief that this has been going on ever since. He never took half so much trouble with you. He did you in a class with all the Ratchet servant girls."

"And he'd have prepared Emily in a class, too, if she hadn't had chicken-pox."

"Well, I'm telling you, it began then."

"I don't think he writes to her. He didn't when he was in Palestine, anyhow."

"No, he wouldn't. He hasn't the gumption. There's the gong! Run along, my girl, or you'll be late."

She was late, but Catherine insisted on their waiting for her, and her apologies, when she did come down, were obviously thought to be insufficient. They drank their tepid soup in a very strained atmosphere, and Trevor came to grief over his first genuine attempt to be pleasant.

"I see," he said, "you've taken down the Leightons. I think it's an enormous improvement."

He nodded toward some bare spaces on the wall.

"They've gone to an exhibition," Catherine said coldly. "I was asked to lend them. Of course, they'll be put back. I wouldn't dream of taking them down for good."

Trevor shrugged his shoulders rather too blatantly, and Charlotte amiably tried to mend matters by saying that the Japanese vary their pictures with the seasons, and that it was an amusing idea. He was grateful to her and reflected that she was really grown up into a delightful creature. Her old, uncouth aggressiveness was mellowing into something fine and strong. It occurred to him that she must have a very poor time of it, living in this dull place, entirely ruled by his mother, and writing novels that nobody ever read. He was sorry that she had not more of a life of her own, that she did not marry. But she was still plain, bouncing, and awkward, with red cheeks and round eyes and prominent teeth; he did not suppose that she would ever get a husband. His mother ought to treat her better. A sense of grievance on Charlotte's account reinforced his own grudge against life.

Catherine, resentful, had determined to ignore her children and their foolishness. For the greater part of the meal she talked loudly to Philip about people whom Trevor and Charlotte did not know. And Trevor revenged himself by talking in an undertone to Charlotte about people whom his mother did not know. Also he described to her the fantastic doings of the twins, with whom he had been roistering a good deal, during the last few weeks.

"I don't understand this enormous *réclame* they have," said Charlotte. "After all, they've written nothing. Only one small book of poems between them, and that wasn't . . ."

"Oh, my dear Car, it's nothing to do with their writing, I can assure you. Nobody reads that. It's simply a success of personality; not what they've done but what they are. They're so—elusively radiant! It's not easy to describe. Partly, of course, it's their lineage. People naturally want to see them because they are the children of Norman Crowne."

At the name of Crowne, Catherine's attention wandered, and she called her garden boy Norman, when she discussed his confirmation with Philip, though his real name was Stanley.

"And of course," pursued Trevor, "there's a sort of *naïveté* about their entire freedom from self-consciousness. They are neither ashamed of *l'affaire* nor proud of it. They don't make capital out of it and they don't conceal it. People begin by admiring what seems to be a marvellous pose, and then they find out that it's no such thing. By some miracle, the twins don't appreciate the fact that they belong to a doomed family and all that."

"My dear Trevor! I don't know what you mean by a miracle." Catherine, unable to contain herself any longer, had finally deserted Stanley. "There's no miracle about it. It simply is that, as children, they came here and led a normal life and never heard any horrid gossip. In my opinion, it's the greatest pity that they should begin to call attention to themselves in this particular way. Especially Emily."

"They certainly call attention to themselves," agreed Trevor. "Partly, I suppose, because they always go about together and look so alike. Of course, either would be striking, anywhere; and the double effect is quite dazzling. He is so handsome, and as for her! I've heard her compared to La Bella Simonetta. Which is nonsense, of course. She's got the features, and that divine purity of outline, but she isn't essentially compelling. There isn't that innate sexuality . . ."

"I hear," said Catherine to Philip, "that they are putting on a new fast train from Ratchet to London, instead of the old 10:49. That will be a great improvement, but . . ."

"It isn't merely their beauty"—Trevor was determined to talk his mother down—"it is that the two of them seem to have, when they are together, a sort of iridescent quality that affects their surroundings. You see it all in a golden haze, don't you know. Anyhow, they've become absolutely the fashion. They go everywhere. They're a sure draw."

For a few minutes he was drowned by the train service, but he took breath and began again when Charlotte asked him if he thought it would last.

"No, it won't last. It can't last. Because they can't last. That's their charm. That's why everybody adores them; because they are made of something that doesn't last. Their career is as romantic as a soap-bubble, and that's the most romantic thing I can think of. You know how you have to watch it while it lasts. And you see all the things of your world reflected in it, only made lovely and strange and quite perfect, in a little, fragile, unreal sphere. And you see it drifting into all sorts of dangers, and just missing them, till it seems an absolute marvel that it can last so long. The whole romance of it is that you know it must come to grief. The solid, ugly things round it, the inevitable chairs and tables and fenders, are bound to collide with it sooner or later. It can reflect them beautifully, but if it touches them, it vanishes. The twins are like that. They sail past dangers. They skim over them. They keep making incredible, miraculous escapes. But they can't always do it. Sooner or later they'll come into direct contact with the vulgarity and snobbery and cold-heartedness that's all around them, and then they'll just . . . disappear."

"Trevor dear! Stop talking for a minute and pass Philip the port. He hasn't had any."

Trevor did as he was told. He stopped talking absolutely and did not utter another syllable until the ladies had left the room. He felt that the absurdity of the position was sufficiently obvious to everyone. He had demonstrated his own conversational powers and his mother's want of sympathy so neatly that even Philip must be aware of it. Also he felt that he had never done better justice to his famous simile of the twins and the soap-bubble.

When the ladies had gone, he apologized for the port.

"I like it," said Philip.

"My mother gets it at the Army and Navy Stores."

"So do I."

A short silence followed this exchange, which Trevor thought fit to break by a direct attack.

"I suppose," he began, "that you and my mother have been arranging my future."

"She has been speaking of it."

"It's very good of you to take so much interest in me."

"I don't know that I do," said Philip, cracking a walnut. Trevor gaped.

"Your mother," went on Philip, "likes talking about you. One naturally hears a good deal about you in her company. But I don't know that I wouldn't prefer it if she talked of something else."

"Well, I'm damned!" exclaimed Trevor. "I'm sure I wish you'd tell her so. It's been my fate through life to be talked over by relations."

"That's the fate of anyone who has relations."

"Yes. But, in my case, it's time it stopped."

"Is there anything so very unique about your case?"

"My relations haven't the right to utter a syllable. They should be sitting about in sackcloth. My career has been ruined through their mismanagement. The world they brought me up to live in has gone to pieces. I've got to start on my own now and make the best I can of the ruins, all on top of this incredible war of theirs. I didn't make it. But I, and my generation, will have to pay for it."

"Oh, dear! Oh, dear! I've heard this so often, Trevor. I wonder you can't even invent a grouse of your own."

"The older generation can't have it both ways. We fought for them. We risked our lives to get them out of this mess they've made. But they can't expect us to come home and sit meekly at their feet as we might have done in other circumstances. My mother simply doesn't realize that there's been a war. She's immense, really! She thinks she can bully me about my future and my profession as if . . ."

But Philip had had enough. He got up.

"I'm afraid I must be going," he said. "Please believe that I don't insult you by being over-interested in your career, Trevor. I'm sure you'll be an ornament to any profession you may adopt. And as for your remarks just now, a little solid reflection must convince you of their cheapness. If the past four years have proved your elders to be foolish and short-sighted, they haven't proved that you are wise."

"You're very glib, yourself, Philip."

"I'm always hearing young men talk as you've been talking, and I'm tired of it. One would suppose that nobody over the age of twenty-one took part in the late war. From the beginnings of history it has been admitted that the sort of anguish that your mother has endured in these years must be a good deal worse than anything you had to put up with. If you can't respect or comprehend the magnificent courage of such a woman, you can at least hold your tongue."

"I suppose you think I haven't played up? I admit it's all fallen rather flat. I admit it's not been heroic; not the traditional 'return of the soldier.' But if I'm to say my little bit, I must have some sort of cue. The first thing my mother did was to scold me for not having a nozzle. I defy anyone . . ."

"I think you've behaved abominably, if you want to know."

Philip was unreasonably angry, and he took himself off without saying good-bye to the ladies, who, for their part, were having a little battle of their own in the drawing room. For Catherine had caught just enough of Trevor's conversation during dinner to make her very uneasy. She began at once as soon as they had helped themselves to coffee.

"Who are these friends that Trevor means to go to Ireland with? I'd hoped that perhaps he might like to ask them down here for a bit, while he is making plans."

"I . . . I don't think you'd really care for these people much," began Charlotte reluctantly.

"Who are they?"

"One of them is Nigel Cuffe; you know, the man who wrote *If All the World Were Paper* and *The Round Pond* and . . ."

"I couldn't get through any of them," said Catherine quickly. "But of course . . . if he's a friend of Trevor's . . . I know he is considered a very clever writer. Who else?"

"His . . . his mistress."

Charlotte felt that truth must out sometimes, and that candour was really best.

"His . . . oh! . . . well, yes. That would be impossible. Will you ring for coffee to go out, Charlotte?"

"It's quite an accepted affair," Charlotte felt bound to explain. "They live together openly, I mean. And go about together."

"Not here. Not in my house." Catherine was quite decided. "I don't accept these ways. One has one's standards. I know that people nowadays feel differently, but . . ."

She was dreadfully flurried and a little excited, as though Charlotte had used an obscene word. It was impossible to hope for any sensible discussion, and Charlotte reflected miserably upon the difficulty of making a plain statement to an elder. It always resulted in getting or giving a shock.

"And who," asked Catherine presently, "is this Mrs. Van Tuyl? I don't think I've heard of her before."

She made a pretence of counting her stitches, but her voice shook a little, and Charlotte thought:

"I knew she was pricking up her ears over that, for all she pretended to be so interested in Stanley."

"I don't know much about her," she said at last.

"Is she married?"

"Yes. I believe her husband was something in the Dutch Legation."

"Was? Is she a widow?"

"I think she divorced him."

"Is she Dutch?"

"Trevor said half French and half Polish."

"Is she respectable?"

"Perfectly, as far as I know."

"And is she going with them on this Irish expedition?"

"I don't think so. She's on the stage."

Catherine mused. Life was getting very difficult. These Mrs. Van Tuyls, these dubious she-friends, had been, in the past, no problem at all. If they existed, it was in their own place. One never heard of them: they involved no lowering of standards. She repeated:

"Not in my house!" And then very quickly, with a little tremor, "He must choose! Trevor must choose!"

For she did not believe, she could not believe, that he would put these new friends before his own mother. If told to choose, he would mend his foolish ways.

When he came in, alone, it was Charlotte's tact that saved the evening from complete disaster. She asked him at once to play for them. He sat down and played Bach Fugues very badly because he was out of temper and had not practised for four years. Neither of the ladies could really have liked his performance, but they thanked him, with nervous civility, in each pause. Charlotte stared at the fire and dreamt of a companion, somebody with a mind like her own, with whom she could discuss all these trying situations. She longed for company. But she was sure that she would find neither friend nor lover until she got away from Water Hythe. And perhaps not then. She knew she was ugly and that she had better learn to like being alone.

Catherine sat bolt upright, knitting very fast. Her lips moved; she was saying to herself:

"Very well, Trevor! You must choose."

2

Trevor's sojourn at Water Hythe lasted rather less than a month. It ended in a complete breach with his mother. He returned to London, having flatly refused to become a barrister. Without delay, he went to tell his troubles to his friend, Tilli Van Tuyl, and as she happened to be giving a tea party, he made a very good tale of it to amuse her guests.

"I've been cut off with a shilling," he told them, "simply because I said the war was all my father's fault."

His hostess did not join in the laughter, because she had not quite made out who Trevor's father could have been.

"He was a man of great influence, Trevor's father?" she murmured to Nigel Cuffe, who was sitting next to her.

"Oh, enormous! Trevor! Tilli wants to know if your father was a man of great influence."

"One of the greatest men of his time," Trevor told her.

"Then he was dead before the war?"

"Dead as mutton."

"That's not a nice way, Cuffe, to speak of a gentleman's father. I shall have to call you out."

"But if he is dead, how has he made the war?"

Tilli was forced to abandon the exciting hope that Trevor's father might have been the Crown Prince of Germany.

"He was an *esprit fort*, Tilli. He wrote books."

"Ah! I understand."

She abandoned the point, which had become dull.

"And now you are to have no money at all?"

"None at all."

"But seriously? That is terrible!"

"Not seriously, Tilli. The truth is that his mother very rightly thinks him an idle dog and wants him to do some work."

"I do work. My notion is that the money which my father made by prostituting his art shall be spent in keeping mine pure. Thus good shall come out of evil and the sin of the Frobishers be purged. I explained this at home. I pointed out that Milton only got £10 for *Paradise Lost*."

"Surely," jeered Cuffe, "our Trevor can beat that!"

"Only relatively," he assured them lightly. "Only relatively. Think how the cost of living has gone up!"

Tilli remembered something of *Paradise Lost;* it was surely an immensely long poem. But vast! And it had been sold for £10! She was scandalized.

"It is terrible!" she said again, very gravely.

She was always sorry for people who were poor, because she hated being poor herself. The insecure Bohemianism of her life was far from being her own choice; she hated living in a flat in a mews, like an obscure cocotte, and she longed for a big house with gold chairs. But the acquisitive, cautious French half of her was often overruled by the Polish element, and this had always involved her in disaster. It was upon impulse that she had divorced her husband, a sudden irrational fatigue for her life with him, rather than any of the very legitimate grievances that she might have had against him.

Bitterly had she rued it since, for freedom had brought her nothing but poverty and loneliness. Still quite young, and not without charm, she found herself stranded in London with no influential friends and no secure position on the stage.

Her attraction consisted largely of a graceful, exotic ugliness. In type she was almost Mongolian, with high cheek-bones and a flat little nose, but with enormous, mournful black eyes. Her skin was clear and pale, and her straight, jet-smooth hair was cut quite short, though the mode of the Eton crop had not yet arrived. Despite her slender means, she contrived to produce an effect of shabby elegance in her person and surroundings. Her flat had distinction, for it was at the end of a mews and the sitting-room window looked up the street. Any vista, even in a town, gives a sense of space, and Tilli's little mews, with a sunset sky at the end of it, achieved sometimes a look of unexpected, delicate romance. Altogether, it was not a bad flat, and several people, including Trevor, were supposed to pay the rent for it.

But the world was wrong. She had, from policy, no lover. She was ambitious, believing that she might still do well for herself, and for that end she kept herself free from petty entanglements. Up to a certain point, Trevor's attentions were permitted, because he was useful to her. He knew the town and could give her a good deal of information. And she had to have some man to pay her taxi fares. So that, when the others took their departure, she kept him back with a faintly possessive air.

"You go to the Martins' to-night? I also. Stay and dine with me and we will go together."

"How about dressing?"

"Your clothes? Where are they?"

"Club. Just round the corner."

"Go now and dress. When you come back, dinner will be ready. It is better, more tranquil, than to go to a restaurant."

The room was empty when he came back, for Tilli was still at her toilet. He was struck for the first time by the impoverished air of the place. The decorations of the flat had little intrinsic merit; they were merely intended to set off a gay crowd. It was all red, white, and black, and the chairs were of club-lounge wicker with many scarlet cushions. A quantity of little inlaid Indian stools were scattered about, with ash trays on them and dirty glasses. Somebody had spilt soda water over the black stained floor and taken the varnish off. There were holes burnt in the curtains, and a fine cloud of dust lay over everything. The air smelt stale.

"Poor little thing," thought Trevor, "hard on her to live like this! Surely, if there was anybody . . ."

For he believed, as a rule, in her virtue. His occasional pricking doubts had no evidence to support them, and he always dismissed them hastily with the reflection that such things were none of his business.

He went across and opened the window on all the strange cries and footfalls of the London night. Fog drifted in from the mews. He leant out and sniffed it. It was the moment, he thought, to write a poem about the buttercup fields and Water Hythe and the clean joys of boyhood. But for Art's sake poor Tilli's ambiguous reputation must be sacrificed. The poem could only have one title: he must call it *The Harlot's Window*.

> Forth from the harlot's window, I
> Lean, breathe, and view another sky.

Water Hytne . . . Time's Scythe . . . he casts it down at Water Hythe . . . And drowsier reaps at Water Hythe . . . brown bodies flashing in the sunlit stream, or white bodies in moonlight? . . . laughing boys . . . small birds in briars . . . rooks in elms . . . the cawing, twittering, lowing and bleating orchestra of a pastoral poem struck up in his head.

"*Voyons*, Trevor! Shut the window! Do you wish the house to be full of fog?"

She had changed her dress and was all in gold like a shining, hard little beetle.

"I'm writing a poem," he explained, as he drew in his head and shut the window.

"And what is it called, your poem?"

"I don't know yet," he said untruthfully.

"It is not of me, then?"

"N-not exactly. Would you like it to be about you?"

"If it is a good poem. And then you will get £10 perhaps?"

"Not ten shillings, I should think."

"No? But I think it is a pity that you quarrel with Madame, your mother."

"So do I."

She stood at the fire, warming her quick, narrow little hands and looking at him out of the corners of her eyes.

"I do not understand it," she said at last.

"Don't mothers and sons quarrel in other countries?"

"They quarrel, yes! But in other countries they do not make a great history of it to the whole world. Except in the family, one does not speak of it. You English have no delicacy."

"We are the most reticent race in the world. I only spoke of it because everybody here happened to be my friends."

"Your friends! You call those your friends?"

"Well . . . Cuffe is."

"That one! He is his own friend; nothing more. I imagine that you and your mother will appear in his next book."

"He is rather a leper," agreed Trevor coolly.

"You think that everyone who laughs at your jokes is your friend?" Her voice was bitter. "I know better. I can tell you that there is no such thing as a real friend. Not one. It is my experience."

"What about you and me, Tilli? We are real friends, aren't we?"

She laughed and told him to come to dinner. He followed her into the tiny dining room, trying not to tread on the long tail of gold drapery that she dragged on the floor behind her, and they sat down on either side of a very small table. Tilli's maid, a heavy-footed Belgian, served them with an omelette.

"Of course," began Trevor when he had helped himself, "you take the woman's view. You can't understand friendship. It's too detached."

"It is humbug," she said briefly.

"Not so much as love."

"But much worse, I assure you. In love we make no pretence of unselfishness. We do not pretend that we want nothing of each other. We know very well what it is that we want. But in friendship we deceive ourselves and each other."

"You simply don't believe in disinterested affection?"

She nodded and said that, if he had led her life, he would say so, too. He was afraid that she was going to tell him how Van Tuyl had thrown her out of a window. It was the best-known fact about her. Everyone in their circle had told it in confidence to everyone else. He said hastily:

"I know, my dear. I know. I daresay you've very good grounds for taking a gloomy view of things."

The table was so small that their heads almost touched over it, and Tilli's eyes, in the flame of the candles, were melancholy and enormous. Seen at close range they were most extraordinary; not bitter any more but infinitely and mysteriously sad. Trevor gazed into them and looked quickly away, with a sense of having very nearly fallen into something. He reminded himself that she was really as stupid as an owl. He would not fall for these stale manœuvres.

"I know of cases to confute you," he said. "I have an uncle, for instance, who has sacrificed his whole life for his mistress."

And he told her the history of Bobbie and Lise, not so much because he thought it a case in point, but because he felt it safer to be talking. Tilli was interested; she liked listening to Trevor, because he was so handsome—just the type she most admired. She studied him while he talked, and thought that she might have been madly in love with him if he had been rich. But his circumstances put that out of the question.

"And yet," she thought, "how easy it would be! One would have only to look at him. Already this evening he is a little disturbed. I must be discreet."

Something in his narrative caught her attention. It seemed that he had an uncle and that the uncle was rich. There were possibilities in this. She made further investigations when they were drinking coffee by the sitting-room fire.

"It interests me very much, this story of your uncle," she said. "He has no children at all then?"

"None."

"And this house . . . Monk's Hall . . . there will be no son to live in it? That is very sad."

"No. But, as a matter of fact, he's having to sell his house. He's very badly off; one of those people who can't manage money."

"Ah."

Her faint hopes were dashed.

"It is very sad indeed," she repeated earnestly.

"Isn't it," said Trevor. "The place has belonged to my mother's family for seven hundred years. But it's an ugly house, outside. Like a stone box."

"Tell me about it."

He described it as best he could, and to her ears it did not sound ugly at all but very solid and magnificent. She hankered after just such a house for herself, for in her fluctuating fortunes she had inhabited many elegant little flats and a great variety of gorgeous hotels, but never a country house. She had a fancy that she might like to live in the provinces, and be dowdy and arrogant and secure; but that sort of thing was only achieved by people who kept their heads. This Lise, who had owned Monk's Hall for a little while, was obliged to give it up, because her man, though capable of disinterested affection, was unable to look after his affairs or leave his property to his handsome nephew.

It all showed how careful people ought to be.

"He has no other nephews but you?" she asked.

"Only my cousin, William Crowne."

"The son of Norman Crowne? Ah, yes. I have heard of him. But is he not very rich?"

"As rich as a Jew. But that's the Crowne side of the family, not ours."

"And he has already a beautiful house?"

"Not very. It's like a nursery."

"Every one speaks of him and his sister. Is he really like that? So handsome? So charming? So clever?"

"He's not clever at all."

"Not?" She raised her eyebrows. "But he has written a play."

"He's written dozens. They're no good."

"They tell me of one . . . an Eastern play . . . my friend Eugene Baxter was speaking of it. He wishes to read it."

"Baxter? That fat fool? Why does he want to read it?"

"Perhaps he will produce it."

"He'd never be so frantic. It's hopelessly undramatic."

"He has said to me that the name of Crowne is in itself a *cachet*. Also he is interested in literature. It is not as a commercial success that he would wish to produce it, but to amuse himself. He wishes to bring poetry back to the drama."

"Oh, I know he likes to pose as the Bayard of the poets, as long as he can find some fool to back him. But nobody in their senses would spend money on this."

"Perhaps your cousin . . ."

"William doesn't want to produce it. He says it isn't written for the stage. Though what use a play is if it isn't meant to be acted, I don't know. You can tell Baxter he'd better stick to Revue and his own side of the Atlantic."

"What is the subject of this play? What is it called?"

"It's called *The Seven Dawns*, or some such title. And it's about Buddha in one of his incarnations. A sort of miracle play. Buddhist theology hopelessly wrong, I should think. A great many very tedious, metaphysical monologues and about half a dozen lines of incredibly good blank verse. This young prince, very successful man of the world, soldier, poet, statesman, hunter, and all the rest of it, gets religion and goes into some sort of contemplative order. That's all there is to it. There are two or three pitched battles in it, if I remember, and a tiger hunt, and a great many arguments between priests in temples."

"Are there good parts for women?"

"I don't remember any."

Tilli shook her head over this. She knew that women, bazaars, and a few references to Allah and Kismet are essential in an Oriental play. She began to see why Trevor thought it a paltry piece of work. But it would be a feather in her cap to be able to say to Baxter that she had seen the Crowne play and that it had no women in it. She heard herself dropping the hint, ever so deftly:

"You waste your time, my friend. I have seen this play. It had perhaps half a dozen lines that will tell, but . . ."

Decidedly it was worth her while to talk to Trevor, for he was a most useful young man. But he must never be more. Her fatal impulses must be checked where he was concerned.

She gave him a melancholy look of farewell as he helped her into her cloak, and swore to herself that in future she would see less of him. But he, unfortunately, did not divine her inward resolutions, and when he had recovered a little he, too, took an oath. He had no wish to entangle himself with any woman.

They drove to their party in Chelsea, cooped up together in the electric darkness of a taxi, and having arrived they escaped from each other as soon as possible. Upon the door-step they had encountered an object-lesson in the matter of entanglements, for Nigel Cuffe was waiting there with the lady whom Catherine would never invite to Water Hythe. This was a person called Sally, and everybody forgot her surname. She always had a very depressing effect on Trevor, and he thought how awful it would be to arrive at parties with her. Of course, she was particularly dank; a little rat-faced girl with weak eyes, dumbly stupid, and dressed shapelessly in the crude materials of poster-art. Tilli, beside her, was all charm, all style and intelligence. It was pitiful to see how through the evening she went about after Cuffe like a little dog, and if she could not get near him, she would stand miserably aloof, patting her hair and looking so forlorn that even Trevor felt compelled at last to go and give her a kind word.

"Good-evening, Sally. Shall I get you an ice?"

"Oh, thank you. If you will do."

"When are you going to Ireland?"

"Oh, dear! We're not going."

"Not going? I thought it was all settled. Why is that?"

"I don't know," said Sally, after thought.

Cuffe was a man of moods, and she comprehended very little of the cyclonic laws that governed her existence.

"How's your puppy?"

"Oh, dear! I had to get rid of him. He barked, you know."

"You must get a kitten."

"They say," she volunteered, "that a dog is more faithful than a cat."

She licked up her ice with a subdued, apologetic greediness. Trevor watched her eat, and offered to take her plate away as soon as she had finished.

"Oh, thanks. If you will do."

He made off with it and took pains not to come back.

"God, what a woman!" he thought, as he fled upstairs. "And to think that she gets asked everywhere! It's my belief that Nigel simply does it to test his prestige. There can be no other tie."

Sally's devotion was the tie, had he but known it. She loved Cuffe with one of those blind, stupid determinations that mould destiny. Her attachment to the man was so much the most positive force in his surroundings that he had come to accept it as a condition of existence. And this might have seemed less ridiculous had she been a handsome creature; she did not look like the vehicle of a strong passion.

Trevor made his way into the large room upstairs and found that the company there had acquired a new vitality, as though a quickened sense of enjoyment had descended upon them. He wondered what had happened until he heard someone say:

"The Crownes have come."

Another voice said:

"Doesn't she look exquisite?"

And when he caught sight of Emily, standing with William in the middle of the room, he was surprised no longer.

Her fair hair was all pulled back from her forehead and plaited with loops of pearl, so that she looked more like La Bella Simonetta than ever. She would have wished, no doubt, to add a chain of live serpents round her neck, like the picture in the Louvre, if a chain of live serpents could be got. For she still adored dressing up, and she had contrived a dress of sea-green silk, all embroidered with little flowers, which flowed round her like a river. There was a sort of magnificence in all Emily's departures from the mode that redeemed them from any taint of artistic dowdiness. She turned extravagance into phantasy; she dawned upon the dullest party with an anticipation of gaiety, a conviction of present enjoyment which few of us preserve beyond our infancy. But it was a suppressed gaiety, because she never forgot her manners. It flitted irresistibly round the corners of her enchanting mouth, it sparkled in her eyes, it quivered in every flutter of her green draperies, but she kept it well in hand. Very sedately she was giving her "imitation of a young lady arriving at a party," and William supported her very competently.

Trevor found that he was being carried toward them by a general concentric movement. He had nothing in particular to say to them, but most of his friends were talking to them or standing close to them. They were the party. He almost wished that he had arranged to arrive at the house with his cousins, so that he might become, automatically, one of this group that always collected all the attention and life in the room. But then he did not want to be perpetually gathering crumbs at William's table. He caught Emily's eye and nodded to her.

"Can you come to breakfast with us on Monday?" she called over somebody's shoulder.

"When do you breakfast?"

"Eleven."

"All right. I thought you got up early."

"So we do. We ride first."

"I see."

"We've got something very important that must be discussed with you."

A voice at his elbow murmured something about hoping to be introduced. He was irritably aware that Tilli had got herself close to him. Out of the tail of his eye, he caught sight of Nigel pushing through the crowd, followed by Sally. Trying not to see Tilli, he began to edge his way round toward William; but she pursued him, and he began to despair of ever getting rid of her. Then a wonderful idea occurred to him and he accosted William in a low voice:

"Look here! I want to introduce you to a friend of mine, Mrs. Van Tuyl. I wish you'd look after her a bit. She doesn't know many people here, and I'm afraid she feels out of it. I think I told you about her once: she's a foreigner, half Polish, and had a brute of a husband who threw her out of a window."

This had quite the right effect. William grew pale with horrified compassion. He was always extravagantly sorry for anyone who was out of it or had had a bad time. At parties he had a way of going round and making himself charming to all the bores, so that Trevor once said that there could be no worse mark of social failure than to be seen talking to William. He saluted Tilli, when they were introduced, with a kind of hushed reverence and asked if she would not prefer to get out of this crowd somewhere downstairs. Tilli lifted her beautiful, melancholy eyes and drowned him in their infinite sadness.

"If you could, perhaps, find me a chair . . ." she murmured.

But it was she who found two chairs in a small recess on the stairs. When they were installed, she lost no time.

"On all sides," she said, "I hear of your play. You will produce it? No?"

"It isn't meant for acting," William explained.

"Ah! The stage is so vulgar! I understand!" She shook her head. "So much that cannot be said. But it must always be so until the poets will write again for the stage. Until some man is brave enough to make the attempt. But tell me, what is it called, your play?"

"*The Seven Dawns*," began William. "It's about India."

"*C'est gentil!*" commented Tilli. "I also have been in the Orient. At Alexandria."

William blinked a little at this, but he had no objection to talking of his work, and she really seemed anxious to hear all about it. So he went on, primarily intending to amuse her, if so broken and maltreated a victim could ever be amused. But presently he warmed to his subject and forgot that she had been thrown out of a window. As he talked, she took stock of him and came to several conclusions. In his way, she thought, he was very good-looking, but not as handsome as his cousin. It was a pity that he should be so rich, for she suspected that he did not know how to enjoy himself expensively. But she was delighted to be seen talking to him, especially by her friend, Eugene Baxter, who gave her a searching glance as he passed them on the stairs. She indicated the broad back of the great man to William and asked if they were acquainted.

"I know him by sight," said William, peering after Baxter with disfavour. "But I generally go away when he comes."

Tilli was silent with amazement, for she had never in her life even heard of a budding dramatist who evaded a millionaire producer on purpose.

"He'd make his fortune in the movies," said William, standing up to get a better look. "I never saw anyone funnier. Look at him being a distinguished Continental! Look at him kissing that woman's hand!"

"He has made his fortune already," said Tilli tartly. "In the theatre. Besides . . . he is my friend."

"Oh, I'm sorry!" cried William, flushing. "I didn't mean to be rude. But he's rather an amusing type, isn't he?"

"In order to produce successful plays, you think it is necessary to be *svelte* and *élancé?*"

"No, no. I'm sure he's a blazing old genius in his way."

She set him right about Baxter and had soon succeeded in making him ashamed of having mocked at physical deformity in a fellow-creature.

She spoke of Baxter's early career, his humble beginnings, and his yearning, in the midst of commercial success, to be of real service to the drama. She admitted that he had very little literary discrimination, but she asserted that he was waiting for a lead from one of the younger men. The grossest vulgarian may sometimes cherish an ideal. And William, as she talked, was moved to a compunction that she would not have understood, but that played into her hands—the delicate, compassionate deference that a rich man pays sometimes to a poor man. If Baxter in the nightmare life he must lead, without education, without tradition, with no shelter from the buffetings of the Philistines, had yet some hankerings after poetry, it was not for the fortunate William to despise him. He should, rather, be respected.

Down in the hall below, a little group of adherents had collected round the object of this discourse. He stood in the middle of them, immense and voluble, beaming at them through his glasses with a most engaging display of childish good-humour. He had sedulously cultivated a fantastically uncouth appearance, like some huge, amusing rag doll. It was his custom to shuffle into a party for a minute or two, wave his hand in acknowledgment of the ovation that he always received, swallow a cocktail, and shuffle out again. And for the upheaval of this departure Tilli was alertly listening, as she wished to have a word with him before he went. She was by his side when he stood on the front doorstep, loudly clamouring for his car.

"Why, Tilli!" he exclaimed. "You're not walking? Let me drive you. Where do you want to go?"

After a moment's hesitation, she was persuaded to let him give her a lift back to the mews.

"I have to-night heard all about Mr. Crowne's play," she told him.

"Is that so?" Baxter's spectacles glittered in the light of a passing lamp. "What sort of play is it, now? Could I do anything with it?"

"Almost. And so much will depend, naturally, on production. It must be greatly altered."

"That goes without saying."

"But do not say so at once," she admonished. "Say you will take it, and then . . . by degrees . . ."

"I haven't seen it yet."

"But you will see it. I have persuaded him to send it to you."

"Well, now, Tilli! That's good." Baxter patted her hand. "I'm very, very pleased if you've fixed that for me. I've wanted badly to see that play. I don't promise, mind you, to do anything with it; but I want to see it. I've an idea that we might make a big hit with that play. We might do something big with it. The plot don't matter so much, if it's an Eastern piece. They're all stolen from the *Arabian Nights* anyway. But then you say it's poetry, and poetry's a big risk."

"He is very rich," said Tilli, looking down at her hands. "If he wished to produce this play, I think it could be arranged very easily. You would lose nothing."

"You bet I wouldn't. And make nothing either. But I don't mind that. I want to cut loose once in a way. You may think I'm crazy, Tilli, but I wouldn't mind so much if it was only a success of esteem. It's just a sort of a kink, I guess. I'm not so pleased with the sort of work I'm doing. I wouldn't say it to anybody but you, though."

Baxter pondered solemnly for a few minutes on the strangeness of it all, and Tilli thought it wise to applaud.

"He has already a name," she pointed out.

"Yes, he certainly has got a name. And he's got people

talking. And it's my experience that people are getting to like something a little serious in their drama nowadays. Personally, I think it's the war. You'll find they appreciate a serious note where, before the war, they wouldn't stand for it. And he's got a name that'll get people interested. I suppose you couldn't say if there's a desert scene? Or a bazaar scene? Or a harem scene? No? What the hell does he go calling it an Eastern piece for?"

"There is a tiger scene," said Tilli quickly.

"Is that so? Well, I daresay I could get tigers." Baxter looked mollified. "And I'll want to have him put in a harem scene, something on a city roof, with a minaret, and one of those guys calling the faithful to prayer, or . . ."

"It's a Buddhist play, not Mohammedan," said Tilli, who had learnt a good deal about Eastern religions that evening.

But Baxter said serenely that it made no difference.

"You must be careful," she admonished him. "He is not very anxious to produce this play yet. Do not make him change too much at once. Be tactful!"

"I wouldn't be where I am, Tilli, if I wasn't tactful. Tell me something easier."

"I shall have a part," she told him instantly.

Baxter was cautious, benevolent, and adamant.

"I needn't tell you," he said slowly, "that I'd be very, very pleased to have you act. But I can't promise. It might be there wouldn't be a part that'd suit you."

"There will be," said Tilli with conviction.

3

Trevor, when he said that William's house was like a nursery, meant probably to deride its taste rather than to epitomize its charm. But it really had something of the unplanned attractiveness of a nice nursery. Its decorations were haphazard and rather shabby, for the twins had been in such a hurry to move in that they would not wait for the painters and paperers, and it had never been properly done up. The furniture was, as a rule, arranged severely round the walls, as though an empty space in the middle must be left for people who wanted to run about. A good many beautiful things were there, for the twins had a certain amount of taste, but nothing had been bought with reference to anything else. The chairs and tables, even the dullest of them, had each of them stood for some romantic purchase, and had acquired thereby the magic of a much-loved plaything, the vitality which distinguishes the battered contents of a nursery cupboard from the new, lifeless toys in a shop window.

Indeed, the whole house looked very much like a toy; it tossed its smoke to heaven from its four little chimneys with the irresponsible gaiety of a doll's-house. It seemed almost to boast of its real knocker and real window-boxes and the lady and gentleman inside eating a real dinner off a dining-room table that could be made larger or smaller in the most amusing way in the world.

Old Mattie, the housekeeper, saw to it that everything was kept very neat. She was, of course, a nurse in disguise. She had belonged to William and Emily very long ago, before they came to Water Hythe, and for many years she had lived in a little cottage where a grateful family had pensioned her off. But when the twins set up house, she came scurrying up to London to see what they were about. She took over the whole business of housekeeping; with the help of a girl, she mended their clothes and fed them and kept everything very bright and clean. She made them put their things away every night in orderly rows on shelves; the house was full of shelves, crowded with tidied objects, pretty things and useful things, all ranged into one engaging matter-of-fact whole.

But if Mattie had not been there, it is to be feared that everything would have been left on the floor.

Trevor had a story that she came to fetch them away from parties, but this was not true. She did, however, sit up for them, and if they were very late she scolded them unmercifully.

"Your shoes is wet, Miss Emily. You've been walking out on the grass with your cough. . . . Oh, I've no doubt you enjoyed yourselves, but you should have brought your sister home earlier, and that's all about it. You've missed your beauty sleeps."

She would brush out Emily's bright hair and put her to bed in the beautiful bed, with four golden angels on its four high posts, that William had bought for his sister as a Christmas present. And then, having slept the short, light sleep of the old, she would be up very early in the morning, long before the girl, getting ready a first cup of tea for her charges before they went riding. Emily woke every morning to her greeting:

"Seven o'clock, my lamb, and it's raining ever so."

"Oh! Oh, dear! Then we can't ride!"

Mattie would draw back the curtains upon bright sunshine.

"But, Mattie! It's not raining at all."

"It will, my lamb. Never you fear. Fine before seven, rain before eleven. And it's been raining all night."

"Oh, no, Mattie. Indeed it hasn't. It was a lovely sunrise. We saw it coming back, and we went down to the river to look at it. The sky was as red as . . ."

"Red sky at night is the shepherd's delight. Red sky in the morning is the shepherd's warning. It's a bad sign. You don't want to go riding to-day. Not to-day. You just turn over and get some more sleep."

"Is William awake?"

"He's as fast as fast. Don't you go riding this morning, my

lamb. If you go on at this rate, you'll tire yourself out. You'll be ill, and that'll be the next thing."

"Oh, Mattie! I had such a funny dream. I dreamt . . . oh, dear . . . I remembered a minute ago . . . it was . . . I forget . . ."

"You go to sleep."

William on his way to the bath would give a loud rap at the door, just to show that he was awake in spite of Mattie's assertions. And at that signal all Emily's drowsiness would be dispersed. She would leap out of bed in a tremendous hurry to begin the day. She chattered incessantly while Mattie brushed her hair and generally fought over the question of a warm woollen vest in the cold morning air. Till at last the pair of them were dispatched to Richmond, where their horses were kept, not without a dispute on the doorstep as to who should drive the car. Mattie would settle it:

"Emily drive going and William coming back. Mind now and be careful at the corners and don't fall out of your motor or off your horses and be home by eleven punctual."

In this way, they had ridden and chattered through the cold dark mornings of winter and into the spring, when the sun was a little higher up every day and Richmond Park looked greener. The almond in the villa gardens at Castlenau came out, and the crocuses and the daffodil . It was in the middle of daffodil-time that William threw the first disturbing pebble into the clear poo of their happiness.

"I've got a plan," he said one morning, as they skimmed in the early sunshine down the street.

"Oh?"

"I've been thinking it over for a long time, and I've decided that I want to produce *The Seven Dawns*."

Emily nearly ran into a milk-cart.

"Oh, William! But theatres are so vulgar!"

"They needn't be. They can't always have been. If they

are, it's because poets won't write for the stage. Somebody has got to do something about it. And not everybody can afford to take risks as I can. In a way, it's my duty . . ."

"But you never meant *The Seven Dawns* to be acted."

"I was wrong. And I've come to see I was wrong. A play can't be a play until it's acted."

"Nobody would go to see it."

"That doesn't signify in the least," said William loftily.

"I mean, no manager would take it."

"If that is the case, I shall produce it myself."

"Do you mean—buy a theatre?" Emily's eyes sparkled. "That would be rather fun, wouldn't it! I've always longed to own a theatre. Do you remember that little toy one that Trevor and Charlotte had when we were small? I did so want to play with it, and they never would let me."

"As a matter of fact, this man Baxter might be of use to me. He's not as bad as he looks, by all accounts."

"By whose accounts?"

"Well, Mrs. Van Tuyl has been telling me about him."

"That woman you met at the Martins'?"

'Yes. I ran across her last night again, and we had a long talk. You must meet her, Emmie. She . . . she's a most remarkable woman. Extraordinarily intelligent, but not in the least annoying, you know. And she listens to what one says."

"What is she like?"

"I'm telling you. She's on the stage herself, and I really think she knows what she's talking about."

"I mean, what does she look like? Is she pretty?"

William could not say. After reflection, he asserted that she was not at all pretty but that she had good eyes.

"She sounds nice," said Emily, with a sudden warmth.

"She's had a very sad history," confided William in an awe-stricken voice. "Trevor told me. She was married to a horrible man who threw her out of a window."

Emily shivered as if a coldness had come over the sun.

"Was it a very high window?" she asked.

"I don't know," said William.

They crossed the river by Hammersmith Bridge, where everything was glittering and newly washed in sunlight. Silver gulls darted over the tide, and the wind was almost like a sea wind. It was terrible to think that people in this same world should throw their wives out of windows. After a long pause, William began again:

"I'd like very much, if I could, to get her into the play. I think she might really be rather wonderful on the stage. She wouldn't vulgarize it. And it might be a good thing for her. I gather she's very badly off. She lives in a mews and gets what work she can, but she's had an awfully hard time. It's not easy to get on when you have no friends in London. Really, people are very unjust, you know. Because she has divorced her husband and lives alone they must needs say the most cruel things about her. A woman in that position is defenceless against gossip. Of course, she could perfectly well have married again if she had liked, but she happens to care for her art more than anything else. That's what people will not understand."

"Did Trevor tell you all this?" asked Emily, surprised.

"N-no. I just gathered it."

"But there's no good woman's part in the play."

"I might manage it," he said dauntlessly. "I've never been really satisfied with it, as you know. It'll have to be altered a lot. I thought the prince might have a sister who became a nun . . . a sort of parallel drama. She said wasn't there a dancing-girl or something quite small. But I don't think that would quite do."

"I shouldn't like it to be altered," said Emily firmly.

"Oh, well . . . it's just an idea, you know. Nothing's settled yet. But I see no harm in just letting Baxter see it, do you?

After all, he's an experienced man, and he might be able to criticize it in quite a valuable way."

They put up their car and mounted their horses, and were soon galloping under the trees in the park. It was, for them, the best moment of the day. The keen air, the swift movement, the sunlight and each other's company were utterly satisfying. Their faces were solemn with delight as they sped away, raced each other, and pulled up at last to admire the view over Petersham.

"This is the best one we've had yet," said Emily.

"You say that every time."

"I know. I think it every time. To-morrow I shall. And the day after that. I don't want this day to end, and yet I want to-morrow to come. William! I'm perfectly happy."

"So am I."

"What did you say?"

"I said: *Verweile doch, du bist so schön.* You know Faust needn't have gone to hell if he could have ever said that at any one moment. Well, I say it every morning."

"Just for luck. To-morrow we might fall down and break our legs and not be able to ride."

He caught her eye and smiled. Their spirits as they trotted back were a little subdued. And as they got near to their gate of the park he gave words to her thought.

"Won't it be horrid," he said, "when we get married?"

"I don't see why we ever should get married. Why can't we always live just like this?"

"Everybody does. I'm sure we shall. We can't go on forever like this. Just think what a couple of mugs we shall look in sixty years' time, being dragged to the top of this hill in bath-chairs every morning."

"Anybody looks a mug in a bath-chair, anywhere, at any time. That's old age, not celibacy, William."

"No, but the only consolation for being in a bath-chair,

that I can see, is to have great-grandchildren to be rude to. When I'm a very old man, I shall be a perfect devil to all my descendants. I can't say that I much want children. But I should like to have grandchildren, and I desire great-grand-children quite passionately."

Emily laughed. The thought of their great-grandchildren had no terrors. It was too far away.

"But you don't want a wife?" she protested anxiously.

"No. Nor do you want a husband. But we shall break into matrimony one of these days. Everybody does."

"I swear I won't."

"What'll you bet?"

"Everything I have. But if you must, please let me choose your wife. She must be very nice."

"My wife," said William confidently, "will be a darling. I sha'n't marry anybody who isn't a darling."

Some of the glitter had gone from the day as they drove home. William steered this time, and Emily talked, and whenever he answered they ran into things. So that it was with their usual air of having triumphantly surmounted an emergency that they drew up at their own doorstep. Trevor was just ringing the bell. He said that he had been invited to breakfast by Emily, because they had something to discuss with him.

"Oh, yes, I remember," she cried as they all trooped into the hall. "We wanted to talk about Monk's Hall. Oh! What a lot of letters!"

"Monk's Hall?" said William. "Yes, that was another plan I had. I'd forgotten. Come into the dining room, Trevor! I want to know what you think before I write to Uncle Bob-bie. Look! Will you have kidneys, or eggs and bacon, or all, or some? Or won't you begin with porridge? And there's grapefruit. We always eat a large breakfast because we work from now till half-past four."

"Oh, William, here's a press-photographer wants to come and photograph my bed! What would Mattie say? Don't you think it would look very bad? I'm sure no honest woman would allow such a thing. Tea or coffee, Trevor?"

"The papers are full of your bed," said Trevor. "I read about it the day before yesterday, and how it has scenes painted on it from the lives of Cupid and Psyche and four angels on the top of it, and how it was designed by William's close friend, Mr. Peter Yates. It was a priceless little par; I meant to send it to you. It began with your being conspicuous among the lunchers at the Berkeley in a *panne* hat, whatever that is, and then it mentioned your parentage, and finally broke out into a most voluptuous description of your bed."

"How could they have known?" she wondered.

"These things get about," William told them. "But it is really a nice bed, though it's a little large for Emily. And the paintings are not very suitable for a virgin: I wanted Yates to do panels of Daphne and Apollo. But about Monk's Hall. I've been thinking of buying it."

"Buying it!" said Trevor slowly. "What for?"

"Why, Lise and Bobbie want to sell it . . . and I want a house in the country. If I bought it, they needn't turn out. They could stay there and run it for me, and I could be there or not as I liked, without any bother."

"Isn't it much too large?"

"I don't know," said William. "If I had a large house, then I could have a lot of people to stay. Peter, for instance. He has no proper workshop. I thought if we took Monk's Hall that he could more or less live there and work in one of the barns. He could paint his beds and things a great deal better there than in a much too small attic in Bermondsey. And then the Hackbutts. You know my friends the Hackbutts? They have to live in a caravan because they can't afford a house. They've had seven children in six years—two sets of twins!"

"They should read Stopes," said Trevor without sympathy.

"Nothing they read seems to do them any good. And poor Mandy Hackbutt tries to write plays. I think they'd be good plays if he could finish them. But he says you'd never guess how difficult it is to write a play in a caravan till you've tried. There'd be plenty of room for them all at Monk's Hall if they liked to come for a bit."

"All seven children! Are you quite mad? Do you want to turn the place into an asylum?"

"Not exactly. But I thought, if I did it up nicely, and could have plenty of room for guests . . ."

Trevor's bacon and eggs were growing cold on his plate. He sat with a deep frown on his face, and the twins looked at each other in dismay. They had feared that he might resent their plan of trying to buy Monk's Hall, and they were determined to get his approval first. For they could all remember a time when he had boasted that the house should be his, though they were too delicate to mention it, and they had agreed to abandon the plan if he was not amenable. It was principally for the sake of Bobbie and Lise that they were anxious to make the purchase at all.

"I don't know what you're asking my advice for," he said at last. "It's your concern. It's nothing to do with me."

"You're one of the family," Emily told him. "It's partly to keep it in the family that we thought of doing this. We'd rather talk it over with you before speaking to the old ones."

"They won't like it a bit," he said, still thoughtful. And then he began to laugh. "Poor Mother! What will she say to the seven little Hackbutts? Lise was hard enough to swallow. If you start this asylum for indigent artists . . ."

"I'm not . . . I don't mean anything of that sort."

"But I think you should. It's a very good idea."

The tempest of anger that had kept Trevor silent at first

was beginning to subside. He felt cool and remote and a little malicious.

"It's a very good idea," he repeated. "I always meant to start a sort of colony there when I was expecting to have the place myself."

The twins looked uncomfortable.

"And as it turns out"—he observed them with amusement —"I'm in quite as much need of shelter as the Hackbutts. More. I've not even got a caravan. I wonder you don't offer to house me."

"There's lots of room!" exclaimed William. "Of course . . . if you'd care . . . ever to make use of it . . ."

He glanced across at Emily, who added eagerly:

"Or any of your friends. We want it to be a sort of family country house."

Trevor laughed again. The idea was really amusing, and it would be such an excellent counter to his mother's ultimatum if he were to settle at Monk's Hall, of all places. For two pins he would ask Nigel and Sally to come, too. And if William liked to pay for it all, so much the better. That would show that nobody was being jealous of anyone.

"I'll think it over," he said, as he turned to his breakfast. "But you ought, you know, to regard it as a definite community with certain stated social and artistic aims."

"Why?" asked the twins in some dismay.

"Because it would be so interesting. I've always wanted to see how a plan like that would turn out. You might make a great success of it: it might be the beginning of an entirely new epoch of the arts. The community spirit has got to come back into life somehow: the world is too large and the artist gets lost in it. Since the monasteries were dissolved, we have had no expressions of a group spirit. . . ."

He talked for a long time, generally with his mouth full, and succeeded in drawing a most attractive picture of an ideal, self-supporting community with its own art and its own laws. Beehives, market-gardening, and hand-looms were mentioned. The profits were all to be pooled, so that no one member of the community need be harassed in his work by any thought of financial pressure. He made out quite a good case for it, and very nearly succeeded in convincing himself, though the twins remained dubious.

"We could turn the drawing room into a common room," he pointed out, "with a stage and a piano. And we'd act there. Only a really strict censor must be appointed to see that only pure music is performed. We can't let any of the inmates go whoring after Wagner."

"All this is going much further than I meant," objected William gloomily.

It was a relief that Trevor should be taking it all in such good part, and he did not like immediately to throw cold water on these plans, though they sounded silly to him and he had himself a partiality for Wagner. He did not know what to say.

"I'll see about buying the house," he suggested, "and we'll settle all these details later."

Trevor found his embarrassment extremely funny. He grew quite determined that William should buy Monk's Hall and that a great deal of comedy should be got out of it. It was not the first time that he had developed the twins' ideas for his own ends, and if his conscience nudged him, he was able to stifle it by the reflection that William ought by this time to be capable of looking after himself. The twins had everything, and he had nothing; if he did not profit by their good fortune, there were plenty of others who would.

"Yes," he said, "you make haste and buy the house first. No, thank you, Emmie. I won't have any more honey I've really done. What magnificent breakfasts you do eat! I don't wonder you miss out lunch. What a life! First riding, then work, then social recreation. It's marvellous how you get it all in. It's positively Greek. You ought to write like all the poets rolled into one, William, leading the good life so strenuously. I wonder why you don't."

"I do," said William equably, for he took Trevor's contempt of his work in perfectly good part. "And by the way, do you know I'm thinking of producing *The Seven Dawns?*"

"Mercy! You're mad! Who put that into your head?"

"Nobody put it in. I thought of it in my bath."

"Mrs. Van Tuyl put it in," said Emily, just a little crisply, as she gathered up her letters.

"Tilli!" Trevor gasped at this amazing sequel to his own diplomacy. "She didn't! The little vixen! Is that what she's after? I won't allow it. I shall have to speak to her."

"It has nothing to do with her," said William. "Emmie doesn't know what she is talking about."

"But he's going to write a part for her."

"She's a daughter of the horse-leech," cried Trevor.

"I've not made up my mind," protested William rather angrily. "And I don't want to hear it discussed."

"I'll speak to her, though," insisted Trevor.

For though he did not mind exploiting William himself, he would not countenance such ways in anyone else. He took himself off with a very long face, and when he had gone, the twins had a quarrel. William accused Emily of indiscretion and prejudice and reduced her to tears. The name of Mrs. Van Tuyl was flung between them like a missile, until Emily began almost to hate her. A shadow had fallen on the day, and no satisfactory work was done by either of them. William endeavoured vainly to graft a good woman's part on to *The Seven Dawns*, and Emily, who was engaged upon a novel about witches in the Seventeenth Century, found herself compelled to burn the first seven chapters.

"It really might be a good thing," she thought as she poked the embers, "if we all went and lived in the country."

CHAPTER III

"THE SEVEN DAWNS"

I

IT WAS impossible to keep pace with the headlong rapidity of the Crownes. They were not unreasonable; they would listen to advice if it was given in time, but nobody had ever been quick enough to catch them in the breathless instant between thought and action. Their boats were always burnt before their would-be counsellors had time to grasp what was afoot, and this was the secret of their singular immunity from family interference.

The news of William's intention to buy Monk's Hall had scarcely reached Oxfordshire before his sister appeared in person to coerce her seniors into immediate, dazed compliance. It seemed that William himself was unable to leave London because he was producing a play, but Emily came down for a week to Water Hythe, set them all by the ears, concluded the deal, and darted off again. Had she stayed a fortnight, the bewildered Bobbie would have begun to ask for time, and Catherine's heavy artillery of criticism and conclave would have been got into action. But a week, as she pointed out to William, would be quite long enough; the initial advantages of the scheme were such as to strike anyone in a moment, and the less they all talked it over among themselves the better.

"I agree," said William. "If once they begin discussing, it'll be endless. All the oldest inhabitants will be called in. It's a funny thing, you know, Emmie. I've often noticed it. The shorter the time that's left to anyone to do things in, the longer he takes to think it over. You'd have thought it would be the other way round. We can afford to take our time, and they ought to be in a hurry. But just think what it will be like if we are all held up till Philip, or somebody like that, has given his considered opinion."

"Philip will be on our side," said Emily quickly. "He always is, really, though he's too polite to say so."

"Oh, I daresay his opinion will be perfectly sound when he produces it, but he'll keep us all waiting. I suppose when you get to be elderly, one day seems so very much like another that you don't notice how quickly . . ."

"He's not really so old . . .   Philip. He isn't fifty."

"Being elderly is a state of mind. I don't suppose poor old Philip was ever anything else. You nip down there and buy that house before anybody has time to ask his advice."

So Emily nipped, and had got affairs well under way by the time that Catherine had posted her first frantic appeal to Philip at Ratchet:

Please come over at once, or go up to Monk's Hall and talk to Bobbie. It is really urgent. Emily has come down on a *most* extraordinary piece of business. It seems that William wants to *buy Monk's Hall*. Of course, the idea delighted me at first; but it is not a step which should be taken without a great deal of careful consideration, and the children seem determined to arrange everything in a violent hurry. I am not surprised that they never consulted me. I am quite used to that. And I am very much afraid that it has all been Trevor's fault. The twins could not have been capable of such an idea if it had not been put into their heads. Of course, it must be prevented. Not the actual purchase, I mean. I daresay we may approve of that, when we have thought it over. But their plans seem to be so extraordinary. I gather that they are going to put the house to a *very shocking purpose*. And Bobbie is so inert. You must talk to him, Philip. Come over and see me first. Come over to-morrow. We really have no time to lose.

Philip could not imagine what was going on, and as he hurried over to Water Hythe he changed his mind several times as to the shocking purpose to which the house was to be put. Sometime she thought of racing-stables and sometimes of a gambling-hell, and then he wondered whether William could have married three wives at once and was proposing to keep them all at Monk's Hall. But, on the whole, it mattered very little. His pleasure and excitement at the thought of seeing Emily were such that he would not have minded if she had proposed to dynamite every house in the countryside.

For some years now he had been devoted to her, but it was romance of a placid, impersonal sort. He looked forward to his rare meetings with her very much as some people look forward to the performance of a favourite symphony. They were tremendous events, keenly anticipated and remembered with thankfulness, but they were governed by forces over which he had no control. He was content to wait until chance brought her in his way. He never sought her out, for to do so would have been to brush some of the bloom off his idyll: it would have given a busy, scheming little touch to a relationship that he liked to believe was entirely passive. He never went to London to see her, nor did he write very often. It was better that her comings and goings should have all the charm of unexpectedness, like fine weather.

In fact, he felt for her all that he was no longer able to feel for Lise, but with the attenuated vigour, the more delicate idealism of his increased years. His attachment to Lise had begun in desire, and with the waning of that flame it had lapsed into mere sentiment. But for Emily he had never felt anything short of passion, and the selflessness that passion breeds. It had invaded him when she was still so very young as to be infinitely remote. She was more unattainable than Lise had ever been, for no mere common obstacle, no husband or friend, stood between them. It was the essence of her, the lovely youth that he had left so far behind him.

It seemed to him as though the flowery lanes between Ratchet and Water Hythe had taken a sudden leap into summer at her coming. He discovered that he had himself been dead all the winter. He had accomplished nothing. His recaptured leisure, the long, quiet evenings by his solitary fireside, had all been so much waste. They were tedious. They petrified him. He supposed that he must have looked forward to it all too much. In Mesopotamia he had longed so terribly to be at home, but now, though he had been repossessed of his kingdom for six months, he still found himself a stranger in his own place. The good things were all there, but the mood to enjoy them had been shattered. He realized that he would have to grow fresh roots, but he grudged the time that it would take, since more than half of his life was already over.

"For, in some ways, I feel younger than I ever did before," he explained to himself.

Like most solitary people, he was inclined to conduct long imaginary conversations with a sort of second self, a mute, sympathetic, but rather stupid auditor to whom everything had to be made exceedingly clear. And to this person he now confided a humiliating truth:

"You know, I've suffered all my life from being two men at once."

"Everybody does," said his companion.

"Not as much as I do," insisted Philip. "My two are deadly enemies. When one cries the other laughs. When one is noble the other sneers. When one is ignoble the other nags. They lead a cat-and-dog life. It's not the jaded contest between good and bad. The truth of the matter is that one is a very old gentleman and the other is a promising young fellow."

At this point he caught sight of Emily, a couple of fields away, running by the river-bank. And his argumentative companion vanished like the flame of a candle that has been blown out.

She had not seen him. She was running and throwing sticks for the youngest of the Water Hythe dogs, a wheezy veteran at most times, but to-day a little above himself by reason of the spring air. The grass beneath her feet was thick with daisies, neat and gay, like the flowery field in some old Italian picture. They seemed to spring up from the earth where she trod. She was bareheaded to the cold laughing wind, the sun and clouds of an April sky. She was almost as lovely as he had imagined her to be.

Ravished at the sight, he stood quite still. For an instant he had made as though to pursue her, but he checked himself in time. Pursuit was not for him; he knew too much. He knew that spring is a flame that burns upon no hearth, and he was glad to be so old and so wise. If he had been younger, this ecstasy in his bosom might have driven him on to commit some folly. And then he would surely have lost her, since it is man's lot to pursue one woman and to capture another, to woo a maid and to win a wife. Because he wished to love her for ever, unchanged, because he wished to keep her perfect in his heart, he let her pass, unhailed.

"And besides," he explained to his companion, who was with him again as he hurried to Water Hythe, "if I had called to her, she would have been bored. I can talk of nothing that would interest her. She has her own friends . . . her own life . . ."

"Very true, Philip. But as a matter of fact, you were shy, and nothing else."

Relieved and yet full of regret, complacent, yet a little ashamed, he passed out of the bright, changing airs of the spring day into the immutable gloom of the hall at Water Hythe. The portrait of Frobisher by Watts glowered down at him from over the fireplace with a forceful vagueness. The past shut him in. He remembered that it was still possible for people to think, in this house, as they had thought in the days of Frobisher. For Catherine, despite years of warfare and disaster, had succeeded in preserving something of the spacious regimen of the 'eighties. And she had done it simply by reason of her invincible obstinacy, her blindness to the new heaven and earth which had come into being beyond her doors. She believed in the ways of her own generation so passionately, was so determined that all innovation must be an accident, that she had really kept, intact and vital, some of the spirit and tradition that had gone to the making of her house. Philip could never visit her without immediately feeling its influence; a desire was sure to rise in him to sing with her a dirge for the good old days.

She plunged, as usual, into her subject, before the polite murmurs of convention had got past his lips.

"Oh, Philip! How good of you to come so promptly. You got my letter, I suppose? I'm afraid, perhaps, I put it all rather strongly, but the whole idea was such a shock. Since I wrote to you, I've thought it over. I've slept on it. And really, I don't feel we need to worry so much. They must come to see for themselves that it's impossible."

"What is it, exactly, that they want to do?"

"Well, in the first place, as I told you, they want to buy Monk's Hall. And that part of it seems to me very sensible.

In fact, between ourselves, it's been largely my doing. I've been working for it for some months."

"Have you?" cried Philip in surprise.

Catherine nodded.

"I gave William a pretty broad hint, the last time he was down here. And I talked to Bobbie."

This was the first that Philip had heard of it. But he was quite ready to believe that she spoke the truth. If William had got a sensible idea in his head, it must certainly have been put there by somebody else.

"Of course," he suggested, "it's a little hard on Trevor."

"Oh, no, no! I don't think of it in that light at all. I don't consider that prospects of that sort would be at all good for Trevor just now: they must encourage him in these silly, idle ideas. And in any case, the possession of such a place, nowadays, must always be a burden rather than an advantage."

"And it would surely be a good thing to keep the house in the family. You must be glad of that."

"Yes. And that is my difficulty. I don't want to stop the actual purchase. To oppose that would be very unwise. One doesn't want to coerce them. I mean, one doesn't want to seem to coerce them."

"What do they want to do?" asked Philip anxiously.

He was beginning already to adopt her point of view. He always did, simply because her ideas were definite and his were not. Although he normally thought of Trevor, Charlotte, William, and Emily as very distinct and individual creatures, he was apt, in Catherine's company, to discuss them collectively, as though the common denominator of their youth had reduced them all to a type.

"They say that they are going to start a Settlement," exclaimed Catherine in an irritated voice.

"A Settlement? For slums or something?"

"No, no. Much worse. For artists, and writers, and that sort of people."

"Great heavens! What for?"

"That's what I asked."

"You mean to say that Emily . . ."

"I'm afraid it isn't so much Emily," Catherine told him mysteriously, "or William. I'm very much afraid it's Trevor. Emily merely talked about buying Monk's Hall, and how convenient it would be for Lise and Bobbie. But then Trevor wrote a letter to Charlotte that cast an entirely new light on the whole idea. It's quite ridiculous, really."

"But does Trevor mean to start a Settlement?"

"It's the merest excuse, my dear Philip. He means, of course, to come down and live here himself. I know he is doing it simply as a sort of childish defiance to me. I asked Emily about it, and she, as usual, was very vague. She said that she and William had merely intended to offer a home for a little time to some friends who were badly off. But even that seemed to me a foolish plan. Why should they burden themselves with these pensioners?"

"It's just the sort of thing the twins would do."

"I said to her, 'You'll merely surround yourselves with a crowd of second-rate hangers-on.' I told her: 'Respectable writers don't sponge on their friends. I've had experience of that sort of thing all my life, and I know the way that class of people get hold of you.' I said: 'Your uncle had a dozen letters a week from starving poets with twelve children.' But, of course, she wouldn't listen to me."

"Poor child! One knows so well. At that age, these things seem so easy to put right."

"And to crown everything, Charlotte is egging them on! She talks of going there, too. She says she will get more time for her work, as she calls it. As if she couldn't write here all day long! But it seems that she finds a difficulty in living her own life, to use an expression that they all seem very fond of. It seems odd, when you think how I've urged her to take up some regular profession, instead of idling away her time here."

Philip snorted. He had no sort of sympathy for Charlotte.

"She doesn't feel that the atmosphere of my house is congenial," went on Catherine bitterly. "Though, as I told her, some of the greatest writers of her father's day did their best work here. 'My dear child,' I said, 'if you only knew how you make me laugh!' Because really it is laughable. When you think of the people who have stayed here. People whom I knew intimately."

"But the whole idea is simply preposterous," broke in Philip, who had begun to grasp it. "Do you mean to say that William wants to buy Monk's Hall simply to house Bobbie and Lise and Trevor and Charlotte?"

"Yes, and that's not all." Catherine's voice sank, and she leant forward, peering at Philip through the shadows of the room. "I'm afraid that's not the worst. Trevor talks in his letter of bringing his friends here. Those people whom I refused to have in this house. He means to bring them to Monk's Hall. To my mother's home."

"As part of this extraordinary Settlement?"

"Apparently. These . . . these people . . . the sort of people that one simply never used to mention, Philip. The . . . the worst sort of people . . . really low, bad women . . ."

"Oh, my dear Catherine!" Philip could not help a protest. "I don't think you can quite say that. You mean this Mr. Cuffe? Even though his affairs are not exactly regular, I think you are making a mistake . . ."

"Oh, I know I'm out of date. I understand from Trevor that this sort of thing is quite usual nowadays. It seems that no writer can be happily married in the ordinary way. They used, in our day, to manage it, but . . ."

"Ruskin," began Philip, "Meredith, Carlyle, Dickens, Thackeray . . ."

And he stopped uncomfortably, remembering that first wife of Frobisher's, who had run away.

"They had domestic troubles," conceded Catherine. "But people nowadays don't even seem to try to be decently married. This Mr. Cuffe . . . I think it's horrible! Taking this girl about with him, into respectable houses!"

"It's an uncomfortable, uncivilized way of going on," suggested Philip.

Her stern eye challenged him: adjured him to keep faith; and he added:

"Yes, and I do definitely agree with you. It's wrong. It's immoral. By all our standards, it can't be accepted. But what are you going to do about it?"

"Nothing," she said slowly. "At least, nothing at present. I've come to that conclusion, since writing to you. The actual sale will take a certain amount of time, and they can't do anything silly until that goes through. If we opposed them too much now, it might lead to their buying another house, not Monk's Hall. We don't want that. We must let them have their own way until the house is bought. After that, we must take steps."

"What sort of steps?"

"One has a certain amount of influence still. It's unthinkable that such a piece of folly should be allowed to go on."

"It is, quite unthinkable. And really, you know, Catherine, I don't think that any particular steps need to be taken. We . . . you . . . need do nothing at all. If you leave them entirely alone, I should have thought . . ."

"I can't allow that woman to be brought to Monk's Hall. I shall speak to Bobbie . . ."

"You've said yourself that the whole plan is absurd. It is. Can you imagine any such scheme as this Settlement lasting for a month? Only the stimulant of opposition will get it together at all. They don't know what they're in for. They'll come to see that life isn't as simple as they think."

"They will indeed, poor children."

"If you leave it to time . . ."

"You mean, simply do nothing and let all their plans come to grief?"

She looked at him with doubt and entreaty, for she was less hardened to the guiltiness of being wise. She was less prepared to accept the thought that her children must, in the end, pay the dire price of experience. Womanlike, she had cherished somewhere the divinely foolish notion that they might possibly escape. She was a better friend to youth than he, despite her many bitter railings.

For a while, they sat silent, in that mute understanding that binds the old when they discuss the young, the burden of knowing so much and believing so little. And Emily, who came in with the tea-things, thought to herself that they looked very bleak. Probably they had been talking about people who were dead, or cancer. It must be awful, she thought, to be old enough to be frightened of cancer. As a very little girl, she had once overheard two old women discussing their symptoms, the impression it made had been acute and lasting. She hoped that she herself might be dead long before reaching this age of whispered fear.

She hailed Philip with a warm-hearted joy that shamed him. Quite obviously, she was pleased to see him, and she spoke with regret of having missed him on the road.

"I can't think how I didn't meet you," she exclaimed, "if you came by Beckett's Lane. I suppose you did? I only turned off into the field for ten minutes, to throw some sticks for Cæsar. I suppose you must have passed by just then. Shall I pour out, Aunt Catherine?"

Philip felt bound to say that he had caught sight of her in

the distance, and she looked puzzled. Why had he not shouted?

"You were too far away."

"Oh, Philip! The next time you come to see me, you'll have to invent a better excuse than that."

Catherine frowned a little.

"As a matter of fact, my dear, Philip did not come to see you at all, strange as it may seem. He came to talk to me."

Emily made round eyes at her aunt and then at Philip. She knew as well as either of them that he was, in his way, her admirer. She hid her laughter behind the tea-urn.

"I never go anywhere unless I'm asked," said Philip, a little heavily.

"Well, and haven't I asked you?" Emily poked her head reproachfully round the urn. "If I've asked you once, I've asked you a dozen times. Ever since we went to London."

"I never go to London, Emily."

"Ah, but you do. I know you do. With Uncle Bobbie to the Chelsea Show. Once a year. You go round and look at everything and you write down, in little note-books, the names of a lot of new flowers that you'll never grow in your gardens, just to flaunt them in the faces of your gardeners. And then you dine at Uncle Bobbie's club. Really, you both hate going, but you've got into a sort of habit of it. Are you going this year?"

"If your Uncle Bobbie insists on it, I dare say . . ."

"Didn't I know it! Well, listen. You must combine it this time with coming to see us. It's not very far from Chelsea to Edwardes Square."

"I shall be delighted," began Philip doubtfully.

She felt impatient, for her advances were not usually received with so much hesitation. For many months now she had lived upon adulation, and she had begun to grow a little imperious.

"You must come and stay with us," she commanded. "And

we'll all go to see William's play. It ought to be on by then."

Catherine again had to take her down, with a suggestion that Philip was a busy man and had a good deal to do on his annual visit to London. But Philip was not grateful to her. He was aware suddenly of a great longing and a great rebellion. It was ridiculous that he should be perpetually grouped with Catherine, whom he did not love, against Emily, who was the apple of his eye. With a look of speaking gratitude, he accepted the invitation to Edwardes Square and declared that he would like to see William's play better than anything in the world. Emily leant back, satisfied.

"That's a promise," she said, nodding at him.

Catherine, looking from one to the other, thought to herself:

"It's a pity he's so old. If he were ten years younger, she really might do worse than take him, poor child!"

For to Catherine's way of thinking, the sooner that Emily stopped being a Crowne, the better.

2

Trevor was greatly put out when he heard that Baxter had agreed to produce William's play. Aghast at Tilli's iniquity, he vowed that the thing must be stopped. Everybody who had read *The Seven Dawns* (and there were few people in London who had not) said the same thing. Its very promise was a reason why so immature a piece of work should be forgotten as soon as possible. Somebody ought to tell William so; his eyes must be opened to the dangers of his own unfortunate surname.

Trevor wrote a long letter to his cousin and forgot to post it. And then he wondered whether Tilli was not the right person to scold, since the thing was entirely her fault. It was well known that she kept the peace between William and Baxter in their frequent disputes, and without her intervention the scheme would have foundered at a very early stage.

It was she who had persuaded William to write in a bazaar scene and Baxter to swallow a long argument between two priests that had, as Baxter complained, "no drama." If she were to withdraw her efforts, the project might still come to nothing.

But the business of reprimanding her was not going to be easy, and Trevor put it off from day to day. He had made up his mind to break with her, and it was most tiresome of William to involve him with her again. If he went to see her once, he might find that he had again become a regular visitor, for she was not the woman to let slip any advantage. He had managed to keep away from the little flat in the mews for nearly six weeks, though it had not been easy. No weeks were ever duller. Funds were running very low, and all his means of amusement were correspondingly straitened. His social diversions were complicated by the fear of meeting Tilli at one of his friends' houses.

He had been forced, in fact, to do some work, and he tried to settle down to a translation of Crebillon Fils.

But he was not comfortable, for the image of Tilli haunted his dreams and disturbed him whenever his thoughts were not resolutely fixed upon something else. Her little figure flitted through all the intrigues with which his pen dealt so nimbly; all conversations on the printed page echoed to his ear in her voice. She had such a pretty voice, and such an air of being clever to speak English at all, that the flat stupidity of what she said could be overlooked. And in French she was sometimes subtle; almost, to his mind, witty. He could hear her saying all the things said by Crebillon's ladies, who talked their reasonable way through amorous adventure as though a seduction were, essentially, an opportunity for conversation. It occurred to him, more than once, that Tilli would talk very well under such circumstances. He had never seen her disordered or embarrassed. He did not think that she could lose poise, or control of situation. She would always be the same dark little mystery.

"I suppose," he thought, ". . . if I'd liked . . . I could have . . ."

And then, in a revulsion, he reproached himself for a fatuous fool. Tilli was an honest woman for all he knew to the contrary, nor could she really be accused of having made advances to him. Of course, she had been kind, and she demanded that personal style of conversation which is inevitable with a certain type of woman; but then she had often snubbed him. She had given him no direct cause for thinking her accessible, and he could not understand his own uncertainty. Perhaps it was simply the effect of living so much in the mental vicinity of Crebillon Fils.

One day, in the King's Road, Chelsea, he met Nigel Cuffe, who said:

"You're looking very yellow! Where have you been all this time? We heard that you'd gone into the country to start a communist settlement."

"I'm going to do that, in the autumn. But the place hasn't been bought yet. You and Sally are coming, aren't you?"

"First I've heard of it."

"I know. I've only just decided to ask you."

"I don't propose, my dear Trevor, to share my royalties with anyone."

"You won't have to. The communism isn't the strong point of the idea. All that it amounts to is that my cousin William is going to buy a house for me, so that I and my friends may live there at his expense."

"Why is he doing that?"

"Because the gods wish to destroy him. Will you come?"

"I'll see. It might be amusing. Where are you going now? What are you looking for?"

"A cure for concupiscence," said Trevor.

Nigel's suggestions did not appeal to him, and he explained:

"You don't understand. I'm suffering from a diseased imagination. Something has happened to shake my sense of proportion: I need a dose of unadulterated reality in some shocking, some startling, form. I want to be made aware of the vanity of man and the smallness of his obsessions."

"I understand perfectly. And I'll tell you what you must do. Go to the Natural History Museum at South Kensington."

"The dead zoo? Why there?"

"Look in the entrance-hall at all the exhibits of human parasites. They're in glass cases, and they jump to the eye the minute you get inside. I often go and have a look at them; they have a wonderfully cathartic effect for a fit of the spleen. You can see the common flea, magnified to a hundred times its natural size; also lice of every sort, liver-fluke, sheep-bot, bugs of all sorts, including the big black bug of the pampas grass. Also some very beautiful and interesting ticks, especially a tick that infests the buffalo, which is enamelled all over in the most exquisite batik, like Sally's Liberty shawl. But in your present state of mind I should advise you to concentrate on the parasites of man."

"Thank you," said Trevor. "I will. I'll go now."

After half an hour spent in the manner recommended by Nigel, he felt very sane, very collected. And he knew a great deal more natural history than he had ever known in his life before. He was inclined to think, as he came out of the building, that the moment might have arrived for going to expostulate with Tilli over William's play. His mind was still primed with facts about liver-fluke, and it would be wise to make use of the opportunity, since so beautiful a detachment could not last for ever.

"But I'll come very often," he vowed to himself. "I'll come whenever I feel to need it."

He looked about for a taxi and remembered, with a slight loss of complacency, the state of his bank balance. Through a drizzle of rain, he walked to the nearest 'bus route.

It seemed to him that the chauffeurs, cleaning their cars in Tilli's mews, grinned to one another as though they recognized him. Very nearly he turned back, but he could not face the return journey under so many mocking eyes. He rang the bell, hoping that she would be out, and heard the flat-footed maid come shuffling down the steep little flight of stairs to the door. Tilli was at home and would see him. Also she was alone, for which he was sorry, for he had selected an hour when she generally had company. He felt that he could have put his points better if he had had an audience to help him, and he feared that she might be reproachful, immediately taxing him with neglect and demanding the cause of his long absence. But the excellent creature did nothing of the sort.

"You have been in the country with your mother?" she asked. "Will you have some tea?"

"Thanks. I will. No, I've not been away. I've been working."

"Aha! I did not know. You did not tell me."

"It's only since I last saw you," he explained.

"Only since then? Quite a little time, then."

"Six weeks," began Trevor, and then checked himself.

"So long as that? I forget; when did we last meet, Trevor?"

"At the Martins' party."

"Ah, yes. I had forgotten."

He wondered, irritably, if she was lying or not.

"I've come to scold you," he explained.

"But . . . what have I done?"

"This play of William's." He now spoke very seriously. "You can't let it go on."

"Cannot go on? But it is all arranged. In one week we shall begin rehearsing."

"'We'? Are you in it, Tilli?"

"I am to play the dancing-girl: the Beloved of the Prince."

"The dancing-girl?" Trevor stared at her. "What dancing-girl? I don't remember one."

"You do not, perhaps, know very much about this play," suggested Tilli smoothly.

"I know quite enough to be sure that it's a mistake to produce it. It won't even be a vulgar success."

"Of that I do not suppose that you are a very good judge."

"It hasn't the vigour or the pace to attract the attention of the average playgoer, however gorgeously you get it up. And as a work of art it simply doesn't exist. It would be fatal for William's future reputation to call attention to this piece of work; everybody says so. It's so very bad. And we all have great hopes of William, you know. Even I have hopes of him, though goodness knows I've called him a fool often enough. It's not so much anything that he's done, but something in him. Something that he is. You must know what I mean. One can't put one's finger on it, and it may never solidify into any concrete expression. It hasn't yet. But some day it may; he's always writing. Some of that personal magic that he has, that they both have, must some day bear fruit, one would have thought. I don't know."

"I am surprised," said Tilli slowly, "that you should think so well of him. You do not often speak well of him."

"I know. He annoys me. He always has. I've always felt an insane desire to score off him, yet it's so easy to do that I'm ashamed of myself." Trevor was still in the candid mood produced by the liver-fluke. "But, in a way, you can never quite score off him, because he never minds. He's an extraordinary fellow."

"I think," said Tilli, "that sometimes you succeed very well."

She had heard rumours of the Monk's Hall plan and had divined at once the self-interest that lay behind Trevor's share in it.

"Of course, his work, so far, has been negligible," said Trevor, without listening to her. "The best that can be said of this play is that the faults are on a grand scale. It takes a certain magnificence to write as badly as that. His critical faculties don't seem to be developed at all."

"Eugene Baxter thinks well of this play."

"Baxter!"

"He is a man of great experience, Trevor. Of more experience than you, perhaps. He has produced . . ."

"Oh, I know he's a successful producer. And I can't think why, for I really don't believe he has a mind of any sort. But I suppose that success was in his stars; it is a gift that people seem to have, quite apart from any special capacity. Probably he'd have done equally well in any profession. Anyhow, he doesn't know a good play from a bad one."

"He has also said that it is immature. It has been improved. They have altered it together."

"You may take it from me that all Baxter can do is to destroy any sort of merit that the piece has got. I shudder to think what it'll be like when he's had a turn at it. No, I can't allow it. And all William's friends agree with me."

"I think you are all jealous," said Tilli calmly. "Because you cannot get your plays taken by any manager at all."

"Nor would William, if his name were Smith, and if he hadn't got more money than is good for him. Don't tell me that Baxter is taking much risk over this."

"I know nothing of all that."

"Frankly, you know, you're making use of William for your own ends. And you're behaving very badly."

"You also."

"I?"

"You have persuaded him to buy a house, that you might live in it."

"I did nothing of the sort. He made up his mind without any persuasion from me."

"But you will profit by it."

"In a way. But I sha'n't be the only one. Other people will live there, too. It's to be a sort of Settlement, you know."

"I have told you," said Tilli, smiling, "that all his friends will make use of him. I am no worse than you."

"He will pay the initial expenses, but you needn't think that we shall all continue to live on him indefinitely. We shall contribute; it's to be communal. Each pays 60 per cent. of his earnings into the common stock. In these days, when the young artist can't live at the expense of any one patron . . ."

"Bah! The people who make money will not come. Or, if they do, they will not stay. Tell me something more easy to believe. No, I do not think I am very much worse than you, Trevor. I make him produce a play because I wish to work, and you make him buy a house because you do not wish to work."

"It won't injure his reputation to start this Settlement. Not as your play will injure him."

"But it is a mad idea. Admit that it is a mad idea."

"It's an experiment. Worth trying."

"Also the play is an experiment."

"I'm thinking of the cause of literature."

"And I," said Tilli, "am thinking of myself."

Trevor laughed.

"Poor William!" he said.

Tilli laughed, too, and looked at him more kindly. Up to a point, she sympathized with him, for really it seemed hard that so clever and personable a young man should have to see his rightful inheritance in the hands of a much inferior cousin. She liked William well enough, but she found that a little of him went a long way. He had none of the qualities that she truly admired, and his want of common sense drove her at times almost to distraction. In her heart she could not blame Trevor for wanting to get back Monk's Hall, especially as the element of intrigue in the affair diverted her.

"In the end," she stated, "you will do him more harm than I. You will spend his money. That is serious."

"Well? He's got more than he can get through."

"This poor William! I find him so agreeable."

"Do you, Tilli? More agreeable than I am?"

"Perhaps. He is more amiable."

"Very amiable," agreed Trevor, "up to a point. But he's a devil when he loses his temper."

"That intrigues me. He does, then, lose his temper?"

"Insanely. But it's soon over. He's never the same two minutes. He's like a cloud that changes its shape while you look at it. Belongs to air rather than earth. They both do."

"Both?"

"He and his sister."

"Ah, yes. He often speaks of her. I have never met a man so much occupied with his sister."

"It's a mercy for him that he is. He'd always be getting into shocking scrapes if he weren't."

"With women? You surprise me."

"Anybody could make a fool of him. He's always ready to worship any woman with the faintest pretensions to beauty."

"He has no mistress, then?"

"None that I know of."

Tilli did not believe him. For though she had found William a little obtuse, she had no reason to suppose that he was sexless.

"He is not in any way abnormal?" she asked thoughtfully. "His father . . ."

Whereupon they disinterred the Crowne case, very cosily, for half an hour. And they were still at it when new visitors arrived, a distraught, rebellious William and a blandly obstinate Baxter, looking very much as Faust and Mephistopheles must have looked in their sinister wanderings through the town. It seemed that William had struck afresh against this infernal companionship, and Baxter had brought him to Tilli for treatment.

Trevor made no effort to go. He was too much interested. He determined to stay where he was unless he was positively thrown out. Making himself as unobtrusive as possible, he watched how she went to work with them.

The small room seemed to be full of Baxter; he existed there so very copiously that the life was almost crushed out of the other three. He produced a sensation of deadness; he talked a great deal, but no quickening idea was ever to be discerned in any of his words. He was like a huge, talkative carcass. And the effect of so much flesh and so little spirit was really appalling because it was not natural, since the very obese are usually supplied with a vitality in proportion to their girth.

He was explaining, patiently, the many advantages of making the play a little shorter, and Tilli supported him.

"I want to have you cut this temple scene, Mr. Crowne. It's not dramatic the way you've got it. It won't help on the story at all. You mayn't just see how it is, and I can't explain it to you. But the whole play loses grip. And personally, I'd like to have you cut it right out."

"I won't cut a word of it," cried William. "It's the crucial scene of the whole play. It's the point that I've been working up to from the very beginning. It's . . ."

"Personally, I'd like to cut it right out," went on Baxter relentlessly. "But I know you have quite a little weakness for that scene, Mr. Crowne. So I won't say cut it altogether. But it's too long, anyway."

"It is a very beautiful scene," observed Tilli.

"Why, yes!" cried Baxter. "You mustn't get thinking I don't appreciate that scene. I do. It certainly is a piece of delicate poetic phantasy. And it creates atmosphere. Even reading it, you get atmosphere. You see this temple and this old priest, and it gives you the East. I've thought a lot about that scene, and, the way it appears to me, the value of it is atmosphere. I had an idea—I don't know what you'll think of it, Tilli; I'd like to have you give an opinion, it's just an idea, remember, and I wouldn't press it on you, Mr. Crowne, but couldn't we have these temple bells ringing all the time this scene is going on? It would all help to create atmosphere, if you get me . . ."

"Perfectly horrible idea!" William was heard to mutter.

"But it must be short, if it's to give any sort of effect. Because, as a matter of fact, it's just a little bit late in the play to have in a scene at all which only creates atmosphere . . ."

"Damn you, it isn't intended to create atmosphere!"

"And, mind you, I'm not in any way talking against the value of atmosphere. It's necessary in all real drama. It was a perfectly right instinct of yours to put it in. But a piece of delicate, poetic phantasy ought to be short. . . ."

"It's not a piece of delicate, poetic phantasy," stated William furiously.

Baxter looked at Tilli, as if to ask what else he was expected to say. He had never, in the whole of his life, met a more unreasonable young man. Tilli asked if some other scene could not be shortened.

"It was short enough," growled William, "before I wrote in that bazaar scene at the beginning. You can cut out that if you like. Or the tiger-hunt. That has nothing to do with the story really. I just wrote it in for fun, and because I wanted to hold the action up a little before the decisive scene in the temple."

"And you were quite right, Mr. Crowne. Your instinct guided you right there. That scene creates suspense, and we want to create suspense. We want to have every man, and (what's more) every woman, in that audience, sitting up and wondering what in hell's going to happen next. Besides, I've engaged the tigers."

William looked about him with a glassy eye. These references to his instinct quite confounded him. Baxter had a way of so describing all his most cherished ideas, the fruit of severest mental toil. It was as though only producers could create atmosphere or suspense on purpose, the work of the playwright being a mere happy accident. For experience was Baxter's stronghold. He had, after all, produced many successful revues, and William had only written one tragedy in blank verse.

But Tilli perceived that the victim's patience was wearing thin, and she began, adroitly, to take his part. She knew, better than Baxter, how likely it still was that the whole thing might fall through.

"Must it be cut?" she asked. "If you begin at eight . . ."

"My dear Tilli!" Baxter was on his own ground now. "That's not possible. When you've been on this job as long as I have, you'll know it's not possible. You can't expect a West End audience to be in the theatre by eight o'clock. There's no sort of use expecting it. . . ."

"Couldn't they eat less?" demanded Trevor suddenly.

Baxter laughed immoderately at this diverting suggestion. The experience of a lifetime had taught him that a West End audience will not be hurried over its dinner. Trevor began to feel uncomfortable, as though he was at William's funeral. He took his departure, and as Tilli came with him down the little flight of stairs to let him out, he said to her:

"Your play will come to grief. He'll never stay the course. Baxter talking about poetic phantasy has a very hypnotic effect, but William's beginning to come round."

"He does not like trouble," said Tilli sagely. "Soon it will be less trouble for him to go on than to give it up. When he is quite disgusted, he will be more reasonable. In the end, he will allow Eugene to manage everything."

"I daresay! The man's stupidity is overpowering. It's crushing. Well! I've said what I could. I wash my hands of it. Don't blame me if it's a gigantic failure."

"Nobody will blame you, Trevor. You have been very noble. You have even taken risks for William."

"Risks?"

"You have so bravely come here."

Her black eyes mocked him, and she added:

"I shall not, I suppose, see you again."

"Not just yet," he admitted. "I have to go a good deal, just now, to the Natural History Museum."

"Why must you go there?"

"To study nature."

"*C'est gentil.* I also, I adore Nature."

He paused in the doorway, irresolute, uncertain before her mockery. Baxter's voice, continuous as the babbling brook, came drifting down the stairs.

"You want to have every man and woman in that audience go home saying . . ."

Very swiftly Trevor caught his charmer round her slim waist and kissed the tip of her nose.

"That'll teach her!" he thought, as he ran out into the mews.

3

Philip had almost persuaded himself into a belief that Emily's invitation was not serious. She could not really want to see him in London; she had spoken on an impulse that was now regretted, if not forgotten, and it would be tactless of him to remind her. It appeared that *The Seven Dawns* was to be produced during the very week of the Flower Show, and she would be far too busy, at such a time, for an old, dull friend like himself. Unless she wrote, repeating the invitation, he would steal back to the country with Bobbie, and he would read about William's play next morning in the newspapers.

But he wanted, desperately, to see her, and his decision was not reached without many waverings. Several letters to Emily were begun. Some of them written in a lightly bantering tone, said nothing at all of the proposed visit, their object being to provoke an answer in which she should again take the first move. Others were grave and fatherly, and entreated her to say honestly if he was really wanted. But in the end he came to the conclusion that it would be better not to write at all. Everything should be left to her. And as the weeks went by without a message, he discovered that he had been a blockhead.

Not until the eve of the show, when all his arrangements were completed did the fatal postcard arrive.

Mattie says dinner at seven, so come any time before then. *Of course* you'll stay the night. And William says to wear a white tie, because we shall be in the stalls. I'm reading *Hudibras*. What is it all about?

Philip knew two tunes; the first was "Pretty Polly Oliver," and he always whistled it when he was very happy. The other, "Loath to Depart," beset him when he was sad. He had given his household a good dose of it during the past weeks. But now, for nearly twenty-four hours, the halls and staircases of Ratchet reëchoed to the adventures of the pretty little drummer-boy. A telegram was sent to Edwardes Square, and the housekeeper was instructed to pack a suit-case full of white ties. Bobbie was told that he would have to dine alone.

At a quarter-past six on the following evening, Philip knocked at Emily's blue front door. It was opened immediately by William, ready dressed for the evening, and in such a state of nervous alarm that he hardly knew what he said.

"I'm afraid I must go! How do you do, Philip? So glad you can come. Emily's there. I have to go. I'm having dinner with Baxter. You're going to take Emily. I'm afraid I can't come with you. I must go."

"It's quite early yet," said Philip soothingly.

They stood in the hall, which smelt of fields and not like anything in London.

"The thing begins at 8:15" jabbered William. "Really, I ought to go. I'm having dinner with Baxter and Mrs. Van Tuyl. I'm afraid she'll be terribly nervous. Some people find these things very upsetting, you know. But I've got her some flowers. We bought some flowers for her this afternoon. Did you get Emmie's postcard? I said you'd better wear a white tie. We've got a party afterwards. But it doesn't matter, you know. You could quite easily wear a black one if you liked. I don't think these things matter very much, myself. I feel it's rather a pity to go too much by what people think. At least, I'd like to be able to think that. But Emmie's got a new dress. She looks very nice. You're to go with her."

Here Mattie appeared and took Philip's suitcase.

"You'll want to dress at once, sir," she told him. "There's not any too much time. Why didn't you show Mr. Luttrell his room, Mr. William, instead of standing talking there?"

"I have to go," expostulated William. "Where's Emmie? She ought to be looking after Philip."

"She's dressing herself. You run along and say good-bye to her, and I'll look after Mr. Luttrell. This way, sir."

She took Philip up to the spare room, which was the most adult room in the house, because the twins never scattered their little things over it. And kneeling down beside the suitcase she began to unpack it for him. He asked after her lumbago.

"Oh, Mr. Luttrell, I don't hardly have it now the warm weather's come. It just catches me once and again. Miss Emily, she got me some wonderful stuff for it."

"How is she, Mattie?"

"She's very well, sir. And looking as lovely as . . . as . . ."

'As usual?'

"Well, now, that's asking! In a way she is, and in a way she isn't. She's very nervous. But she's got this new dress, and she looks like a little queen in it."

"I suppose, even with Emily, a dress makes a difference."

"She's the same whatever she wears. Always was. Such a lovely little girl she used to be! And William! Such beautiful children! People used to turn round and stare in Kensington Gardens, when I took them out in their pram. And I used to feel so proud. Everyone staring at *my* children. I always call them my children. I had them, you see, from the first month. And now they call Miss Emily the most beautiful woman in London."

"Who calls her that?"

"The papers, sir. I have a bit that I cut out and kept that

said, 'Among the early arrivals was Miss Emily Crowne in silver lammy. Miss Crowne is the daughter of Norman Crowne, the poet, and is said to be the most beautiful woman in London.'"

"How does she like that sort of thing?"

"Oh, I didn't show it to her. It's beneath her. She'd scorn the impidence of it. You'll excuse me telling you all this, sir. I wouldn't, only you,—you've known them for so long and prepared Miss Emily for confirmation, and give her that lovely prayer-book, it seems like speaking to one of the family. You'll ring, sir, if you want anything?"

She hurried off upstairs to Emily's room at the top of the house, where William was taking a final, distraught farewell of his sister. The new dress, of gold tissue all brocaded with jewels, filled the room with its glitter. Emily wore it nobly, like a robe of state.

"I'm very beautiful," she said placidly, as she glanced over her shoulder in the glass.

"Humph!" said William. "You keep your cloak on, or nobody will look at my play. Sha'n't you wear earrings?"

"Mattie! Shall I wear earrings?"

"No, my lamb. Your ears is so lovely without."

"I must go!" said William for the hundredth time. "Is my tie straight? Oh, Mattie! Where's my new hat?"

"I've put it in the hall for you. Have you got a handkerchief? Clean?"

"Three. Good-bye, Emmie! I'll come round afterwards and fetch you. Wait in the foyer."

He kissed Emily and Mattie and rushed downstairs. From the hall a loud bawling was heard.

"Mattie! Mattie! Where did you say my hat was?"

"On the chest!" called Mattie over the banisters. "Right under your nose!"

"Here? Oh, thanks! I must go!"

He crushed his hat on to the back of his head and burst out of the house. The blue door banged behind him.

Dinner was rather a mournful little meal, for Philip and Emily had not very much to say to each other. He looked at her a good deal, and she smiled whenever she caught his eye, but they were both oppressed by the importance of the occasion, and Emily exclaimed at last:

"Oh, dear, I'm being very bad company. You must forgive me."

"You're excited, and no wonder."

"I wish I weren't so . . . nervous."

"That's natural."

"It's been so hard to hide from William. I've been in dreadfully low spirits all day. Silly of me."

"You don't really approve of this play, do you?"

"I don't like the way he's altered it. No, and I never did like it. But I'm sure he's right, and one ought to see it acted to judge. I've never been to any of the rehearsals, so I've quite an open mind about it."

And in the car she turned to him suddenly and took his hand, exclaiming:

"Oh, dear!"

He realized, for the first time, that an element of courage had gone to make the twins' success in life. Somehow, he had always thought of them simply as children of good fortune, beautiful, rich, prosperous, accepting their luck serenely, as a matter of course. But now he perceived their fundamental isolation: they shared a unique misfortune that cut them off for ever from the rest of mankind. They were shockingly vulnerable. The boldness of their attack upon the world had been born, in some degree, of a spirit of despair. Emily's radiance was a torch, deliberately brandished, not so much in defiance of external dangers as against some half-realized, inward doubt.

"I don't believe," she murmured, looking out of the window, "that it is at all a good play. But I sha'n't say so. Is that dishonest, do you think?"

"Not always. Won't you say it to William?"

"Oh, yes. To him I shall. In a day or two, when it's all calmed down. But to other people, you know, we always pretend that everything we do is quite right. It makes us feel safer."

"Families ought to back each other up."

"Yes. And then, you see, we are such a very small family. We've only got ourselves. Look! Just look at that awfully thin dog!"

It was with a new comprehension that he watched her sweep into the theatre. In the face of the world, she made the usual sensation. Everybody looked at her and everybody knew that she had come. But as they crowded round her he thought for a moment of some fine, defenceless creature at bay among wild beasts. He found himself under the wing of Trevor, who was being very ubiquitous and important, and managing to look as though he must have written *The Seven Dawns*, and produced it, and be going forthwith to write all the criticisms thereon. He had been talking successfully to seven people at once in the vestibule, but he managed to detach himself in time to become associated with Emily's entrance into the stalls.

"I wish," he murmured into Philip's ear, "that it were bedtime and all well over."

"Tell me who everybody is," whispered Philip.

Trevor had some satisfaction in pointing out his acquaintances. He felt that he had never liked Philip so well.

"I'm glad you've come with Emily," he said. "I'm sorry for her."

"So am I."

This annoyed Trevor, who felt that such sensibility was

out of place in a dullard like Philip. At the moment, his
cousin appeared to be in small need of compassion, as she
walked down the gangway, giving little bits of herself to
everyone in her orbit.

"She looks quite pleased with herself," he said quickly.

Just then the lights went down, and they sought their
places. An orchestra struck up a tune, feverish with a heavy
languor, full of queer chromatic cadences, the throbbing of
tom-toms, and the tinkle of little bells. Philip, as he stowed
his hat under the seat, was reminded of pale hands like lotus-
buds and the nightingales in Damascus. He was too un-
sophisticated to know why he thought this, but the associa-
tion was immediately established in his mind.

"This isn't . . ." he whispered to Emily.

"No, it's not," she replied. "But it's dreadfully like, isn't
it?"

She drooped a little and added:

"It's a pity, I think, to have music at all."

The curtain went up on the gorgeousness of a city bazaar
in northern India. Priests, beggars, Brahmins, and veiled
women jostled one another. A weaver wove a real carpet in
the foreground, and a small boy sold melons.

Solitary amid the throng, the young disguised prince
watched and mused over the human tide, its uneasy ebb and
flow, its small drama, its nothingness. Deaf to the world-
wise counsels of his faithful friend, he cried out that all was
vanity. As soldier, statesman, scholar, husband, and father
he had played his part, but the secret of existence was hidden
from him. He questioned one and another, in the throng,
and heard many words of folly, but met with nobody wiser
than himself.

A company of hill-women, sold for their beauty into the
courts of southern rajahs, were carried through the crowd
in litters. And, breaking loose from one of these, a sinuous,

lovely creature flung herself without warning at the feet of the disguised prince, hailing him as her deliverer and beseeching him to set her free. He raised the woman and questioned her; she told him of the hill country whence she had come.

Tilli's voice was beautiful when she talked of the mountains. Her features, already Mongolian, seemed to have taken on a Tartar look: she belonged to China rather than to India. Having won the price of her freedom, she fell into the dust at the feet of the young man, and the extravagance of William's blank verse was drowned in the clamour of a nautch.

Philip had been thankful that the lights would remain down between the scenes, for he felt that the obscurity might be a kindly shield for his companion. But in the end he was sorry, for a group of people with loud voices, who had come in late, were sitting in the row immediately behind. It was obvious that they did not, in the darkness, perceive any reason for taking care.

"Nearly as bad as one expected," said a voice, emerging from the faint applause at the fall of the first curtain. "What a waste!"

"Of promising talent?"

"Of expensive production. All you can say is that it isn't as good as a pantomime. And the literary pretentiousness of it makes one feel a little sick."

Emily, turning her head to Philip in the gloom, nodded slightly, as though she were forced to agree.

"I said you wouldn't like it," a woman behind them was crying. "But you would come."

"I had to come," said the first voice, in tones of some pride. "I've a record to keep up. I always attend the Crowne shows. I didn't miss a day of the trial."

"That dates you!"

And somebody else said warningly:

"Ssh! You never know . . ."

"Only twenty years ago. Less!" The voice was a little huffy. "It was more amusing than this."

"You knew him quite well, didn't you, Mr. Saule?"

"Who? Crowne? Oh, intimately, poor fellow. I used to dine with him, on an average, once a week at one time. Of course, you don't remember it, my dear Betty. You were in your cradle."

"Trials nowadays aren't half so interesting."

"I suppose all his friends went."

"Everybody went. I assure you, the audience at that trial was a very distinguished audience indeed. And it would be again, if this young Crowne here were to . . ."

"I think that's disgusting."

"Not at all, my dear child. You'd go yourself if . . ."

"I don't think I would. He dances divinely. And, after all, his father's trial was so peculiar. . . ."

At this point they really did drop their voices, as they went over, in memory, the details of the last Crowne show. And Emily said to Philip that the carpet-weaver should not have sat so near the front of the stage. One watched him instead of listening to the prince. Her calmness showed her to be not unpractised in such a situation. Perhaps she was quite used to it.

The short interval came to an end, and the curtain rose again, but Philip had lost all interest in the piece. His thoughts were for the girl who sat so very still beside him. He was dreading for her the long interval between the acts, when she would have to face the light. On the stage, he was conscious of an uninterrupted, vulgar brilliance of production. There were tiger hunts, and temples with silver bells, and sunsets in the Himalayas. A great deal, meanwhile, was said. The young prince, after several very long speeches, decided to become a hermit. His musings were haunted by the woman from the hills, who pursued him everywhere like a bright gadfly. At length she bathed in the marble tank of a palace garden, under a canopy of burning stars. The audience began to get excited, and the prince, from being an inveterate looker-on, was roused into something like an active frame of mind. He retired with the lady into a pavilion hung with cloth of gold. Emerging shortly afterward, he stated that he was weary of the flesh. And the curtain fell on the first act.

There was some little applause, and Philip wished that it might last longer. He observed, however, that Emily was going to carry it all off with a high hand. She had grown rather pale, but her eyes were very bright. She stood up, gathering her cloak about her, and, turning round, she studied gravely the people in the row behind her. An instant's petrified silence showed that she had been recognized, and then he heard sounds of a stampede. He, too, turned round, to behold the party, scurrying off to smoke a cigarette outside, and scattering a few panic-stricken nods and smiles in Emily's direction as they went. The last to escape were a pretty girl and an old-young man of the type that is born a little past middle age. Emily bowed to him and said "How do you do, Mr. Saule?"

"Miss Crowne! How brave of you to come! We thought you'd be pacing the Embankment with William. Where is he?"

"Behind somewhere."

"Ah, well. No doubt we shall see him before the end of the evening. A most remarkable performance . . ."

He fled, and his pretty companion added, as she followed:

"My complaint is that so *little* of your *brother* is left in it. That seems such a *pity*."

"That's Betty Beamish," said Emily to Philip. "William

is a little in love with her. She's very pretty, don't you think?"

She left him and went to scatter pale vivacity among another group of vehement friends. Philip's heart bled for her. He kept by Trevor, who began at once:

"Isn't it awful? And yet you know, in a way, it's quite extraordinary how impressive the little bits of William are. Of course, it's only grand language, and he uses it much too recklessly, but now and then, for a line or two, it's magnificent. I've never felt quite so certain that William, for all his sins, is a poet. Once he gets going . . ."

"But how could he ever have allowed such a thing to be produced?" broke in Philip. "I should have thought that he must have seen, right at the very start, how unsuitable . . ."

"Baxter and Tilli did it between them. They're both determined creatures, and William's got no sense of humour. Nor has he any guts. He does what he's told rather than fight. What does Emily think of it all?"

"I don't think she's altogether happy," said Philip cautiously.

"She always had the more common sense of the two. But William is bound to come off badly in an affair like this, because he has no vulgarity. If you are to cope successfully with vulgar people, you must have a pinch of it yourself."

"Then he oughtn't to lead this sort of life."

"You're right. He oughtn't. He'd much better join us down at Monk's Hall. We'd never let him in for this sort of thing."

The interval was cruelly long, but it came to an end at last, and Philip was once more beside Emily in the darkness. They were listening to that temple scene that William had refused to cut. It stood out bleakly from the rest of the play, free, for a few minutes, of the luxurious trappings provided by Baxter. Philip became almost interested. It seemed to him that the rest of the piece had a dignity and a sort of sedate dullness, distinct from the earlier passages. The hill-woman, scorned by the prince, flung herself from a high precipice, and they all got on very comfortably without her. Their friends in the row behind spoke with guarded criticism, in the short intervals, but in a manner that need hurt no feelings. Emily was quite silent.

The play came to an end before a little mountain shrine. The prince, in the guise of a holy man, sat there in meditation, withdrawn at last from the stream of life, while before him, on the steps of his shrine, two wayfarers squabbled endlessly over the possession of an earthenware pot. They came to blows, and one slew the other. The curtain fell on the splendours of a mountain sunrise, the shrine, the saint, and the dead man. Under cover of the clapping, Emily turned to Philip and said hurriedly:

"Let's get away from this . . . quickly!"

He recognized some urgency in her tone and knew that she could bear it no more. Luck, however, was against them, and they could not immediately get away. Philip groped for his hat; his coat was stuck between two seats. They were in the middle of the row, and their departure was blocked. While they were fighting their way out, the curtain went up once or twice upon a bowing prince. Some people began to shout for William. The last glimpse they had, as they left the theatre, was of Baxter dragging on a white-faced, ashamed young man, to face these plaudits.

"Didn't he tell you to wait for him?" asked Philip in the *foyer*.

"Oh, I can't . . . not now! I don't want to see him. I don't want to see anybody. Take me away. I want to go home."

He found the car and put her into it, and then he dispatched a messenger to William, saying that Emily was very tired and had gone home. It was all that he could do for the

helpless pair. He drove back with Emily, through streets
that had changed from sunset to blue night in the time that
they had been in the theatre.

Emily spoke when they were nearly home.

"He was quite right," she said.

"Who?"

"Mr. Saule."

"When he said that it . . . wasn't very good?"

"Oh, no! Anyone might say that. But when he said that
. . . that all the same people would be there if William . . .
if William . . . Oh, Philip! So many of them are friends
who . . ."

"My dearest child," babbled Philip, "you mustn't take
this sort of thing too hard. Everybody gets a shock, at one
time or another, over the callousness of human nature.
Some people become obsessed with it. They let themselves
forget that there is such a thing as real kindness and sympathy."

"I looked at their faces in the interval. I couldn't help it.
I seemed to see, suddenly, how cruel they could look. Oh,
Philip, I'm so frightened of people, really. Just think what
it must have been for my father! To be there, day after day,
and see his friends . . . his *friends!* Oh, I don't want to see
any single one of them ever again."

"Don't be foolish. Your father had real friends, like any
other man. I know he had. And they suffered with him. They
didn't go to gape at him in his misery. But not all agreeable
companions are friends in that sense. Only an imbecile or an
infant would expect it."

"Oh, I know. I know. But I think that we . . . William and
I—have no real friends at all. Except, perhaps, you, Philip.
Everybody draws away from us. They won't forget . . . they
don't want to forget . . ."

"Here we are. Come in, my dear, and let Mattie put you

to bed. Try to realize that William, both as a man and a poet, will have to come out and hold his own in a very hard world. It's no worse for him than for anybody else."

"Oh, yes, it is. It's unbearable. I . . . can't stand it any longer. We'd much better both jump into the river and give them another Crowne show. We've tried . . . it's no use . . ."

"Get out, Emily! Don't keep Fordyce up late. There's no reason why he should be kept out of his bed because you are feeling discouraged about things."

"I suppose there isn't."

She got out of the car and suffered him to lead her up to the drawing room. Then she broke out again:

"If only anything could ever be over! But it's all still going on. We are part of it. Nothing is ever done with as long as it goes on in people's minds."

Philip stood by the window and looked away from her, out into the clear green twilight of the square. A few lamps twinkled among the trees and in a distant house a piano and violin were playing the *Frühlings* Sonata, a clear, gay stream of melody flowing out into the night. Its limpid melancholy reminded him of Emily when she was a little girl. The undercurrent of pathos had been there, always.

"My dear," he said, "I wish that I could help you."

"Nothing . . . nobody can help us."

"Ever since you were quite small, I've been dreading a moment like this for you. A moment when you might feel that it was all too hard."

"A moment! It's all my life. I can never get away from it. We neither of us can. We've tried to live as if it just . . . wasn't so . . . but there's no end to it."

Philip could see no end to it either. The long martyrdom, begun for Crowne, was by no means over yet.

"I can't . . . go on with this life. I haven't any more courage. I won't bear it any more."

"You've got William to consider, besides yourself. He has the same trouble to bear. And you can help him."

"No, I can't. I make it worse for him. We ought never to have tried living together. We aren't any protection to each other. We're only more of a target."

"But you wouldn't be happy apart."

"Could any wretchedness be worse than this? And we couldn't be really apart, Philip. Not if the whole distance of the world were between us. Distance is only an imaginary thing. I used to feel that when he was away in the war."

"Then you really want to run away from this?"

"I must get away."

"Where to?"

"Ah, that . . ."

"Your safety will have to be in yourself. No place will do it for you."

"You mean I must get away . . . to being another person?"

"It's not as hard as you might suppose, my dear. Time does it for all of us."

"Was there ever a time . . . did you ever say 'I can't bear it. I can't go on any more'?"

"I have said it."

"But you went on?"

"Yes."

"How?"

"I grew tougher. You'll have to."

"I don't want to change. I don't want to be different. I want to stay the same and have outside things different."

"Baby!"

"If I can't live in this world on my own terms, I'd rather not live in it at all."

"It's a choice, and we all have to make it."

"Whether we'll go on living or . . ."

She leant past him, out over the street, brushing his arm with the soft folds of her cloak. The faint, limpid stream of music was still flowing out into the darkness.

"They're playing very well in that house!" she said.

Philip took her hand and pulled her back into the room.

"My heart's love! If there were anything ... anything in the world that I could do for you ..."

"Would you really do anything, Philip? Really?"

"You know I would."

"Why?"

"Because I love you so much."

"I know." She searched his face intently. "I know. Then will you marry me?"

"Emily!"

He fell away from her aghast.

"Are you ... are you serious?"

"Most serious. If I married you ... I ... I would be another person, wouldn't I? I'd be your wife. And I'd go away from here, to Ratchet. A place I know. All safe and settled."

"Marriage isn't very safe, as far as I know. When did this idea occur to you?"

"Just this minute."

"Then you should think it over. You should consider the drawbacks. I'm much too old for you. And are you sure that there is no one ..."

"No, indeed. I'm sure I shall never be in love with anyone. I've thought that for a long time."

"At your age, that's a highly dangerous conclusion."

"And if I married you, there'd be one person happy, anyway."

"Who?"

"Why, you! You want to marry me, don't you?"

"No!"

He had told the truth before he could stop himself. It burst out of him in a single, disastrous ejaculation, and he saw her flinch away from it.

"But if you love me . . ." she stammered. "If you love me . . ."

"You don't love me, Emily."

"But that isn't the reason why you don't . . . you don't . . ."

As he had begun, he had better go on. He tried to explain:

"It's because I love you so much. Because you are, to me, like a flame—like poetry. That feeling has nothing to do with marriage. I'm too old to deceive myself. If I were a younger man, the risks . . ."

"I see. I understand. I'm so sorry, dear Philip. I wouldn't for the world have involved you in such an embarrassing discussion if I'd understood. I . . . I know it's a great honour that you feel like that about me. Please believe that I'm not hurt. And we'll forget all about this. We won't ever speak of it again. I was stupid. Do let's forget it. Good-night."

She spoke dizzily; her humiliation was so terrible that her whole body ached with it. But she managed a difficult little smile as she took his hand again.

"Good-night, dear Philip. And please don't let this worry you. It's nice that we can be such friends as to talk things over in this way, without having to be insincere. It's a great comfort. It has been a great comfort to me, having a friend like you. God bless you."

But he knew that she had needed other friendship than that. He remembered, with bitter self-reproach, his own un-meaning offer of help. He had failed her. He cried after her like a man in danger:

"Emily! Oh, Emily! Help me!"

"Help you? How?"

She turned back.

"I've been a fool all my life. I was a fool not to ask you

to marry me a long time ago. You've heard . . . I've just explained to you why I didn't. There's a part of me that wants to marry you very much. And now I'm losing you."

"Oh, no, no! I quite understand. You were quite right."

"I've been such a stick-in-the-mud all my life. All these doubts and difficulties! They've stood between me and happiness. And they will again unless you'll give me a chance. You must forget what I said and marry me. You must . . ."

"You just say this not to hurt my feelings. I've told you. They're not hurt. I understand . . ."

"No, you don't. At least, only part of it. You don't understand all of it. I've never had my life. I never shall, unless you can manage to see what I mean. I've got so used to arguing with myself instead of doing things. It's been the curse of my life. Whenever I've wanted anything, I've always begun by cataloguing the reasons against trying to get it. Because I'm afraid of getting what I want."

He took a little time to convince her, but for the moment he really was so very anxious to marry her that she began at last to believe him. She yielded before the evidences of his distress, and when they parted for the night they were plighted lovers. Too much distraught to sleep, he went out and walked round Edwardes Square. Dire anguish pursued him, but extravagant elation drew him on. He had won a wife, and he was very proud. He was determined to be happy. But never again, in any spring, would he behold this lost Emily, this airy virgin, running lightly over the flowers and the grass.

4

"I am a fool. I have deserved it all," said Tilli to herself. And she mopped her eyes on a little lace handkerchief, the only present that she had ever got out of Eugene Baxter. It was not usually her way to cry in private, but it was a wet Sunday evening, and there was nothing else to do. A conversation on the telephone with Baxter had been the chief event of the day, and this had been enough to dash the gayest spirits. It had given the death-blow to her hopes.

The Seven Dawns had run for a week and was an absolute failure. Baxter took it all with tolerable cheerfulness: he adopted a tone of rueful but good-natured martyrdom and said to Tilli, with a shake of the head, that the public did not seem to appreciate delicate poetic phantasy as much as it ought. But she understood that a flat in a mews must be her lot for life for all that this play would ever do to get her out of it.

It seemed to her that, during this week, the whole world had deserted her. Nobody came to see her, not even William, and she supposed that he must be blaming her for the whole affair. Very bitterly did she regret her own obstinacy in disregarding Trevor's warnings. He had been right, and she should have listened to him.

Now, in the long chilly English dusk, she sat and sobbed for Trevor. At the end of the mews a church bell tolled, in a perfunctory monotone, a dirge over her hopes, and the footsteps of late worshippers went pattering through the rain. If it had been a Catholic church she would have run out and prayed; a little religion would have done her a lot of good. But she knew better than to seek consolation at a Protestant Evensong. So she cowered in the obscurity, among the scarlet cushions of her divan, and lamented the bad luck that seemed, through life, to have pursued her.

Tilli's past had been discouraging. She had never been a child; she was born grown-up. Her first recollections were of work, devastating, unsparing effort in a ballet school at Prague. Her mother took her there in the morning, and brought her home in the evening, and whipped her if she had been lazy. There had been, of course, occasional holidays when, with red bows on her black hair, she drove out with her mother into the country. But even in those days the business of gain and bargain was begun, and she learnt that an engaging display of pretty ways would bring in a harvest of sweets and trinkets from her mother's cavaliers. She was a useful little messenger, and she knew how to hold her tongue; by nature, she understood the elements of intrigue.

At fourteen she had been sent to a convent to finish her education, and of that epoch she could remember little, save that it had been acutely boring. She was enchanted when a marriage was arranged for her some three years later, though at the time she was puzzled to know how it was that her mother had contrived to make up so good a match. Van Tuyl was rich and well-born, advantages which, in the eyes of both mother and daughter, outbalanced the fact that he was an elderly rake. He had seen Tilli for a few minutes when she was home from her convent on a holiday, and from that moment he had taken an unceasing interest in the child. But she could never make out at what point he had been driven to offer marriage. She only knew that he was a man, and that from men must come all the good things that are most to be desired on this earth. They were to be her eternal opponents, and success, for her, must lie in giving as little and getting as much as possible in the conflict of sex.

Pondering upon all the squalid woe of her married life, she made a little grimace of disgust. For Van Tuyl had done worse things than throw her out of a window; he was vicious, brutal, and very mean. The bare necessaries of life were scarcely allowed to her; when her baby was born, he would not pay for proper attendance. He shut her up in a horrible gloomy old farmhouse that he had bought, and when she was very ill he would not send to The Hague for a good doctor but called in the local apothecary, a dirty little man who pulled out the kitchenmaids' teeth for sixpence apiece. Tilli always believed that her baby's death was due to his carelessness.

Nobody in England knew of this child that she had had. Her other wrongs were freely canvassed, and she never spared her friends any detail of Van Tuyl's ill-treatment. But this one sorrow was a secret that she kept. As far as she had ever loved anybody, she had loved her son. Dimly, during the months before he was born, she had thought and planned for him. She had groped after the idea of a better life somehow; a conviction that there must be, for this child, finer things than she had ever known. But all that he ever got was a little grave in his father's garden, and his memory became a fount of bitterness. Somehow, at the bottom of her heart, she blamed all the men in the world for the cruelty of one man, and she meant to pay them out.

In this mood she had first formed an intimacy with Trevor. She had meant to make use of him and to cast him aside, with Van Tuyl, with William, with Baxter, with all the others who had served her turn. But he had got the better of her, and she began to be aware of it. She could not hate him, as she hated all the rest. To begin with, she had merely admitted to herself that she might have loved him if he had been rich, and it was not until he had kissed her, mockingly, upon the doorstep, that she repented of this vain boast. Rich or poor, she wanted that young man, and she could not get him out of her head for two minutes together. He was so amusing and so clever and so handsome.

For a little time, in her excitement over the play, she had succeeded in forgetting him. But now, in her disappointment, she had no protection against his dangerous image. She was beginning to regret her vow of coldness, of caution. For prudence had not, after all, served her very well in the past; if she was not to be rich, she might at least be happy. He was an easy conquest and she had foreborne, yet she would have been no worse off if she had indulged herself. Now he had deserted her, and that was because she had been so unkind.

"I am a fool," she sobbed. "I have deserved it all."

Darkness crept into the room. The lamps of the mews, shining in an aura of wetness, cast faint spots of light on the ceiling. The church bell stopped, and the hurrying footsteps. Tilli wept in a silence broken only by the soft whisper of rain in the gutters.

A shattering ring at the door startled her back into practical efficiency. She remembered that the maid was out, and that she was alone in the flat. Either she must ignore this ringing or answer the door. She half decided to ignore it, but a second peal sounded so like the sort of ring Trevor used to give that she could not help going to see. A man was standing in the rain upon her doorstep and she cried out joyfully:

"But, Trevor! It is you, then! Come in!"

"I'm so very sorry to disturb you, Tilli!" He made no effort to come in. "I came to find William."

"William? He is not here. I do not expect him."

"What a nuisance! I must get hold of him. I rang up Edwardes Square and they said he was probably here. And then I tried to get him here, but they said your line was out of order. I've chased over half London, looking for him."

"Perhaps he is already on his way here. Come in and wait a little while."

"Thanks very much." He paused, irresolute. "I'm in a violent hurry, as a matter of fact."

Tilli looked up at him. In the light of the street lamp, he was startled to see that she had been crying. Everything about her was soft and sad; the old mockery was gone. He remembered the last time that they had stood there. For he had not been to her house since the night when he had kissed her upon this very spot. It struck him that, for the first time, he beheld her pliant and off her guard.

"Ah," she murmured, "you do not wish to come in. You are like the others. They all desert me now. But you have more right than the others, for you have warned me. You have always said that this play is a mistake. I wish now that I had listened to you."

"Poor Tilli! Cheer up! I won't throw it up at you."

"I have deserved it. Trevor! Will you not come in? Will you always be angry because I would not take your advice? Even though I now say you are right?"

He felt so sorry for her that he came in. After all, she was a good creature; she bore no grudges. He hung up his wet hat in the little hall which he thought to have deserted for ever and went with her into the quiet warmth of the sitting room. She made him sit on the divan and sank, herself, upon a low hassock at his feet. Her humility touched him, and he spoke as kindly as he could of the play and her part in it. They were in darkness, save for a distant, faintly rosy lamp.

"It is strange," she said, "that you, who were so angry about this play, are the first of my friends who have come to me since the failure. All the others!" She made a gesture to show how far they had run. "Even William."

Trevor forebore to say that he himself had merely come in search of William. He patted her shoulder.

"Have you seen William?" she asked. "Does he also hate me since this play has failed?"

"Oh, my dear! I'm sure he doesn't. But he's been very busy. His sister is going to be married."

"The beautiful Emily? And whom is she to marry?"

"An old parson, down at Ratchet. Near where my mother lives. Very dull. Nobody can think why she's doing it. She went off down there yesterday, and she's going to be married in three weeks' time."

"That is very soon! It is a sudden engagement?"

"Positively a thunderclap. I think she's crazy. He's the sort of man no right-minded girl would marry unless she had no other choice."

"Marriages of that kind are often made very quickly," observed Tilli drily. "Perhaps she has some very good reasons."

"I hadn't thought of that. It may be. The Crownes can certainly never do things like anybody else. It'll be a devastating sort of wedding, but not without its humours. I hope I shall behave."

"You are going down, then?"

"Yes. In fact, I'm off to-morrow."

"To-morrow? Then your mother . . ."

"She's practically sent for me. In a gathering of the clans, like this, it wouldn't do for me to be away. She wouldn't like it."

"And after the wedding, where will you go? You will come back to London?"

"I don't think so. I may stay down there for good if this Monk's Hall plan comes off."

Her heart seemed to turn right over, and she gave a little gasp.

"I am very sorry that you are going away," she said, in a low voice.

Trevor patted her shoulder again; he liked to feel that he would be missed.

"Poor little Tilli! There'll be other plays."

But she drew herself away with a cry of despair:

"Plays! What do I care for plays! It is the loneliness of my life that is insufferable. I cannot endure it any longer. What have I done that I should always be alone?" She started to her feet and turned on him. "What have I done that you should despise me? Have I asked for so much, then?

Go! Go away! If you are so much afraid of me, I shall not ask you to come here any more."

He sat rigid, his thoughts taking a great leap forward into darkness. The cosy pretence of sentiment had fallen away from them. He knew that she was his for the taking, and that in a moment all the torment and unease of the past months might be assuaged. They were quite alone in this quiet, warm place. At last he got to his feet and approached her.

"Tilli?" he whispered. "Tilli?"

And in the same tone she answered:

"Now."

The dream of many broken nights was coming true. She was ardent and unresisting, as he had never quite dared to imagine her. He began to tremble.

A bell, shrilling loudly in the passage, caught at him and held him back.

"What is that?" he asked.

"Nothing. The door. Let it ring."

But the outer world and its thousand complications clamoured to him. The bell rang again, and he pushed Tilli away. She saw that her moment had gone by, and she went sullenly to open the door. Trevor could hear her talking to William in the passage.

A cold wind blew from the street into the room. The turmoil of his senses subsided. Reason nagged at him. He looked with startled eyes at the drawn curtains and the tumbled scarlet cushions. And as William came in, he turned on all the lights, flooding the room with a hard glare. Tilli had run into her bedroom to powder her nose.

William, on the threshold, blinked a little, for the passage had been dark. He greeted Trevor with that deceiving mildness of his which always signified the brewing of a storm.

"Haven't seen you to speak to, Trevor, since my first night."

"No."

He peered at Trevor, aware of something amiss. Tilli had been odd, too, when she came to the door. Before that, when he was waiting on the step, a premonition had come to him, and he had nearly gone away between his first and second ring. It occurred to him now that Tilli and Trevor might have been . . . but he dismissed the idea. He knew how Trevor disliked entanglements, and he was accustomed to think of Tilli as an honest woman.

"Seen the notices of my play?" he asked.

"Some of them."

"Aren't they bad?"

"Awful!"

"I'm sorry for Baxter."

"Baxter! I don't suppose he's suffered much."

"No. But I'm sorry for him."

"Why?"

"It must be awful to be him. I don't know how he ever keeps alive at all. I've always an uncomfortable feeling that he may begin to go bad, somewhere. I mean . . . it's not natural for anybody to have so much body and so little mind. After all, it's mind that keeps people alive: that makes the difference between a man and a corpse. He hasn't enough to go round. I believe that one day he'll begin to putrefy."

"Personally, if I were you, William, I wouldn't waste any pity on Baxter. I should be much more sorry for myself."

"I was sorry for myself on the night," said William with a grin. "I said to myself, as soon as it had begun: 'It's as bad as it can be. Nothing can be worse than this. I always knew something like this would happen to me.'"

"I told you it was a bad play," said Trevor peevishly.

"Yes. But I had an idea . . . it was partly Baxter's fault . . . that it might seem better when it was acted. And then, once I'd got started with it, I didn't like to let him down.

After he'd got all his elephants and tigers! However—it's over now. And I can never make a worse fool of myself."

"One would hope not."

"But I wish you'd been behind on Wednesday, when I told Baxter that the tigers had got loose. I've never laughed so much, though I was as sick as mud all the time."

"What did you tell him that for?"

"Just to see him sweat. He quite believed it, and you should have seen him edging away down the passage, turning round every other minute to see if a tiger hadn't nipped a bit out of his backside."

Trevor was a little scandalized at William's levity.

"I think the whole thing was a ghastly mistake," he said severely. "You can't expect to persuade people that you did it all so as not to hurt Baxter's feelings."

"I never expect to persuade people of anything," said William, suddenly lowering. "Their minds were made up before I was born."

He laughed again, and Tilli, who had come in and was sitting by the fire, looked up quickly. She did not see William as Trevor saw him. She knew how diverse the effects of a sudden disaster can be. To her mind, the young man was brokenhearted. He was half stunned, as though he had fallen from a great height: he seemed scarcely to know what he was saying.

His despair surprised her, for she had never supposed that he set any great store by this play. But she hardly cared, one way or the other. She had too many troubles of her own, and she could not forgive him for this untimely intrusion. Her whole being was still shaken by that delirious moment he had interrupted. She tried to make Trevor look at her, but he would not, and she began to suspect that he was drifting away from her with every moment of delay.

Her fears were justified, for Trevor was longing to make

an escape. His thoughts had swung back to Monk's Hall, to all his plans and resolutions. His brief madness was over, and he wanted to remove himself as soon as possible. It was not safe for him to be alone with Tilli.

"I'm glad you came," he said, turning to William. "I wanted to see you. I think that Monk's Hall should be entirely redecorated, and I want your views."

William looked blank and said that he had no views.

"Well, but you'd better have some," expostulated Trevor. "Seeing that you've bought the house."

"Do it up any way you like. I sha'n't live there. I'm going to Japan. Now that Emmie . . ."

He jerked his head toward an imaginary Ratchet.

"I shall go to Japan," he said again.

"Then shall I get on with it on my own responsibility?" asked Trevor briskly. "I'm going down to-morrow, and . . ."

"To-morrow?" said William.

"To-morrow?" said Tilli.

"Yes. I've no more use for London than you have. I expect I shall stay at home until we can move into Monk's Hall. You'll be coming down for the wedding, I suppose?"

"I suppose I must."

"Well, we can discuss all this then. Meanwhile, I'll get some estimates made." Trevor got up. "Good-bye, Tilli! Good-bye, William! No, don't bother. I'll let myself out."

She had made a move to come with him to the door. But she saw in time that it could not avail her, so she let him go. There were small sounds in the passage, while he found his coat and hat. The street door banged.

Tilli and William, equally bewildered and forlorn, sat together in the cheerless room. She looked at him with a smouldering animosity because he had driven Trevor away. If she could have hurt him more than he was already hurt, she would have done so with the greatest satisfaction. He and Trevor! They were both of them her enemies. She almost believed that they were allied against her. She remembered that she had heard William laughing when she was in her bedroom, and in her distorted fury she imagined that Trevor had whispered the whole story to him. They should be sorry for it. They should not laugh over her humiliation for very long. They should find something else to make them laugh.

"It's very late," said William at last.

"I suppose that it is."

"I'll have to go."

He thought of the empty house in Edwardes Square, and shivered.

"Can I have a drink?" he said.

"But surely. It is over there. Bring one for me, too."

He mixed a brandy-and-soda for himself, and one for Tilli, at the rickety little table between the windows.

"You're very tired," he said, observing her. "You ought to go to bed."

"It has been a fatiguing day." She sipped her brandy and looked at him sourly. "Why did you come to see me?"

"Why? Oh, not for anything special. Just to pass the time of day. I haven't seen you since Wednesday, and I thought we ought to condole with each other."

"I thought, perhaps, you would not come again."

"Why ever not?"

"We are companions in misfortune; it is not likely that we should love one another. The same blow has fallen upon us both."

"The same blow? But you hardly knew my sister."

"Your sister?"

"Oh, you mean the play!"

He smiled again. The play, to him, was getting to be nothing but the faint, ludicrous memory of Baxter and the tigers. But his smile enraged Tilli.

"To you it is a small thing that this play has failed. To me it is everything. I am ruined. I shall not easily find a new engagement. And I lost a good one when I took your part."

"Did you? Tilli! Why didn't you tell me? I'm most terribly sorry. I hadn't the least idea. . . ."

"It is nothing to you. You will go away now. To Japan. You will forget it."

"If there were anything that I could do . . ."

"You are going very soon?"

"In about a month."

It flashed upon her that Trevor would thus be left in complete possession of Monk's Hall. And that was intolerable. For she knew very well that Monk's Hall and not William had been the immediate cause of her failure. If Trevor had not had this refuge, he might have stayed with her.

She looked contemptuously at William, who was standing before her with a face of compassion and apology. It was plain that he knew nothing of her relations with his cousin. He was a fool, a mere gull, whom anyone could cheat. He was accepting, without question, her statement of advantages foregone. She could have no difficulty in getting a fortune out of him simply by asking for it. It was ridiculous that anybody with so little capacity for self-protection should be so rich.

Her own criminal stupidity was suddenly borne in upon her. She could scarcely believe it. From the beginning, she ought to have been aware of the possibilities in William. But for the last weeks she had been so much occupied by Trevor's image that she had not thought with fit seriousness of any other man. She had viewed his cousin simply as a playwright. In their first conversation, she had set him down as a bad subject, easy to deceive but not easy to attract. And she had not considered him again. She had been quite mad. But if she was to snatch anything from these ruins, she must waste no time now.

"If there were anything I could do . . ." he was saying.

"My poor friend," she murmured. "We are both in trouble together. But no one is to blame. It is life. I am used to it. I have been already so unhappy."

"I'm very sorry, Tilli."

"And you, perhaps, are not so used to it. Perhaps it is the first time that you have known what it is to fail."

"Oh, don't worry about me. I'm all right . . ."

He knew that he was miserable, but he would not say so. When the world goes to pieces, it is safer to insist that nothing has happened at all. And the shock of Emily's desertion was still so recent as to be almost unreal. Tilli saw that he was in need of another kind of comfort. Really, he wanted to laugh, and, if possible, to laugh at Baxter.

"Eugene has rung me up to-day," she began.

A small, irrepressible giggle burst from William. He came and sat down beside her on the divan. It was difficult to go away. His house was so cold and empty; not even Mattie was left, for Emily had taken her to Water Hythe, and for company he had only a charwoman with a cold in her head. It was better to be sitting in the warmth with Tilli. It was wonderfully soothing. He had never realized that she could be so nice. Simply to be with her was like coming into a temperate climate after hours of cheerless cold. And she was so amusing.

She was more than that. Dimly he felt that she had something which he had always needed. Soon he would need it more than ever before. While they made merry together, his mind moved imperceptibly toward imagined caresses, the narcotic, the warm oblivion of sensual enjoyment. He had thought of these things before, spasmodically, but other vital occupations had crowded them out.

At last, when the church clock near by had struck midnight, he tore himself away.

"But to-morrow I'll come and see you," he said. "Can I? We might go into the country, if it's fine."

Tilli reflected, and said that on Monday she would be busy. He might come on Tuesday. She took him to the door and put him into his coat. And on the step, where Trevor had once kissed and left her, she whispered a laughing farewell.

"Why are you laughing?" he asked her in the darkness.

"Because it is raining, and you do not wish to go away."

"Do you want me to go away?"

"For our reputations, it is better."

"Well . . . good-night."

"Good-night, William. Dream of . . . pleasant things."

"I shall dream of Tuesday. What'll you dream of?"

"Of Eugene."

"No, don't; he's a nightmare."

The clock struck the quarter.

"William! Positively you must go."

"All right. I'm going."

But he lingered, standing beside her in the darkness. Half protesting, she seemed to sway into his arms. They kissed closely, desperately, as if they were in love and about to be parted for ever. And then, with a sob and a laugh, she pushed him out into the rain. She heard his footsteps going away up the mews. They were very slow.

PART TWO

"Il n'y a qu'une manière de refuser demain:
C'est de mourir."

CHAPTER IV

PANIC

I

"OF COURSE," said Catherine to Charlotte for the hundredth time, "Philip will make a splendid husband. And everything about him is all right. He has money. He comes of nice people. But I did so want you girls to make interesting marriages."

Disappointment fought with relief in her heart; for though Emily might have done better, she might equally have done very much worse.

"The difference in age is not important," she proclaimed. "It's often a good thing. I was a great deal younger than your father. And Emily wants somebody sensible to look after her. I'm sure Philip will do that. But he's so . . . so . . ."

"Dull?" suggested Charlotte.

Catherine would not agree. She had always disliked the attitude of her children toward Philip.

"No, he's not a bit dull. That's nonsense. I only mean that I'm afraid, now, that he's too old to have much of a career.

And in a way it's a pity she should marry so young. She's so pretty and sometimes quite clever. If she had only waited, instead of rushing off with William like that, I might have taken a house in London for the winter and gone about with you both."

Charlotte could not help a shudder at the idea.

"And then you might have married me off at the same time," she said rather bitterly.

"Charlotte! Don't be so vulgar! Such an idea never entered my . . ."

"Oh, I know it's not called that. It's called taking the child about so that she gets the chance of knowing nice people. But it means a hunt for a husband, all the same."

"It means nothing of the sort. I know perfectly well that you don't want to marry."

"But I do, Mother. I'd be a fool if I didn't. Only I'm so ugly that I don't expect anybody will ever want to marry me, so it's no use thinking about it."

"My dear Charlotte!"

"If we both worked very hard for it, I might conceivably get a husband your way. But it's so unlikely that it's not worth the waste of time and self-respect."

"What do you mean by my way?"

"Going up to London and meeting nice people. But you know I dance so badly. And my nose gets shiny, whatever I do to it. Any little chit can beat me in that field. If I ever do marry, it will be because I've met somebody who can forget my face. And that's too small a chance to build on. I will not get old and haggard and bitter with disappointment, the way some women do. It's not necessary, nowadays. I know plenty of girls like me, who can't get married, but who have a very tolerable life of their own, with lots of interests in spite of it."

"This is a way of talking that I cannot understand. I

must say I think it's rather coarse. I had no idea you were so anxious to be married."

"I want it as much as any normal woman wants it."

"When I was a girl, one didn't . . . one didn't . . ."

"That's humbug, Mother! Really it is."

"You're very frank," said Catherine coldly. "I never met a girl before who talked about herself in such a way; who openly admitted that she wasn't . . . that she couldn't . . ."

"I only admitted it to myself after a struggle," said Charlotte, flushing. "It isn't, even now, a very pleasant thing to feel. It's humiliating. But it's true. And I'm sure that the truth is best if only one can bring oneself to stand it. These things are ever so much more upsetting if you won't look them in the face."

"You get morbid, living here with nothing to do. You should go away and take up a regular profession."

"My writing is a regular profession. I know it doesn't support me. If it did, I shouldn't live at home. I would rather write than do anything else. It makes up . . . for what I'm missing. If I went away, I'd have to work so hard for a living that I'd get no time for writing. Rather than that, I prefer the ignominy of living here and being a burden to you."

"You aren't a burden. You know that very well." Catherine spoke more kindly. "I like having you here. But if you earned your own living you might respect yourself rather more."

"I do respect myself. And I think I earn my bare board in all the messages I run for you. All the notes I write. I'm very lucky to have work I really care for. Many girls in my position haven't even that. I'd rather be myself, with all these handicaps, than be Emily, who is rich and free and going to marry a man she doesn't love."

"Charlotte! Even jealousy doesn't justify . . ."

"I'm not jealous, Mother. But I can't help seeing it. And you know quite well what I mean."

"Girls are often out of spirits when they are in love."

"Their spirits are unequal, perhaps. But she's absolutely lifeless."

"She likes being with him. If a day goes by without his coming over, she gets restless."

"I think she's fond of him. That's quite different."

"Is it?"

Catherine sounded a little amused, as though she doubted whether Charlotte could know very much about it.

"I think, my dear, that you judge life too much by books. A great many people get along very comfortably without ever being passionately in love with anybody at all. I know it's disappointing and unromantic. But it's true."

"I've no doubt it's true. But Emily will never be one of those people. And, what's more, Philip knows it. He's miserable, by the looks of him."

"He's devoted to her and always has been. I've seen it for years. It will all settle down when they have been married for a little while. It's the love that comes after marriage that counts, Charlotte, as you will find if you ever get married yourself."

"Oh, well . . . if they ever get as far as being married . . . I daresay you are right. But I'm very doubtful over it all, and so, I'm sure, is he."

"He's repainting his house," Catherine pointed out.

"Which needed doing up, in any case. So one good thing will come out of it, even if the marriage doesn't come off."

"But why, in Heaven's name, should she marry him, if she doesn't love him?"

"For safety."

"Safety?"

Catherine found this a very alarming word.

"What do you mean? Is there . . . was there anyone else, you think? Has she had a disappointment?"

"I never heard of anyone. But I'm sure she's had some kind of shock that's shaken her nerve."

"I wonder," said Catherine thoughtfully, "what I ought to do!"

"Do?"

"I can't think you're right."

"But you do think it! You've thought it ever since . . ."

"She's so anxious for the marriage. Why should she be in such a hurry if . . ."

Charlotte said nothing, and Catherine dismissed from her mind the memory of other young women she had known who had married men they did not love, in a hurry.

"I wish," she said nervously, "that one knew more of the people she's been seeing this spring. William was not a good chaperon." And in a final burst of foreboding she added, "I do hope all this is being quite fair to poor Philip."

"He's old enough to look after himself," said Charlotte. "He must know he's taking some risks, marrying a Crowne."

"Risks?" said Catherine. "Risks?"

But Charlotte would say no more. She regretted the moment of bitterness in which she had spoken her thoughts. She had been exasperated by the life of small, decently-veiled bickerings that she was forced to lead, but she wished with all her heart that she had held her tongue. Such confidences were dangerous.

And Catherine, nursing her fears in solitude, grew more uneasy every day. It seemed to her that something was really very much amiss with this marriage, although, for once, she was able to manage the whole affair in her own way. The complete absence of any argument or opposition was a disappointment to her. It was almost dull. She had no occasion to be masterly or tactful. Nobody consulted her, or disagreed with her. Emily, with a baffling indifference, assented to everything, stood passively, like a doll, to be fitted for clothes of Catherine's choosing, and wrote dreary little notes of thanks for her presents. Trevor and Charlotte were tiresome, and said that weddings were vulgar, but they offered no interference. And William never came down to Water Hythe at all. He sent to his sister a beautiful present, an Aubusson carpet, and a telegram to say that he would be writing, but that was all that was ever heard of him. Nobody knew whether he was still in London or had gone abroad. It was all very odd. Catherine had to fall back upon the formula that young people did not seem to care for weddings as they used.

It was with a heavy heart that she sat alone, on the eve of the marriage, making the bridal wreath without any tiresome disputes with the younger generation. Nobody interrupted her except Lise, who came with a diffident offer of help. And she disliked Lise too much for any confidences.

"I just wondered, Catherine, if we could send over any flowers. We have masses of syringa."

"Too kind!" murmured Catherine. "But I'm keeping the church decorations just to clematis and honeysuckles. I detest the bedizened look so many churches have at weddings. And we don't care for orange-blossom, mock or otherwise."

Lise saw that it had been a mistake to offer flowers from Monk's Hall. She indicated a vague, amused good-will.

"Well . . . anything that we can do! I'm sure I hope Emily is grateful for all the trouble you are taking."

"Grateful!" Catherine gave a short laugh. "One doesn't expect that, does one? Well, Charlotte? What is it?"

Charlotte had poked her head round the door. She made a slight grimace when she saw all the litter of greenery and myrtle sprigs.

"Jane wants to know how many for dinner," she said.

Catherine considered.

"Seven. Better say eight, in case William turns up. He might come by that train the Brandon Crownes come by."

"Mr. Cuffe's coming," volunteered Charlotte. "He's coming over from Oxford this evening to look at Monk's Hall, and I believe Trevor asked him to stay to dinner."

Catherine would make no comment on this in the presence of Lise. And Charlotte, flushing a little, came to the point.

"Mother! Can I speak to you for a minute?"

Catherine shook the flowers out of her apron, excused herself to Lise, and went with Charlotte into the dining room.

"Well? What is it?"

"Emily says she won't," said Charlotte solemnly.

"What?"

"She won't get married."

"Oh, that's nothing," said Catherine quickly. "Girls often say that. Where is she?"

"Up in her room."

"Tell her to stay there. I'll have dinner sent up to her. I'll see her presently."

Catherine's spirits were rising. She was able to tell herself, a little triumphantly, that she had half expected something like this.

"Then it'll be seven for dinner? What about Mr. Cuffe?"

"He won't be having dinner here. Send Trevor to me at once."

Trevor was, as it happened, hanging about in the hall, prepared for battle. He had been waiting all day for this explosion, and he was in no mind to listen to Charlotte, who recommended compromise.

"Do remember that it's her house!" she pleaded. "I don't think, knowing how she feels, that you ought to have invited him."

"If she insults him, she'll regret it. She's got to understand that she can't bully me. That's what it is. It's bullying. She likes to keep us dependent because it gives her power."

"It isn't even as if you liked him much."

"No, but it's a precedent. If he comes to Monk's Hall this autumn, she must learn either to put up with him and Sally, or do without me. You ought to back me up in this, Car. You get no sort of life of your own, simply because you won't fight her. If we're firm now . . ."

"It's not a good moment for fighting. She's worried with the wedding. Emily says she won't go through with it."

"Does she? By Jove! That's interesting. Why?"

Charlotte shrugged her shoulders.

"Has Siegmund turned up?"

"Who?"

"William."

"Why do you call him that?"

"Don't you think it's a good name, Car?"

"No, I don't. If I hear you making that sort of joke again, Trevor, I . . . I'm through with you. I'll never come to Monk's Hall . . . I won't back you up over this Cuffe business."

"Oh, keep cool. I don't make jokes like that to anybody but you."

And he went off to his mother, feeling a great deal less brave than he looked.

She was quite resolute, having also determined that this was a precedent. If once she gave way, she would be powerless: it was the thin end of the wedge, and she might never be able to assert her principles again. She began at once:

"I think you will admit, Trevor, that this house is mine. I have a right to choose my own guests."

"And I my friends."

"Certainly. But unless I approve of them, they don't come here. Mr. Cuffe is not the sort of person I have ever . . ."

"Why not? His morals are no worse than those of many people whom you have been perfectly ready to entertain. Do you mean to say you've never given dinner to a man who kept a mistress?"

"That has nothing to do with it. It's no concern of mine what people may do in their private lives. I'm not as unworldly as you think, Trevor. I'm perfectly ready to ignore a great deal. But this Miss . . . Miss Whatever-you-call-her . . . one is expected, I understand, to receive her, too."

"You mean you've no objection to a man who keeps a dozen women and is ashamed of it, but an open relationship . . ."

"I don't pretend to judge. But I simply don't ask people of that class to my house."

"You asked Lise before she married Bobbie."

"That was for your uncle's sake."

"Well, if you waive your principles for his sake, can't you for mine?"

"I'm not certain, I can never be certain, if I did right then. I've often regretted it. If one gives way in a case of that sort . . . Good heavens!" She stared out of the window. "What is that coming up the drive? Is it gipsies?"

Trevor looked, and saw a large yellow caravan.

"Up to the very house! What impertinence! Go out, dear, and warn them off."

"It's raining," said Trevor peevishly.

Catherine pursed her lips.

"Very well," she said. "I suppose I'll have to go myself."

"There's a car coming, too," said Trevor, leaning out of the window. "I believe it's Nigel's car. Am I to warn him off, along with the gipsies? I say! I know them! Look! Lord bless us! It's the Hackbutts! William's friends. What a day for them to turn up! I'd heard they were coming to camp hereabouts until Monk's Hall was ready for them."

Catherine could say nothing: she could only stand at the window and stare at the invading forces drawn up in front of her house. She saw Trevor go out and bid them welcome. He helped Nigel Cuffe to extract from the car a bunchy little female who must be the unspeakable Miss Whatever-her-name-was. A vast horde of little Hackbutts, all about three years old, were tumbling out of the caravan, and a bedizened woman with a yellow handkerchief over her head was climbing off the driving-seat. They were greeting Mr. Cuffe: it was evident that they all knew one another. The drive looked like Hampstead Heath on a Bank Holiday.

Her last defences were down, and the rabble was upon her. She had no hope, seeing them, that the Monk's Hall scheme would fall through. Having come, they would never go away. Like some rank, persistent weed, they would overrun the neighbourhood. Nothing would be safe from them. They would take possession of her old home—the house where she had been born, and where she had led the safe, ordered life that seemed to her the right sort of life. At her and her principles they would snap their fingers. It was nothing to them that she was the widow of Charles Frobisher, and that a lost generation had paid deference to her. They sneered at Frobisher.

She made no distinctions among them. For all she knew, the Hackbutts might be as improper as the other two. They certainly looked very unpresentable, and the enormous number of their children did them no credit. A fierce, helpless resentment was all that she could feel in contemplating any of them, a hatred of their indecorum, their want of order and purpose, their detestable, strident complacency. But on one point she was resolute: they should never enjoy the hospitality of Water Hythe. Monk's Hall was enough. They might live there, bang doors, sprawl, swear, wrangle, and scatter cigarette-ash. Cuffe and his Sally might invade her mother's bedroom. But into her own citadel, the shrine of a decent and orderly past, they should not come.

Her elderly parlourmaid appeared, with a very bleak look on her face.

"If you please, Madam, Miss Charlotte says is there any more to dinner?"

"No, Louisa. No more."

"And Mr. Luttrell is here, Madam. He's at the garden door. He's on his way to Ratchet, but he just stopped to ask if there was any chance of his seeing Miss Emily."

Catherine remembered, with increased irritation, the obdurate bride upstairs.

"I'm afraid he can't," she said. "Miss Emily is tired, and I am sending her to bed early."

She set off to deal with her niece. As she climbed the stairs, a great clamour in the hall told her that the invaders had got into the house. She supposed that they were sneering at her pictures. Her patience, as she gained the attic floor, was wearing very thin.

Emily sat on the little bed in which she had slept for the greater part of her life. She had begun to dress for dinner, and she was still in her petticoat, with her fair hair loose over her shoulders. She crouched, her arms about her knees, staring in front of her. To all the exhortations of Charlotte, she offered a mute obstinacy of regard. On the floor, a heap of childish possessions lay all tumbled together. The new trousseau was already packed and locked away in boxes labelled for the Swiss hotel where the honeymoon was to be spent, and these were just old treasures that must be sorted and sent across direct to Ratchet.

"If you'd help her to pack instead of talking so much," said Catherine to Charlotte, "you might be of more use."

"She's not even sorted out what she wants to keep," explained Charlotte.

"There's no need," observed Emily. "I've made up my mind not to get married at all."

"That's nonsense."

Catherine began briskly to sort out the heap on the floor.

"A good deal can go to the jumble sale, I should think. You can't want, for instance, to keep this china jug?"

"William gave it to me."

"Oh, well . . . but this half-finished bit of knitting . . ."

"Really, it's of no use, Aunt Catherine. I've changed my mind."

"Why?"

"Because, when I started to go through these things, I got afraid. I don't want to change."

"Change?"

"They reminded me of when I was a different person," explained Emily. "I admired that jug once. I don't now. Well, I don't want to change any more. I think I'll be a nun."

Charlotte took this up.

"We all change, whether we marry or not. We can't help it. But sometimes we get nicer."

"I know. But I sha'n't get nicer. I've had the happiest time in my life. I'll never be so happy again as I was this winter. If I marry, perhaps I shall leave off being sorry. I don't want to leave off. It's . . . it's like being disloyal."

"It does seem like disloyalty to recover from things," agreed Charlotte. "But everybody does it."

"I don't mean to."

Catherine scarcely listened to this passage. She had been pondering upon her niece's first statement about change.

"I think I understand," she said gently. "Charlotte, you can go downstairs."

"You don't understand, Mother. It's not what you think."

Charlotte was banished with a look, and she went off, cursing herself for the unguarded moment when she had put ideas into her mother's head. She knew that words like *change* and *safety* meant one thing to Catherine and another to Emily, and she felt sure that they would come to grief on these rocks of words. To the older woman there was still a possibility of safety in concrete things. She thought of it in terms of fire-escapes and razors and sound investments. But for Emily it stood for something infinitely more elusive: self-confidence and the integrity of her own judgment meant everything. She could trust to nothing else. She had seen the reckless dissipation of millions, the bankruptcy of nations, and the collapse of all civilized society. She knew that man, when he has constructed a perfectly safe ship, will never rest until he has invented a torpedo to destroy it. And this knowledge had impressed itself upon her dawning intelligence, not as an immense accident, but as a natural condition of life. She accepted it, not as a disaster, but as a commonplace. For safety, she turned to the hard, scornful self-reliance that is the shield of her generation.

"My dear," said Catherine, when Charlotte had gone, "you mustn't upset yourself. This is nothing so very dreadful. I know how you feel. Girls often feel a little nervous at the idea of getting married. I did myself."

"Did you?" asked Emily, gaping.

"It isn't anything so very dreadful. All . . . all that . . . is really so very unimportant. You'll find . . ."

"All what?"

"The . . . the physical part . . ." began Catherine bravely.

"Oh, that!" Emily looked contemptuous. "I don't worry about that. What do our bodies matter, anyway? They're only worms' meat."

Catherine was shocked to the marrow by this speech. Apparently there was no limit to the disagreeable ideas which these young people could entertain. That a girl on her marriage eve should talk so was almost depraved. She cried:

"Then what on earth is the matter with you? Have you thought of Philip at all? Why did you accept him if . . ."

"I didn't. He accepted me."

"He accepted . . . Do you mean that you asked him?"

"Yes."

"Why?"

"Because I wanted to be safe," said Emily sulkily.

"Safe?"

Catherine thought of Charlotte's suggestion that this marriage had been an escape. And then she thought of the licentious crew downstairs who were some of them Emily's friends.

"Safe! Were you in danger?"

"I can't tell you about it," said Emily.

"Had you any reason," demanded Catherine, "for . . . for getting married so quickly?"

"Yes. The same reason for getting married at all."

"Philip . . . does he know of all this?"

"Oh, yes. I explained it all to him."

That was, at least, a relief. But Catherine scarcely knew what to make of it all, and she shrank from asking further questions. She preferred not to hear any more. If Philip, knowing the circumstances, was willing to marry the girl, he had much better do so. Of that she was very sure, nor did she like to imagine the consequences, the terrible predicaments which might arise, if the marriage was broken off.

"I'm afraid, my dear," she said, "that you must marry him. You can't get out of it now; the thing has gone on too far."

"No, no . . ."

"What do you propose to do?"

"I don't know."

"Will you go back to London?"

Emily shivered.

"For you won't stay here, you know."

"Oh, Aunt Catherine!"

"Not for a moment could I countenance such behaviour. Either you marry Philip to-morrow or you leave my house. Think of the scandal . . . the publicity . . . if you break it off now!"

Emily grew very pale. This had evidently frightened her.

"You know what people will say? It will simply be regarded as another effort, on your part, to make yourself conspicuous. Of course, if you want that . . ."

"Another Crowne show!" muttered Emily.

"Exactly! Another Crowne show."

"Oh, what shall I do? What shall I do?"

The dinner bell, clanging in the house below, reminded Catherine that the enemy were still on the premises. She must lose no time in clearing them out. But she was undaunted. She liked having to fight two battles at once. She turned to go, saying very firmly:

"I'll leave you now to think it over. Your dinner will be sent up to you. And remember that it's not a bad thing to ask yourself where your duty lies. Perhaps you have always allowed yourself to be governed a little too much by inclination. If you have given your word to Philip, you will dishonour us all by breaking your promise."

"I wish I could see him," said Emily mournfully.

But Catherine held out no hopes of this. She saw that it would be more easy to frighten Emily than to persuade her. Repeating her injunction as to unselfish reflection, she hurried downstairs.

They were all assembled in the hall, and her coming put an end to their jovial chatter. She was like a cold north wind blowing into the house. With an air of faint bewilderment she submitted to an introduction to the Hackbutts, as if wondering why they should be there. She was quite civil to them, and apologized for the absence of William; and they, being simple people, unversed in the finer shades of manner, were at first unable to locate the sudden fall of the social temperature. Their heartiness had subsided a good deal before she had done with them.

Trevor, with an attempt at bravado, introduced Nigel Cuffe. And then it was the turn of Sally, who had been standing on one leg in the background. He remembered with horror that he ought not to have left her to the last.

"And this is Miss . . ."

He broke down. For the life of him he could not recollect Sally's surname. Perhaps he had never heard it.

"Miss Green," said Cuffe, coming to the rescue.

"Oh, yes," said Catherine, and turned her back on Sally.

"Mr. Yates," said Trevor, introducing a very young man in a Fair Isle jumper.

Catherine gave her hand to Mr. Yates. And then she stood waiting politely for them to go. Trevor was forced to say:

"They're all staying to dinner, Mother. I knew we had enough food in the house, with all the wedding baked meats, so I took it upon myself to invite them."

Catherine started, looked grave, and murmured something about regret and being sure that Mrs. Hackbutt would understand. But she did not endorse Trevor's invitation.

"Indeed, there are too many of us!" exclaimed Mrs. Hackbutt. "I told Trevor so. But menfolk don't understand these things, do they, Mrs. Frobisher? We'll all go out and get our own dinner in the van. I'm sure it would be an outrageous thing for you, with a wedding on your hands and all."

"I'm afraid it is rather . . . I'm very sorry . . . If William . . . if I'd had more notice . . ."

"We shouldn't have come!" cried Mrs. Hackbutt.

Catherine did not contradict her. She looked instead at Nigel Cuffe, and Trevor said immediately:

"You'll stay, won't you, Nigel?"

"Thanks!" said Nigel, who found it all very funny.

"I'm afraid," said Catherine gently, "that I can't do with any more guests to-night. Mr. Cuffe will understand."

"Do you mind?" asked Trevor furiously of Nigel.

"Oh, not at all." Nigel could scarcely conceal his mirth. "I think I understand. But where are we to get anything to eat? Sally's hungry."

"We'll go over to Monk's Hall," said Trevor. "Lise will give us something."

And when the invaders trooped out, he went with them. He wanted the whole world to know that war had been declared again between Monk's Hall and Water Hythe.

2

Emily's wedding took place in the queer little old church that flanked the Water Hythe garden, so that there were no carriages or pushing crowds. The guests strolled across the lawn to the church in the most delightfully informal way. The sun shone all day, and if the bride had not been so very late, it would have been a perfect wedding.

For Emily was such an unconscionable time dressing herself that many of the congregation, fidgeting in their pews, began audibly to wonder whether anything had gone wrong. Philip, stuck up for them all to gape at, suffered tortures. He grew more and more sure that she must have changed her mind and that he would be jilted in public. He had spent a miserable, sleepless night, full of regret and anxiety. The thought of marriage depressed him infinitely. But now that he was at the altar it was imperative that he should get married. If Emily did not turn up, his heart would break.

The church was so small that he was obliged to stand in
the very midst of the congregation. He took no notice of
anybody, having previously determined that it would look
more dignified. He would try not to be a grinning bridegroom.
But he was embarrassed by Lise and Trevor, in the front
pew, who were doing their best to make him laugh.

"It's a pity," whispered Lise, in a hushed boom which
could be heard in the vestry, "that the poor man can't be
veiled, too. Or draped somehow. It would be so much easier
for him, standing there, if he were covered up."

One of the little Hackbutts demanded shrilly to know
what the funny man was for.

"He's waiting for a fairy princess," whispered Mrs. Hackbutt dauntlessly. "You'll see her in a minute."

"But, Mammy, why is the funny ma-an waitin' for the
lady?"

"Because she's a little late, darling."

"She is late!" boomed Lise. "I hope she hasn't . . ."

"Not so very," Trevor assured her. "They always are."

"But, Mammy, is that a fairy prince?"

The stifled explosions which greeted this question struck
Philip as being in particularly bad taste. The village school-
mistress, at the harmonium, struck up a voluntary consisting
of three common chords and a dominant seventh rhythmi-
cally repeated. It drowned the din a little, and he was glad
of it. He knew now how it was that people managed to get
themselves married. He had often wondered at the courage
of his parishioners in thus undertaking obligations which
they were so little likely to fulfil. He had heard froward
scolds promising obedience, libertines and wantons promising
fidelity, the brutal engaging to be tender, the destitute to
provide a maintenance, without a whisper of incredulous
protest from anybody. The overpowering silliness of their
fellow-creatures provided them, for a time, with a protection

against reality. Their own rashness lost significance when everybody round them was intent on being as foolish as possible. All these festive imbecilities were designed to nerve a man in taking an otherwise insupportable risk.

The windows of the chancel were made of clear, unstained glass, and Philip could see out across the lawn. The pigeons strutted and spread their tails there, on this day as on all other days that he could remember. They had been there before the Frobishers came to Water Hythe, when the place was a farmhouse and Monk's Hall a Benedictine foundation. He thought of other weddings in that church, of the munching yokels in the hall kitchen, the heavy drinking, the broad jests, the flung stocking, the horseplay. The same folly was always there, but it had once been simpler and more direct. He could see the garden door, open on the shady blackness of the hall, and the sun-baked warmth of the stone porch, where the house dogs lay snoring. Two maids in black dresses came out and hurried into the church. They had been helping to clothe the bride, and their coming was a sign that everything was nearly ready. The veil and the wreath were pinned. In other days, it would have been their task to assist, later, in a hilarious undressing; in putting her jovially to bed. Society, having entrapped a bewildered pair into this coil, was at least good-natured enough to see them most of the way through it. But for Philip and Emily this support was to be withdrawn at a much earlier stage. They were to be left in petrifying solitude, in a foreign country, to finish the business as best they could by the light of their recaptured wisdom.

Catherine came out of the hall door, a little battered, but triumphant. Her wedding hat, plumed all the way round with small black ostrich feathers, sat rather askew on her head. She looked as though she had done a hard day's work, and as she chattered to a grizzled Crowne relative, she fidgeted with the eternal eyeglasses in the lace at her bosom. The sight of her reminded Philip of something unpleasant that he had been trying all the morning to forget. He had had a shock, when dressing, at the number of gray hairs upon his own head. They seemed to have doubled in the night.

Charlotte, also emerging from the house, looked bouncing and ill at ease in a bridesmaid's dress that did not suit her. And immediately afterward came Bobbie with the bride upon his arm. They had muffled her up in so much drapery that she was scarcely recognizable as Emily. Her frozen panic was hidden beneath a veil, just as Philip's melancholy was for the moment obscured by a buttonhole and a new suit. They were the chief figures in a public function, and that got them through it. They were married and found themselves standing side by side in front of old Canon Frobisher, who had done this to them and who wished to say a very few words before they left the church.

"Now when I see two young people just starting upon their Great Adventure, there is just one thing that I always want to say to them . . ."

For the first time, Philip caught the eye of his bride. There was a gleam in it. He thought:

"We shall laugh at this. After all, there may be a future . . . a way out. We may be sane some day."

Small jokes, an infinite number of small approaches, might some day make them one. Nothing else could. For these things were life. He felt a little safer as they listened to Canon Frobisher, who told them that Roman Catholics called marriage a sacrament, which it was not, and yet in a sense it was, so that they must make allowances for one another.

They knelt for a blessing, and the congregation sang a hymn. In the little pauses between the verses, pigeons could be heard cooing on the roof, and the soft, sleepy murmur of them seemed to Philip like the voice of eternity. He remem-

bered having heard that swans mate for life, and he wondered if this was true. He thought of the Swannery at
Abbotsbury and wondered if he would ever go there again.
He thought that it was foolish to think so much and do so
little. He thought that he was too old.

They had no Wedding March to help them out of church,
because Catherine had justly decided that it would sound
silly on the harmonium. So they walked soberly across to
the Manor House and ate a meal with their friends. They
smiled a great deal, were kissed, slapped on the back, rallied,
jostled, and put into a car. It took them away to London
before the powerful anæsthetic of all these festivities had time
to abate. They drove for the greater part of the way with the
same fixed smiles on their faces, though there was no need for
it. It was not until the western suburbs had begun to spring
up round them that they gradually relaxed and began to
take notice of their plight.

"How do you feel?" said Philip to Emily.

"Rather cold."

He tucked the rug more closely round her.

"Do you like being married . . . Mrs. Luttrell?"

"Yes and no, to quote the Brontës."

"No? Why no?"

"It goes too fast."

"It shall go," said Philip, "as fast as we choose. I'll tell
it to go slower."

He gave an order, and the car slackened its pace. He, too,
had the feeling that they were being whirled very fast,
straight into the future. This car was taking them into time
as well as into space, and it was rather terrifying. Both of
them, in the depths of their hearts, heard a frightened voice
whispering:

"And what is going to happen next?"

Philip, braving the future, took her hand. But she shrank

away, with the plea that the driver could see them in the wind-screen. His anxiety took a menacing step toward him. Until that moment, it had been overshadowed by regret. All night, in his soul, he had lamented the necessity of marrying Emily. When his, she would inevitably lose her magic, as the spring ripens into summer. The idea of her would no longer have power to enchant him, and he knew this because he was too old for her. No young man could know a tenth part of this passion of his which shrank from possession.

But it signified, now, very little what he had thought or what he had felt, since it was all to come to the same commonplace conclusion. The emotions are many and complex, but they lead us to few and simple ends. His relation to Emily, beautiful and rare though it had been, was now the prelude to the ordinary domestic activities of marriage and procreation. Nor was this well-trodden path to be easy before them. It was, on the contrary, full of pitfalls. She was not yet won. He had scarcely begun his wooing. A thousand responsibilities overwhelmed his imagination. It came into his head that she might not, after all, change so very much, but live with him, invincibly cold, a hostile stranger in his house. This idea was so definitely frightening that he fled from it into a survey of the foolish, confused day stretching away behind them. He asked suddenly:

"Who were all those odd people in church?"

"What people?"

"A lot of rather dirty children I never saw before."

"Oh, the Hackbutts."

"Oh, were those the Hackbutts?"

"Yes. They're camping in the park till they can move into Monk's Hall. Of course, they expected to find William."

"It was a thousand pities that he never came."

"I don't know. I was quite glad he wasn't there. It was all so silly and muddled."

He had an impression that she did not like to think about William.

"But, Emily," he said, "it's not serious, this Monk's Hall idea, is it?"

"Serious?"

"He doesn't really mean to start a Communist Settlement?"

"Well . . . not exactly. It's an experiment. You see, Philip, all modern life is much too complex."

"I agree."

"The only hope of the creative artist," said Emily very glibly, "is to have a little world of his own, something smaller and simpler, where he has more control over all the conditions of his life. At Monk's Hall they are to be almost self-supporting, you know. They are going to do their own gardening and keep cows and bees and things. And they are going, in time, to do their own spinning and weaving. Peter Yates is going to make all the furniture and the earthenware. It will all give a sort of unity to existence, which the creative artist must have if . . ."

"Stop quoting Trevor, darling, and say it in your own words, if you can."

"I can't," she confessed. "In my own words, I should say that I think it all very silly. But I wouldn't say that to anybody but you, because it would be rather disloyal to the others. I'm sure they won't write any better for living at Monk's Hall and wearing homespuns."

"I can't think that any of them really believe in it."

"No. I'm sure they don't. But it happens to suit them all. Trevor has got to live somewhere, and he loves managing things. It's convenient for Bobbie and Lise and Peter and the Hackbutts. And Charlotte will have a better time there than at home. As for Nigel, Sally has persuaded him to come. She's so lonely in London. She has no real friends."

"It may be convenient for them all. But why all this talk about creative art? Of course, I'm a plain man . . ."

Emily giggled. "Oh . . . oh! Don't say that. You aren't a plain man."

"Yes, I am. A very plain man."

"Don't boast."

"Is that boasting?"

"Yes, it is. It means that you think yourself more sensible than Trevor."

"Does it? Well, perhaps it does. And I am. Much more sensible."

"I think so, too. But please don't call yourself a plain man or I shall have to laugh."

"And I sha'n't mind a little bit. I like it when you laugh, Emily. You don't do it quite often enough."

They were getting on very well. He could almost imagine that it might be possible to steer this course without disaster. He thought with a new warmth of pleasure of his house at Ratchet, all newly painted and ready for lovely young Emily. She would make her home there and learn to laugh at him, with him, lured by laughter into intimacy. And then again he fell into doubt. The abyss was not to be bridged as easily as that.

They had got, by now, into London and were part of the traffic in its streets. They dodged among the trams in Hammersmith Broadway, in the sun and dust of the summer evening, and took the road that William and Emily had travelled so often in the early mornings. She saw, like a little picture, that queer London life of theirs, very remote and exquisite and unreal. It was over, and had the timeless quality of all past things. Because it had seemed eternal then, she felt as though it must still be going on somewhere. Inevitably, they drew up at last before the hotel where they were to spend the night. Upstairs in their room, all the new luggage was piled up at the foot of a large double bed with brass knobs and a black-and-gold eiderdown. The hotel porters went stumping away down the corridor, and the sense of motion was succeeded by a blank, dismaying pause.

Philip came out of the adjoining dressing room and looked glumly at the impersonal cheerfulness of their surroundings.

"I ought to have got some flowers," he said. "Fool that I was, not to have arranged it."

"We can go out now and buy some."

"Emily! Can I kiss you?"

"If you like."

As he kissed her, he would have given his last penny to be fifteen years younger and less uncompromisingly aware of the difficulties before him.

"Poor Philip!"

"Why 'poor Philip'? I'm happy. Aren't you?"

"I don't think I want to be happy," she said, frowning. "It's a little smug."

"Because you're young, you think that."

"Did you think it ever?"

"Once, perhaps, I did."

"When did you stop?"

"I can't remember now."

"How odd!"

"Do I look smug?"

"No. But then you're not really happy."

"Oh, Emily!"

"But are you?"

"I'm going to be."

"So am I. We'll both be happy and smug together."

She caught him to her heart with a new warmth, comforting him as a mother comforts, full of pity for his forlornness.

And then she told him to let her unpack before they went out to buy flowers. Obediently he took himself off, leaving her alone in this strange place. She thought:

"Oh, dear! What is going to happen next?"

Of course, she must go on with it. A failure in resolution could never be permitted; it was too late now. She should, perhaps, have been firmer last night. But she had let them persuade her, and she must try to be very good to Philip.

Opening the window, she leant out of it, her elbows on the ledge. Far down below her an endless stream of traffic flowed in two rivers along the street, and people, like ants, hurried and jostled on the pavement. It was odd to think that each one of them had a destination and a name of his own. Each one was as real as herself.

But then, she did not feel very real. She was Emily Crowne, she was Emily Luttrell, a virgin, a bride, hanging for a moment between two lives, above the sunshine of this busy street. Soon she would be gone, like an image seen for a moment in a mirror, swallowed in the vast, uncomprehending abysses of time. She flew to her unpacking with a little gasp of fright.

In the tray of her box was the dress she was to wear that night. Catherine had chosen it for her, and it was all soft and silvery, like moonlight. Silver shoes and stockings lay beneath it, and a gray velvet cloak. Under a layer of tissue-paper she came upon fine silken underclothing. She put all the things out on the bed, but she did not want to wear them, for they were not hers. They belonged to the woman who would replace her—to Emily Luttrell. She began to search through her trunk for something that she had worn before. But everything was new. A faint spasm of terror shot through her. It had begun.

The strangeness of her dressing-case was even more appalling. She pulled out brushes, combs, and bottles. Nothing looked familiar. Nothing of her own was left. Panic invaded her; she grew frantic, and called to Philip. He hurried in from the dressing room to find her standing, wild-eyed, among her fine, new possessions. She was muttering:

"Oh, I can't! I can't."

"You can't what, my love?"

"Go on with this."

"With your unpacking?"

"With being married."

He had been waiting for this moment all day. But he made an effort and fought back his despair. He must be wise for both of them.

"What has made you change so suddenly?" he asked.

"It isn't sudden. I've felt like this ever since last night. But I was weak. I let Aunt Catherine bully me."

"Did you feel bad last night? So did I. I nearly jumped into the river. I didn't want to be married a bit."

This desperate move was a good one. Emily's surprise mastered her terror.

"Philip! Didn't you? Why didn't you tell me?"

"Ask yourself if it was possible. Why didn't you tell me?"

"Isn't it silly? We've let ourselves be trapped into it. We neither of us wanted it. What are we to do now?"

"We can do whatever we please as long as we keep our heads and don't get panicky. Let's talk it over quietly."

"Not here! Not here!"

"Certainly not here, if you don't like it."

He spoke so calmly that she was reassured. And he put on her hat and took her out at once, hoping that a change of scene might steady her nerves. Out in the street they became part of the throng of human ants, who ran about and were so greatly concerned about nothing at all. They strolled on aimlessly for a little way, and Philip suggested that they might dine somewhere in Soho, so as to postpone their return to the hotel.

He was just a little elated at his own cleverness, and she detected the complacency in his tone. Stealing a secret look at him, she saw that he was smiling. The smile enraged her. She knew that she was still in a trap. She said nothing, but she became dark and subtle like a slave, or like an animal that has known for a long time the mastery of man. She plotted an escape, and when they passed a flower shop, she said suddenly:

"Aren't you going to get me some of those?"

Philip was delighted. He said that he would get her some at once. He hurried into the shop, and left her outside because she complained of the heat. The moment he was gone she took to her heels. A taxi turned the corner of the street, and she jumped into it, trying at the same time to pull off her wedding ring. But her finger had swelled with the heat, and she could not get it off.

Philip came out of the shop two minutes later, red, grizzled, and beaming, with a bushel of roses in his arms. He could not find her.

3

She forgot that she had no latchkey until she found herself actually standing upon the doorstep. And a qualm of uneasiness assailed her lest there should be nobody at home. For, if William was away and the charwoman was out, there would be nobody to let her in. She rang the bell hastily and heard its faint tinkle die away in the basement. Nothing stirred.

Peeping through the slit of the letter-box, she could see the empty hall and the stairs winding away up into sunlight. On the half-landing a bowl of roses stood on a little table in front of a window; they looked fresh, and she concluded that

William must be at home, for the charwoman would never go putting flowers about. The smell of the hall, of the polish that Mattie used for the floor, and a whiff of cedar from the old chest, were wafted out to her through the letter-box, and she grew quite faint with her longing to get in. This time she thumped with the knocker in case they were upstairs. It made a shocking noise, up and down the empty sunlit Square. But when its echo had ceased, a watchful silence settled down once more upon the house.

She could not be absolutely certain that nobody inside was listening. It almost seemed as though she could hear distant steps. Standing back, on the pavement, she scanned the windows. They had a secret look, though they were still hung with curtains of her choosing. Her door, with its bright knocker, remained mutely shut. Again she listened at the letter-box, and again she thought she could hear light foot-steps moving about somewhere upstairs. But perhaps it was the beating of her own heart.

The sudden clamour of a dog-fight, across the road, made her start violently. And then her eyes filled with tears. She was so tired, and she was shut out of her own home. Soon it would be night. The long sunbeams were losing their power, and half the Square was in shadow. She longed to be at rest.

At last she went down to the basement and tried the kitchen door, but, of course, it was locked. Peering through the kitchen window, she saw Mattie's rocking chair and the old nursery rag rug, and all the Delftware on the dresser shelves. The window was not latched, and with a good deal of tugging she managed to get it down. Two minutes later she was inside.

The dogs in the Square were still yelping and scuffling, but the kitchen was as silent as a tomb, its quietness mea-sured for it by the loud clock that ticked on the mantelpiece.

Everything was unchanged, but it seemed to be waiting for something to happen. She sped up the dark little stairs into the hall and cried for joy when she saw a letter on the mat addressed to Miss Emily Crowne. It was only a circular, but she was reassured to know that Emily Crowne could still receive letters. Her spirits bounded upward, as she flew from room to room.

There was no sign of William in the drawing room, but the place had a used look, as though people had been there lately. Some of the cushions were tumbled, and there was cigarette-ash in the fireplace.

"He's been here," she thought, "since Mrs. Masters dusted. But why—why didn't he come to my wedding? What a fool I've been, all this time! What's the matter with me? Oh! What was that?"

It could not, this time, be her heart. It was too loud. Unmistakably it was someone walking about upstairs. She had been half certain already that the house was not empty. She ran out on to the landing and called:

"Mrs. Masters! Mrs. Masters! Is that you? William?"

The footsteps stopped, but nobody answered.

"Who is that?" she called again, a little uncertainly.

Of course, it was Mrs. Masters, and really the old woman was getting to be very deaf. Emily began to run upstairs again, but grew so tired halfway that she had to take the last few steps at a walk. The landing was high and hot and bright. Sunshine had poured in all day through the skylight. Its untempered light now fell upon an object that brought Emily to a standstill: a wardrobe trunk, very new, very expensive, such as continental ladies keep in the corridors of hotels. It looked horrid in the bare brightness of the landing, and she stared at it in doubt and dismay. She could not believe that it belonged to William.

Inside her own room she could hear the rustling of tissue-

a very distant sea. Emily stared at the sky, which was all
that could be seen from the bed, and saw how it grew clear
and gold with the late sun. The day had been very long. She
remembered how the dawn had found her sobbing in her
room at Water Hythe.

At last she turned her head away from the window and
looked into the room. It seemed quite dark, after the brightness outside, but in the glass over the dressing table she
caught the black sparkle of Tilli's scrutiny. The little woman
had been sitting with her back to the bed, peering into the
glass at the reflection of the tumbled pillows and the long pale
young creature lying between the four angels.

"*Ciel!* But how she is like William!" thought Tilli. "In
bed he also looks so long."

When she saw that Emily had moved, she got up at once
and came across to the bed.

"You feel better now?"

"Yes, thank you."

"I am so sorry. You are *énervée*. I can see that it has
been a shock. You will understand that we wished this marriage to be secret. I have a horror of publicity. It was, of
course, necessary to write to you, but . . . William will be
so happy to know that you have not got his letter. He thought
that you were angry."

"Why should I be angry?" said Emily. "I have got married myself."

Tilli smiled, a little maliciously.

"It is not for getting married that he asks forgiveness,"
she said, "but because he has not told you before."

"I'm sure," said Emily simply, "that it was your wish."

She intended no attack; she was too much stunned to speak
with any purpose. And Tilli, after a quick look at her,
agreed:

"But, yes. Perhaps. I did not wish it to be known."

She had wished to keep her marriage secret, especially from Emily, until it had become irrevocable. In this sister of William's she recognized the one influence that was likely to be stronger than her own. But she could not have staged their first encounter better.

"How are you feeling?" she inquired politely.

Emily rallied her powers and sat up. She was beginning to comprehend, dimly, the menace and importance of this queer little woman. It was as though some victory were being gained over herself and William for every moment that she lay weakly there.

"I'm better," she said.

Tilli looked into her face and then at the ring on her hand.

"You also are married?"

"To-day."

"And you have come here . . . to fetch something, perhaps? Some book or dress? Can I help you?"

"No."

The front door banged loudly, and someone was heard pounding up the stairs. Tilli smiled.

"That is William," she told Emily. "You will excuse me?"

She tripped downstairs to meet him and Emily heard her, replying to his call:

"Here, beloved! Here I am!"

The drawing-room door closed on them.

William was in very good spirits: he had for the moment forgotten his depression over Emily's silence.

"Oh, Tilli!" he cried, "what do you think? I've sold the house. And listen! I've heard of a villa near Syracuse, going quite cheap. Don't you think it would be rather fun to spend the winter in Syracuse?"

"No," said Tilli. "I wish to live at Monk's Hall."

William made a face.

"You don't, really? We'd never get a moment to ourselves.

The place is full of mouldiwarps . . . Cuffes and Hackbutts."

"That is not necessary. It is your house."

"I can't turn 'em out now," he said, shaking his head.

"All the same," she persisted. "I wish to live there."

"I can't think why. You've never seen it. It's ugly. When you have all the beautiful places in the world to choose from . . ."

"Why, then, did you buy it?"

"Trevor . . ."

"Ah! I forgot! You have done it to please Trevor!"

She was determined never to go on her travels again, and she had coveted Monk's Hall ever since the first time she heard of it. Even an account of its ugliness had caught at her fancy, for she liked permanence, and the most durable things have a way of being ugly. It was a symbol to her of the advantages which this marriage had brought to her. She had quenched her passion for Trevor and married William chiefly because William owned Monk's Hall and Trevor did not. She would call herself a fool for ever if, after all, Trevor was to be left in possession of the place. He must be sent packing, and the Hackbutts with him. If she had once established herself as mistress there, they would go away; and, if she was clever, William would believe that they had gone of their own accord.

"I have been to Syracuse," she said. "I do not like it."

"Then let's go to China. I don't mind where as long as I'm out of England and alone with you."

"I know . . . I know," she murmured. "For the honeymoon, let us go. But afterward, I think we shall live in England."

Since every month was an advantage to Trevor at Monk's Hall, she wanted the honeymoon to be short.

"I don't see," said William, "why our honeymoon should ever stop."

"Don't you?"

He had pulled her down on to the sofa beside him, and they very soon abandoned all show of argument. For he still felt a little dizzy, when he had got her quite close to him. It was as though he led two lives, and each life was like a dream to the other. The domination of Tilli and her world had grown upon him so rapidly that all his other life, his work, his friends, his freedom, seemed to have lost value and conviction. They could never recapture him for long; for his touch on these realities had always been a little uncertain. He saw them through a fog of dreams.

She was like a new country, a vast region of experience, entirely sensual, revealed to the young man for the first time. As a person, an individual, she was difficult to apprehend; he scarcely thought of her save in a confusion of images. He found her mysterious and wonderful and disturbing, because she had soft breasts and eyes that drowned him. These things were sublimely exciting because they were discoveries. But he could not fit them into any existence that he had already known, and he imagined that their life together might acquire more coherence if they went away to some new place like China.

To Tilli, these transports were incredible. She had always known that the English are an extraordinary race, but she could not have believed that, in any country, a young man of so much vigour and charm should have spent his youth to so little effect. His inexperience surprised her into something very like resentment, for she felt that her sex had been slighted. If she could have believed that other women had preceded her, she might have despised him less.

But she liked him well enough. As a husband, he was a great deal better than Van Tuyl. He was generous and considerate and easy to please. She lay in his arms and thought of that detestable little flat whence she had fled and how lonely and poor she had been, and how lucky she was to have made so good an escape. The image of Trevor was still like a bruise on her heart, but her new prosperity might do much to cure it. And then she wondered what was to be done with Emily upstairs. William was saying:

"And all your lovely new clothes? Have they come? Let's go up and look at them. Let's try them all on."

"They are nothing . . . a few chemises. My clothes I will buy in Paris, not here."

"But I want to see them. Let's go and . . ."

"In a moment. Kiss me."

The telephone rang, and William swore.

"No. Don't take any notice. Let it ring."

But it takes a good deal of fortitude to ignore a telephone. It goes on. At length, conquered, he took up the receiver.

"Yes?" he said crossly. "Yes? William speaking . . . who . . . oh, hullo, Philip! Are you married yet? Oh? . . . this morning . . . where are you speaking from? . . . No! . . . No, she's not here. Why should she . . . Isn't she with you?"

"She's left me," squeaked the telephone.

"What? What? When?"

"About an hour ago. I thought she might have come to you."

"Well, she's not here."

"She is here," said Tilli.

"What? Here, I say, hold on a minute!" He covered the receiver with his hand. "What's that, Tilli?"

"Your sister is here."

"Emily? Where?"

"Upstairs."

"In her room? Why didn't you tell me?"

He flung down the receiver.

"In my room," said Tilli.

But he was gone. She took the receiver and resumed the conversation with Philip.

"Are you there, Mr. Luttrell? It is Mrs. Van Tuyl speaking. Will you come here? Your wife is here, and she is not very well. Perhaps you would come and take her away."

"I'll come in a quarter of an hour," said the voice.

Tilli hung up the receiver and followed William upstairs.

He had rushed up, without an instant's reflection, to the room above, where his sister still lay upon the bed. When he saw her, stretched pale and still between the four gold angels, on the bed that he had given her, which was now his own marriage-bed, he was filled with a violent, unreasoning remorse. It was as though he had done some great injury to Emily. He fell on his knees beside her and cried:

"Oh, forgive me!"

"It wasn't your fault," said Emily drearily. "The letter missed. I never got it."

"Emmie! Are you ill? You aren't going to die, are you?"

"Oh, no! It was the hot day."

"But why . . . why . . . I didn't know you were here. I didn't know you were coming."

"Oh, William! I . . . I came back."

"To me? But aren't you married?"

"Yes."

"Then . . ."

"I . . . I've changed my mind. I don't want to be married."

Tilli came in and stood apart, looking at them.

"She doesn't want to be married," announced William.

"Ah!" said Tilli.

"But I didn't . . . I wouldn't have come here disturbing you, if I'd known," said Emily, sitting up.

"But my letter . . ."

"Your letter, beloved, never reached her," put in Tilli.

"My letter?" William looked astonished.

"Perhaps it was lost in the post."

"Let me remember." He groped among the confused, exciting events of the past week. "Where did I write it? At your flat, wasn't it? After we'd had a long arg—discussion whether I should or shouldn't. And then . . ."

"You took it to the post," suggested Tilli, "when you left me? I think it is still in your pocket."

"But no, Tilli! You sent your maid with it."

"Berthe," said Tilli, "was a careless girl. I have sent her back to Belgium. Perhaps she forgot."

William looked unhappy, and Emily, glancing from one to the other, saw very well how it was that the letter had never reached her. But it was of no consequence. The need to get away at once was the most important thing in the world. She got up, a little uncertainly, and went across to the dressing table. William, in extreme distress, demanded:

"What's to be done now?"

She did not answer. She began to smooth her hair, occupied by nothing more relevant than a vague disgust at the sight of Tilli's brush and comb. She was sick and tired. Tilli beckoned William outside on to the landing.

"The husband is coming," she whispered.

"But what on earth do you think has happened?"

She shrugged her shoulders.

"It seems that she has run away from him. Perhaps she is afraid. Perhaps he has been too . . . *emporté*."

"I shouldn't think it's that, Tilli. I know Philip. He's all right. Still, if she's thought better of it, she sha'n't go back to him. She shall stay in my house."

"But, my dear William! Consider . . ."

"I never approved of the marriage myself. She's much too good for him."

"What folly! What folly!"

He was beginning to understand why Emily had run

away. He thought of her again, as he had seen her, lying on Tilli's bed. He thought of her yielding herself to Philip as Tilli had yielded to him, and the idea enraged him.

"She sha'n't marry anybody," he exclaimed.

The doorbell rang, and he set off downstairs proclaiming that Emily should never leave his house.

At the sight of Philip, pallid and shaken, upon the doorstep, he was a little mollified, but he stood blocking the threshold as though to hold the house against an invader.

"Well?" he asked truculently.

"How is Emily?" demanded Philip.

"Very ill," said William at once.

"Let me come in."

"All right. But you can't see her unless she wants to see you."

"All right, I won't." Philip followed him up the hall. "You needn't look at me like that. She's quite in the wrong over this. I've done nothing to justify . . . Of course, I won't force myself on her, if she doesn't like it. I love her. I've married her."

"I love her, too," said William coldly.

"But I've married her. Twenty thousand brothers . . ." He broke off, with an attempt to laugh. "But how ill is she? Have you sent for a doctor?"

"No."

"Then I must insist that you do."

"I'll get a doctor," said William, "if I see fit."

"You'll get one, whether you see fit or not. I must be satisfied about her health. She is behaving very strangely. I don't really think she's fit to look after herself. She left me to-day without a moment's warning. I had gone into a shop for a moment, to buy her some flowers. When I came out she was gone. I thought at first that she had gone back to the hotel, but when I went back and couldn't find her . . ."

His anguish gripped him and he turned away. He did not want to weep in front of William.

"I must know," he said, "that she is under proper care. She can't be treated like anybody else."

"No," said William, "she can't. But I promise you that she will be all right. She will stay with us. I ought to tell you, Philip . . . I . . . I'm married myself."

"Good God!" Philip was stunned. "I never knew a word of this!"

"Nobody knew. We wrote to Emily, but Tilli . . . the letter seems to have missed. I expect I forgot to post it."

"Tilli?" repeated Philip, with an uncomfortable memory of all that he had endured on the first night of *The Seven Dawns*. "Tilli?"

"Mrs. Van Tuyl," explained William. "You've met her?"

"I've seen her on the stage," gasped Philip.

"Well, now you'll see her off, for I hear her coming downstairs. Tilli! This is Mr. Luttrell! Philip—my wife!"

Philip and Tilli shook hands, taking a swift measure of each other. In that first moment they became allies and enemies at the same time. They were leagued against the madness of these Crownes to whom they were married. Their eyes promised mutual support. Yet neither trusted the other. Philip thought:

"What a little baggage!"

And Tilli knew it.

"Emily," she told them, "is coming down. She knows that Mr. Luttrell is here, and she wishes to go away."

"But she mustn't! She isn't well enough! She must stay here with us," protested William.

"I think she is quite determined," said Tilli smoothly.

"Anyhow, I'll see her," suggested Philip. "I'll make sure of her real wishes. I can't think," he turned to Tilli, "that it can be very convenient for you to receive her at this moment, unless she very much desires it."

"Of course, we are enchanted to have her"—Tilli kept an eye on William—"but——"

"She can't go!" repeated William.

Emily, very pale but determined, made her appearance on the stairs. When she had got to the hall, she paused between Philip and William, and looked from one to the other.

"Do you want to go?" said William.

"Do you want to stay?" said Philip.

"I want to go."

"But, Emily . . ."

"No, really, William. Have you got a taxi, Philip?"

"I have one here waiting."

She turned to Tilli and held out her hand.

"I'm so sorry," she said, "that I have disturbed you like this. But, you see, I didn't know. Good-bye!"

She found that she was going to have to kiss Tilli. It was difficult. She put her face near Tilli's cheek for a second. And then she embraced William hurriedly. On Philip's arm she left the house for ever.

"Where would you like to go?" he asked, when he had put her into the taxi.

"I don't mind."

He took her back to the hotel.

CHAPTER V

WET WEATHER

I

CHARLOTTE lay flat upon her back. She could see nothing at all save the ceiling and a little bit of sky through the window. She could hear nothing save the contented quacking of ducks in the yard below and the occasional irritable scream of Peter Yates's saw. But this noise, though not agreeable, was at least reassuring. It meant that somebody, somewhere, was getting on with their work. The large quantity of chairs and tables made by Peter down in the outhouse was symbolic: it stood for the vast stream of literature proceeding from Trevor, William, Charlotte, Mandy Hackbutt, and Nigel Cuffe, inside the house.

Her mind was bleakly void. She lay on her back because she believed that her best thoughts came most easily in this position. There was about it something lowly that ought to placate the Muses. Since coming to Monk's Hall she had writhed a good deal upon her bedroom carpet, for she was anxious to produce immediately a much better book than

213

any she had ever written at Water Hythe. But her very anxiety seemed to make her mind sterile. Her old inspirations, once so nebulous and radiant, floated far beyond her reach, now that she was free to pursue them. Daily she lay on the floor, conscious that no mother would upbraid or interrupt her, rejoicing in the amplitude of her leisure, and getting nothing done. Sometimes she rose in despair and tried to record, doggedly, some of those remembered inspirations of the past; but her writing had a flat deadness about it for which she could discover neither cause nor cure.

Trevor's gramophone, grinding very triumphantly in the next room, brought her, with a start, out of her agonized trance. She sat up and cursed him. It was the ninth time since lunch that he had turned on the last movement of the Kreutzer Sonata. He had no business to make such a noise at all, in work hours. She was sure that she might have secured an idea in a few minutes, if it had not been for this interruption. Very crossly, she knocked on the wall, and Trevor came round to see what was the matter.

"Was that you knocking?" he asked severely.

She was still sitting on the floor, scowling at him.

"How do you imagine," she asked, "that anyone is ever going to do any work?"

"Were you working?"

He looked round for signs of it.

"I was thinking," she explained.

"So was I. And I had to drown the noise of Peter's infernal saw. Really, I must ask William if I can't be moved to the other side of the house. It's most distracting."

"Did you say you'd ask *William?*" demanded Charlotte with sarcasm.

"If I'm changed, one of the others'll have to be moved, too, and they mightn't like it. William had better be the one to be blamed for it."

"Or Tilli."

"Tilli," he said immediately, "has nothing whatever to do with it. She refused the keys when Lise offered them to her, and in doing that she virtually . . ."

"That's merely because she regards Lise as a paid house-keeper. She doesn't mean to be bothered with the details; but she does intend to run this house; to be mistress."

"She can mean what she likes. She's nothing of the sort, and she never will be. Oh, I know she's William's wife. But before he married her, he gave us this house, and if he comes here, or brings her here, it must be on the same footing as the rest of us."

Having made this statement, he was preparing a dignified withdrawal to his own room when Charlotte gave him a shock.

"Did you know she'd moved the Hackbutts?"

"Moved the Hackbutts? She didn't dare! When? Why wasn't I told? I won't have it."

"It only happened this morning. She went to Mrs. Hackbutt quite nicely and asked her if she wouldn't mind changing. She put them into those rooms in the old nursery passage. It's really better, for it's like a little flat all of their own. They quite like it."

"But what did she do it for?"

"She wants their rooms for herself. And she said to Lise that they must be put away at the back because they will hang horrid baby clothes out of the window to dry, and it gives such a squalid look to the front of the house."

"What confounded cheek!"

"But, Trevor, you said yourself that they were very uncontrolled over their laundry. And, after all, it is her house. I mean, legally, there's no . . ."

"But it isn't, blast her! Oh, blast the woman!" Trevor fairly gobbled with rage. "I knew, directly William brought that woman here, that we were in for trouble."

"There hasn't been trouble. It's all been arranged perfectly peacefully, and everyone is quite satisfied."

"No. But she means . . ."

The Kreutzer Sonata, next door, paused suddenly and Trevor hurried out. Charlotte followed him, and while he reversed the record and put on another needle, she told him that Tilli had also refused to sleep in the bed made for her by Peter Yates because it was ugly and uncomfortable.

"Like her impudence. She can sleep on the floor, then."

"She's sent to London for a bed."

"Where from? Shoolbred's? Come *in*, can't you?"

The person who had knocked at the door would not come in, but scuffled about in the passage until Trevor went himself to see. He found Sally there, timidly plaintive.

"It's Nigel," she explained. "Of course, if it was me, I wouldn't say a word. But he says he'll really have to move his room or something. You see he's always been used to absolute quiet, and he doesn't seem to care for gramophones, anyhow . . ."

"Does he object to mine? Is that what you want to say?" asked Trevor uncompromisingly.

"Yes, that's it." Sally grew a little bolder. "You see, he needs absolute quiet. His writing is such a fearful strain."

"Did he send you?"

"He wants it stopped. He says he'll have to speak to William."

"Why can't he come himself instead of sending messages?"

"He's never had to put up with so much noise before. His work's so important, you see. It's such a strain . . ."

"All writing is a strain. I know that perfectly well. Nigel isn't the only person here who's doing important work."

"Pardon?" said Sally offensively. And then she added: "He simply must get that article off to-day to the *New Critic*."

Nigel was the only member of the community who could write with a certainty of publication, and Sally lost no opportunity of letting the rest of them know it. Trevor felt that his temper was getting very short.

"I'll stop when this record's done," he said.

And he shut the door in her face. Charlotte, with a cigarette in her mouth, was listening to the music and lolling in Trevor's armchair. This, being one of the very few chairs in the house not made by Peter Yates, was comfortable. She stared up into her brother's face with unconcealed amusement, and he turned his back on her.

"I wish you'd stay in your own room," he said.

"Not when yours is so much nicer."

He pounded over to the window and looked down at the yard where hens were pecking about in the frosty sunshine. The Hackbutt move must have already taken place, for a row of unseemly rags hung out of one of the upper windows in the left wing of the house. Peter Yates, in his workshop, was whistling the Kreutzer Sonata, and Bobbie, who crossed the yard with a bucket of pig-wash, whistled it, too. Trevor used a loud-toned needle.

"In fact," Charlotte was saying, "it's the nicest room in the whole house."

"I don't see why you say that," he contended, without turning round. "The only view is of middens and pig-sties."

"No, but it's nice inside. You've bagged the cream of all the nice things that were turned out of the rest of the house. Why do you make us all have Peter's furniture and not have any yourself?"

"I don't like his furniture."

"Nor do we. I loathe my wardrobe. The drawers all stick. I don't think the painted panels make up for that."

"We must patronize home industries. I didn't bring the fellow here."

His back and shoulders became intent, and she wondered what he had seen. But she was too lazy to go and look.

"Who's down there?" she asked.

"Nobody. Only a hen."

For a moment he had seen his enemy, stepping delicately through the mire of the yard in those absurd little high-heeled shoes that were so unsuitable for the country. She wore no hat, but since the wind was cold, she had put on a wide, modish cloak of French military blue. It made a vivid patch among the tertiary colours of the farmyard. For a short interval, it was lost to sight behind some outhouses, and then it emerged again. She was talking to Bobbie beside the pig-sties. Probably she was tricking him into doing something for her. Trevor was sure of it when he saw that she was taking notice of the pigs. Bobbie was a simpleton not to see through that sort of thing. But then, Bobbie did not know the type as Trevor did.

He craned yet farther out, in some hopes that the bright, keen wind might carry their words to him. He saw her throw a quick glance up at the house and at his own head sticking out of the window. She said something to Bobbie, who looked up, too, and they both laughed. Trevor drew in his head with so much haste that he hit it on the sash.

"I can't think . . . I cannot think why William brought that woman here!" he stormed. "It's upsetting everything."

"Where could he bring her? They have no house now."

"He could have bought another for her. This isn't in the least her style. I never thought for a moment, when they got married, that they would want to live here. I expected them to stay abroad for at least a year."

"There's plenty of room here."

"Not for her sort. We're all workers. Idle, disturbing women will be the ruin of us."

"Sally isn't a worker," Charlotte pointed out.

"No, but she will be. When we get the hand-loom and the printing-press, Sally will be worked to death. She'll weave all our cloth and print all our books, poor girl."

"I'm sorry for your books, then, for she's practically illiterate, and idle into the bargain. But you can make Tilli print and weave, can't you?"

"I will. I'll teach her to hang around the place, wasting our time. She makes Bobbie ride with her when he ought to be feeding the pigs. She keeps Peter on the run, in and out of Oxford, doing her commissions. She sits up with Nigel half the night. It was positively thirteen minutes to two when they came upstairs on Tuesday night. I looked."

"Trevor! I believe you're . . ."

"I'm what?"

She was going to say jealous, but she thought better of it.

"You sound bilious. It's the east wind. I can't understand your prejudice against her. On the whole, she's been very civil to us all."

"She's not been here three weeks. You wait."

"Once you used to like her. I was always hearing how intelligent and alluring she was."

"I've got to know her better since."

"How well did you get to know her?"

"Well enough to see through her."

"Trevor!"

"Um?"

"What happened?"

"What do you mean?"

"What's behind it all?"

"Nothing's behind it, I tell you."

"Did you never have . . . any sort of quarrel? Before she married William?"

"Why, yes, I suppose we did have a sort of quarrel. It's my belief, you know, Car, that she only married him to get this house."

"But she'd never seen it!"

"No, but, like a fool, I told her of it. She knew how set I was on the whole idea. And to pay me out . . ."

"To pay you out? What for?"

He made no answer, but drifted back again toward the window and glanced out casually. The blue cloak was nowhere to be seen. But Bobbie was still there, and talking to Bobbie was the very last person Trevor had ever expected to see at Monk's Hall. The spectacle took his breath away.

"Gracious heaven!" he exclaimed at last. "Car! Come here and look! Look what's in the yard!"

"What?"

"It's Mother. And, what's more, she looks as if she meant to come in."

Charlotte leaped up and came to look, too.

"Now what on earth can she have come for?" pondered Trevor. "I thought she would never come near the place while all this Nigel-and-Sally is about."

"Philip told me that, when somebody asked her about Monk's Hall in his hearing the other day, she said it was empty and William away. Just as if we none of us existed."

"What scheme can she have got in her head now, do you think? It must be something quite new."

"I'll go down and find out, I think," declared Charlotte.

"Do. And send up word to me if it's peace or war. Then I know what sort of face to put on when I come down."

Charlotte hurried forth, and at the drawing-room door she met Lise, who explained the whole situation in a hurried whisper:

"My dear! She's come *to call on Tilli*."

"On Tilli?"

Lise nodded.

"State call. Nephew's bride. All that."

Charlotte saw it all, and she could not help admiring the strategic adroitness of it. For three months her mother had ignored their household entirely, because, in her eyes, the place was empty and the proprietors away. Now, on their return, she was prepared to call on them, but she was not thereby giving any countenance to such other odd inmates as the house might contain. On the contrary, she was carrying her non-recognition to a yet completer stage.

"I do hope," thought Charlotte, "that she will take a good quick dislike to Tilli."

She opened the drawing-room door and peeped in.

It had been fitted up by Trevor as a sort of common-room. All the old furniture, the harp, the china cabinets, and the Récamier sofa had been cleared out, and chairs and tables had been imported from Peter's workshop, all painted in bright blue and yellow. The walls were washed a rich ochre to match, and the floor was strawberry-pink.

Catherine and Tilli were sitting on two hard little blue-and-yellow chairs upon either side of the fireplace. They were exchanging courtesies, with brief, thoughtful pauses, and looking one another over. At intervals, Catherine would throw a distracted glance at the golden walls and the pink floor, and then she would look again at Tilli, whose neat dark elegance went so oddly with this startling room. It was evident that something had surprised her very much, so that, in her guile-less honesty, she was forced to stare a little.

Tilli, on the other hand, was much more discreet in her glances. Indeed, she scarcely removed her eyes from the large feet, plastered with mud, that Catherine had planted well in front of her. Never, save among the lowest order of peasants, had Tilli seen such feet on any woman before. She scrutinized them, while Catherine, in ungracious, jerky sentences, explained that she had not called before because she had been uncertain of the date of their return.

"I understood from my niece, Mrs. Luttrell, that you were going to be abroad for some months longer," she said. "In fact, I thought she told me that you were never going to live at Monk's Hall. It was quite a surprise when we heard that you had come back."

Tilli sighed out that William was so lazy. She was sure that she had told him to write and tell Mrs. Luttrell that they were coming back to England.

"But if he is to write a letter, Mrs. Frobisher, I must stand beside him all the while, or it is never done."

Very slowly she removed her eyes from the boots. Her regard slid up to Catherine's lap. She took notice of the gnarled, rheumatic hands, the beautiful rings, and the ancient leather card-case that her visitor was clutching tightly as though it were some sort of weapon. She looked at the thick gauntlet gloves, and the eyeglasses, tangled in the gray woollen scarf. And at last she looked Trevor's mother in the face. It was so that she thought of this woman: Trevor's mother, and not William's aunt.

She found much to deride and something to respect. The absurd hat with its wreath of black feathers, blown awry on the gray hair, struck her as ridiculous. But how formidable were those peering, short-sighted eyes! Here they were all afraid of her. Tilli had found that out very soon. Because this old woman was secure. Her triumphant dowdiness indicated an almost arrogant security. No woman of Tilli's world would have dared to look like this. But Catherine had never been obliged to please anyone in her life, and to be sitting with her on terms of civil equality in a drawing room was a mark of status. It came of being married to William, and it was new enough to be amusing to Tilli.

She bowed her neat little head and was cooing away about

her pleasure in making this acquaintance when Charlotte joined them, and the real battle began.

"Well, Charlotte!" Catherine half raised herself in her chair to kiss her tall daughter. "How long it seems since we've seen each other. I've just been explaining to Mrs. Crowne how it was that I did not call sooner."

At last she had succeeded in extricating her eyeglasses from her scarf, and she planted them firmly upon her nose. After a good look at the two young women before her she decided that Tilli was too much powdered but a great deal more presentable than Charlotte, who had a spot of ink on her nose.

"And how," she said, turning to the bride, "do you like Monk's Hall?"

"You would say the house?" faltered Tilli cautiously. "For the building, I think it is ravishing. You, who have lived here so much, I think you must agree with me."

"Oh, yes, it's a nice house," conceded Catherine, in a grudging tone that belied the approval in her heart. "Some people criticize it, of course. They say it has a northern aspect. But that's a matter of taste."

"Besides," Tilli pointed out, "the rooms at the back, they look to the south."

"That's what I always say," Catherine threw a quick, triumphant look at Charlotte. "But then, perhaps, I'm biassed."

"The house, the garden, they are most perfect," Tilli repeated. "But the furniture I do not like, Mrs. Frobisher. I must admit that I cannot like it. Perhaps my taste is not very good."

"You've never said you didn't like it before," put in Charlotte sharply.

"I was never asked."

"Ah, well . . . the furniture!" Catherine dismissed the blue-

and-yellow room with a last, contemptuous glance. "Of course all that's been changed since my poor mother's day. All her beautiful old things . . ."

"William has told me of them," cried Tilli eagerly. "He has described this room as it used to be. I much regret . . ."

She broke off and sighed. Catherine looked at her with sympathetic interest and, for the first time during the interview, smiled a little.

"Perhaps," she suggested, "you may be able to collect some of the old things again. They must be somewhere about."

"They're in the loft over the garage," Charlotte told them. "Trevor had them put there."

"With these walls, with this floor!" Tilli shrugged her shoulders. "*À quoi bon?* Beautiful things need a beautiful room, I think. I can do nothing with a room that looks like this."

"It was a pity," agreed Catherine, "that William allowed so much to be done in the autumn while he was away."

"He told Trevor to decorate the place as he liked," insisted Charlotte.

"Before he married, yes!" said Tilli. "He is not interested in wall papers, William. But I . . . I have very positive ideas."

"Still, you know," Catherine consoled her, "you can alter things gradually, and redecorate more to your taste."

"That is my intention."

For a moment the two women looked full at one another. In Catherine's gray eyes and in Tilli's black ones the same mute reassurance was reflected. And in that instant, despite the yawning gulf of age, race, class, religion, and taste, they knew themselves to be united in at least one purpose. On either side, there was an equal determination to clear all this rubbish, human and otherwise, out of Monk's Hall. But nothing further was said at the moment, and Tilli, after a short pause, turned to other topics. She spoke of Frobisher and of her anxiety to visit Water Hythe. This she was able to do because she had, on her honeymoon, read about one seventh of every book written by Frobisher, in order that William's relations might not be in a position to taunt her with ignorance. She realized now that this undertaking had been well worth while, since praise of Frobisher was the surest way to captivate his simple-minded widow. She spoke warmly, and she managed to convey that she spoke for Poland, France, and Holland. In fact, she dispensed her adulation in so subtle a manner that even Charlotte was impressed and forced to the conclusion that Tilli must be a great deal cleverer and better read than they had all of them supposed.

As for Catherine, she was enraptured. She had come upon this visit in no mood to expect a favourable reception. She knew but little of Tilli beforehand, and that little was unpromising. The woman had once formed part of Trevor's disreputable London circle and was probably no better than she should be. It was in no hopes of forming an alliance that Catherine had come, but simply to annoy Trevor. And she was taken altogether by surprise.

Tilli was not what she had expected. She had no sort of resemblance to Sally or the Hackbutt tribe. She was entirely free from their loud assertiveness. Of course, she was a foreigner, but her voice was soft, her manners respectful, and her clothes quite sensible. Catherine hitched her chair up a little closer to the stranger and called her *my dear*, whereat Charlotte, appalled, slipped off to warn Trevor of the unnatural coalition that was being formed.

"My dear," said Catherine, "you ought, of course, to have come to Water Hythe long ago. William should have brought you over."

Tilli could not help wondering what the old lady would

have said if Trevor and not William had brought her into the family.

"She is not beautiful, Trevor's mother," she thought to herself. "Nor is she very clever, *par exemple! Dieu! Que Monsieur son père a dû être intelligent!*"

"I think," she said aloud, "that Mr. Frobisher must have been a very great mind."

"Have you read his life?" asked Catherine. "I will lend it to you."

They were interrupted by Mrs. Hackbutt, who burst in with a tea tray. It was the custom of the whole community to take tea in the common-room at half-past four. Provisions, cups, and urns were put upon the centre table and everybody helped himself. Catherine, when she had sufficiently snubbed the warm greeting of Bertha Hackbutt, was invited by Tilli to stay and partake of this meal. She accepted, feeling that it would strengthen her position, but she hoped very much that she would not thereby be forced to break bread in the company of Sally. And she saw with approval that Tilli had taken the tea-pot away from Bertha with a decided gesture of ownership. Upon this occasion, at least, the common-room was to be Tilli's drawing room.

Bertha, chilled by Catherine's manner, was afraid of intruding. She took herself and her cup and her plate away to the farthest corner of the room in order to leave Tilli alone with the visitor. But this they would by no means allow. She was recalled.

"Do not sit so far away, Mrs. Hackbutt!" commanded Tilli with a smile. "Will you not sit by me?"

Meekly, Bertha came back and sat between them. Without knowing why, she felt unhappy. She wished she had known that old Mrs. Frobisher was coming. She would have tidied herself a little. She would have taken off her old red smock. Aware that Catherine was peering in polite surprise at her head, she remembered miserably that it was still tied up from the dust in a yellow handkerchief.

"I must look a proper guy," she thought.

And she felt worse when Tilli mentioned the change of rooms as if to explain and excuse her appearance.

"My poor guests! I give them no peace. To-day I have changed all the rooms. I hope, Mrs. Hackbutt, that the servants have moved everything without trouble for you."

"Oh, yes, rather. Thanks very much. It's all quite straight now, and in some ways it's nicer than the rooms we had before. All those cupboards are so handy. We've just got the rhyme sheets to nail up. You must come in and have coffee with us one night soon, Mrs. Crowne."

"Thank you. I shall be delighted," murmured Tilli faintly. "Mr. Hackbutt has spoken to me about a table . . . that you wish for another table . . ."

"Ah, yes! For Marmaduke. He really needs a table to himself. And if you had a little one to spare . . ."

"Marmaduke?" asked Tilli, puzzled.

"The typewriter, you know. We call him Marmaduke."

Catherine gaped at this, and Tilli again had to explain.

"It is so amusing," she commented, "to call the furniture by *petits noms*. I think it is an English custom. I had not heard of it before."

"Nor had I," said Catherine. "I don't think it's typically English at all."

Bertha nervously attempted to make herself clear.

"I don't suppose anyone does it but us. It's just a joke, you know. We used to call the caravan Archibald."

"Why?" asked Catherine.

Bertha got more and more flustered.

"Just . . . just for fun. Childish of us, but . . ."

"Where there are so many children," Tilli helped her, "one speaks their language . . . yes . . ."

Bertha felt that she would never make them understand. And for the first time in her life it occurred to her to wonder if it was really so very amusing to call a typewriter Marmaduke. Until then it had seemed deliciously whimsical. Perhaps it was childish. Perhaps the valiant, undiscriminating sense of fun, which had helped them through so many hardships, might be, after all, a mark of inferiority. She drank a large gulp of tea and wished herself away.

"So many children! Ah, yes," pursued Catherine. "How are they all, Mrs. Hackbutt? Let me see . . . I don't remember quite how many . . ."

"Seven," mumbled Bertha.

"Oh, yes. Seven. And where are they all now?"

"Here," said Tilli.

"Here?" cried Catherine, as though this were news to her. "Why, you must have a houseful!"

Poor Bertha felt obliged to say that it was very good of William to have them all. For the first time, it seemed to her as though she and Mandy were not quite ordinary guests; as though they were more like pensioners. It was not a nice feeling, and she was glad enough when Trevor came in with Peter Yates and Nigel Cuffe, doing his best to look like a host.

"My dear Mother!" he cried, as he kissed her. "They never told me you were here. I hope they've given you some tea?"

Catherine, as she returned his salute, replied that she was just going away, as a matter of fact, and that she had been fortunate to find Mrs. Crowne at home.

"But now that you are here," pursued Trevor, "I hope you will let us show you the house."

"Oh, yes, you must," urged the guileless Peter. "You'd be surprised at what we've done to the old place."

"I daresay I should," said Catherine drily.

And Nigel Cuffe, who understood the state of things rather

better, suggested that their improvements might not be entirely to her liking.

"They express *us*," he said, "but that isn't a recommendation to everybody."

"It is true what you say," observed Tilli with a smile, as she gave them all their tea. "It is a good expression of Trevor and his friends. But, of course," she turned to Catherine, "it is not . . . expensive . . . how they have done it."

"And expense in these days is a thing that one is bound to consider," agreed Catherine quickly, "however much one may dislike cheap things."

"It isn't so very cheap," protested Trevor. "Hullo, Sally! Come in and have some tea. We've nearly finished."

Sally had got well into the room before she saw who was there. Her terror at the first moment was so extreme that she was quite paralysed. She just stood and gaped at Catherine. And then she scuttled out of the room as fast as ever she could. But Trevor made after her and could be heard haranguing her in the hall.

"Come back, Sally! Don't you want your tea?"

"Oh, no, thank you! Not really! Thanks!"

"You silly girl! You're afraid of my mother!"

"I'd much rather not."

"She can't eat you. Come back."

"She looks at me in such an insulting way."

"That's the way she looks at everybody."

"I don't want to have to be rude to her; but one of these days I shall have to give her a bit of my mind."

"Oh, do! It'll be delicious. Come and do it now."

But she would not, and Trevor came back to the drawing room by himself to find his mother preparing to depart. Tilli accompanied her to the front door, and Trevor, determined to maintain the pose of proprietor, went with them. They all walked round the house and through the wood to the point where the path turned downhill. Trevor had inwardly sworn to go every step as far as Tilli went. So that when, at length, they parted from Catherine, the rivals had to walk almost a quarter of a mile together, back to the house. Since their parting in Tilli's flat, they had never been alone together for so long a space of time. She told him how charming she found his mother.

"Did you not expect to find her charming, then?"

"But, no. From your descriptions I had imagined someone very different. I was so nervous at this meeting, when I thought how we might be close neighbours for all our lives, perhaps. It is so necessary that we should understand one another. In the country, where one is so much alone, to have a friend near is everything."

"You'll never be so very much alone here," he reminded her.

They came out of the wood and stood on the lawn in front of the house. Tilli looked at it and thought how dreadfully like a jail it was. The bare trees round it and the winter sky above it did nothing to temper its structural bleakness.

"I should like," she said thoughtfully, "to make a winter garden."

"A what?"

"A large conservatory . . . upon the other side . . . out from the dining room."

"Do you mean one of those places with wicker chairs and palms? My dear Tilli!"

"I shall speak to William."

"You'd better! Oh, Tilli! You'll be the death of me."

He laughed so much that she was disconcerted. For though she was in a position to interfere with his comfort, she was after all a stranger, a foreigner, in the midst of a set of people who all disliked her and who understood each other better than she understood them. Catherine really belonged to them, and so did William. In spite of her recent triumphs she felt forlorn and lonely.

2

"And will you kindly tell me," finished Bobbie, after a harangue that had lasted nearly seven minutes, "how long this state of things is going on?"

"I'm not Old Moore," mumbled Lise sleepily. "Drink up your tea, dear, before it gets cold."

She heaved herself up in bed and handed him a cup from the tray on the little table beside her. It was half-past seven in the morning, and the only hour at which Bobbie was ever known to talk. It was his habit to wake then and to begin a sort of lament on life and its misfortunes, which usually lasted until he had drunk his early cup of tea. Then he would sleep again for ten minutes before getting up and going out to the pigs. But this second awakening was always taciturn: he had done his talking for the day.

On this morning he was complaining neither of the climate nor of his pass-book, but of the consummate folly of all the other people in the house.

"Confound it!" he was saying when Lise woke up. "I'd much rather have sold the place and gone right away. A lunatic asylum would be peaceful compared to this."

"It won't last."

"You've said that all the winter. I see no signs of its coming to an end."

"Don't you? I do. Tilli thinks there's too much of a crowd here."

"And the end of it'll be that she'll turn us all out just when the Duchess is going to farrow. You see."

"If we are turned out, it will certainly be just then, for the Duchess is always going to farrow. I never knew such a sow. If her offspring didn't always die, she'd have made our fortunes. But we sha'n't be turned out. William won't let her. He's a man of his word, whatever else he is."

"He's a fool."

"Poor William."

"What's he want to marry a foreigner for?"

Lise, stirring her tea cheerfully, agreed that foreign blood can never be trusted.

"It'll be Nigel that'll have to go," she added.

"Nigel? That's nothing. You may take it from me there's nothing in that."

"What does she make those eyes at him for, then?"

"Pure devilry. She wants to make trouble between him and Sally so that they'll go. And she wants to make Trevor jealous."

"Trevor? You mean William."

"No, I don't mean William. I've eyes in my head."

"My dear Bobbie, you're not properly awake. Tilli and Trevor loathe each other. It's their continual bickering that's getting on my nerves more than anything else."

"Ever seen him watching her and Nigel?"

She pondered. Bobbie was nearly always right about people.

"Of course," she mused, "when first William brought her here, I remember saying to Charlotte that she was much more the sort of person I'd have expected Trevor to marry."

"You were wrong. People like Trevor don't get caught like that. They're too sensible. She's exactly the sort of person I always expected William to marry."

"I never expected him to marry at all."

"I don't suppose he did. He just woke up and found that it had happened. Some sort of a knock he'd had; I don't know what it can have been. Some other woman, I suppose. And he took to this Tilli as a man takes to whisky. Now he's got into the habit of her. And he'll never catch her out. She's too clever. What time is it?"

"A quarter to eight."

"Wake me again at eight. It's raining, I suppose?"

"Cats and dogs," said Lise, leaning forward to look out of the window.

"Ah-ugh!" He yawned. "Infernal weather. Never seen such a spring. Rained every day for . . ."

He was asleep again, and Lise knew that when he woke up he would profess the blankest ignorance of the motives, characters, likes, and dislikes of everyone in the house. He would only tell the truth before eight in the morning.

She lay down beside him, wide awake, and wondering if all men talked more expansively in bed than at other times. Both her husbands had done so. Grainger, once between sheets, was more startlingly candid than Bobbie because, at other times, he was more untruthful. And she remembered that Philip, when she mentioned this point to him in the course of some discussion, had laughed and said: *In lecto veritas*. Now that Philip was himself married, he might not think it so funny. Probably he gave himself away to Emily every morning, in a torrent of sleepy prattle. Only that Philip and Emily did not, by common report, sleep together. And while Bobbie snored, Lise turned over in her mind the much-discussed topic of the Luttrell marriage, and the rumour, whispered through the family, that it was positively no marriage at all.

The soft, continuous swish of the rain mingled with her reflections, and everybody at Monk's Hall, waking to the sound of it, groaned at the prospect of yet another wet day. In poor Tilli's ears it sounded like a dirge, like the actual voice of this horrible, cold, monotonous country and this sombre house which was no better than a prison. She thought that she would always remember Monk's Hall whenever she saw rain anywhere in the world.

She could not have believed it possible that she should be so acutely bored. Nor could she remember now how it was that she had ever coveted such an establishment. Not even a long experience of England had helped her to imagine so dismal a picture as this. The house of her dreams was a very different affair,—a building with many pinnacles, gables, verandas, porticos, towers, and coping ornaments, green shutters, stone vases of geraniums on a terrace, some ornamental water and an avenue of poplars. When first she saw this bleak gray box with its wet woods and encroaching farm buildings, she had told herself that only her vow to get it away from Trevor could keep her for half a day in such a place. And now she was beginning to wonder if revenge would be as sweet as she had hoped, or worth the trouble.

As she lay on her back, listening to the rain, she reviewed these things in a series of little pictures that passed before her mind. She believed that she was thinking.

"And what wonder if I am becoming thoughtful?" she said to herself. "In this terrible place one is obliged to think. There is nothing else to do."

At last, with a groan of impatience, she sat up in bed and looked at William. He had said that her feather mattress stifled him, and he slept beside her on a camp-bed. When she called to him, he rolled over and muttered something about trench mortars. The thought of guns and battle seemed to haunt his sleep, and he often spoke of them in anxious, broken sentences.

"William!" cried Tilli peevishly. "Wake up, then! What is the time?"

"What . . . a . . .?"

He reared his fair, tousled head from the low pillow and looked at a watch on a chair beside him.

"Half-past eight."

"But really? As early as that? How terrible! In this place it seems that I cannot even sleep. I shall not sleep now again, and it is an hour till my breakfast will come."

"Have it up earlier."

"That is impossible. I do not give orders to the servants in this house."

"Don't talk nonsense. They're your servants."

"Yes, they are my servants. I pay them. But I am to understand that Mrs. Trevor gives all the orders."

"Still, it's silly to say you can't have your breakfast earlier. You know as well as I do that it isn't true."

"Not true? Not true? Am I then a liar?"

"Oh, Lord!"

William roused up completely, realizing that another day had indeed begun.

Their room was very fine now that Tilli had succeeded in banishing all the handiwork of Peter Yates. She had imported an enormous bed of white and gold and her dressing table had a petticoat of purple satin with a triple glass wreathed in purple silk roses. There was a great abundance of cushions, little tables, and brocaded stools; by the fireplace stood a broad divan, covered with skins, on which were sprawling, with a sort of limp depravity, two impossibly magnificent dolls. One of them was not unlike Tilli herself, with her changeless pallor, and her oblique, inscrutable regard. She crouched in the middle of her bed, exotic and hostile, glaring at William, and the doll on the sofa glared at him, too.

He was out of place in such a room. His uncompromising camp-bed and his hearty slumbers beneath the army blankets were most unsuitable. He felt it himself. Every morning he woke up with a shock of surprise, remembering that he was a married man, and that this gorgeous room, and the two dolls and Tilli and her lavender sleeping-suit and her gold

cap, were all his undoubted property. But as the day wore
on he seemed to get used to the idea.

"It would be just as odd," he reflected, "whoever one was
married to. Marriage is really an extraordinary thing. Well,
now! But it *is* extraordinary."

His bed gave a rickety lurch and a squeak as he climbed
out of it. He came across the room and leant over her. She
used a scent called *Nuits d'Amour*, and it struck him as he
kissed her that it would be quite a shock if one day, for a
change, she were to use lavender water instead. His morning
embrace would have a little variation; it would be like finding jam in the marmalade dish.

"It is most extraordinary," he said aloud.

"What is extraordinary?" asked Tilli petulantly.

"Being married."

"You find that extraordinary?"

"Yes, I do. What do we really know about each other? I
know you smell of *Nuits d'Amour*. I remember I was ravished
when first I found that out."

"It is very expensive," said Tilli thoughtfully.

"The things you find out first are the things you take for
granted soonest," decided William. "But I suppose it's the
same with everybody."

She moved herself away from him, rather sullenly. The
prospect of another wet day was more than she could bear.
Excitement of some sort she must have.

"You do not love me," she muttered.

"Now, Tilli!"

"You do not understand me. You do not sympathize with
me. You despise me. You have only married me for one thing,
and now that you have it, you are tired of me. As far as
possible, you try to forget that I exist. You neglect me.
You leave me alone all day . . ."

William denied all this with the eagerness born of inward

doubt. For he could not help suspecting that these re-proaches might contain an element of truth, and that, driven by the appetite of a moment, he had really undertaken a charge which he was now neglecting. He asked how much oftener he was going to have to deny these accusations.

"You love your friends, your cousins, your sister so much better than you love me."

"You can't say that I neglect you for Emmie. I've only been over to Ratchet once since we've been here. I've only seen her three times altogether."

"What is that, when all the time you think of her?"

"I never think of her," stated William heatedly.

"And if you do not go more often to see her, it is because you are jealous of that poor husband."

"That's a new idea. When did you think of it?"

"I did not think of it. Trevor is making everybody laugh with that story. It is his idea, not mine. But I think that it is true."

"Trevor?"

"But, yes. Trevor. I can assure you that he is most amus-ing. When we are dull, we ask him for a Crowne story."

"I'll kick his behind for him, one of these days," mused William.

"One of these days!" cried Tilli vindictively. "I think you will do more than kick him one of these days. But not to-day. That is understood. To-day he will live in this house, and he will spend your money, and he will laugh at you."

"Haven't we had all this out before? Must I tell you again that I can't turn him out? I promised him this house before I married you. If you want another, I'll buy it for you."

"What folly! How could you give such a promise? You are mad. Why should you promise houses to that man? He is not your friend. Since I have known him, he has never spoken one good word of you, behind your back. He only thinks of getting money from you, and he despises you because it is so easy."

"You don't understand. I've known Trevor longer than you have. I know he never speaks to me without a stream of Billingsgate. I know he talks of me as if I were an escaped lunatic. But that's how one does generally talk of a person one's been brought up with. And it's very hard on him, really, about this house. He ought to have had it."

"He has got it. He can have anything that is yours, it seems. Wait, then, and see what else he will take."

She nodded at him with a dark look. For a moment he hesitated, debating inwardly the danger of completely understanding her words. Then, with a sigh, he took himself off into the bathroom. Once there, and free of the airless, scented confinement of their bedroom, he felt his spirits rise. He was never depressed for very long at a time. Soon she could hear him splashing about and singing very loudly:

> *"Siegmund heiss' ich!*
> *Und Siegmund bin ich!*
> *Bezeug' es dies Schwert,*
> *Das zaglos ich halte!"*

"Mother of God," muttered Tilli. "What a barbarous noise!"

For if she was getting tired of the house, she was getting a great deal more tired of William. The half-scornful tenderness which she had, for a short time, been able to feel, was doomed to evaporate very quickly. She had run through all his capacities for emotional entertainment long ago, and now he bored her. He would not even quarrel with her. Van Tuyl, for all his brutalities, had never irritated her like this, since she always understood him. William, though he would do anything she liked save turn his cousin out of Monk's Hall, was far less easy to manage. She had less real power over him. Nor was it any consolation to know that she could exasperate him, since a quarrel is only useful as a prelude to strategic reconciliation, and he always recovered his good temper at the wrong moment. He would wander off by himself into the woods, or go fishing with the little Hackbutts, and when he came back he would be as serene as ever.

She became aware that the sensuality which had betrayed him to her was, after all, an intermittent and impermanent force in his character. He could frequently escape from her, and her dominion, into a world to which she had no clue. It was quite true that he did not love her. And yet, if it had not been for Trevor, she might have been happy enough with him.

After a little while, she got out of bed and went across to the window to look at the sheets of rain that blew across the lawn. Even the early daffodils, sprinkling the grass in the park, looked draggled and broken, as if all this downpour were really too much for them. Not a cat was stirring, and the mournful silence was only broken by William yelling, "*Nothung! Nothung!*" in the bathroom.

Listlessly, she pattered back and got beneath her warm quilt. Since it was impossible to sleep any more, she might as well read and improve her mind a little. She drew a book from under the pillow and composed herself to study. It was not a Frobisher book, but it was very interesting, and full of information, since it dealt with the worship of Isis under the later Roman Empire. Though the text was erudite, the illustrations were highly pornographic, and Lise had asked Tilli not to leave it about in the common-room where the little Hackbutts might get hold of it. Sally however had expressed a wish to borrow it with a hope of improving her French, and Trevor had vowed that he could not put it down.

Tilli spelt her way contentedly through the description of a Priapic Saturnalia, and presently she felt her cold little body growing deliciously warm again. Now that William had stopped singing, the house seemed deathly quiet. She heard him tramp out of the bathroom and down to his breakfast. Then there was a great stampede of little Hackbutts along the passage. She began to grow sleepy, and into her drowsiness there crept faintly the distant strains of Trevor's gramophone. She smiled to herself. Her dreams were wafting her to another, warmer, more genial country, and she forgot that she hated Trevor. Or perhaps, in those dark caverns of the soul that we explore between sleep and waking, she discovered that love and hatred are two names for the same thing. The rain fell, the wind blew, and the world swung on, as through long hours she lay dozing, sentient, mindless.

It was late in the morning when she roused herself once more. After a very hot bath and a leisurely toilet she was delighted to discover that it was almost lunch-time. Really the day was going past very well. She decided that she would lunch downstairs, and as she came into the upper gallery the big gong sounded in the hall below. Most of the household were lounging at the bottom of the stairs, waiting for the meal, and she paused for a moment, looking them over unseen before she came down. They struck her as an unkempt and shabby crew. Peter Yates had not taken off his dusty overalls. He believed so firmly in the dignity of manual toil that he liked to bear the marks of it and would never wash. He was sitting astride the banisters, pushing back his mop of red hair from a sweating brow, arguing loudly with Nigel, who never looked like anything but a draper's assistant. As for Mandy Hackbutt, with his ragged clothes and his ragged beard, he need not masquerade as a tramp, for he was a tramp. Trevor was the only presentable person among them all; he took some pains to dress well, even in the country, and he had kept that air of alert amusement that so captivated Tilli. With a fresh shock of rage and anguish, she stared down at his round, black head, thinking how very handsome he was.

"But what types!" she said to herself, as her eye wandered over Charlotte, Bertha, and Sally, in their home-knitted jumpers and their beads.

She came slowly down the stairs, producing among them that atmosphere of uneasy courage that a wasp creates at a tea-party. They paused for a few seconds, and then tried to go on talking as if nothing had happened. Lise, who had just come into the hall, asked her what she intended to do with herself that afternoon.

"I am going to Water Hythe," said Tilli, "to call on Mrs. Frobisher."

"You'll get very wet," said Trevor instantly.

"I shall take the car."

"I'm afraid you can't. It's got to go into Oxford, hasn't it, Lise?"

"It can do that while I am with your mother, or after."

"Fordyce has several commissions. He'll have to be in Oxford all the afternoon. Don't you remember? I announced it last night."

"It must go to Oxford another day."

"Not at all. You will have to put off your call to another day, or else walk."

"I will tell Fordyce. He must go another day."

Trevor was silent. He did not like to fight with Tilli before an audience, aware that all the others were listening curiously. He waited until after lunch, before he sought an opportunity to have it out with her. She was standing on the steps, just outside the front door, and he went and stood beside her, away from all the racket and babel that was going on in the hall.

For a few minutes no actual rain was falling, though heavy

black clouds were drifting so low over the house that they seemed almost to touch the chimneys. It was clear that another downpour would very soon begin. Tilli shivered and hugged her thin arms to her bosom.

"What a country!" she muttered.

"Look here, Tilli! You can't have the car to-day, you know. The Morris Oxford is the house car. It's not yours, and you mustn't treat it as if it were."

"Is it yours?"

"It belongs to the house. If you want to drive, you must give sufficient notice to me. Or you can buy a car of your own. There's plenty of room in the garage."

She said nothing to this, and after a short pause he began again:

"You're adopting a line that none of us can understand. You make it perfectly impossible for this experiment to be a success. Lise offered you the keys when first you came, and you wouldn't take them. Either you ought to run the place entirely or you should let it alone. You've no business to make all these difficulties. Why do you do it?"

"I shall do what I please in my husband's house."

"You only came here to make trouble. It's not just the car. You're doing all you can to wreck my plans. You can't deny it."

"I do not deny it."

"But why? That's what I want to know. What have I ever done to you?"

"It does not please me that you should have this house."

"William won't turn us out. You needn't hope to make him do that. I know you've tried."

"That we shall see. I am cold. I am going in."

"No, no. You mustn't go in just yet." He caught her by the arm and kept her on the doorstep. "You must give me a plain answer. Why are you doing this? You can't look me in the face and tell me that you really care a pin for the house. Confess that you're doing it to score off me! Now, why? What have I done? We used to be such friends."

"That was before I married William. It is impossible, I think, to be married to William and to be your friend. You have never behaved well to William."

"I see. When you learnt to love William, you began to hate me. What a humbug you are, Tilli!"

"Let me go in."

"You don't care a boot button for William. You never have. You only married him for his money. If I'd had it instead of him, you'd have married me, now, wouldn't you?"

"If it pleases you to think so . . ."

"You care, or you did care, a great deal more for me than you ever cared for him. Why should you suddenly take to hating me? Isn't it very silly? Can't we be friends as we used?"

But she had shaken him off. She drew herself up and spoke very sternly.

"You are mistaken. You will please control yourself, Trevor. I cannot allow you to speak to me in this way. If you continue, I must tell William."

"What? What?"

He gaped at her blankly.

"I must insist that you do not suggest such things to me."

She swept into the house with her nose in the air, leaving her companion in considerable disorder. The fresh raindrops spattered round him as he stood on the doorstep, trying to determine whether he had in fact made dishonourable advances to his cousin's wife. He thought not, but he could not be absolutely certain, and if there was any doubt in the matter, he supposed that he ought to take himself away from Monk's Hall.

Tilli, meanwhile, marched upstairs to her room. On her

way she passed her husband, who was standing by one of the windows in the upper gallery, reading. As usual, she was annoyed at his habit of standing up to read, instead of sitting down to it like a solid-minded person. She told him, as she passed, that she was going to Water Hythe, but he was so much engrossed that he did not reply. She stopped for a moment and peered over his shoulder. He was reading Sophocles. She stared at the outlandish characters, without the slightest desire to know what they meant. A slip of paper had fallen out of the book and lay on the floor at her feet. She picked it up and turned it over, but she could make nothing of what was written on it. William's writing covered it all over, so scored and scratched that she could only decipher one line: *O Delos, gentle Isle, to me be kind. . . .* From the paper she looked to William and from William to his incomprehensible book. She shrugged her shoulders and passed on.

She changed her dress before she went to Water Hythe, realizing that a flame-coloured jumper suit was not likely to inspire Catherine with confidence. Only by looking as discreet as possible could she hope to preserve the impression she had made upon Trevor's mother. She chose a little travelling dress of dark blue cloth, and then decided that none of her hats was shabby enough.

"The next time that I am in Oxford," she thought, "I will buy a hat for Water Hythe. Perhaps I shall ask Charlotte to choose it for me."

She managed at last to contrive a makeshift by removing the paste ornament from a little velvet turban. And when she was quite ready, she took a long look at herself in the glass over her purple satin dressing table. Her cheeks were as pale as ever, but a black and secret sparkle in her eyes betrayed the intensity of her inner excitement. She was charged with it, despite her deliberate stillness. For her situation bored her no longer: since her short passage with Trevor, she had discovered it to be full of enchanting possibilities. She was still determined to be even with her enemy, but she was not quite sure, now, that she wanted to turn him out.

"Perhaps he will go away," she murmured, "and perhaps he will stay. But if he stays . . ."

She smiled, and the pale face in the glass smiled briefly back at her.

3

The bride's room at Ratchet was very large and rather dark. Philip had wished to do it up, but this Emily would not allow, for she liked its sombre distinction. There was a huge mahogany four-poster, hung with greenish tapestries, and an old Chinese paper of many birds in obscure, bosky groves. The dressing table was Sheraton, and so were the few chests and cupboards that stood about against the walls. Three long windows, looking out upon the lawn, could not perfectly light all the dark recesses of the room.

The place smelt of lavender which Mattie put among Emily's linen, and of the scented apple-boughs that burned all day upon the enormous hearth. But penetrating everything was a smell of damp earth, which was the abiding smell of Ratchet. It drifted in continually from the rain-soaked lawn outside, where many water wagtails ran up and down but where no other living thing was ever seen. For the room was very quiet; only when all the windows were open could there be heard the distant whir of a mill-wheel, a faint, whispered hint of all the rushing waters that turned the garden into an island.

Emily's writing-table, strewn with scribbled manuscript, stood between two of the windows, and often when Mattie came in at seven she would find her charge up and sitting at this table. For Emily, lonely in her great bed, had got into the habit of waking very early. She would lie for hours, waiting for the gray morning to break and listening to the whisper of the mill-stream. And when she could bear it no longer, she would get up and write. Mattie would scold her and wrap her in a shawl and revive with a bellows the smouldering ashes of last night's fire.

"For, after all, Miss Emily, you've got the whole day to write your verses in. You've plenty of time."

"Very true, Mattie. I've plenty of time. I've got my whole life."

There was a flat finality about this statement that silenced Mattie.

The great mirror in a tarnished gilt frame, which hung over the fireplace, held the room in its heart like a picture—a dim old picture, for the glass gave an unreal, bluish tinge to the lights and shadows. The two people mirrored there, the gray old woman and the fair young one, were not more silent than were Mattie and Emily over the toilet. There were no squabbles now about warm vests and early rides. No change of routine broke in upon the monotony of these mornings, except the one gradual, relentless change, which, to Mattie's uneasy glances, became more frightful every day, the sense that her nursling was leaving her. Each morning she was to miss a little more, in tone or gesture, of the old Emily; until a constraint fell upon her solicitude as though they had been strangers.

Punctually at eight o'clock a faint hum, which thickened into a roar, was heard in the depths of the house. It was Philip's gong, an institution of his bachelor days. He had bought it twenty years ago because it was the loudest gong he could find, and he could hear it even if he was fishing at the bottom of the garden. Emily had changed nothing at Ratchet so the gong still deafened the house four times a day. She always went downstairs at once at its signal, and

Philip was always waiting for her in the breakfast room.
First she would kiss him good-morning, and then she would
blow out the little flame under the massive copper tea-
urn.

In this room, which faced north, the sound of the mill-stream
was much louder. All conversation was blent with its subdued murmur; it sang a dirge each morning, as the long slow
day began. Philip would open the *Times* and read the news to
Emily as she poured out his tea. He had made a rule that
she must not touch the paper until he had done with it, because she muddled up the sheets. Although forced to do this,
he had courteously offered to order another copy especially
for her, but she was not enough interested in public affairs
to make this worth while.

A long and particularly damp winter, middle age, and
recently frustrated desires were having a curious effect upon
Philip: an effect of slow petrifaction. He was far more set in
his ways, far more of an old bachelor, than he had ever been
before his marriage. He was fussy and fidgety, apprehensive
about his digestion and inclined to be put out over small dis-
locations. Emily's unpunctuality threw him into an agony.
Sometimes he was aware of this; on one occasion, just after
Christmas, he made a single, half-hearted attempt to save
himself. He suggested to Emily that they should go abroad
for the rest of the winter.

"Abroad?" she said, startled. "You don't mean it? You
used to say you hated going away. You used to say that you
would never willingly leave this house, even for a night."

"At my age, one gets stuck. But it's different for you. I'm
so afraid the life here is too dull for you."

"Me? I'm all right. I'm not dull."

"Are you sure? I ... I don't think you look quite as well as
I should like. You've got so pale."

"Have I?"

"And thin. Have you been weighed lately?"

"You're as bad as Mattie. She thinks I'm going into a decline, whatever that is."

"What?" cried Philip in alarm.

"She thinks I ought to drink ass's milk. She says my mother had to drink ass's milk when she was my age, and it did her a lot of good."

"Ass's milk? Well, I daresay we could get . . ."

"No, no, *no!*" cried Emily impatiently. "I won't drink ass's milk. And I won't go away. I'm quite all right. There's nothing the matter with me. I like this house. I'd be quite happy never to stir out of it again in my life."

"It's just that apathy which is so unnatural, at your age. And so unlike you. I remember that you used to want to travel and see the world. Why don't you now?"

"Because you don't."

"I don't know that I mightn't like it very much, with you. I don't want to turn into an old fossil before my time. I think, if we made the effort, that we might find it did us both a lot of good."

"Of course, if you wish it. Where should we go?"

"Wherever you like. Where would you like to go?"

Emily pondered. She could not think of any place.

"You used to talk about Rome."

She saw herself in Rome, accompanying Philip and his Baedeker. She heard all his affectionate inquiries as to whether she was tired and if she had seen enough that morning, his attempts to be cheerful and interested in a strange land where he could never quite digest the food. And then there would be all the careful preparations, passports, tickets, *wagons-lits*, frontiers, exchanges, and hotels. Philip would be bound to take those things so seriously. The mere paraphernalia of travel would fill all their foreground.

"No," she said distastefully, "not Rome."

"Then Greece? Weren't you planning to go there last year, you and William? I should love to see Greece with you."

"Oh, no! Not Greece! It wouldn't be nice at this time of year. Let's go somewhere warm, if we go at all. Hyères, or San Remo."

"We should both hate it. What about Madeira?"

"Just as you like. It's all the same to me, really. If we go, you'd better choose."

"All I want is to get away from this everlasting rain. It's crippling me. Say what you like, this house is infernally damp: I don't wonder that we all get rheumatism."

"Rheumatism?" cried Emily, concerned. "Have you got rheumatism?"

"Touch of sciatica. It's in the family."

"Oh, it's horrid! Poor Aunt Catherine gets it. Of course we'll go away, if it would do you good. But hadn't we better go to some spa, or cure place?"

The idea of a spa did not enliven him. He had never heard of a spa that provided a cure for old age. Probably it would finish him altogether. He had no doubt but that Emily would force him to go about in a bath-chair, and she would walk beside him, being dutiful and attentive. He lost heart and gave up the idea of going away. Also, after this conversation, he began to care less how things fell out between them. But the rheumatism was constantly mentioned, and sometimes he complained of it when he had not had it. The winter seemed endless.

Very few visitors disturbed their solitude after the round of bridal calls was over. Emily had found no friend among the ladies of the neighbourhood: she shrank from the compassion latent in their advances. Since her panic and flight from London in the summer she had taken a great dislike to society, mistaking all kindness for hypocritical curiosity. If Philip had not insisted, she would have returned no calls.

Catherine came sometimes, but her visitations were a nightmare to them both, and she was unsparingly inquisitive. They had the greatest difficulty in the world in persuading her that their marriage was entirely happy, since she invariably assumed that it was not. Why, otherwise, should Emily be growing so thin? And when was she going to have a baby? For Catherine had been talking to Mattie who, harassed beyond endurance, had poured out in secret a long catalogue of fears, hopes, and conjectures, beginning with ass's milk, and ending by a reference to separate bedrooms. Catherine had then scolded Philip for not giving Emily an object in life.

"What sort of object?" asked Philip wearily.

"Something to rouse her—to take her out of herself. She's getting silly and morbid because she hasn't enough to do. Is there a Women's Institute in Ratchet? I thought not. Why shouldn't Emily start one; or a troop of Girl Guides?"

"I shouldn't think she'd care about it."

"Well, then, she rides, doesn't she? Why doesn't she hunt? Remember, Philip, you can't go against nature. Nobody can do that without paying for it."

And Philip, who did not perfectly understand the gist of these remarks, said later to Emily:

"Your aunt wishes you to hunt, because it will be going against nature if you don't. I don't myself see why, but she seems very positive about it."

Emily, to whom Catherine had spoken a good deal more plainly, laughed a wintry little laugh and changed the subject.

Of the Monk's Hall party, they saw nothing at all, although they knew that William and Tilli were there. Emily would never, willingly, speak of her brother or his wife. By her very avoidance of their names, Philip came to guess that she thought of little else. At first he was sorry for her. But as time went on, this preoccupation, this ceaseless brooding, began to annoy him. He longed to scold her a little, to reproach her for injustice to himself. His mouth was shut, however, by the memory of their wedding day and of her disappearance. It was all too recent and too terrible. He could not speak of it, and yet he longed for some crisis that might clear the air. It was with this thought in his mind that he suggested one day a visit to Monk's Hall.

"What for?" she asked, opening her sad eyes in astonishment.

"Just for the walk. And to see how they're all getting on."

"I'd like to go for a walk. But not so far."

"Nonsense. It's no distance. You don't take nearly enough exercise; that's what's the matter with you. Your aunt is quite right."

"Let's ride over to Lyndon and see the Clewers," suggested Emily rather desperately.

"If you have any dislike of going to Monk's Hall, I think you should try to overcome it."

She was silent. She gave him no help. He continued nervously:

"You allow yourself to be governed by your feelings too much. Because you dislike William's wife, because you are hurt that he married without telling you, you've no business . . ."

"Oh, stop! You don't understand. I'll go to Monk's Hall, if you like."

"I wish it."

"If you wish it," she said in a voice of exasperating submission, "of course I'll go."

"Very well, then."

"When do you want to start?"

"Let me see!"

He took out his watch and deliberated. "It's half-past two now. Shall we say in half an hour?"

"In half an hour."

"At three."

"I'll be ready."

She made a great point of obeying all his small behests, yielding with an almost apologetic haste to his little fads. Had a happier relationship existed between them, she might not have been half so biddable. But the fact that she was cheating him of happiness lay heavy on her conscience, and she tried to make up for it by humouring him in small things. An unadmitted, yet potent, sense of guilt and injury lay for ever between them, until Philip, trading unconsciously upon his grievance, had got into the way of taking these disastrous submissions for granted.

She hurried now to her room and sought about in the large, orderly cupboards for a green leather hat and a coat. Positively, it was six days since she had set foot out of the house. She made violent efforts to be ready by the time that Philip had appointed. Her shoes seemed all to have disappeared. She found at last a pair of brogues, but they pinched her feet. She was still hopping about in her stockings when the clock struck three and Philip's voice summoned her.

"Emily! Are you ready?"

"Oh, dear!" said Emily. "Oh, dear!"

Hurriedly she thrust her feet back into the pinching shoes and ran downstairs. Halfway down, remembering that she had got no handkerchief, she ran up again. Philip, when at last she joined him, was walking up and down the hall with his watch in his hand.

"I thought I said three," he remarked to her coldly.

"I'm so sorry."

"You've had half an hour, and nothing to do but put on your hat."

"I'm so sorry."

He set off down the avenue, under the dripping trees, at a great rate, and Emily, in her tight shoes, panted at his heels.

"It'll take a good hour and a half to get there," he was cal-culating, "and we're bound to stay to tea. We sha'n't be able to start home till . . ."

"But surely it doesn't matter when we start home?"

"We shall be late for dinner."

"Well? After all, we're by ourselves. I should have thought we could be late if we wanted to."

"I've no doubt you thought so."

He talked about the time for ten minutes, scolding her again when they heard the Ratchet church strike half-past three. An exasperation that had been gathering impetus for months seemed to have inspired him, and he kept on nagging at her.

"You walk so badly," he complained. "You don't take enough exercise. You're walking lame already."

"My shoes hurt."

"Why did you put them on?"

"I was in a hurry."

"You had plenty of time. You had half an hour."

"I know. I'm sorry."

Their walk was bleak enough, for, when they had got too far to turn back, the rain began to fall again. Emily had forgot-ten to provide herself with an umbrella or a raincoat. Her leather hat, soaked in a few minutes, flapped dolefully over her ears and streaked her face with green tears. Her limp grew worse with every mile. Philip, grimly turning up the collar of his Burberry, strode on in front. Floods had cut off the field path, and they plodded along the tarred, shining high road until they came to Water Hythe village. Emily made a timid suggestion:

"Shouldn't we go in to Aunt Catherine's and shelter for a bit? This may be only a shower."

"No," snapped Philip.

Presently a car passed them and drew up a few yards ahead. Lise, with a surprised expression, was peering out through the flap of the hood as they came up.

"It is you!" she cried. "I thought I recognized you as we passed, and I told Bobbie to stop. But then I wondered if I'd been right. Can we give you a lift anywhere? We've been lunching in Oxford."

"Well, thank you, Lise. We were on our way up to Monk's Hall, as a matter of fact."

"Jump in, then."

Bobbie had by this time climbed out of the front of the car and was unbuttoning the hood. He, too, looked at them with a sort of furtive curiosity. It had been quite difficult to recognize this woebegone and bedraggled pair; he had thought that Lise was wrong when she insisted upon stopping. Emily, smiling wanly, hung back a little from their offers of a lift, saying that she was too wet to invade any car, but Philip told her sharply to get in at once, and she obeyed. They shot through the rain, over the stone bridge in the village, up the long hill, and were at Monk's Hall before Lise and Bobbie had recovered from the shock of hearing the golden-hearted Philip speak in such a tone to his wife.

The house was full of music, for Trevor's gramophone was playing in the dining room. They had taken down the long trestle table, sprinkled the floor with powder, and were dancing a little before tea, a diversion which had grown upon them during the past wet weeks. Three couples were revolving in the large, garish room, Tilli and Nigel, Peter and Charlotte, Trevor and Bertha. Sally stood uneasily by one of the windows, looking on. When she saw the newcomers, her little eyes snapped. Philip, after one hasty glance round the room, withdrew to smoke a quiet pipe with Bobbie and left Emily to fight her own battles.

"They dance all the afternoons, nowadays," commented

Lise. "Well, there's nothing else for them to do. It's been so wet."

Tilli had abandoned Nigel, and she now came across to welcome her sister-in-law. All down the long room she walked, slowly and beautifully, as though she were receiving a royalty. And when she was quite close to Emily, she smiled a very little, and put her pale, powdered cheek for a second beside Emily's cheek, which was damp and streaked with green raindrops.

"My dear," she murmured, "I am enchanted that you have come. Will you dance?"

"I have no shoes, I'm afraid," said Emily, looking at her feet.

They ached intolerably, and the mud was over her ankles. Tilli looked at them, too, with raised eyebrows.

"You are very wet," she said. "Have you walked? What courage! Can we lend you anything?"

"No, no," cried Emily. "I'm not wet, really. Only damp-ish."

It would be awful, she felt, to have to wear Tilli's clothes.

"And Mr. Luttrell, too? Is he here? You make me ashamed that you walk through the rain to see us, and it is so long since we have come to see you. I will send for William. He will wish to know that you are here. He is upstairs, I think. He does not dance: I think he despises these frivolities."

Trevor, Nigel, and Peter had now come up and were asking Emily to dance. But she said that she would sit and watch with Sally until William came. Trevor put on a new record, and Nigel turned to Charlotte. Peter flung an arm round the stalwart waist of Bertha and set to work on a step consisting of two long paces and a little jig, which was the only step he knew. Trevor, after the smallest of pauses, went gravely across to Tilli. They took the floor together in silence.

He liked an excuse for dancing with his enemy, since their

hostility gave a sort of piquancy to the perfect rhythm of their steps. Emily, watching them, was disturbed. She had never seen such a performance. Trevor had always danced well, but never like this. And Tilli's grace was scarcely human. It had the slow, voluptuous beauty of some exquisite, cat-like animal. Trevor was lord of all her movements, of every nerve and pulse, as they stepped backward and forward over the floor, glided, paused, and swayed, with but a single existence, as it were, between them. Both were very serious and intent, nor was one word exchanged between them. The dance went on for a long time.

"I suppose they've practised together a good deal," said Emily to Sally at last.

Sally sniffed.

"Is it a sort of tango they're dancing?"

"I'm sure I don't know," said Sally. "It's a pity that William doesn't dance. We all think so."

"But he does. At least, he used to."

"Did he? Well, he's given it up now. I suppose he can't compete with Trevor."

The record came to an end for a second time, and Trevor, stepping hastily away from Tilli, put the needle back and went on dancing. For the few seconds while she was alone, Tilli stood quite still, just as he had left her, the surrendered posture of the dance unbroken, until she swayed once more into his arms. The other couples, growing weary, came and stood beside Sally and Emily in the window embrasure.

"I thought," said Emily, "that there was to be nothing but Morris dancing at Monk's Hall. Trevor used to say . . ."

"That was before he'd tried to Morris dance," Charlotte told her. "We did it one evening, but never again."

"It made him sweat," explained Nigel. "And Madame," with a nod at Tilli, "told him that he was disgusting."

"No, she didn't," contradicted Charlotte. "She merely

came in to watch us doing it, and said she was sure it was very healthy."

They all watched Trevor and Tilli for a little while, and Emily said ballroom dances were quite good exercise if they were properly done. She could not be quite sure, but she thought that someone behind her repeated the word "properly" in a derisive whisper. She looked round and saw that Nigel was scowling at Sally, but she thought that she must have been mistaken, for Sally would never dare to criticize anybody.

"Tilli makes all the rest of us look clumsy when she dances," said Bertha good-naturedly.

And it was quite true. For Tilli danced, and the rest of them jigged about, innocently and a little ridiculously. She seemed scarcely to belong to the same sex as Bertha and Charlotte, or to be young as they were young. Her youth was simply physical; and her sex was a force, dark and mysterious through centuries of inherited experience. Emily, watching her, thought suddenly:

"I know why William married her. She is the opposite of us."

He came running down at last, flurried and genial and pleased to see his sister. He kissed her wet, cold cheeks and asked her to dance with him. But she said that her feet hurt her, and they sat down side by side.

"How's your book?" he asked.

"I burnt it."

"Why?"

"Because it was bad."

"It wasn't when I last saw it."

"It went to pieces after. What are you writing?"

"Another play. A comedy."

"A comedy?" Emily frowned. "You aren't old enough."

"It isn't very funny," confessed William.

"You ought to write a play about all of us here," advised

Sally, behind them. "That would be funny enough, I'm sure."

They both started slightly, for they had forgotten her. William said:

"You ought to write it, Sally."

"Well, now . . . I often say to myself . . . the books I could write if I had the time! I see a lot going on, though I know some people think I'm stupid. That's what I like. Sitting in a corner and watching. I notice a lot. But I wouldn't ever try to write a play. A novel I might, but not a play. You need technique for a play. Nigel says . . ."

William nodded amiably at Sally. He was not listening. He was learning how to do that: to smile and nod and think of something else. Nowadays, he never listened to anything any of them said. He could be quite happy whatever was going on. But Emily found it almost intolerable. She longed to get out of this stuffy, noisy room, away and alone with William.

"It's stopped raining," she said. "I think the clouds are lifting. Perhaps it will be a fine evening."

William nodded at her. She perceived, with a little stab of pain, that he was not listening to her, either. But presently he seemed to collect his wits again, and he suggested that they should go into the garden.

Her feet ached, and she had had quite enough fresh air for one day, but she went with him out on to the lawn. It had stopped raining, and the birds set up an optimistic chorus that drowned the noise of the distant gramophone. The air was very fresh and clean.

She took his arm as they wandered along the dripping garden paths. He talked, perfunctorily, about his play: how far he had got, his difficulties, and what he hoped to do. He knew that she would want to know, and he wanted to tell her, but he was not feeling inclined for conversation. She saw how unreal this existence at Monk's Hall was becoming to him.

The impact of an uncongenial world had roused him to no rebellion: it had merely driven him deeper into himself. It had been so at school and in the army. His geniality, his acquiescence, were the fruit, not of contentment, but of permanent abstraction. After this long silence, this severance, though he still loved her, it was not easy for him to return or to make any communication to her. She was part of the reality that he had avoided.

Her sorrow was no longer a cloud, hanging obscurely over all the horizons of life. It was herself: her whole existence. She walked beside him, listening, saying nothing, beholding truth. She could keep it at bay no longer. They were parted, not in time and place, but absolutely.

They came out at last upon the top of Ash Hill, and he spread his coat for her on the temple steps. They sat with their faces turned away from Monk's Hall and all its uneasy cares. The country below them was bathed in yellow light, for the sun had struggled through the clouds and was splashing the world with thick, molten beams.

"Are you happy?" asked Emily suddenly, after a pause.

"No," he said, and looked away from her.

She knew that he was not, he could not be happy. And yet his answer gave her courage. Something strange, new, and irrevocable was happening to her. She seemed to be living more vividly, more actually, than she had ever lived before. She was conscious of his life, and his suffering, going on so near to hers, and yet apart. She was sharply aware of the significance of this joint yet separate existence. It was so because in each life there is prisoned something that is larger than self, that transcends the boundaries of sensual perception, that clamours to be free and universal. By passion and suffering it is revealed, because all passion springs from it. In her grief, she had escaped the margins of identity; the self from which she had fled no longer bound her; she was not

Emily, not a woman, not a sister; she was impersonal and comprehensive. And that other self beside her had vanished, too. He was all humanity; he was everybody in the world, for in the beginning they had all been one, and to that wholeness they would all one day return.

A deep sigh escaped her as these urgent tides flowed through her being. The vision, in its clarity, fell away from her. She returned to solitude, surrendered, changed. It was as if she had come to some long-delayed moment of quickening.

She shivered. In spite of the sunshine, it was growing cold. The skies had deepened into a wild and lovely sunset, with great red banners of cloud flung high up into the heavens. There was colour everywhere. The air, cool as wine and preciously clear after the rain, was full of sounds coming from a long way off. The pausing moment was over. William said:

"It'll be fine to-morrow. A red sunset is a good sign. D'you remember Mattie? 'Red sky at night: shepherd's delight.'"

They watched it as it flamed and glowed, until a voice below them called their names:

"William! Emily!"

And the echo that always haunted Ash Hill called them, too. Tilli had come from the house to look for them, and was standing on the gravel path a little way down the hill. Perhaps she had stood there for some time watching them. Her lifted face was pale and small; she was like some goblin peering out of the bushes. A dimness fell upon the sunset like a faint cloud.

"Is it tea-time?" asked William.

"But tea is finished! We have looked everywhere for you. I am so sorry. Mr. Luttrell is impatient to be going."

They got up a little stiffly, for they had sat upon the temple steps much longer than was wise, and walked back to the house with Tilli, who continued to observe them in sidelong glances. At the front door they met Philip, manifestly put out and complaining that it would be dark in half an hour. Emily was hurried away before she had time to swallow so much as a cup of tea.

The light made everything look strange. It was as if the world had caught fire. The pools along the road and the flooded fields were all splashed with the same crimson. Far off, they could hear the Lyndon church bells coming faint over the fields. Emily lagged intolerably. At last she sat down upon a field stile and said that she could go no farther.

"Is it your shoe again?" asked Philip. "Why don't you get new ones? It's no earthly use keeping them if they hurt. Let me see!"

He took the shoe off and held in his hand her small foot in its stained and muddy stocking.

"Why, it's all bleeding!"

"It's much easier now the shoe is off."

"My poor child! Why didn't you tell me before we started? Of course I'd have . . ."

"I forgot how bad it was, up at Monk's Hall," she explained.

And she smiled at him.

It was something in her smile, and in her little bleeding foot, that broke his heart. He was kneeling on the lower step of the stile where she sat, and he tried to get up. But a sort of weakness seemed to come over him and he bowed his head in her lap. He could not restrain his tears. Above his head he heard her sigh deeply, and then her arms were round him, and she pulled him up to her. He could not speak.

"Philip! Poor Philip! Dear Philip! Don't!" she whispered. "I love you."

"I can't stand this life any more, Emily. I can't stand it. Don't mind! I'll be all right. I'm sorry for this. I don't know what's happened to me . . ."

"That's all right. It's all going to be all right."

"You don't love me. I can bear anything but that."

"I do! I do!"

He turned and looked up into her eyes. They were serene and ardent, the eyes of a visionary. Yet he knew that she spoke the truth and that she loved him. She was feeling for the first time all that he felt—his loneliness, his grief, and his need. With a great effort, he mastered his tears and moved away from her, a little ashamed.

"I'm sorry," he said again. "I've been a brute all day."

"Never mind. It'll all be better after this, I promise."

"No, but how are you ever going to get home? Can you walk, do you think, or shall I try to carry you?"

"I shall walk without my shoes."

"You'll catch a chill."

"My feet couldn't be colder or wetter than they are. I'll drink hot punch when I get in."

She took off her stockings and the other shoe and put them into his pocket. Then she got over the stile.

"At least take my arm," he entreated.

She said she would not mind doing that. They scurried on. Her toes sank deliciously into the wet grass, and Philip left off wondering what his parishioners would think if any of them happened to be walking in the fields. Luckily, it was getting dark.

Bats wheeled and fluttered over their heads as they limped up the avenue, and the voice of the mill-stream grew louder. Ratchet, with some of its windows already lighted, glowed at them through the trees. Philip whispered as they drew near:

"I'm going to carry you this last bit. It's rough."

He caught her up. She was very light. He could have borne her easily over a score of fields. With a heart full of strange comfort, he carried her over the threshold.

CHAPTER VI

THE CACTUS

I

SALLY was not happy at Monk's Hall. In London she had been very lonely, and she had persuaded Nigel to join the Settlement because she hoped to make friends there, and to secure some recognition for her precarious little liaison. But, since the advent of Tilli, her hold on him had weakened and she had formed no other ties. At the best she was treated with contemptuous good-nature by the more tolerant members of the party, and to many she was an object of open mockery. Nigel had always been inclined to bait her, even in the old days, and the rest of them caught the habit from him. Her cowardice was a standing joke with them, especially her terror of an encounter with Trevor's mother. They used to invent pretexts for sending her over to Water Hythe with notes and messages. She was too timid and too anxious to propitiate them ever to refuse, as they were well aware, but her desperate stratagems and excuses were extremely entertaining. And if she was forced into going, she would dawdle

263

about in the fields for hours in the hopes of finding an envoy who would do her business for her. If she caught sight of Catherine in the garden or by the river, she would scuttle round under the lee of hedges and do her business at the back door in peace. But, generally, as she slunk back past the house, all the dogs would rush out at her and try to bite her, as they did to no one else except tramps. She never needed to ring a bell, even if she had dared, for the whole household ran out when she came, to quiet the uproar.

Sometimes Catherine would come out at her, too, and then Sally would spin round in an agony of terror, unable to tell her business or to run away.

"Oh, Miss . . . Miss . . . er . . . Down, Cairny, down! Be quiet, Patsy! They won't hurt you. They didn't know who you were. Have you brought a note from Mrs. Crowne?"

"Oh, no, Mrs. Frobisher, thank you very much."

"Down, Cairny! Bad dog!"

"It was nothing, Mrs. Frobisher. It was just . . . Lise just wanted . . ."

"Down, Patsy! Come in, please . . . Miss . . ."

And Sally would follow Catherine helplessly into the hall, delivering her message with many apologies and self-contradictions. Once, inspired by a sort of abashed defiance, she plumped herself down uninvited into a chair, thinking: "I will not be treated like a servant. I won't stand her insulting ways."

"It's nothing, Mrs. Frobisher. I just said I'd drop in and give you a message, as I happened to be passing this way."

"Yes?"

Catherine did not sit down, and Sally was sorry for her bold move, since the stander has an advantage over the sitter. She stared up into her enemy's face and wriggled.

"Lise wanted to know . . ."

"You mean Mrs. Trevor? Yes?"

"Lise wanted to know if you had any plums this year to spare, because our crop has failed and she could do with some for jamming."

"Plums? Dear me! I must speak to my gardener. I don't know . . . one doesn't know how many she'll be wanting."

"I think she wants all she can get."

"I'd no idea their crop had failed. Of course, I know it's been a bad year. Our own crop hasn't been . . ."

"Because, if you haven't any to spare, I'm to go over to Ratchet and see if Emily has. We'd have asked her in the first place, only we didn't know she was coming back from abroad so soon."

"I don't think Mrs. Luttrell would care . . . I daresay I could manage . . . perhaps I shall be seeing Mrs. Trevor in a day or two, and then she can give me the exact particulars."

"She wants to know at once, Mrs. Frobisher. She's writing out her order to the stores for jamming sugar."

"Then perhaps she had better send me a note. A note would be best. A message of this description is so very vague, isn't it?"

Catherine always pretended that Sally's messages were in some way inadequate, partly to discourage the woman from coming to her house, and partly from a general wish to be offensive.

"She can't write anything more than I've told you, Mrs. Frobisher. She wants to know if you're likely to have any plums to spare, because she's writing her stores' order and she's had plums from you other years."

"Thank you. I'll write to her. She's writing her stores' order, and she's had plums from me other years," repeated Catherine vaguely. "Good-morning!"

Sally got up. She wished that she could say to Catherine, "You're no lady!" But she said nothing except to repeat with a pale smile:

"Then I'm to say you'll write, Mrs. Frobisher?"

"If you will."

"I just dropped in as I was passing," insisted Sally as she edged toward the door. "I thought I'd save Lise the trouble."

The dogs in the porch began to growl at the sight of her, and she got herself out of the house in the usual tumult. As she scurried back across the fields, she rehearsed inwardly a scene with Catherine in which she should give the old lady a piece of her mind.

"And will you kindly tell me what right you have to treat anybody like you do? I could tell you a thing or two that would make you sit up. If you knew all I do, perhaps you wouldn't think such a lot of yourself. Up at Monk's Hall they simply laugh at you. You ought to hear the way they talk about you behind your back. I'm not respectable, am I? And what about Lise? Oh! I beg your pardon! *Mrs.* Trevor. Didn't you once used to treat her like you treat me, and didn't you have to climb down about it? Think I don't know? And what about Norman Crowne? He was a relation to be proud of, wasn't he? I've got ears. I can hear what's said. I've eyes. I can see what's going on as well as anybody else, and better than some people, I daresay. I could tell you a pretty story if you were to ask. I must say, Mrs. Frobisher, I don't think you've brought up your own children so very well. You're so busy picking on me, you don't want to know what they've been up to, I suppose. But I always say that a man that goes on like Trevor does is nothing but a dirty rotter. Carrying on with a married woman! It's a pity nobody ever wrote and told you about it. Somebody ought. It ought to be known. I've a good mind . . ."

And Sally pictured Catherine getting a letter one morning which might begin: *Dear Madam, you will pardon a word of warning from a friend.*

"I've a very good mind," she said to herself, as she began to climb the hill.

Made bold by indignation, she strode along without looking where she was going, and in the wood she nearly fell over William, who was lying on his back under a beech tree. She begged his pardon with fewer apologies than usual.

William removed his gaze from the leafy roof over his head and blinked at her sleepily.

"Been for a walk?" he asked.

"I've been taking a message for Lise," said Sally, speaking rather quickly and panting a little. "And I must say I do wish you'd ask Lise not to send me any more on those sort of messages. It's not what I expected when I was brought here."

"What sort of message?" began William, sitting up.

"I'm quite ready, I'm sure, to do all I can to help and all that. But I don't like going where I'm not wanted, and the way your aunt treats me! I won't stand it. As if I was so much dirt."

"I'm sure Lise wouldn't ask you to go anywhere if she thought you didn't like it. Why don't you . . ."

"I didn't come here to be insulted, and I don't care who I say it to."

As a matter of fact, she would only have dared to say it to William. For they were fellow-sufferers; he also was ignored by the other inmates of Monk's Hall, and knowing this, she was not afraid of him.

"I've as good a right as anybody in the place," she declared, "and a great deal better than some. I don't see that she's got so much to be proud of, I'm sure. I wouldn't be proud of Trevor if he was my son. But then, there's none so blind as those that won't see. She's not the only one."

"I'm sorry if she was rude," said William distractedly. "You must simply refuse to go there again."

"I certainly sha'n't. Not if it was ever so. Not if you all

begged and prayed me to. But it's funny the people she does ask to go and see her. I should have thought . . . Oh, well! One mustn't say what one thinks, I suppose."

She tossed her head and flounced off into the bushes, leaving William to make out what all the storm had been about.

He pondered for a few minutes, and could come to no conclusion save that Sally looked like a weasel. Perhaps he had better not go on guessing at what she had meant. He rolled over on to his back again and stared upward into the flickering green shadows. The broken mood had escaped him: it was floating away. He could catch nothing of it. Sally had upset him.

These invasions of his tranquillity were becoming more frequent; or else his own capacity for withdrawal was diminishing. Twenty times a week he would find that he was involved in some reverberating passage of words. He could no longer sit for hours without hearing anything of the discussions that raged about him: he had begun to listen, and though he seldom followed any conversation with continuous attention, he heard enough to make him dumbly resentful.

Presently he got up and made his way moodily back to the house. Nobody was indoors. All the large rooms were empty, their doors and windows open to the airs and sounds of the summer day. For a few minutes he stood uncertainly in the hall, like a visitor, and then he went into the common-room, which was full of toys belonging to the Hackbutt children. These he began to put away, carefully, for the want of anything better to do. He was as quiet as he could be, because he did not want to be drawn into the discussion that was taking place on the terrace outside. Charlotte, Lise, and Bertha were sitting there in the sunshine, shelling peas, and it sounded as though Trevor had lounged out from his work to tease and contradict them. They made a noise, intermittent and clamorous, like starlings in a winter hedge. It was the permanent noise of Monk's Hall from ten in the morning until midnight, and William had grown very wary in evading it. Now, as he put the ninepins softly back into their box, he heard Trevor say:

"But when was all this? They haven't been back so very long."

"Yesterday. I went over there with Mother," said Charlotte.

"I must go, too. I must see it for myself. Go on, Car! Tell some more."

"Well . . . they take in the *Spectator*. And he is reading aloud Mahan's *Life of Nelson* to her in the evenings."

"I always said she'd settle down," proclaimed Bertha placidly. "I always knew they'd be quite happy once they'd . . . once they'd . . ."

"Quite! We take your meaning, Bertha."

"No, but it's wonderful what a difference being happy makes to her," pursued Charlotte. "She's a different woman."

"I think she always was a happy little person," said Bertha. "Before she married, anyhow "

"Oh, no!"

This burst from the other three simultaneously, and Trevor added, "That was all bluff. But how, exactly, is she different now, Car?"

"Oh, she's getting so dull. Quite wrapped up in all the dull things he likes. The garden and all that. They do nothing but tell you that their cactus has flowered and it's only supposed to do it once in a hundred years. I expect they'll write to the *Spectator* about it."

"Well, I always did think him one of the dankest creatures on the face of the earth. But in her it's positively depraved. It's a tragedy of the bedroom."

"Really, Trevor, must you talk like that?"

"I'm quoting Tolstoi. It's in Gorki's conversations, and

I thought it so true and helpful that I copied it out into my little book: 'Man survives earthquakes, epidemics, the horrors of disease and all the agonies of the soul, but for all time his most tormenting tragedy has been, is, and will be—the tragedy of the bedroom.' "

"Do you copy things down into a book?" asked Bertha, in the short, embarrassed pause that followed this quotation.

"He copies things that apply to himself," Charlotte told them. "That's why he calls them helpful. And I am asking myself what bedroom . . ."

"Anything that applies to me applies to the whole of the human race. I have a genius, really, for being normal: I'm a sort of common denominator of all the passions. If there ever was such a thing as *l'homme moyen sensuel* . . ."

"If everyone in this house using a French expression were to pay a fine of sixpence, we could very soon pay off our obligations to poor William."

"Well, the mean, sensual man, if you like. But it's a phrase you can't translate."

"In this case," put in Lise, "it's a very good translation. It has gained in truth what it has lost in . . ."

"I used to keep a commonplace book at school," Bertha told them. "But I never kept it up."

"Trevor means to tell us that he has survived the Great War, but that he's bound to succumb in the end to some designing female."

"Not designing. Very few women are capable of anything so coherent as a design."

William had left off listening. He knew that they always ended by talking in this way whenever they began to discuss their friends. They would go on until it was time for another meal.

He had begun to play, quite intently, with the wooden bricks on the floor, making them into a little theatre with an apron stage. It struck him that it might be fun to write a play for puppets, and he could, in Peter's workshop, construct a proper theatre for them with a curtain and scenery and footlights. He remembered that Trevor had once owned such a toy; it had been an object of keen envy to himself and Emily. And a play for puppets would be the best sort of play, since it could be presented without any complicated dealings with other human beings.

As he crouched on the floor beside his bricks, the conversation outside, with its laughter and pauses, floated in and out of his consciousness. He was aware, vaguely, that the same couple were still under discussion when he heard Trevor say:

"The long and short of it is that she's lost her virginity."

He wished that Trevor would not talk like that and was glad to hear a protesting snort from Lise.

"Your interpretations are so gross," said Trevor. "I am referring to a state of mind. Some women remain virgins all their lives, however often they marry."

"As, for example?"

"But some seem to lose their very identity when they change their names. This is a case in point. Here you have a woman who is temperamentally a virgin. She is capable of an absolutely concentrated devotion; she can worship with the undissipated passion that is possible to a nun and nobody else. All the forces of her nature are centred upon one object. All right, Car! I've my own views on the matter, but I'll keep them to myself, though I expect you all know what they are. There's nothing like being discreet."

Bertha was heard to utter, shyly, a few remarks about the value of experience. But he talked her down.

"No, Bertha! No, no, no! All this talk about experience is wrong. Believe me. No woman survives her experiences. They take up all her foreground. They aren't of the slightest use to her, because she doesn't live long enough to get over them. All inspired women are virgins. Our forefathers knew that. It's the only condition in which their inevitable sex is thrown into the balance with them instead of against them."

"Funny," said Charlotte. "I said much the same thing to Mother, coming home yesterday."

"What on earth made you say such a thing to Mother?"

"Oh, she annoyed me so. She's so triumphant about it all. I think old women are terrible. They talk of life beginning when it's really over."

"And you said that inspired women are all virgins?"

"Practically that. One uses different words to Mother."

"What did she say?"

"I don't think she listened. She would keep maundering on about their cactus and how she's sure it isn't true about it's flowering only once in a hundred years, because she remembers it in 'eighty-two. But she did say that she'd never come across any inspired women except perhaps Sarah Bernhardt. I don't think she meant it as a retort. She was just in a mood for reminiscence."

"Still, I expect it shut you up, just the same," said Trevor.

"God!" thought William. "How they talk! I wish they'd all get lockjaw."

His theatre was not finished, but he had used all the bricks. He sat back on his heels and stared at it morosely before he took it to pieces. The group outside the window was silent for a moment, and then Charlotte said, in a lower tone:

"Perhaps there's nothing in that story of Tilli's, after all."

"She doesn't always speak the truth," said Lise.

"She never speaks it," said Trevor.

William got up from the floor and prepared to make an escape. He did not mind what they said about their own friends, but he supposed that he ought not to listen in silence while they called his wife a liar. He peered into the hall and saw Sally sitting on the stairs doing a cross-word puzzle. Panic-stricken, he bolted back into the room. Bertha was asking what story of Tilli's this might be.

"Why! Surely you've heard," said Trevor. "I thought it had gone the round of the house. Everybody has discussed it with everybody else in strict confidence. It seems, or rather Tilli asserts, that Emily ran away from Philip on her wedding day. And went—where do you suppose?"

"Back to William!"

"Got it in one."

"Emily!" thought William. "Emily! Is it Emily they've been . . . Christ! I must stop it."

He went across to the piano and began to play upon it very loudly. He made a horrid noise, for he was full of fury. Fragments of their discussion kept returning to his mind. He thumped discordantly, half blinded by rage, until the voice of Trevor called him to order.

"Look here, William! You mustn't make that noise."

"I shall if I like."

"Not in this house. Now, don't swear. And pray don't lose your temper. I know you like strumming, but we've all got to sacrifice something."

"Have we? Then you can sacrifice your bloody gramophone."

"Not at all. In playing the gramophone, I am considering the greatest good of the greatest number. Most of us like it. In fact, we are all just going to dance to it."

"No, you aren't."

"Cousin William, you forget yourself."

At that moment the gramophone was let loose by Tilli in the dining room. William jumped up, strode furiously through the echoing rooms, and commanded her to stop it.

"But why?"

"I won't have that noise. It disturbs me."

She gaped at him, and then exchanged glances with Trevor, who had strolled in casually after William and was looking on with an expression of extreme amusement. A rising excitement coursed through the three of them that was to Tilli pure pleasure.

"I had thought," she said, "that nothing could do that."

"Nothing can," Trevor assured her. "He's merely peevish because I won't let him play the piano. Come, Tilli."

They began to dance. William stopped the gramophone and took off the record.

"Take care!" Tilli started forward. "That is a new one."

"Is it?"

He looked at it for a moment, and then he threw it out of the window on to the hard path outside. Tilli screamed with satisfaction. The sight of anything being thrown out of a window reminded her of Van Tuyl and the good old days. William threw all the records within reach out of the window, one after another. Trevor tried to pull him away. The little Hackbutts, playing outside, were astonished at the hailstorm of records on the path and set up a squeal of excitement. The two cousins scuffled and swore and belaboured each other. Tilli shrieked for help until the rest of the household rushed in and put an end to the fight.

"What is it? What was the matter?" asked Bobbie, looking from one furious young man to another.

Tilli was repeating, again and again:

"*Mon Dieu! Mon Dieu! C'est un assassin, cet homme. Mais un assassin!*"

"I don't like his gramophone," explained William, panting.

But nobody believed him, and Bobbie said very sharply

"We can't have this sort of thing in the house. If you want to fight, you must go out somewhere."

Trevor, whose nose was bleeding, repeated in a muffled

voice, from behind a pocket handkerchief, that he would play the gramophone whenever he pleased.

William turned to Tilli, who had never ceased to hiss the word *assassin* at him.

"Stop that noise!" he said. "Go upstairs. And you, Peter, clear this thing away." He pointed to the gramophone. "I won't have it in the house. And some of you had better wash the floor."

There were spots of blood on the strawberry paint where Trevor had been standing. And in the hall there were more spots, and up the stairs to the bathroom, where he had fled to hold his head under a tap.

William went after his wife, up to their room. She had left off hissing and was standing in sullen silence before her purple dressing table. In the glass, she saw William come into the room and stand behind her. He was no longer scowling; his equanimity was almost reëstablished.

"I lost my temper!" he remarked pleasantly.

She turned round and looked him in the face.

"I think you are always a little late," she told him. "If you had been wise, you would have lost your temper sooner."

2

"If you don't believe me," said Sally, "come and see for yourself."

Nigel joined her by the window and looked down into the garden.

"What am I supposed to be seeing?" he asked.

"Haven't you eyes?"

"I see Trevor and Tilli sitting under a mulberry tree. I've sat with Tilli under that tree myself before now; but she wasn't my mistress, for all that. So I don't think it proves that she's Trevor's. God, Sally! What a mind you've got!"

"Oh, yes! I know it's all my dirty mind. You would say that. But don't you be too sure. She's very deep. And he's deep, too. I shouldn't be surprised if they weren't playing a very deep game between them."

"I've seen Peter sitting under that tree with Lise. Of all the public places . . ."

"That's just it. They go on in this open way just to put everybody off."

"You're quite mistaken. Trevor is too much set on making this settlement a success to get himself entangled with her. And besides, he's got an odd puritanical strain. I've noticed it. I suppose it's the Frobisher taint coming out. He'd have scruples; obligations to William and all that. I know Trevor and his scruples. He's ashamed of them, but they're there."

"You haven't any of that yourself, have you?"

"What d'you mean?"

"You don't worry much about your obligations to William, do you? If it was you . . ."

"It isn't me. It never was me."

"Oh, yes, it was. Once upon a time. Only it turned out that she was only playing you up to make Trevor jealous."

"Or you. And she certainly succeeded."

"If she'd been serious, you wouldn't have thought twice about William, or me either."

"I never could stand a jealous woman."

"I never trusted her. The very first day she came here, I said to Lise . . ."

"She's a married woman, anyhow."

"Nigel! How dare you? After all I've done for you."

"Well? What have you done for me?"

"I've given you the greatest thing a woman can give."

"So you're always telling me. I can't see so very much to it."

"And now you throw it in my face. I'm respectable. I'd always been respectable till I met you."

"It does you credit, I'm sure."

"And you bring me here to associate with people like that Tilli. Why, she never has a bath but once in a blue moon."

"You can always go, if you don't like it."

"Oh, if you want to turn me out!"

"You're perfectly impossible. You know very well it was you who insisted on coming. I was against it. I didn't think you'd get on with the other women. You're too . . . respectable."

"I didn't think I was to be treated like this. But, of course, if you're tired of me . . ."

"By God, I am tired of you and your eternal caterwauling! And what's more, if it goes on, Sally—do you hear this?— if it goes on, I won't stand for it. You can do what you like about going or staying, but I've done with you."

"After all I've . . ."

"You talk as if you'd got nothing out of it. Haven't I kept you these three years?"

"I suppose you grudge me my food now. Not that you pay for it here."

"All right. Say what you like. But you'll only have yourself to blame if I leave you one of these days."

"After all I've done for you. I'm sure I wish we'd never come near the place. I'm sick of it."

"You couldn't be more sick of it than I am. I'm sick of it and I'm sick of you."

"I've given you the greatest . . ."

The door slammed behind Nigel, and Sally burst into tears. She cried in miserable half-hearted little sniffs, for she had not the power to be effective, even in rage and despair. But there was a real passion of hatred in her eyes as she looked down once more at the garden where Tilli sat with Trevor.

"All right," she muttered. "All right. You just wait. You've taken him away from me. That's what you've done.

But we'll see. You're a lousy cat, but I'll get even with you. Just you wait."

And from that hour she kept her enemy under a strict watch, waiting her time. Her position in the household gave her plenty of opportunity for this surveillance. She had come to be regarded as a sort of unofficial assistant to Lise, a congenial task, full of small secrets, confidences, and responsibilities. She ran errands, wrote lists, and told tales of the servants. She liked to be obliging, and to be thanked, and to hear people say, "Oh, ask Sally." The care of the linen cupboard was given over to her, and she gave out the clean sheets and bullied the little Hackbutts when they spilt tea in their beds, and was able to tell Lise in a whisper that William always slept in his dressing room.

"And Trevor's bed often isn't slept in, either."

"They all sleep on the roof in this hot weather."

"They'll spoil the mattresses."

"Well, if William doesn't mind . . ."

"William's as blind as a bat. And a good thing, too, I should say. If he wasn't, he might see some funny things going on in this house. Of course, foreigners have different ways to us."

"You'd better not let your imagination run away with you," Lise advised her.

"Imagination! You don't need much imagination where some people are concerned. No! But I'll just tell you one thing I saw. You're to let this go no further, mind."

"You see so much, Sally."

"I've always been pretty sharp, if that's what you mean. If there's anything going on, I always seem to notice it. But, mind you, I wouldn't say this to anyone but you. I just happened to be looking out of my door when she was coming down from the bathroom . . ."

"She? D'you mean Tilli?"

"Yes. And I was thinking to myself, 'Well, it's a wonder she's had a bath for once.' She had on that dressing gown of hers with the green dragons. I must say I don't think it's very nice, do you, Lise?"

"It's only a kimono."

"But it's all open under the arms. I wouldn't wear such a thing. But, anyhow . . . Trevor was coming up the stairs and if you'll believe me . . . well . . . I hardly like to tell you."

"You'd better, now you've begun, or I shall imagine the most dreadful things."

"I suppose it was an accident. It must have been. But she dropped her soap or something, and stooping to get it you know, this kimono fell right open!"

"I know, it's a way they have."

"I could see perfectly plainly. She was . . ."

"Oh, well, it was an accident!"

"That's what I said to myself. But if it had been me, I must say I wouldn't have passed it off with a laugh. I couldn't."

Lise made very little of this story, but Bertha Hackbutt was rather shocked when it came round to her. She retailed it to Mandy, and said doubtfully that it must have been an accident. Mandy replied that he was not sure.

"Why, Mandy! How can you? You mean——"

"I mean"—he nerved himself to speak the thought that had nagged at him for weeks. "I mean, Bertha, that the sooner we get ourselves out of here the better."

"Oh, Mandy!"

Bertha looked quite dazed, as if somebody had knocked her on the head. She scanned his face anxiously, and then she looked round the sitting room where they had been so snug. The caravan had been great fun. She had always insisted on that. But her heart sank at the thought of going back to it, and her tired, patient eyes filled with tears.

"Oh, Mandy!" she said.

"I know, my dear. It's hard on you. But I don't like the way things are going here. It's not what we expected, not what we understood, when first William invited us."

"After all, it's none of our business what the other people do here, is it?"

"I don't like this communal life. William said nothing about it, when first he asked us to stay; and you know we were in two minds about coming when we realized what we were in for. But we were in such straits."

"We are still."

"My play is finished now."

"I know, dear. But that won't feed us or keep a roof over our heads."

"I'm bound, some day, to get it taken, and then . . ."

"But, Mandy, where could we go? How could we live? We've sold the caravan."

"People do live," said Mandy desperately. "Nobody ever actually starves nowadays. At least, I never heard of such a thing. If other people manage to get along, I suppose we shall. Oh, Bertha! Don't cry! You're generally so brave."

"I can't help it. It's all too much. It's too much for me. Just when we'd got a little peace and quietness and decency. And the rooms look so nice with the rhyme sheets all pinned up. I could almost pretend it was the little house we planned to have when we got married. And Dorrie's croup was so bad last winter, I know she'll never get through another if we have to go back to that awful, rough life, and it was such a comfort to know that they were getting enough to eat, anyway. I'd never been so happy before. I might have known it was too good to last. Oh, Mandy! We must wait! We must wait until there's some hope of you making some money. We can live on very little, ever so little, but we can't live on nothing at all."

Mandy groaned. It was all quite true. He wandered miserably about the room, the battered, useful room that was, to Bertha, a palace. He paused for a moment, beside the special writing-table that was now his, where Marmaduke the typewriter might rattle all day without disturbance. And he remembered how hard it was to type on an upturned packing case.

But it was Bertha's gallant little attempts at decoration that smote him most bitterly. She had tried so hard to make the place look pretty, and it was a marvel to him that she should have kept the heart for it. He knew very well that the vagrant, uncertain life of the caravan was hateful to her, though she had tried to make a gay picnic of it all, because she loved him and because she was a woman of enormous courage. In her soul, she hankered after some trim little house in a garden suburb, with art shades in distemper, and Monday washing-days, and a local dramatic society. In that life she would have been happy and contented, despite all their grinding anxieties and their seven hungry children.

"Do at least wait until one of your plays has been accepted," she was entreating.

"That may be never."

It burst from him unexpectedly, and they were both a little shocked. For he was usually the most hopeful of men—always on the point of making a fortune. But the truth had, in this moment of distraction, escaped him.

"If you feel like that," she said slowly, "if you really feel like that, you've no right, *no right*, to take us all away from here. You ought to hang on as long as you can, for my sake, and the children's."

She faced him accusingly.

"I'm very fond of William," he began.

"So am I. But I don't put him before my children."

"I can't stand this life any more, Bertha. I can't go on

living on him, and thinking . . . as I do think . . . of his wife.
Talking as we've just been talking."

"I don't believe anything at all," cried Bertha, valiantly
blind. "I don't believe a word Sally says. It's just her spite.
She wants to make trouble. I'm sorry I told you. I didn't
know you'd take this line about it, else I wouldn't have. After
all, we know nothing."

"We know nothing now. But it's jumpy, the way we all
live on top of one another. I'm frightened of what we may
come to know before we're through. Supposing (I'm just
putting it to you), supposing we all found ourselves entangled
in some ugly scandal. We might be dragged in as witnesses."

"Do you mean . . . a divorce, or something like that?" she
whispered.

"That sort of thing. It might happen. And think what a
horrible case it would be. The whole circumstances . . . the
publicity . . . Crowne is such an unfortunate name. Think of
the figures we'd cut, living here on William, supposing we
had come to know any really damaging facts against Tilli . . .
holding our tongues because it paid us. We must get away
before it comes to that. We know nothing, as you say. We
must go while there's time."

"It's William's fault. He ought to take her away. He ought
to see . . ."

"Why should they go? This is their house."

"But couldn't you speak to him? Couldn't you point
out . . ."

"What could I point out? Nothing that he couldn't see for
himself if he wanted to."

"Still, it's Trevor that ought to go, not us. If he had any
decency, or any sense, he would go."

"I daresay. But he hasn't. No, it's we who will have to go,
I'm afraid."

"You may. If your conscience is so tender, you can. But

I sha'n't. I shall stay here with the children. They sha'n't starve, if I can help it, just because you're a failure and can't support us."

"Bertha!"

"I must look out for myself and the children, if you won't."

"A failure! You never threw it at me before."

"There's a limit to everything."

Mandy had turned quite green, as though he were going to be sick.

"In our worst times," he said at last, "worse times than this, you never turned on me. Oh, I know it's true, but it's awful to hear you say it. I wish to God we'd never come here. A roof and food we've got, but that's all. You hate me, don't you?"

She flung herself on the floor beside him, repentant.

"Oh, Mandy! Mandy! Forgive me! I'm sorry. I didn't mean it. I oughtn't to have spoken like that. It was wrong. I was wrong. Do forgive me!"

"You only spoke the truth, my poor girl."

"You were quite right. This house has done us nothing but harm."

"My poor Bertha! If it would do you and the children any good, I'd jump into the river and be thankful."

"No, no, no! Don't talk like that. Of course our ship will come in some day."

"It won't. You know it won't, and so do I. I am a failure, and I always shall be. I've tried. God knows I've tried. Other men seem to get on, and I never could see why I shouldn't, too. But I don't, though I can't quite understand how it is. And you have to suffer for it."

"I don't suffer, because I've got you, and that makes me happy. I was wicked to speak like that. It was just in a moment of exasperation. You must forgive me. You must forget it. I'm sure I don't want to stay in this horrible place one minute longer than we need. But oh—it's the children, Mandy! What is going to happen to them?"

"I know."

"Do at least speak to Trevor. Couldn't you? Couldn't you? It's him or our children. Try to make him go away. He ought. He must go away, if he thinks it out."

"I'll try," said Mandy heavily.

He kissed his wife and assured her many times that her hasty words had not hurt him. But they had, and she knew it. They never spoke of this dispute again, and they never forgot it. For the rest of their lives, they thought of Monk's Hall with shame as a place where life had been too much for them.

Mandy waited a few days in a mood of miserable uncertainty, and then he went to Trevor, driven by a conviction that no more time could be lost.

"I detest coming to you about this," he began. "But I've been talking to Bertha, and we agreed that I'd much better come straight to you."

"Well?" asked Trevor crossly, adding: "The people in this house are always talking things over and then coming straight to me. I never saw such a place. Is it about the use of the bathroom, because . . ."

"Oh, no. We've come to an agreement about that. It's . . . it's something much more disagreeable than that, I'm afraid. I . . . we . . . you . . . we think you ought to know that a good deal of gossip is going on in the house about you and Tilli."

"Oh, really? No, I didn't know. What sort of gossip?"

"The usual sort."

"Who's gossiping?"

"I gather that Sally is responsible for most of it."

"Sally! What does she say?"

"Nothing very definite. I haven't heard her. I only hear of it through Bertha. I suppose it's the sort of thing that's bound to go on among women, anywhere. But she hints at an accusation which would be very serious, if it were true. The sort of thing which, as William's friends, we can't allow to be said."

"I see," said Trevor thoughtfully. "I agree. I'll talk to Sally. I'll shut her up. Fancy Sally! That little rat of a woman! Who'd have thought it?"

"I don't believe that talking to Sally will do much good. The harm's done now."

"Well, then, what do you expect me to do about it?"

"We thought you ought to know. It makes the atmosphere of the place very unpleasant for any friends of William's. We don't want, of course, to go away. In fact, it would be a disaster for us if we had to go just now, but . . ."

"Go? You aren't thinking of going, are you?"

"We don't want to," repeated Mandy miserably. "But I'm afraid we'll have to unless this sort of talk is stopped. And it won't stop while Tilli and you are both here."

"Then what's the alternative?"

"Well, we just wanted to know . . . you did mention, the other day, that you would like to go to Dalmatia this autumn. And we wondered if you really had any plan of that sort."

"Are you suggesting that I should go away?"

"Even if it was only for a time, it would mean that all this gossip might die down."

"Well, I'm damned! Look here, Mandy! Are you suggesting that you believe any of Sally's tales? Because, if you are, say so."

Mandy swallowed twice, thought of Bertha, and toiled on.

"We don't believe a word of it. We know you well enough . . . but we don't trust Tilli. That's the long and short of it. Of course, we don't know her very well."

"My dear fellow, either you believe this story or you don't. If you do, you must believe it of both of us. You can't say that you believe it of her and not of me. Unless," he added suspiciously, "there's another man in the case. And if there is, my going away wouldn't improve matters."

"There's no other man," said Mandy, driven on to speak the truth. "But we don't like the way things are going. We think you spend too much time with her: that you behave in a way that is bound to give rise to talk. We think the situation is the sort of situation which is bound to end in trouble of some sort. It's giving the place a bad name in the neighbourhood already, so I'm told. I'm sorry. We don't want to think this. But we can't help it. And if we think it, we'd better go. Only Bertha was so unhappy that I promised her I'd speak to you before we made up our minds."

"In case you could persuade me to go instead," exclaimed Trevor bitterly. "Thank you, Mandy. It was very good of you. But don't make up your minds in too much of a hurry. I'll think it over. I'll speak to Sally. I'll make her take back every syllable of it."

He went off, quite dizzy with rage, to have it out with Sally. But he got very little satisfaction from her.

"I never said a thing that wasn't the truth," she asserted. "Besides, I don't know what you're talking about."

"Yes, you do. You've been slandering Tilli."

"No, I haven't."

"Well, you've been criticizing her."

"What if I have? It's no business of yours."

"I won't have gossip of that sort going on in the house."

"Pardon?"

"If you haven't definitely accused her, you've hinted at a very shocking thing. You know that quite well."

"What sort of thing?"

"That she has been unfaithful to William."

"With who?"

Trevor avoided the trap and said that accounts, on that point, seemed to differ.

"Well, you do surprise me!" said Sally.

"But you must understand that you can't stay here if you talk in this way. If I hear any more of it, I shall have to ask you to go."

"Go? I'll have to go, will I? I'll go when William tells me to, and not before."

"You came here, you and Nigel, as my friends, not his. And I won't have . . ."

"You'll turn us out? I like that! Because you think I see too much. But the Hackbutts, and Lise and Bobbie, that daren't say a thing for fear they'll be turned off to starve, they can stay, I suppose. You can do what you like, and they won't say anything. That's a nice idea, I must say."

"If this is the way you talk, the sooner you go the better."

"Oh, really? It's you that ought to go, let me tell you. Everybody says so. But, of course, you'll turn us all out rather than go yourself."

And she flounced off, leaving him speechless with surprise. He had never expected her to hold her own so well. And he remembered wrathfully that he had once been sorry for her. He had even taken the trouble to talk to her at parties because she looked so lonely. He wished now that he could wring her neck.

In spite of himself, he began to wonder if she was right, and Mandy was right, and whether he had not better leave Monk's Hall. The very idea of it was heart-breaking to him, for he knew that the Settlement would fall to pieces at his departure. His hopes and schemes, begun at first in idleness, had come to mean so much to him. He really believed that he might have made something of Monk's Hall, if only Tilli had left him alone.

He had not betrayed his cousin, and he was still trying to persuade himself that he never would. The possibility was fantastic. He did not love this woman. He was quite sure that he hated her. She no longer appeared to him as beautiful, amiable, or intelligent. He still desired her, but he could in no way deceive himself as to the brutality of his relation to her. The hours spent in her company had been hours of degradation and torment.

Nor did he believe that she would ever yield to him. She was cold. She was playing with him. It was part of her infernally clever campaign to get rid of him. In time, he would tire her out, and then she would go away. He would remain: he would survive the storm she had brought into his life. She should not beat him in a duel like this.

But he had not foreseen the publicity of this affair, or the threatening of a scandal that would mean the ruin of all his plans. If in the minds of the whole party he was already Tilli's lover, then she had succeeded in her aim just as surely as if he had really surrendered to her. The only course before him would be to pack up and go. He felt this so strongly that he got out his suitcase and began to study a continental Bradshaw for convenient boat trains. By lunchtime he had even put out all his ties upon a bed as a first step toward packing.

At lunch, however, all the reasons against departure came flowing back on him. Peter Yates was full of a printing-press that was to be set up in one of the barns. And this scheme reminded Trevor of all that Monk's Hall was to have been. He recollected that his plans had scarcely begun to mature; that this group of people was but the nucleus of a future community which he had in mind. The very meagreness of this first year's achievement had roused him to a much more passionate belief in the possibilities of his idea. But if he went away now, he would never see a day when Monk's

Hall would rank as a sort of Kelmscott. And how his mother would triumph!

"Yet one of us must go," he thought.

He took care not to look down the long table, past the litter of food and flowers, to the place where Tilli sat silent at the bottom. But he knew exactly how she was crumbling her bread. He knew all her gestures by heart with a precision bred of hatred. He was aware that she had never glanced at him. And he wondered what was passing in her mind. He wondered what she would say when she knew that he was going. She would be pleased. And as soon as she had got rid of him, she would go away herself, for he was sure that she disliked the place.

Perhaps, if he went to her and said that he was going, confessed to surrender, she might, impossibly capricious as she was, wage war no longer. He thought that he knew the secret of her bitterness against him: it was because he had once rejected her for the sake of Monk's Hall. Now she was avenged. She had the house. She had ousted him. And their quarrel had never really been over the house, but over his defiance of her power. On this score, she was also even with him; his departure would prove it. She would know that he fled from her, and knowing this, she might forgive him. A confession of his own subjugation might end this long duel, and she, satisfied, might go away. An interview of some sort might be worth trying before he packed that suitcase upstairs. And he could not in any case go away until he had raised the price of a ticket, for he had only half a crown, and that would not get him nearly far enough.

He thought that lunch would go on for ever. And in the midst of his perplexities he felt a sudden disgust for this herd life, with its noisy, disorderly meals. He was revolted by the great plates of pudding dealt out by Lise, the flat contradictions that Peter was shouting across the table to Nigel, the want of any real coherence. A picture of Water Hythe in its hushed security rose up before him. It would be very cool on a day like this. He almost wished himself there, in his mother's dining room, eating one of the very excellent salads that she used to make for him. She always made one on the first day of the holidays because he loved them so and never got them at school. Suddenly, he was sorry that things had fallen out so badly between them. She was a wonderful old lady, in spite of her faults. Her life was all in a piece; she knew exactly what she wanted. It was a pity that she wanted such impossible things.

At last the meal was really over, and they all trooped out into the hall. Although he did not look, he was aware that Tilli had taken a red silk parasol and was gone into the garden. Outside, it was very hot; the lawn danced in a dazzling shimmer of light. He took up a newspaper and pretended to read until the last of the chattering groups had disappeared. Then he went in search of her.

The sunshine was like a blow, it was so fierce. Even the children were languid and stayed indoors. He could not think that she had walked far, though he knew that she loved it. No day could be too hot for her, after the long winter that had so chilled her little bones.

He tracked her to the kitchen garden, where the four red brick walls threw back the heat like a furnace. Fruit ripened everywhere, in an abandoned profusion, but everything seemed motionless and dead in the glare, even the clusters of glutted wasps on the plum trees. Tilli sat on an old wooden seat at the end of a long, box-edged path. Under the ruby shade of her parasol, her pallor glowed warmly. She said nothing when Trevor came and planted himself in front of her.

"I've come to say good-bye," he said.

"You are going?"

"Yes."

"I did not know."

"Nobody knows. I've only just made up my mind."

He liked the discomfort of this interview, in the glare. It would keep him to the point and make him brief. Nobody can talk for long in an oven.

"You know why I'm going," he said, "and I hope you're satisfied. You always wanted to drive me away, didn't you? Well, you've done it now. You've got your house."

"When are you going?" asked Tilli thoughtfully.

"To-morrow."

"And you say that I have driven you away? How is that?"

He hesitated. The whole truth would be inopportune. He could not tell her that he was running away from gossip. She would laugh at him.

"You know quite well how it is," he said at last. "I only want to tell you that you've got the house."

"The house? But I do not want it."

"That's no affair of mine."

"Quite soon I am going away. Perhaps at once. Then, Trevor, you could stay."

He was unable to repress a start of eagerness. Smiling slightly, she went on:

"I think you have been very foolish. A year ago you ran away from me."

"Yes."

"And yet, if you had not been in such a hurry, you could have had this house, just the same. And perhaps I should not have married William. But now you will lose it all. But yes! You will lose it all. For I do not think that I shall go away just yet."

"Tilli, what do you want? Do you want me to say I'm beaten? I've said it. Do you want me to apologize for my behaviour a year ago? I will, if you like. Do you want me to say that I daren't go on living in the same house with you? I've practically said it already. You know I daren't. What more do you want?"

"I do not want you to go away," she said.

"I must, if you stay. I want you. I've always wanted you. Every moment here is torture to me. I can't stand it any longer."

"I do not want you to go away."

"I daresay not. You like to see me suffer."

"It is not necessary that you should suffer, as you call it. I have been angry with you. That I admit. But also I have loved you. Perhaps a great deal better than you deserve. But still I love you."

"No, you don't. You don't."

"I do. I would go away with you, if you would take me. But you wish to stay here; so I also shall stay here. You torment yourself for no reason at all."

"Do you mean . . . But then, there's William."

"William! He is nothing to me any more."

"I know. But I've lived on him for a year."

"He has been foolish to allow it. Many times have I warned him."

"Have you?"

"He should have sent you away, Trevor."

"Of course he should."

"But he would not listen. He will not see. I don't think that he wishes to see."

"I know. But still . . ."

Suddenly she lost her calm. She jumped up and faced him furiously.

"Still, still, still! You would rather go away! William will not know. But you would rather go away. Very well! You can go! Since you would prefer it, you can go. For me, I shall go, too. I shall not stay with you or with William. You are both mad. I would rather be poor; I would rather live in London . . ."

"Don't speak so loud! I hear people coming."

"You think only of yourself. You are not so mad as you pretend. What do I care if they come? I don't want to stay here. If I am going, they can say what they like. I shall be amused."

"Oh, Tilli, do for heaven's sake be quiet. I think they're coming into the garden. Listen!"

There was a sound of voices beyond the brick wall. Sally was saying:

"What I tell Lise is this: she ought to count the pillow-cases *before* they go to be aired. It's not a bit of good . . ."

Tilli began to laugh softly.

"She is coming to pick fruit," she said. "How it will interest her to find us here!"

They were trapped, for there was no way out of the garden but a door through which Sally must, in a few seconds, enter it. Trevor looked round wildly for cover. He could see none save a small potting-shed at the end of the path where the seat was. He touched Tilli's sleeve.

"Come in here a minute," he whispered hoarsely. "We must settle this."

Tilli followed him, still laughing. And he could not help laughing himself. They scurried along the path, quivering with secret, intimate laughter. Trevor felt as though all his power of resistance was drowned in it. He pulled open the rickety door and drew her in after him. A hot, damp smell of earth and roots blew out at them, and as they shut the door a voice inside said:

"Why the hell didn't you knock? You might have spoiled my whole day's work, letting the light in like that."

They remembered that this shed was sometimes used by Peter as a dark-room. Helplessly they stood in the sweltering darkness, beside his ruby lamp, while he showed them the negatives that he had been developing. It was plain that Peter took their visit as a compliment.

3

After tea, Trevor decided to pay a call upon his mother. It was many weeks since he had been to Water Hythe, and he hardly knew how he should behave when he got there, but an obscure hope drove him on. He told himself that he might induce her to help him, but he wished, really, to make her responsible for his ultimate decision. His suitcase was not yet put away, and, thanks to Peter, he was not yet finally committed with Tilli. If his mother would advance him a little money, he would stick to his plan of leaving Monk's Hall immediately. If she refused to do so, she must be regarded as to blame for anything that might occur.

The unfairness of this arrangement was not apparent to his mind, for he had convinced himself that his situation was entirely due to his mother's parsimony. If she had been more liberal, he would never have been forced to live in William's house, in the dangerous neighbourhood of William's wife. But he wanted the reassurance of knowing that she had once more refused to assist and understand him. For it was quite plain that he could not leave Monk's Hall with a bare half-crown in his pocket. He had borrowed too much from William, and nobody else in the house had any money at all.

So he set off in a curious mood of bitter detachment, pretending to himself that his fate had been already taken out of his hands. He was so much detached that he was even able to argue with himself—with that small section of himself that retained, exasperatingly, a trace of Frobisher, a narrow, nagging rectitude of outlook that never had much effect upon his conduct, but that existed in his consciousness and made him uncomfortable.

"How can I help myself?" he inquired. "How can anybody help himself? Look around you! Look at Bobbie, with his career ruined. Look at Mandy, drowning with eight stones round his neck. Look at Nigel! Look at William!"

"Bobbie," said that inner voice, which was so like Catherine's voice, "is suffering from his want of enterprise. He'd have done all right if he'd sold the place long ago and gone out to the colonies with Lise. Mandy shouldn't have married without prospects. William is so self-centred that he ought never to have married at all, and Nigel deserves all he gets. You, Trevor, didn't want to work for a living. Therefore, you have got yourself into this mess. It is character, not circumstance, that shapes our lives."

"I didn't choose to be born. That was a circumstance over which I had no control whatever. And very important, too. If I had been born to a different mother, I might have been a different man. And this worship of character is pure Frobisher. I'm bound to react from it. In my father's day, it was a fashion to be earnest and striving and to go about proclaiming that one's head was bloody but unbowed. If I hadn't been forced to wallow in it as a boy, perhaps I shouldn't have taken such a dislike to it."

He was a little put out to find that Philip and Emily were sitting with his mother when he got to Water Hythe. They were all closeted together in the pleasant, shady gloom of the hall, and as he came in it struck him that they looked up with a sort of resentment at his intrusion. He wondered what family discussion was being interrupted.

Catherine, however, received him cordially and showed no surprise at his sudden visit. She gave him the feeling that she had been waiting for it. She even looked complacent when Emily asked him for news of Monk's Hall.

"Not much news," mumbled Trevor. "The little Hackbutts can't get rid of their hay fever, and Nigel got stung by a wasp yesterday. One of Bobbie's pigs got into the kitchen garden the same day that one of Charlotte's poems got into the *Adelphi*. Tuesday last week, I think it was. We began to rehearse *Rosenkavalier*, but we've decided we won't act it, because I haven't time to learn the part of Baron Ochs. That's all. How did you get on abroad? You went to mountains, didn't you?"

"Yes. The Tyrol."

"Did you climb?"

"No. We walked up some."

"You mean," said Philip, "that we ran up. I never saw anyone go so fast as Emily does up a mountain. I couldn't keep up with her. It nearly killed me. We aren't going to mountains again, for if we do, she will certainly come back a widow."

"I see. And what is this rumour that your cactus has flowered?"

"Oh, you haven't seen it!" cried Emily. "You must, before it's over. They only do it once in a hundred years, you know."

Catherine contradicted this, and for a few minutes they all grew very warm about the cactus. Trevor observed Emily curiously. He was aware of a change in her, but he did not think that it was for the worse. He would have said that she was even more beautiful than before; she had acquired a poise and placidity that were very compelling. Charlotte had found it dull, but then, Charlotte was a woman. In the old days he had admired Emily as he might have admired some beautiful picture or statue. He had been cold to her. But now it occurred to him to wonder that he had never been in love with his romantic cousin. No other woman of his acquaintance could compete with her. It was strange that this ripening of loveliness should have lain in wait for dull old Philip, who had not changed a bit. Philip was like a house or a hill. As one remembered him in childhood, so he remained.

Catherine beamed upon them both. She liked exhibiting the domestic concord of the Luttrells. It would be a good lesson for Trevor, a sermon on the futility of rebellion. Presently she took her niece away with her upstairs, with a mysterious reference to some things that she wanted Emily to see. The two of them went out with an air of secret importance, like two priestesses performing a rite, and Trevor turned vengefully on Philip.

"Is Emily writing another book?" he asked.

"No. She's taking a rest from her writing."

"She hasn't given it up?"

"Well, I don't know at all if she will go on. She feels, and I agree with her, that her work up till now has been very poor. It was striking, but too immature to be taken seriously. Not worth going on with."

"And now she has the cactus to water."

Trevor spoke low, and Philip, who was getting a little deaf, did not catch what he said.

"Very true," he said. "But that reminds me. We were wondering the other day where all those early poems of hers can be. The things she wrote when she was quite a little girl. Some of them were most amusing. I should like to make sure that they are kept. She thinks that they are all in some old box together, but your mother has no idea where it can be."

"I know. All our first efforts are together, somewhere in the attic. At least, it was there I last saw them. If they haven't been moved, I could lay hands on them any time."

"Well, I wish that you or Charlotte would have a look for them some day. I'd like to have them. I like to think of Emily when she was a little girl."

His tone struck Trevor as being a great deal too complacent. And it was odd that he should like to think of Emily when she was a little girl unless he had entirely forgotten what she used to be like.

"I'll go and look for them now," said Trevor. "I've nothing to do. If I find them, I'll post them to you."

He knew that he had better not sit with Philip any longer; the old temptation to be impertinent was nagging at him. So he hurried off upstairs, and as he passed the open door of his mother's room, a fragment of conversation drifted out to him.

". . . those are matinée coats. You'd better take them all, for you can't have too many."

"But, Aunt Catherine, aren't they any use to you?"

"My dear child, I've kept them all these years, hoping that you or Charlotte . . ."

"Matinée coats!" thought Trevor as he raced up the noisy attic stairs. "What a ridiculous idea! Why does she want so many? Nobody goes to matinées."

The attic was large and stuffy and full of old-fashioned luggage. Last year's apples, spread out on wooden trays, had made it smell like a cider press. Long ago it had been a play-room for four children in wet weather. Their tramping feet, their laughter, had shaken the old beams. But now it was given over to silence, dust, and the sleepy buzzing of blue-bottles. Emily's skipping-rope still hung on a nail by the door, while under the window there was a heap of rusty skates, stringless tennis rackets, and torn butterfly-nets. All the ghosts of the household were collected in that room under its roof, and nothing looked as though it would be used or wanted any more. Yet a faint halo of romance, an immediate sense of the past, lingered over the broken musical instruments, the stamp-collections, typewriters, fishing-rods, and framed school groups.

Trevor stood for a moment in the doorway with a sense that the room had been waiting for him. There had been a childish legend that it was haunted. Nobody ever used to go up there after dark. And now, though it was bright day, the little window was so thick with dust that a sort of twilight seemed already to have fallen. But it was not so dim that he could not perfectly descry the young man who sat on the trunk by the window. A smooth, round head was very clearly outlined against a beam of dusty light. It was bent forward intently, and after a second it turned upon Trevor a face that was familiar to him. He grew very cold in spite of the airless warmth of the attic. Time paused, while he stared, and his companion stared back at him, through the shadows, with a gaze full of meaning.

The panes of the window, a crack in the plaster on the wall, began to glimmer through the stare. The bent head was a dim shadow against the light. It was gone. Nobody was sitting on the trunk by the window.

Trevor breathed again, in a great sigh. At last he pulled himself together and went nearer. He told himself that it had been the heat and the closeness of the attic. In so faint a light it would be possible to imagine anything. Nor was it the first time that his sight had deceived him in such a way. Once he had seen a school friend, standing at the edge of a pool where he was bathing. At his call the figure vanished. It was a trick, an illusion of shifting lights among the bushes beside the pool. And this also was an illusion. But it is never comfortable to see one's self . . .

For some time he could not pluck up courage to open the trunk by the window. He nearly went away. But at last, a little gingerly, he pulled up the lid, and a great blast of camphor rushed out at him. A snowstorm of loose pages, all scrawled over in a round hand, fell out on to the floor in a cascade. It was *The Pollipantos, an Imaginary History of an Island, by William and Emily Crowne*. The whole tray of the box was full of it. Trevor picked out a page and read:

Now when we had sailed 50 leaugs we sounded and it was 30 fathums. And by the bits of driftwood and leaves floating past us and by the appearance of the birds flying over the masts which were robbins, wrens and etc., we congectured that land must not be many leageus away. So we sent up the cabbin boy, an ajile and noble youth called William, and he cried out Land I see! so that all hands broke into a cheer.

This was Emily, and he put it on one side for Philip. But the next sheet was William's. He knew it by the Greek E, an affectation that had prevailed at Bassett's in those days.

The blackness of the night the denseness of the pathless virgin forest and the loud roaring of savage beasts the hissing of serpents the buzzing of deadly poisonous insects smote upon our terrified years. Our spirist qualed but the corage of the dauntless William encoraged us a good deal. Follow me! he cried dashing fearlessly into the pathless virgin . . .

Trevor read on, rummaging among the strewn sheets on the floor. They carried him back into the past, until four lost children, emerging from these scribbled sheets, were sprawling beside him in the dusty sunshine. And as his mind ranged back over the years, he was fain to ask himself whether any trace of those children could still be discerned, or whether any germ of their present selves had been at work, shaping them, in those former days. He wondered if their growth, their inevitable change, had ever been conscious, and if they had had any sort of choice.

It seemed to him that they had not. There had been no real freedom. Irresistible, uncomprehended forces had been at work on them. Passion had broken up the single divine vision of childhood. Distrust and danger had stolen on them unawares. At no point could they have helped themselves, because at no point could they have known what was being done to them. The uselessness of struggle, of flight, was borne in upon him overwhelmingly.

With a heavy heart, he sorted out Emily's work from the rest. For Emily was the only one among them who had ever, consciously, defied her fate. And now she was the most lost of any. She was married. She was happy. Happiness had engulfed her.

He took his way downstairs, with a last backward glance to make sure that the attic was really empty. The Luttrells had gone, and the time had come for him to make his request to his mother. Perfunctorily he made it, as they stood in the porch together, though he knew very well that no good would come of it. But he thought:

"I'd better try. I don't know for certain till I've asked her. If I'm going to escape, I shall. If not . . ."

"Mother," he said, "can you lend me a little money?"

"Why, Trevor?"

"I want to go away. I want to go abroad for a time. I think it would be a very good thing if I did."

"You want to leave Monk's Hall?"

"Not exactly. I want to get away from it for a time. Things aren't easy there."

Catherine was aware of this, for Tilli's tales had not been carried for nothing.

"It's what I've been expecting," she said. "When you are my age, Trevor, you'll learn to foresee things more."

"I daresay. But one never learns that until it's too late to be much use."

"You can always take the advice of older people, you know."

"What's your advice to me now?"

"You know very well. Adopt a profession and work hard at it. If you will undertake to do this, we will discuss the question of money. You must know that I don't grudge you anything."

"I know, Mother. But I want to get away at once."

Catherine paused and reflected. She did not think that it would be wise to make things too easy for Trevor. It might be better that he should stay at Monk's Hall, until he was heartily tired of it. If she kept him waiting, he might learn to be a little more reasonable.

"Why are you in such a hurry to go?" she asked.

"I can't explain. There's been a certain amount of quarrelling, and I can't work."

"Ah!" She repressed a smile. "I'll think it over."

"You won't give me anything now? To-night? I'll pay it back later on. I haven't a penny, and I can't get away unless I can raise a few pounds."

"Certainly not to-night, Trevor."

"Oh, very well."

He turned on his heel and was gone. Nor would he pay any attention when she called after him. As he strode across the lawn, she stood rather sadly in the porch, watching him. She was inflexible, but tormented. The long martyrdom of motherhood was as heavy on her as it had been on the first day that she had let him walk by himself and he fell down and cut his head. There were tears on her cheeks as she turned reluctantly back into the house. The portrait of Frobisher by Watts looked down with an impassive woodenness upon her gray and shaking head.

Trevor hurried through the fields and over Ash Hill. The woods were full of children's voices, and as he crossed the grove he came upon a peaceful group. Emily and Bertha Hackbutt were sitting together on the grass. They were tired, after the long day, and they sat silent, their busy women's hands lying idle in their laps. Round them, on every side, young children were sprawling and staggering. Bobbie's hen-coops, put out on the hill for the summer, were close by, and hens pecked about in the grass among tumbling babies. A herd of little pigs went grunting through the bushes. Pigs, hens, and babies seemed to be massed together in one fine confusion of livestock. It was a teeming, fertile picture. The two women sat in the midst of it, immobile, ruminative rather than thoughtful. They surveyed the country with blank eyes. Bertha would sometimes cast a word of command to one of her boys, but her chidings were languid. She looked like a farm woman, a great russet cow, chewing the cud. Emily's beauty was asleep. She, too, in her fecundity and her silence seemed to be mindless, benevolent, and calm, like the earth that bore her.

And Trevor, looking at them, pondered once more upon the immense secret strength of women, their immutability, the folly of resistance to their hidden forces. He felt that he had known it all in some other life. He had seen before, with the same pang of dread, a group of women and children sitting on the ground amid possessions, cattle and livestock. Since those days he had changed. But these would never change. They were stronger than men in their resistance to time and circumstance. They moved to a rhythm of their own, the slow rhythm of the earth. They hearkened to a wisdom of their own, a terrible, ancient, wordless wisdom. Man, in his brief agonies, may sow and reap and build cities and name the stars, but he comes at last to lay his bones in those fields which he has called his own.

CHAPTER VII

FOOTPATH TO RATCHET

I

WILLIAM was at the door when the postman came, so that he read his letter in the hall. It was the only one for him in the whole bundle. He handed the rest to one of the young Hackbutts, who took them and stuck them into the right pigeonholes in the common-room. William's letter was written upon cheap, thin paper, and he read it standing in the doorway, half in sun and half in shadow. It began abruptly:

You will pardon a word of warning from a friend. Take your wife away from Monk's Hall before it is too late. There is a person there who you cannot trust though this person calls himself your friend. It is an open scandal to everybody but you. She's very deep. But not so deep that some people can't see through her tricks. And I'll just tell you another thing. You'd better ask how much there was between her and this person before she married you. Look out! Look out! Look out!

Having read this letter once, William looked at the post-mark. But he learned nothing from that. It had been posted from Paddington at 6:15 the night before. He stood for a few minutes, holding it in his hand, between the sunlight of the garden and the blackness of the hall. And into his mind there floated from very far away a little picture of something that he had once seen and then forgotten. He remembered Tilli's flat on a wet spring evening and how he had come in from the rain and found Trevor with her. As he came in, he had known that they must have been in one another's arms a moment before. He had known it. But only for a little time. He had forgotten it before the end of the evening, since it was upon that very night that he first kissed Tilli himself. Putting the thought of it away, he went out into the garden. He was still a little stunned, as though he had fallen from a great height.

It had been a harassed morning. He had slept in the woods, as was his habit upon hot nights, and from his first awaking he had known that the day held a menace. As the sun swam relentlessly higher into the hot sky, he had thought about breakfast. But a weakness of resolution seemed to attack him, and a great repugnance at the idea of returning to the house and facing the others. At last he went to the kitchen door and got bread and coffee from Lise, which he took away with him to Peter's workshop. But he had been forced to go into the house to find a book, and there he encountered Mandy Hackbutt with a tale of trouble. It was a most incomprehensible thing: the Hackbutts were going away. They wanted to live nearer London. But William did not believe that story. He knew that they were flying from the vague, undefined discomfort that seemed latterly to have spread over the household. He would have liked to escape from it himself. But he was very sorry that it had ousted the poor Hackbutts, for he had hoped to do them a service when he invited them to Monk's Hall. And he was angry, too, with a slow, formidable anger, which smouldered in the bottom of his heart whenever he thought of Trevor and all that Trevor had done to make his house intolerable.

Why did he always think of the Ash Grove when he thought of Trevor? Half consciously he turned his footsteps that way. Long ago there had been a fire and a thunderstorm, and two boys running round and round the little temple, hating one another. He remembered a weapon, a blazing stick, and Trevor's pale, laughing face. That was the first time that he had wanted to kill Trevor. But he was not quite sure if it had really happened, or if he had dreamt it.

The day was very fine. The morning sun shone with a sick brightness that half dazzled him. He plunged into the thick shade of the plantation with relief, half walking, half running, as though some enemy were coming after him. And presently he found himself upon Ash Hill, looking down over the well-known country. He sat upon the temple steps with an empty mind, and scanned the changed face of the earth. The fields, the sky, and the river were bright and threatening and unreal. He saw them as a man sees objects in a nightmare.

Small fragments of things seen and heard drifted through his head without order or consequence. Because they came from long ago, and seemed to take him away from the stress of the moment, he clutched at them. He remembered that he had sat like this once before, at the edge of a hole where a shell had burst, himself and not himself, groping among pictures and shadows, not thoughts, until someone had dragged him, with curses, into cover.

Childhood was a dim time. It began in darkness: there were great caverns of dark stairs in their London house, and huge shadows on the ceiling of the night nursery when the firelight danced, making a criss-cross pattern of the high guard. And then there had been a great door, opening into the night, and leaves blowing in on a stormy wind. The phantom fears of infancy flowed back over him, the terrors that lurked in dark cupboards, the muffled whispers, the strange faces mopping and mowing over his head.

"My house is so dark," he thought. "I can't go back there."

He felt as though he were two people, and one of them were waiting for him if he went back to the house, a blind, fettered creature, waiting for release, a self that had been shut up in the dark. He was afraid of that creature, for always, even when he had been most safe, even in the Edwardes Square days, its muffled howlings had not been quite inaudible to his inner ears.

He must escape from this darkness before it overtook him. Soon it would be night again. He must seek his safety in daylight. He looked upward to the sun. Already it was a little over to the west. He had been in that place for many hours, and the morning was gone. Suddenly he shouted very loud:

"Oh, night! Oh, night!"

He got up and went down the hill, stumbling a little, and shouting. The echo of his cry came back across the river and frightened him. His shouts sank to a mutter. Whispering and stumbling, he crossed the bridge into a field and came to a stile in a hedge. It was a long time since he had been on that path, and somebody had put up a new signpost that he had not seen before. On a very neat, white little board the black letters confronted him slyly, like an intimate dig in the ribs. It said:

Footpath to Ratchet

William stopped muttering and looked at it, reassured by its air of anonymous friendliness. Then he jumped over the stile and started across the Ratchet fields in long, purposeful strides.

2

"What did William come for?" asked Philip, as soon as he had seen his guest off the premises. "Is he in any kind of trouble?"

Emily shook her head.

"He didn't say anything to me," she said. "I thought perhaps he might have been talking to you after dinner."

"Not about himself. We talked about his father. He seems to have begun to be curious about that business of the trial. But all the while I had an idea that something was on his mind and that he couldn't bring himself to speak of it."

"So had I. But it's no use. I mean, we know what the trouble is. It's Tilli. We can't do anything about it."

"I suppose not. But I felt somehow that we ought to be more helpful. I almost asked him to stay the night."

"That wouldn't help him very much, poor dear."

"No. But when I went with him to the gate just now, it was as if I was turning him out. I don't think he wanted to go. He kept looking round all the time, as we were going down the avenue, back at the house and the light."

Philip went across to the window and peered out into the warm night, as though he expected to find William still hovering close to the house, like a disturbed spirit.

"I don't believe," he added, "that he went back to Monk's Hall at all. I watched him to the turn of the lane, and he went over the stile into Ratchet fields instead of keeping straight on. I shouted. I don't know if he heard me."

"It's a hot night," suggested Emily. "I expect he'll sleep out in the fields. He often does."

"It's a good deal colder than it was. There's a heavy mist

coming up from the river, and the moon'll be down in an hour. He'll lose his way or get an ague."

"Oh, if he's cold, he'll go home. He can get in by the scullery window. He's done it before."

"I wish I'd asked him to stay. I wonder if he heard me when I called."

Philip felt that he was foolish to be so concerned when Emily, for once, was not. She knew best the wild ways of her brother, and she took it for granted that the boy should go straying off into the night without home or goal. To Philip it had been disturbing. When he ceased shouting after William and turned up the avenue again to the solid security of his own home with its open door and lighted windows, he had felt ashamed, almost guilty.

"Poor William!" he muttered.

Emily rejoined with a little sigh.

"An unhappy marriage must be a dreadful thing," she said.

But she spoke with detachment. He looked quickly across at her. She was sitting in the lamplight, her knitting in her lap, a sight to please the heart of any man. When he came in, a few minutes earlier, and saw her there, the thought had crossed his mind that all the radiance of his life seemed to come from her as light comes from a lamp.

"It must be dreadful," he agreed.

A vagrant moth, flitting in from the garden, beat its wings against the globe. He caught it, took it to the window, and flung it out again into the dark expanses of the night. Then he waited, listening, half expecting to hear footsteps among the trees. But he could hear nothing save the whisper of the mill-stream and the faint, far barking of a dog.

"A happy marriage has its dangers, too," he said at last.

"How?"

"It narrows our hearts. One should fight against it."

Emily began to wind up her ball of wool.

"The dangers of happiness don't frighten me," she said. "Very few people run that sort of risk. I'm going up."

"All right. I'll shut up. I won't be long."

She kissed the top of his head as she went by and said:

"No, don't be long."

He heard her in the hall, and the little sputter of her match as she lighted her candle, and the soft footsteps going up-stairs. But still he waited by the window. The fog rolled up quite fast; it lay in long, low wreaths round the trunks of the apple trees in the orchard, so that he could see no grass at all. Its chill breath crept into the house. The moth flew in at another window.

He thought of William, at large in the foggy fields, and remembered with amazement his own alarm when, coming in that afternoon, he had first seen William's hat in the hall. For a moment he had imagined, fantastically, that Emily might be going to leave him again.

Lately he had got into the habit of calling for her whenever he came into the house. He would stand in the hall and shout once or twice, not because he wanted anything, but just to make sure that she was there. Her reply, from the drawing room or upstairs, convinced him that no thunderbolt had struck her while he was away. If she did not answer im-mediately, he would suffer a fleeting pang, a faint echo of the shock that her first desertion had given to him. But he rather liked this small spice of insecurity. It gave a flavour to his domestic contentment, which might otherwise have been so perfect as to be almost dull. He chose to imagine that she might still run away, because of a certain elusive-ness in her, which had once enchanted him, and which he liked to think she had not lost. His real certainty that she would never leave him any more gave him scope and freedom to dally with the fancy that she still, possibly, might.

His happiness at times was too sure to be quite credible. She was his so entirely, with him all the time, a constant companion in all the daily small things of life, bound to him by a thousand minor surrenders. A fitful but deep abstraction was, now, the last of her old ways. A fixed look would come upon her face sometimes, and she would sit, for a few moments, mute and blind. But he found that he could always rouse her by exclaiming "Mrs. Luttrell!" very sharply. She would start and smile and answer him. But no other name would bring her back.

Since their return from the Tyrol, she had been very happy. She was like continual music in the house. She laughed oftener than before and upon more reasonable occasions. Sometimes she made very sensible remarks. And every day she grew more lovely, like some exquisite, secretly closed bud that has come into flower over night. She was now a part of his life, so that he had almost left off thinking about her, save in rare, precious moments of alarm like this.

For when he had shouted two or three times in vain, his first thought had been that she must have fallen into the mill-stream. And then he saw on the hall table a hat that could only belong to William: a hat that filled him with uncomfortable memories. Looking into all the rooms for traces of the pair of them, he saw with relief that the supper table had been laid for three. And on the garden path he found her weeding basket, a pair of leather gloves, pruning scissors, and a note to himself, weighed down with stones. He read it, still in some slight agitation. It said:

W. is here and will stay to supper. We have gone down to the stream at the bottom of the orchard. Come and fetch us when you come in.

Relieved, he called himself a fool. Of course they would have gone down to the river. They would be sailing little boats. When they used to pay him visits long ago, they always sailed boats on the smooth swift stream at the bottom of the orchard. He was glad that they should do it still. He remembered how eager she used to be, as a long-legged little girl, skipping along the bank with a stick to guide her craft.

He made for the bottom of the orchard and found them. But they were sailing no paper fleets. Emily was knitting with an eternal placid industry that was growing upon her. Sometimes she annoyed Philip by counting her stitches before she answered him. William lolled beside her and chewed grass.

"Here you are," she said. "We were wondering if you'd found my note."

"I saw William's hat. How are you, William?"

"I'm well. We've been looking at your cactus."

"It's a wonder, isn't it?"

"I think it's awful," said William. "It's got no neck."

"How's Monk's Hall?"

"Still there."

"The Hackbutts are going," said Emily, looking up.

"Oh, really? Why?"

William said, rather gloomily, that he could not think. Emily rose and gathered her knitting together.

"I'm going in to make a salad," she said as she moved off among the trees.

The two men followed her and William said:

"She's told me."

"Good!"

"I was very much surprised," confided William.

Philip, with difficulty, suppressed a grin.

"I mean, the idea seems so odd somehow. Like a sort of miracle. But she seems very pleased."

"So am I."

"You must be. It's a fine thing to have a son."

"Perhaps it will be a daughter. I don't mind which. But she wants a boy."

"So she said." William looked after his sister as she disappeared into the house and added, almost in a voice of dismay: "She *is* pleased with herself, isn't she?"

Perhaps it was this new baffling serenity of Emily's that had so daunted William that he could not begin upon his tale of trouble. Philip was sure that something had been left unsaid. And yet at supper they had been gay enough. A sort of wildness seemed to have invaded William's spirits and he ran on in an extravagant way that reminded Philip of other days.

He had almost forgotten how lawless this pair had always been. And yet, until he took it into his head to be alarmed for them, their childish exploits had always given him pleasure. They were not like other naughty children; their recklessness, their beauty, and their innate good manners combined to temper his disapproval. But still, they never knew when a joke had been carried too far. He remembered one piece of iniquity that they had confessed to him and that had frightened him very much. They had been sent for a walk with a very stupid and unobservant French governess and they took the opportunity to open all the canal sluices along the towing path for half a mile, thereby flooding over twenty fields of standing corn. In spite of the hue and cry, the real culprits had never been discovered, and Mademoiselle would have answered for their good behaviour and particularly fluent French throughout the walk.

Philip had been really shocked at the senseless folly of this deed, and by the want of any idea of real proportion that lay behind it. And for all the change in William, it was not impossible that he might do the same sort of thing again at any moment. William was not vicious, but he was, nevertheless, too much like his father.

"One can't judge him by our standards," thought Philip. And by that he meant his own standards and those of the regenerate Emily. For he was no longer forced to feel like a stranger in the company of the twins. He was now the host at his own table and Emily was his belonging. William was the stranger.

After dinner, Emily got out her guitar and they had a little music. The twins sang together, as they used to sing in Edwardes Square. Old songs were pulled out and new ones tried over. Philip, released from the duties of conversation, could loll comfortably in his favourite chair and listen. He thought it a pity that William did not come oftener, for this singing was very pleasant. The bright evening, paling into a long green twilight, made him sleepy. He dozed off, as was his custom when Emily sang to him after dinner, and drifted at once into ridiculous dreams of Lise, and bright sunshine, and some old, forgotten misery. He was with her; he was trying to tell her something, but she would only laugh at him.

A pause in the singing brought him back with a jerk to the shadowy room and the memory of the shadowy present, where sleep was creeping peacefully, like a slow tide, over all the shores of his life. Late sunset burned beyond the orchard trees, with pools of light and long bars of purple cloud. The grass glowed like a fiery emerald. Beside the window, their fair heads very close together, sat the twins. They were silent, the guitar between them.

"That was pretty," said Philip. "Go on."

Emily struck a note off her guitar like a faint, deep bell. It reminded Philip of the harp that had fallen slowly into ruin in the Monk's Hall drawing room, of the dead days of his own first love, and of the twins at ten years old, fair-haired, wild, unconquered.

"I must go," said William. "It's getting dark."

Philip got up to light the lamp and told them to sing one more. The green dusk changed in a moment to night, and two voices floated mournfully away into the darkness:

> "The silver swan, who living had no note,
> When death approached unlocked her silent throat.
> Leaning her breast against the reedy shore
> She sang her first and last, and sang no more."

William stopped singing. He was watching his sister as a man on an alien shore will watch the boat that bears off a friend, seeing nothing but a widening waste of deep waters. And Philip, as the old enchantment caught again at his heart, thought bitterly:

"He's lost her. But then . . . I've lost her, too."

For she was gone now, and they were both bereft. But her voice was the same—a child's voice, clear, soft, and without passion:

> "Farewell ye joys! Now death come close my eyes!
> More geese than swans now live, more fools than wise."

He had always known that he must lose her. He had told himself that it is man's fate to woo one woman and to wed another. And in his happiness he could forget his loss. But he was sorry for William, who was to be left desolate, wandering on the shore of a barren country. For William there was no promise in the future: it was Philip's children who would be fair-haired and wild and unconquered.

The moth found its death in the flame of the lamp. He shut the shutters, lighted his candle, locked the front door, wound up the clock, and turned out the lamps. As he creaked up to bed he hummed softly and hopelessly the song of the times:

> More geese than swans now live, more fools than wise.

3

Charlotte started awake with a cry and a sense of immediate calamity.

"Yes? Yes? Who is it? What is it?"

"Hush!" A whisper came in the darkness. "It is I. It is Tilli. Light the candle."

Charlotte groped for the matches, but her hand was shaking so that she could scarcely strike one.

"What is it?" she asked. "What do you want?"

"Oh, hush! Hurry!"

A flame leapt in the darkness and Tilli's white face peered at her over the end of the bed.

"Are you ill? Is anything the matter?"

"Oh, I do not know. I think . . . yes . . . it is terrible! I cannot think what to do. I shall faint."

She came and sat on the bed while Charlotte lighted the candle. The flame burnt low and then very brightly. Charlotte's sleepy panic subsided. She sat up, large and healthy and tousled, looking at Tilli.

"Why, you're . . . you'll catch cold! Wrap the eiderdown round you. Have you had a bad dream? What has happened?"

She huddled a counterpane over the lace and chiffon which seemed to cover so little of Tilli. There was a small pause, broken by the hooting of an owl in the trees outside. Tilli started up with a cry of terror and burst into tears.

"Oh, I am afraid! I am afraid! I think I am the most unfortunate creature in the world. Have pity on me, Charlotte. I have married a murderer!"

"Are you mad?"

"But a murderer!" Tilli's voice rose to a shriek. "A murderer! And I have married him."

"Hush! You'll wake the whole house."

"I do not care. Everyone will soon know it. I have married..."

"You've been dreaming?"

"No, no! If only it had been a dream. Oh, my God!"

"Tilli! Control yourself! Tell me what has happened."

Charlotte leaned forward and grasped Tilli by the wrists. She shook her a little. In spite of the fixed, glassy eyes she could not be quite sure that this frenzy was genuine. The shaking seemed to have some effect. Tilli grew calmer and presently she said, in a more collected voice:

"He has come back."

"Who? William?"

"He is a murderer." She repeated it this time quietly, almost sullenly. "It is terrible for me."

"Who has he murdered?"

"Trevor."

Charlotte got up and put on a dressing gown. She drank some water and made Tilli do the same. Then, having mastered her terror, she asked, as carelessly as she could:

"But where are they now?"

"Out there."

Tilli jerked her head toward the window.

"In the park? Trevor? And William, too?"

Tilli nodded.

"And what makes you say that William has murdered Trevor? Did you see him do it?"

"No, no." Tilli shuddered. "But he has taken a gun. He has gone to shoot him. And if you had seen his face, as I have seen it, you would know why I am so afraid. He is like his father. He is a..."

"But why has he gone after Trevor with a gun?"

"Why? Why? Because he is jealous. That is why. I don't mind who hears it. Everybody shall know. He neglects me. He does not love me. But he is jealous. Everybody shall hear what I have suffered since I am married to that man."

"Hush, hush! When did they go out?"

"Ten minutes . . . five minutes ago. Not longer."

"And they have not come back?"

"I have not seen them."

"Then how do you know that anything of the sort has happened? Where did you last see them?"

"In my room."

"Both of them?"

Tilli said nothing. She sat crumpled up on Charlotte's bed and blinked at the candle.

"William came back in the middle of the night and found Trevor in your room," hazarded Charlotte. "What then?"

"Am I to blame?" exploded Tilli. "He has never loved me."

"Never mind that. Nobody's blaming you . . . yet, I want to know exactly what happened."

"I can tell a pretty story of William. These Crownes! They are all alike. And I will tell it. If I am to be blamed, I will tell it."

"Do stick to the point. We'll discuss that afterward. What was Trevor doing in your room, anyhow?"

"I swear that I am innocent."

"I know. But what was Trevor . . ."

"He came to borrow some aspirin. But William would not wait to hear that. He is a murderer. He will listen to nothing. I tried to explain, but he would not listen. It is nothing to him that Trevor is his cousin. He is mad! Like a wild animal."

"Why did they go out?" pursued Charlotte patiently.

"When William tried to open the door . . ."

"Was it locked?"

"Always at night I lock my door," said Tilli superbly. "It is, I think, more decent. I told Trevor to go out by the window. It is quite easy to jump on to the workshop roof. Because I knew how William is unreasonable and I did not wish for a quarrel. But I think that he heard, for he began to kick the door and to shout. I was afraid that everyone in the house would wake up, so I let him in. And at once he went to the window that I had shut. He opened it, and I think he saw Trevor on the roof, for he called out in such a terrible way: 'Wait! You wait! I'm coming for you!' And he took the gun from his dressing room. The gun that he keeps for the rabbits. And he went out of the window, too. I thought at first that he would shoot me. If you had seen his face! Oh, my God! Oh, my God!"

"And they're both out there now?"

Charlotte went across to the window and drew back the curtain. Leaning out into the night, she strained her ears. It was a little foggy and as black as pitch save for the flame of a few doubtful stars over her head. The moon had set. A dense silence hung over the vast, shadowy masses of wood. Blackness and quiet had swallowed the world for miles. An owl hooted far away. There was a smell of morning about.

"It all sounds quite quiet," she said. "Are you sure that they are still outside?"

"How could they come in? All the doors are locked."

"How did William get in?"

"I do not know."

"Shall I go and wake Bobbie? Perhaps he would go out and find them before more harm is done."

"Yes! Oh, yes! Before anything terrible happens."

Charlotte put on shoes and stockings and a thick coat over her nightdress, while Tilli, becoming excited again, repeated that she was innocent.

"You can stop that, Tilli. It doesn't impress me."

"Do you dare to say that? I tell you . . ."

A shot, fired some way off, rang through the stillness of the woods. Tilli screamed and flung herself face downward on the bed. Charlotte flew back to the window. The last echoes of the noise were drifting from the Ash Hill direction. The silence afterward was worse than ever.

"I'll have to get Bobbie," she said.

She ran downstairs to the room where Lise and Bobbie were sleeping, and burst in with her story.

"William came home in the middle of the night and caught Trevor with Tilli. And he's gone out after Trevor into the woods with a gun, and I think he's shooting him."

"What's the time?" asked Lise, sitting up in a fright.

"Half-past two, about. Did you hear what I said? William came home . . ."

"Yes, we heard. What do you want us to do about it?"

"Bobbie must get up and go after them."

Bobbie was already out of bed and hunting for his shoes. Under his breath, he was cursing his nephews. Lise, also climbing out of bed, swore no less fluently, and asked why William had not shot at Tilli instead of Trevor.

"You don't mean to say he's really hurt him?" she asked, catching sight of Charlotte's face.

"I don't know. I heard a shot, out in the woods."

Charlotte was shivering violently.

"That's nothing," called Bobbie from the dressing room, where he had gone in search of his trousers. "William never hits anything. As long as he's the only person with a gun . . ."

"Yes," said Lise, "it's a safe rabbit that's shot at by William. You're sure Trevor didn't have a gun, too? Oh, well! But did she have the impudence to tell you all this herself?"

"She's terrified out of her life."

"She told you that Trevor . . . How did she explain it?"

"She said he came to borrow aspirin."

"Aspirin!"

"But her door was locked."

"Little——!" Bobbie in the dressing room was still cursing, softly and steadily.

"I can't think how William can have got into the house," added Charlotte. "It was all locked. I locked it myself. I didn't know he was still out."

"I suppose he got in by the scullery window. He did one night in June, when he was sleeping out and the rain came on."

Bobbie made his appearance, rather sketchily clad, and asked where he was now to go.

"The shot sounded as if they were Ash Hill way. I'll come with you."

They hurried down the shallow, slippery stairs, and Lise, in the gallery, lighted them with a candle held high. The hall looked like a cavern and smelt abominably of all the stale cigarettes which had been smoked there in the past months. The chain of the front door rattled, and they stepped out into the cool mystery of the night. Lise, faintly visible in the doorway, watched them as they ran across the lawn into the denser shadow of the larch woods. For a few minutes they groped and hurried, stopping every now and then to listen.

"What the devil can we do? Shall we shout?" asked Bobbie at last.

"We don't want to make too much noise," demurred Charlotte.

"Noise enough already. Besides, if they have a gun, they might hit us by mistake."

And suddenly he began to yell: "William! Trevor! Are you there? Hullo!"

Instantly the plantation was filled with clamour. Another shot was fired, close at hand, and a pandemonium of shouting began. Charlotte thought that Trevor had answered Bobbie, and immediately there came a yell from William. "Got you, have I? Got you! Got you!"

There were crashes in the undergrowth and a grunt from Bobbie.

"Nobody dead yet, anyhow."

He plunged forward toward the noise, stumbled over a tree trunk, and added forthwith to the babel of curses that made the night hideous. Charlotte wondered that the whole countryside was not roused. She heard Bobbie entreating somebody to let the gun alone, for the love of heaven, and then a sound of blows as though somebody was being thrashed. She thought that she had better get back to the house. Nobody seemed to be very much the worse, and their language was appalling. She was best out of it. As she recrossed the lawn, a man broke from the wood and came running past her.

"Is that Trevor?" she called.

He was making for the front door, but, seeing Lise on the steps, he sheered off and ran round the corner of the house. Lise, statuesque in the ample draperies of her kimono, looked after him with interest.

"Was that Trevor?" she asked when Charlotte came up.

"I think so. It was too short for William."

"He's all right, then?"

"He must be."

"And where is William?"

"In the wood still. Bobbie's with him."

"I hope Bobbie's safe," said Lise anxiously.

She withdrew into the hall and put down her candle, saying:

"I suppose William fired that shot *pour encourager les autres*."

A gale of laughter seized Charlotte. She leant up against the doorpost, in a sort of hysterical reaction, shaking and heaving.

"I see nothing to laugh at," grumbled Lise. "What on

earth is going to happen now? A nice breakfast we shall all have!"

"Oh! Oh! I ca-can't help it. I don't want to laugh. But I was so fri-ightened."

"You're hysterical," said Lise, catching the infection and giggling, too. "Come into the dining room and have some damson brandy."

Stifling their paroxysms, they stole into the dining room and foraged in the sideboard for a decanter and some glasses. Gusts of laughter shook them whenever they tried to speak, and they grew more helpless than ever when, through a crack in the doorway, they saw Bobbie and William come into the hall.

"But I've lost my gun," William kept saying. "I dropped it. I left my gun outside somewhere. My gun is in the wood. It'll get rusty. I can't leave my gun out all night."

"That's all right," Bobbie soothed him, as he hung up chains and shot bolts.

But the frantic young man hurled himself upon the door.

"I must find it," he repeated. "I dropped it somewhere."

"You leave it till to-morrow," advised Bobbie. "You'll never find it in the dark."

"Let me out, Bobbie!"

"No. I won't let you out. Go up! Go to bed! You've made quite enough noise for one night. We'll look for your gun in the morning."

William stopped arguing suddenly. He turned from the door, bounded upstairs, and was lost in the darkness above.

"Will he be all right?" asked Lise, coming out into the hall to look after him. "He won't go for Tilli now?"

"No such luck!" Bobbie assured her. "He's quieting down. And his gun is outside, fortunately. Lord! What a night!"

Charlotte, between peals of laughter, was trying to say:

"It isn't that I'm not sorry for William. I am most t-terribly sorry. It's all awful. But I c-can't help it."

"I know," said Lise. "Come in and have a drink, Bobbie."

She led him into the dining room, with her single, starry candle, and poured him out a little glass of the damson brandy that was a specialty at Monk's Hall.

"I'd sooner have a brandy-and-soda," said Bobbie. "I never spent such a night in all my life. Where's Trevor? He came in, didn't he?"

"I saw him running round the house," said Charlotte. "I think he was making for the garden door."

"He won't be able to get in. It's locked. Lord! Lord! I suppose I must go out and find *him* now."

"Let him cool his heels outside for a bit," said Lise indignantly. "It's been mostly his fault. What right had he to go on in this way? In William's house, too. He ought to be ashamed of himself. He should have gone away rather than let this happen."

"Still, I'd better let him in," said Bobbie, going off.

But in the hall he paused and asked suspiciously:

"Do you hear anything?"

They listened.

"Nothing! What?" whispered Lise.

"I thought I heard a . . . There it is again!"

They all heard, this time, a sound like a faint moan. It was just outside the drawing-room window. Lise had the shutters back in an instant and was wrestling with the heavy sash. Bobbie helped her. It slid up, and the light of their candle made a splash in the darkness outside. The night was so still that the flame burnt steadily even when they held it over the window-sill.

"Who's there? What is it?" asked Bobbie of the night.

A groan answered him.

Trevor lay where he had fallen in the midst of his run,

sprawling on a flower-bed under the window. His face was hidden in the earth and in the gay flowers crushed beneath him. Charlotte, who had got the door open, ran round and dropped upon her knees beside him. It was plain that he was badly hurt.

"Hit, after all!" gasped Bobbie, craning out of the window. "Bring that brandy, Lise! Quick!"

They hurried out, taking the candle with them.

"But I saw him running," wailed Charlotte. "I saw him! How can he be hurt? Oh, Trevor! Trevor!"

"Hold him up and give him a drop of this," commanded Bobbie. "I've known men run farther than this, after they were hit. Get more lights!"

Lise brought a lantern and put it on the path beside them. It made a round patch of light in the void of the darkness, a small world of terror and pain. They pulled Trevor over and put a coat under his head. He had stopped groaning and breathed in heavy, gurgling gasps. Bobbie pulled open his shirt and saw the wound.

"No good," he said. "He's done for."

"He can't . . . it's not . . . he ran!"

"Get a doctor!" urged Lise. "Go, Bobbie! Find someone!"

"I know. I'll go."

He ran into the house as Trevor, for a moment, opened his eyes and looked at Charlotte. His lips moved.

"Oh, Trevor!" she whispered. "Don't . . . don't . . ."

When she put her ear close she caught the words.

"My fault . . . entirely my fault . . . accident . . . William and I . . . out after poacher . . . I had the gun . . . I tripped . . . mind that . . . it went off . . . accident . . . tell them . . ."

He choked a little, and they held him up, out of the marigolds and geraniums. There was blood on the flowers. Lights were moving in the house; voices on the stairs, in the hall, came nearer. The whole night woke up to panic. Somebody lit lamps in all the lower rooms, so that the great shadowy building sprang into life, with orange squares of windows. Light, too, was collecting in the sky and a morning wind whispered among the trees.

Trevor, raised up on Charlotte's breast, seemed just to breathe. She signed to Lise to keep the rest of them away. She heard him whisper again. She thought he said:

"Sorry . . . Mother . . ."

His white face took on a secret look.

4

An exclamation, a summons from Emily, broke in upon the dreamless peace of Philip's night. He found himself awake and blinking at a stormy sunrise. A dazzling carmine light made everything in the room look new and strange. Dawn airs, soft as milk, flowed in through the uncurtained window and over the bed whence Emily, wild-eyed, had started in alarm.

"Emily! What is it? What is the matter? Don't you feel well? Get back into bed."

"William's there!" she was saying.

"William?"

"Yes! Yes! He's out in the garden somewhere. I woke up. I heard him singing."

"You were dreaming."

"No, no! I heard him."

She ran across to look, leaning on the window-sill, her long hair tossed back over her shoulders.

"Well!" Philip climbed out of bed a little wearily. "Put on your slippers and your dressing gown. You'll catch cold."

And as he could not persuade her to leave the window, he wrapped a shawl round her shoulders and leant out beside her to scan the dawn-flushed garden.

"It was a dream," he assured her. "He's not there."

"But I heard him! I've been dreaming about him all night. But this was different. He is looking for me. He wants me. He was under the window singing: *More geese than swans . . .*"

"Go back to bed, my sweet."

The garden was dewy and empty and quite silent save for the sleepy twitterings of a few birds.

"But he was standing on the lawn, Philip!"

"If anybody had stood on the lawn there would be footprints in the dew. Nobody has been."

"But why was he singing?"

"You were dreaming. Look at the time! It's only just after five."

"He's been out all night in the fields, as we thought. And now he wants to come back to us."

"Well, if he does, we'll let him in."

Reluctantly, she let him put her back to bed. But she insisted that he must go down and search for William. He tucked her up and put on some clothes. Taking a last look out of the window before he went down, he saw that there were really footprints across the lawn. Bobbie was there, uncertainly scanning the front of the house. When he saw Philip, he beckoned mysteriously, and at the same time enjoined silence. Philip was not surprised. He had been full of dread at the moment of waking. He knew that Bobbie had come with evil tidings. Emily was lying in her bed, staring idly at the strip of crimson sky. He said to her:

"I sha'n't be long. I'll just take a look round and make sure he's not there."

"If he's there," she said rather sleepily, "mind you give him something to eat."

Philip went down into the dark and shuttered house, past the loud-ticking clock on the stairs. He opened the door upon the chill radiance of the morning. Bobbie, on the door-step, was looking like a funeral.

"Is—what is it?" whispered Philip. "Be very quiet! I don't want Emily to be disturbed."

"Can you come up to Monk's Hall?"

Bobbie's whisper was like the roar of a distant ocean.

"What has happened? Is William all right? Emily . . ."

"It's not William. At least . . . it's Trevor. There's been an accident."

"How? What?"

"Shot."

"Not dead?"

Bobbie grunted.

"But how? What happened?"

Bobbie took a long breath. It was the first time that he had given any account of it to anyone. But he knew that it would not be the last. Lise had told him what to say. He hoped that he had got it right.

"Tilli heard noises in the night . . . footsteps going round the house. She thought that somebody was trying to climb in, and she was frightened. William was nowhere to be found . . ."

"He didn't leave here till late last night."

"I know. It turned out that the person they heard was him. But that didn't come out till after. She routed out Trevor. And he went off to see if everything was all right. He took William's gun with him. We don't think he can have known that it was loaded."

"*William's* gun. Where was it, then?"

"I don't know," said Bobbie rather crossly. Lise should have told him where the gun was when Trevor took it. "But when William came in, a few minutes later, and heard of the mistake, he went off to find Trevor. They roused me and I went, too. We hunted, and shouted, but we were too late.

We heard a shot and found him badly hurt. He only lived a few minutes, poor boy. He said that he tripped over a root or something in the dark and the gun went off. We found it this morning, over on Ash Hill."

Bobbie came to an end and mopped his forehead. He looked at Philip to see if it had sounded all right.

"Somebody must tell Catherine," he added anxiously.

"You must tell her yourself, Bobbie. You're her brother."

"Philip! I can't."

Bobbie felt that he could tell his story to Philip, and, if necessary, to other, more official ears. But he could not tell it to Catherine, and he wished very much that she should hear it for the first time from somebody who believed it.

"Won't—won't you tell her?" he asked anxiously.

Philip hesitated.

"Is that really what happened?" he asked.

"Why—it seems to be that. Everyone has a different story. It was all such a muddle."

Philip did not believe him, but he thought that he had better not say so.

"Sally," began Bobbie, and stopped.

"What about Sally?"

"Oh, nothing. But she's making trouble. We'll have to shut her up somehow. You must come, Philip."

"All right. I'll come. As soon as I've told Emily and seen that she's all right. She'll be frightened if I go off without telling her why."

"Ah, yes! Poor girl! I hope she won't be too much upset."

"She's bound to be. But as long as William is all right . . . What does Sally say?"

"No good repeating it."

"William's gun," thought Philip. "It doesn't hold water."

"Does Sally say that it wasn't an accident?" he asked.

"Yes."

"I see."

"I must be getting back," said Bobbie.

"How did you come over? Did you ride?"

"Umhum! Horse just outside the gate."

Philip went with Bobbie down the avenue, postponing as long as possible the moment of facing Emily. He stood by the gate, listening to the trample of hooves in the lane till it changed to the regular clip-clop on the high road. The sound, in the clear early silence, lasted for a long time. It would be lost, and then it would come back again across the fields like the faint ticking of a clock. He waited until he could hear it no more.

Very slowly he turned back toward the house. The sun was now quite up, and the red banners of cloud had turned to black. There was a smell of rain in the air; a hint, already, that the brightness would not last.

"Storms!" thought Philip, as he made his way up the avenue. "I don't wonder, with the sky that colour."

Bent, a little grizzled, he stood in front of his house and wondered what he had better do, and how it was possible to go to Emily. Perhaps he had better say nothing until she had had her breakfast. It did not seem likely that she should believe this story, any more than he did. For long years, they had been waiting for it. The thought of death, of violence, had always lurked in her mind and in William's mind. It had been their inheritance.

His eye fell on a little piece of groundsel that destroyed the stony order of the carriage drive. He pulled it up before he went indoors.

Steeled against her questions, he went upstairs. But he found her asleep, breathing deeply and tranquilly, her pale cheek pillowed in her hand. He sat down in a chair beside her bed and waited.

She looked very lovely asleep, and very young. She was

as untouched as the dew upon the grass outside: a child herself, and yet she was carrying his child. All her helplessness
lay there, revealed to him, and all his old unhappy thoughts
of her. As he sat beside her, watching and waiting, he found
it almost possible to wish that she might sleep for ever.

THE END